WALK THE
PROMISE ROAD

A Novel of the Oregon Trail

Anne Schroeder

Walk the Promise Road
Copyright© 2018 Anne Schroeder
Cover Design Livia Reasoner
Prairie Rose Publications
www.prairierosepublications.com

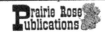

Chapter One

March 4, 1848. My whole world has ended. How I shall bear up, God alone knows. Mama, Papa, Toby—all gone with the fever. My only hope is that I shall be next. Oh, glorious childhood, over. How shall I fill this void when my heart lies broken?

THUD...THUD...THUD. The dirt clods rebounding off three fresh graves claimed the attention of a young woman as she fought the wind whipping her skirts into a sodden mass. Each bite of the shovel resonated in the pain pounding her eyes; each hollow thud shamed the wind howling overhead. Beneath the naked branches of a giant elm, a pair of burly Irish gravediggers eyed her uncertainly then doffed their caps and waited, arms pressed against the hickory handles of their shovels.

The wind carried a muffled shout. "Mary, come on."

Her cousin Philip waited impatiently, his hands struggling to hold her mare as it struggled against its traces. When crashing thunder followed a second later, the mare reared; its eyes wild and fear-crazed. In a stupor, Mary Rodgers watched Philip wrap his silk scarf around the horse's eyes and murmur in its ear, calming it. A fat raindrop fell on her outstretched hand and she walked blindly toward the horse and buggy, her skirts twisting in the gathering wind

"Mary, there's nothing you can do for them now. They're gone. Let the men finish." Philip reached to support her, tenderness belying his harsh words.

Mary peered over her shoulder at the gravediggers and focused her tear-swollen eyes on her cousin. "Oh, Philip, I've been so selfish. I didn't think. They'll get soaked and it'll be my fault." It was hard to know whose soaking she cried for: her mother's, her father's, Toby's, or the men's.

Silence rode between them like an uninvited visitor. When Philip pulled into a circular drive and leaped from the buggy, Mary saw the two-story clapboard house as though for the first time: gingerbread trim framing lace-curtained windows and an ornate brass knocker that her mother had carried from Philadelphia as a bride. Each fixture seemed strangely new, detached from the family that had once claimed it.

"We should have left a lamp burning," she said.

"Maybe the woodstove will still have embers."

She followed Philip inside and turned when she heard a raspy nickering behind her. Her mare was still hitched to her father's surrey, rain matting its mane while mud ran down its forelocks. When she could speak, her voice seemed little more than a croak. "Philip—the buggy."

Philip had already found a hook for his rumpled overcoat and was bent over, removing his overshoes. He tried to mask his chagrin with a cough. "Sorry, I forgot."

Forgot? Anger seared her insides. Maybe *he* could forget, but this day would be etched into her memory forever.

"Never mind," she called over her shoulder. "I'm already soaked."

She returned to the yard, glad for the chilblains in her sodden toes that matched the numbness in her brain. She jerked the reins and started toward the barn where pickets of the old fence were barely visible in the fading light. She saw her father's cattle standing in a tight huddle against the driving rain. She made out the forms of the huge oxen that Philip had unyoked from his wagon a few days earlier. Thank God he had stopped to say good-bye on his way west. If it weren't for his help she might have worked herself into her own grave by now.

"Poor beasties," she crooned "You're so eager to start for the Oregon Country. Probably no more so than Philip. I know he thinks his westering journey is a distant dream now, but we'll have to think of something. Soon." Dropping a bucket of oats into the feeding bin for the horse, she closed her eyes and relived the events of the past five days.

Her brother Toby had spotted the Conestoga wagon hidden in the thicket alongside the lane and had come bouncing in with mud all over his boots, full of fifteen-year-old zeal over the new friend he'd met. Her mother had gone over the next morning with preserved peaches and a ham, wanting to find out about the family that seemed to have neither childbirth nor slippery roads to justify their camping alongside the public road. Indeed, as Ruthie Rodgers reported to her husband Henry that night, she was fearful they might be hiding a case of illness. But even knowing the situation, she persisted in aiding the strangers, as one after another, they succumbed to the influenza they had brought with them.

The townspeople were already wary and worn from their own illnesses and they spared little sympathy for the outsiders. After the last member of the little family died and was hastily interred in the cemetery, Toby and Henry saw to the burning of the wagon and all its contents. They led the mules into a nearby river, scrubbed them, and took them to auction to repay the township for the costs of burial.

"Just like that, an entire family wiped from the face of the earth," Mary muttered aloud to her horse, nose-deep in the oat crib. "But they deserved what they got for the misery they caused us."

Three days later, the first signs of sickness showed up in their own farmhouse. First Toby, then her mother came down with the nausea, chills and wracking fever that sent Mary begging for help. When none arrived, she donned the cotton gloves she used to prune the roses, wrapped her father's clean handkerchief around her face and set to doing what she could. She wanted to put her mother and Toby in one room so she could better care for them, but her father was adamant; he slept each night beside his Ruthie, cradling her in his arms until he caught the sickness, as well.

• ♥ •

Mary dried her teacup, covered the raisin cake and wiped the table while everything in her protested that this was her mother's table, her mother's task. It felt unbearably lonely to brew a cup of tea for one. She caught her reflection in the shaving mirror above the stove and studied her thick black hair, set about her shoulders in tousled curls. Wan and spent, her cheeks were devoid of their usual vitality. Gone was the healthy girl who lived to escape outdoors. But what did it matter? With tears blurring her vision, she walked to her room and closed the door behind her.

Night stole over the farmyard as she waited to sleep. In the distance, an owl hooted its wake-up call. "How familiar and dear this place is. But everything's gone. I just…can't…stay," she sobbed into her pillow. "I need to go away where everything doesn't remind me of what I've lost." She heard Philip climb the stairs on his way to bed. It was late when the sounds of the oxen lulled her into uneasy slumber.

Sunrise brought no answers. At least the rain had stopped, although the eerie silence made the house seem even more desolate. She woke with a start; snatched from a restless dream by a loud thumping at the back stoop. For a moment, her father was bringing a load of cord wood into the kitchen as he had done every morning of her life, but when she shook the sleep from her brain and peered outside, it was only Philip scraping his boots. She finished dressing and made it to the kitchen in time to see him enter in a rush of cold air, his blond hair dripping from the eaves.

She stirred oats into a pan of boiling water, hiding her tears in a rush of good cheer as had been her mother's way. Philip had donned her father's trousers in order to feed the cattle, and the familiar clothing brought a lump to her throat. She heard herself babbling to fill the silence. "Look at you, Philip, dressed in common work clothes." The dimple in his chin disappeared as he scowled at the puddle of water he had left on the floor, but she continued, undeterred. "How your fiancée could see her way to travel all the way to Oregon Country without you, I just can't fathom."

"What choice did she have?" He pulled back a chair and slumped into it.

Everything she said was making it worse, but she couldn't help herself. "I know you would do anything to keep from being drawn into the war that's coming between the states, but the newspapers hold that maybe we can still come to an agreement.

"Holding slaves or killing another person—both are wrong in my eyes. I won't put myself in the fight. Better I leave before I'm put in that position."

"It takes courage to hold to your beliefs. You should have fought as hard to keep your precious Laurel by your side. Long trip across the plains, anything could happen. Here you are, fancy-free, and your intended is twenty-five hundred miles away. For a whole year now, too."

His voice was nearly a growl. "Her father didn't trust me to keep his daughter safe. Thinks I'm a city boy."

Mary felt a flash of anger on his behalf. "You're too easygoing for your own good. People take you for a dreamer, and not a doer. Show him he's wrong. Laurel's your perfect match."

He looked relieved. "Her letters from Oregon City say she's not changed her mind."

"Then go to her. The wagon trains start for Oregon in a month. You can still make it."

She didn't realize she'd spoken aloud until Philip glanced up, frustration in his voice. "Too late now. I promised your father I'd see you settled before I go."

"You don't mean *settled*. You mean married off." She looked up to see his blush. "Philip Rodgers, I don't intend to be packed off like I'm in your way!" The last words were spoken in a rush of tears.

She served up his portion of oats and took a seat opposite him. The thought of eating turned her stomach, so he ate in silence then escaped to the barn while she collected the dishes and rinsed them. When the kitchen was clean she wandered aimlessly about the parlor, pausing to run her fingers over the organ keys while her heart broke. She was weak from crying when she heard a vigorous knock at the door. For a moment, she considered not answering, but that would not be honest. Instead, she dried her eyes on her apron, not caring that her eyes were swollen and red, and opened the door to find the florid face of her neighbor, Mr. Claus Vandevender.

He ducked into the farmhouse looking shy and out of place in the company parlor where he stood twisting his worn coalman's cap between work-roughened fingers. Smelling of earth, fresh rain and a splash of bay rum, he said, "Miss Mary, I beg a moment of your time."

She felt her eyes tearing up. He had been her father's friend for as long as she could remember. A short, barrel-chested man in his mid-forties, he had come from Denmark long before she was born, with nothing but a worn carpetbag and a head full of dreams. By dint of hard work and luck he bought the farm on the northwest side of the Rodgers's three hundred acres. Neighbors in every sense of the word, they shared the shearing of the sheep and harvesting of the crops, working together whenever the need. He was the first to respond when he got word of Henry Rodgers's illness. It seemed to Mary that he was always laughing as he worked beside the other men at barn raisings and road buildings. He was the first to pick up a hammer, and the first to lift a tankard of his beloved beer when the work was done. He was a worker—of that, she was certain—but whether he was the man she should marry, she knew otherwise. Still, with red face and careful pronunciation, marriage was exactly what Mr. Vandevender was proposing.

"Miss Mary, the timing is all wrong, but this your Papa would want for you, no?" The cap he was twisting in his fingers showed danger of coming apart at the seams. "Marrying me would be a good thing. I would soothe your sorrows, for I know the way. Later, we could share the land and have much together, yah?"

The idea of seeing the preacher again after yesterday's heartache nearly brought her breakfast up. Surely he would understand this. Looking frantically around the room, she searched for inspiration in her mother's whatnot shelf, in the spider's web that graced the corner, in anything but his wide-eyed, hopeful eyes. "Mr. Vandevender—"

"Please, call me Claus." He smiled, his cap still revolving in his hands.

"Claus," the name stuck in her throat like undercooked taffy candy. "Um, Claus…you have been a good friend to me and to my family."

"No more family do you possess now, Miss Mary. It is only you, looking so much like my dear Hilda when she was a girl. But she is gone, two years now, leaving me with the three little ones to rear alone. So here I am with hat in hand to do the asking."

His sincerity unleashed a flood of tears. "Oh, Mr.—er, Claus. I'm so sorry. But it's too soon." Her voice broke and she could not continue.

"Time will be taking care of the sadness. This, I know from my Hilda."

"Claus, I will always think of you as a good friend." She spoke gently, forcing herself to meet his clear blue eyes. "But I don't love you." She watched his trusting smile fade.

"I…" He paused, then slowly continued. "I have feared to hear this, but I had to say my piece." His eyes shifted to the floor while his eyes registered disappointment. "Maybe in time you will change your mind about us? About being a mother to my children?"

She shook her head, not trusting herself to speak while the seconds ticked by in the corner. He glanced up at the time-piece on the wall as if the minute hand was warning that he not overstay his welcome. "Well, then I'll say my farewells, Mary Rodgers. I am so sorry for your loss. And for my family's, as well."

"Thank you, Claus, for everything." Mary covered his rough, trembling hand with her fingers.

He mustered a weak smile, his eyes dewy with disappointment. "If you are set on leaving, I mean what I say to your Papa about buying the farm. I have cash money. I would be happy to help you out." He bobbed his head in a quick, respectful gesture and turned to the door.

Mary watched from the steps as he drove his wagon away, back straight and cap firmly atop his head.

Chapter Two

March 5, 1848. For however long life flows within me, I must make every day count. My mind knows this, but my heart is without direction. I pray for Mama and Papa to guide me.

MARY WAITED FOR Philip to return from the barn before she poured two cups of coffee and took a seat across the table while apprehension clenched her belly. "Philip, I am not entirely helpless. I'm grown, now. And I have a plan." Despite her firm words, her coffee cup trembled.

"You got a husband in mind, already?" Philip sounded unflatteringly relieved.

"I said I have a *plan*, not a husband. Now, hear me out. Before Papa died, Mr. Vandevender promised to look out for…everything."

"Are you interested in the man?" Philip glanced up in surprise.

She snorted, "No, Goose. But he's willing to buy the farm. In hard currency. He's been saving for years and we could close the transaction in a day or two. He might have need of Mama's things, too. Wouldn't that be wonderful?" Her voice cracked and she took refuge behind her coffee cup, masking her tears.

"But, Mary, honey, think carefully, here. You'll be feeling

better one day, and you'll be wanting her fine things." Philip's voice took on the calm reasoning of a man explaining to a child until he saw the sudden shift in her expression. "Okay, what's your plan?"

"Well, actually, I figure to go to Oregon with you."

Mary watched Philip react as though she had suddenly turned into a snake. His heavy oak chair crashed to the floor. He lunged to his feet and stood fuming. She raised her calm, uplifted face, hoping to check his ire. It worked, to a point.

"Now, listen here, Mary. I won't even consider it. Your life's here."

"No, Philip. My life *was* here. I buried it yesterday in the Wedgewood Cemetery. I haven't had time to grieve, and that will come, but I won't be left to shuffle around in this house, making my life a shrine to those I've lost. I'm too upset to face these walls another day. I need a fresh start." She moved toward the dry sink, hoping to appear calm.

"No. That's surely not possible. No!" His flushed, angry face said it plainer than his words.

"Why not?"

"You need a list? For one thing, I promised your Pa I'd keep you safe. You know as well as I do the reports making their way back. Diseases, floods, Indian attacks and just plain misery are besetting folks on that trail. I worried myself sick over Laurel. There's no way I'm going to risk losing the only family I've got left."

She shook her head so vigorously that her curls bounced against her ears. "Not reason enough. There's calamity right here in Illinois. At least on the trail we could face the dangers together. What's the next reason?"

"All right—my wagon's packed full-up. There's no room for your things."

"I'll sell them to the ladies in town. They've always admired Mama's organ and her whatnot cabinet. I can think of half-a-dozen ladies who would jump at the chance." Mary ignored the pain stabbing at her heart.

Philip eyed her apprehensively. "You'd give them up?"

"I'd trade them for a chance at a new life. That's not giving them up. Mama would agree."

"What about Buttercup? Can't take your filly with you." A flat statement made harder by the unyielding look in his eyes.

"Then...I'll sell her too." Mary's heart sank. "Philip, I don't eat much. You know I don't. I wouldn't take up much room. I'll sleep under the wagon. I'll pay my share of the provisions. I'll cook for you and I won't ever complain. No matter how hard it gets, I won't forget that I forced you to take me. Oh, please, Philip, it's the only way."

"Mary, the answer is no. It's just not possible."

"But—"

His face flamed. "Besides, how would we explain ourselves? We may feel like we're brother and sister, but we aren't. We're first cousins, and our traveling together in that little wagon would be mightily frowned on. Folks would shun you for the scandal. I've seen it happen before."

Truth to tell, she, too, had witnessed cases where the townspeople banded together to rid the sinner from their midst. There was no arguing with Philip on that point.

Her silence seemed to indicate her surrender, at least to Philip. Gulping a last swig of coffee, he gave her a pat on the head on his way out the door. "Don't you worry, Mary-girl. We'll think of something."

Mary collected the dirty dishes, preoccupied with Philip's reasoning. As she tossed the dishwater into the sodden backyard, she was struck with sudden inspiration—they could pose as husband and wife. Who would know? After all, they shared the same last name; all they had to do was introduce themselves as *The Rodgers family*. And she had her mother's wedding ring. If she chose to wear it on her finger—to keep it safe—that was her choice. When people got to know them, she would request that they call her *Mary*. Sleeping arrangements would be a problem, but people would be crowding together in all kinds of conditions and she could hang a blanket between them when they slept under the wagon. Later, as provisions dwindled, she could sleep in the wagon. It was perfect. Somehow though, she knew Philip wouldn't think so.

On her way to the outhouse, Mary made a furtive trip to inspect Philip's Conestoga wagon. She stepped onto the wheel spoke and heaved herself onto the seat. It was higher than the old farm wagon. She thought of the women she knew who had started the trip in various stages of pregnancy and wondered how they managed. Peering into the back, she saw that Philip hadn't lied when he said it was packed. It was filled to overflowing with three, two-hundred-pound barrels of flour, two wooden boxes each holding two-hundred pounds of salt pork. She had seen the way he double-wrapped the bacon in heavy burlap sacks, pouring cornmeal over the bundles until the boxes were full. He said it would prevent the bacon from turning rancid in the summer heat. Reading his description, it hadn't occurred to her that she might be eating any of it.

Her inventory continued: fifty pounds of coffee, the same of rice, thirty pounds each of lard, dried fruit, and lead, one hundred pounds of sugar, thirty-five pounds of salt and pepper, five pounds saleratus, a tent, a bedroll that must weigh forty pounds at least, all stowed against the high walls of the sturdy wagon. Philip had included various cooking utensils, matches, candles, soap, harness fixings, axes, rope, tools of every kind, extra wheel rims and spokes, and a fiddle. Other boxes held seeds and cuttings for the farm he planned to homestead. Water barrels and a plowshare were strapped to the sides of the wagon.

Philip had read everything he could get his hands on in preparation for the journey. Even his clothing supplies came straight from the pages of the *Prairie Traveler:* two red flannel shirts for him and several for trading, two wool undershirts, two pairs of thick cotton drawers, six pairs each of cotton and wool socks, two pairs of stout walking shoes, a coat and a greased canvas rain slicker. Various personal items completed the list, not the least of which, repair and sewing kits made up by Ruth Rodgers, months ago. Mary had heard her father and Philip discuss his supplies so often that she could recite them by heart. Now, her heart sank as she viewed the collection. Neatly boxed and properly secured, the supplies filled the wagon. The wagon itself was a simply-built but sturdy affair for which Philip had paid eighty-five dollars to the local wagon maker. The wheels were white-oak. More expensive than pine, but worth the expense, he claimed.

Mary fingered the box containing three rifles and two sets of pistols. She glanced at her father's fields and tried to visualize a land so savage that men were forced to kill one another just to survive. Even with such an arsenal, could Philip— or she—fire on a fellow being? She had seen too much life stolen from the unwilling; she would not be quick to take a life. She peered out over the farm, but the Illinois landscape held no answers.

After returning the guns to their nest, she made her way to the front of the wagon and jumped. Halfway to the ground she jerked against the wooden spokes and heard the rending of fabric. Her skirts were entangled on the axle knob. With a twist she pulled herself free and leaned against the wagon until her legs stopped shaking. She ached where her hip had struck the axle knob, but the pain was a relief compared to the numbness that filled her body. Heart and soul, she was numb.

Thoroughly discouraged, she sauntered over to the chicken coop where half-a-dozen hens pecked the toes of her shoes. Nestling a warm egg against her chin, she caressed the shell and tried to find a solution. For once in her life she resented Philip's conservative nature. He had thought of everything, had forgotten nothing. Probably even over-packed.

"Wait—that's it!" Egg-gathering forgotten, she grabbed her skirts in both hands and ran into the house, up the stairs and into her parents' bedroom where Philip had spent the night. On the bureau she noticed his dog-eared copy of *The Prairie Traveler,* his bible for the past winter. Hurriedly scanning the pages, she found what she was looking for: a list of recommended supplies for three people journeying west.

"Five barrels of flour," she read aloud, "but he's taking three—just for himself." As she skimmed down the page, a slip of paper fell to the floor. Stooping to pick it up she glanced toward the door with a guilty flush, but she continued reading the list he had compiled in his neat, precise script.

A moment later she sank to the edge of the bed, weak-kneed in excitement. "Trust Philip! He's packed almost enough for a whole extra person." She double-checked the lists for numbers that would prove her right—or wrong. "If we pack some extra jerky and dried beans, a little more coffee and an extra barrel for water, we might just have enough. We'll be pretty lean by the time we reach Oregon, but from the looks of it, we could manage." From the vanity she found his stubby pencil and began her own calculations. "And besides, this list for three people is probably for big, strapping fellows. I don't eat very much, and I can eat less if I have to."

Carefully replacing the list and the book where she found it, Mary closed the door to Philip's room and remembered her chickens, still waiting. While she sprinkled grain in the hen house and watched the Plymouth Rocks peck right up to her skirts, she felt like she was seeing them for the last time. Each time she glanced at the apple trees, rested her arms on the old board fence that corralled the milk cow, hung damp towels on the clothes line or carried a bucket of water up the back stoop, she felt like she was saying 'good-bye'. Going into the springhouse to fetch a crock of buttermilk, she said good-bye to the coolness. Listening to the drone of the fat bees sipping on the crocus, she said good-bye to them. Watching the sparrows dog the hawk that threatened their nests, she was reminded that one did not have to be the biggest to succeed—only the most persistent.

She was ready with more than supper when she called Philip to the table that night. As she passed the boiled potatoes, she kept her gaze on the bowl, took a deep breath and said, "Philip, I noticed you've packed far more than your handbook says you'll need."

"Oh? And how'd you be knowing that?" He raised questioning eyes and speared a potato with his fork. "Been reading up on Oregon, have you? I never suspected you harbored a passion for travel."

Mary felt her face heat. "Well, things have changed, and so have my opinions. Anyway, listen. You have nearly double what you need. I only eat a little bit, and I won't even drink much water. I would take the clothes I need and nothing else."

"And your mother's things? I don't intend starting out with fancy knickknacks and mirrors and rocking chairs that get tossed out somewhere in the Kansas prairie when the oxen get too tired to pull them."

"I'll make arrangements to leave them with Mr. Vandevender. He can have them shipped around the Horn to San Francisco and we can pick them up there."

"Cost twice what they're worth. Doubt your father would approve."

"Maybe not—but Mama would. Once the farm sells, I'll have the money. Papa had an account in the bank, besides." Mary's voice lowered and her eyes pleaded intensely, "Please, Philip. We can do it."

Philip studied her face as he weighed each word. "Can't pass ourselves off as brother and sister. We're as far apart in looks as two people can be—you with black hair and green eyes and me, blond and blue. Folks would think our Ma dallied over the neighbor's fence."

She caught her breath just in time. "We'll travel together as husband and wife."

His fist pounded the table so hard that her coffee cup rattled. "What in tarnation's got into you?" He looked so incredulous that she had to smile. "In case you've forgotten, I've a bride waiting in Oregon."

"But Philip—"

"Don't you 'but Philip' me! The wagonmaster's word is law. If he said we had to marry proper, there'd be no getting out of it. I'd be double cursed, loving Laurel and married to you." He spun off across the room, his fair skin a ruddy blaze of fury.

Mary bit her lip to hide her trembling. He could only think of why her plan wouldn't work. She could only think of why it must. "All we have to do is be nice to each other and people will assume we're shy. Do you have a better suggestion?"

"What if we get found out?"

Mary could feel his resolve waning. "How? How could anyone find out if we don't tell them? We don't know anyone who's going west right now." She hoped she was right.

Looking down at his cold dinner, Philip lowered his head into his hands with a weary sigh. "Well, reckon it might be worth thinking on. I'm not making any promises."

"Does that mean I can go? And Buttercup?" Mary waited while the big clock in the parlor ticked its cadence.

Finally, his eyes returned to her. With a shrug of defeat, he agreed. "Your father'd have my hide for this. But no matter what, we play the roles we set. That clear?"

"Oh, yes. Yes! I promise, dear Philip, you won't regret this."

Chapter Three

March 10, 1848. Today we set forth on our West-ering. Henceforth all my thoughts will be sur-rendered to one outcome. May God go with us.

AS THEIR WAGON rolled past the Vandevender farm, Claus and his three children pulled into the lane on their way to their new property. Mary called out, "Good luck. Thank you for everything."

Claus's answering smile turned wistful. "Good-bye, Miss Mary...Philip. Godspeed to you both." Then he was gone, left behind in the track.

The creaking wagon had not traveled a mile when they recognized a buggy coming toward them. The Klaumanns, neighbors from two farms over, eyed the loaded Conestoga wagon with Buttercup tied to the tailgate.

Mrs. Klaumann hailed them with her customary thin smile. "Well, landsakes, so you're bound for the Oregon Country. Gonna help expand the reach of the States clean to the Pacific Ocean. 'Manifest Destiny,' President Polk and his cronies call it. I feel we should be unfurling the flag for the two of you." Her husband nudged her, but she continued. "Set your minds to that westering whimsy, did you? Thought you'd have better sense. The two of you traveling alone?"

"Oh, no," Mary replied in her sweetest voice. "We plan to stop by nightfall at our spinster cousin's house in Merriam. She is a teacher, and has wanted to start a school in Oregon for the longest time." Her fabrication sounded good, if she did think so.

"I wasn't aware you had a cousin living so near. Surprised we've never seen her. What's her name?" The woman was tenacious.

"Anne."

"Rose."

Mary and Philip spoke in quick, nervous unison.

"Uh, Roseanne is her given name," Mary improvised quickly. "She's sensitive about her age. Goes by Anne, now that's she's older."

"See that you don't abuse the Sabbath. Your mother would turn over—"

Philip suddenly found much to occupy himself as another horse and buggy came trotting toward them. "We best be going, ma'am. Blocking the road." Tugging the brim of his felt hat, he urged the oxen on.

• ♥ •

They made camp that night in a driving rainstorm and spent the hours until daylight under the wagon, wrapped in a tarp while rivulets of rain soaked the ground beneath them. For her dinner, Mary munched on a cold biscuit and tried not to think about the leftover beef stew she had left behind for Claus Vandevender. As darkness descended, a panther screamed from a nearby treetop and small feet padded past on the other side of the camp, leaving Mary to stare out into the darkness at the dense forest with its mantle of cover that made her feel trapped and vulnerable. "I'm not going to give Philip the satisfaction of hearing me complain, no matter what I have to do," she muttered to herself. But in spite of her resolve, her tears fell.

Sometime after midnight, she awoke from a troubled dream where her father and mother stood at the farmhouse door pleading for her to return.

At sunup she arose, stiff, weary and filled with apprehension. Her eyes were swollen from crying, but she kept her head down and prepared the meal in silence. For the rest of the day, spring rain fell in thick sheets of misery while she slogged along, draped in a poncho of thick gutta percha. No matter that she dressed for the elements or that she tried not to move in her stiff poncho, her muslin dress became a mass of clammy layers that soaked her to the bone.

Philip fared no better. He developed a blister from his new boots.

The Pilgrim House Inn appeared at a misty crossroads, offering a hot meal and a chance to dry off. Mary bit her tongue to keep from asking for the favor, but she felt like hugging Philip when he guided the wagon to the shoulder of the road and motioned for her to follow him inside. The inn was nearly full. At home it would be an early hour for supper, but on the trail people ate whenever it was convenient. From the comfort of a window table, they watched wagons pass. Everyone seemed filled with the apprehension as they hurried to make it to the setting off point in Independence, especially the children who peered at the bright windows of the inn with ill-concealed longing.

She glanced around the room hoping that she would not recognize any of the diners, or more correctly, that none of them would recognize *her*.

At a nearby table, a stranger was applying himself to his meal with gusto. She stared while he sipped his coffee with an ease that revealed twin hollows beneath high cheekbones.

His left eyelid drooped slightly, giving him a lazy, nonchalant appearance that contrasted with the feral leanness of his body. She found herself unable to shake off the image of his black hair, worn long and straight over his shoulders. His bronze skin was smooth and unlined, and it reminded her of a charcoal drawing in one of the frontier guide books that Philip owned.

A man with Indian blood, his face held a scowl for the room and anyone who might be watching. She felt compelled to study the manner in which his lips closed around the morsel of bread he had stabbed with his knife blade. She wondered if they would be required to share the road for long. If he owned the string of horses tied to the rail outside, he would be heading west along the same road, a solitary horseman in tanned skin britches and a fringed hide shirt. She gave an involuntary shiver and was glad when the waiter brought her coffee.

Between bites of beef pie, Mary felt the man's glance on her. Judging from his scowl, he did not approve of women going west, or possibly the color of her dress, or maybe he disliked beef pie. Flustered, she tipped her cup too quickly and managed to slosh coffee onto the table covering.

Across the table, Philip was calmly finishing his meal. Swallowing his second cup of coffee he politely inquired, "You going to finish your pie?"

She shook her head. "I couldn't eat another bite." The scowling man had ruined her appetite. As they left the room she pressed her lips together at the pungent whiff from the man's cigar.

• ♥ •

Lucas Sayer glanced at the girl with the mane of ebony hair framing her ivory face and frowned. He hadn't gotten close enough to find out, but her Irish coloring made him pretty sure her eyes were green. Her skin had a glow of health that spoke of travel in the open air. She was another eastern girl unprepared for the trail ahead, probably destined to be dead before her time. Framed in the doorway, she caused his blood to burn with frustration. He made himself a promise. He wasn't riding the emigrant trail this time as a scout. If he did, he would end up watching her die—whether of thirst or childbirth, it didn't matter, but she would die—he could almost count on it. The man sitting across from her was a tenderfoot who should have stayed in the city. He'd seen hundreds just like him.

At least the woman wouldn't be his concern this trip. He was traveling to Independence to meet a friend, nothing more. He wasn't exposing himself to the troubles that a trainload of strangers brought with them. Wasn't going to stand by and watch as they brought their diseases to a hundred Indian camps, including his own people. Fury darkened his irises to granite black. He had stopped at the inn to rest and it had been a waste of time. For a young man, he felt old. Maybe he was destined to share his mother's heritage, death by white man's disease, but his father's trapper blood kept him riding from place to place, trying to find a reason to care about something.

He watched the dark-haired girl walk away with a swish of her skirts, apparently intended to let him know that she did not approve of him, but if that were the case, she could stand in line behind the girls in his white school who had already sent the message that he wasn't suitable husband material. At least, this one wore her hair like an Indian maiden, unfettered and natural. She was not his concern; he told himself a second time.

• ♥ •

When Philip insisted they make camp next to another wagon, the sun was still high in the sky. "Why are we stopping so soon?" Mary kept her voice to a murmur.

"Because the book says the animals need time to graze."

She watched Philip struggle with the unfamiliar yoke as he narrowly escaped an oversized hoof. By the time he finished, he was sweating, even in the chill air. One of his boots had a gash in the side.

"Does the book say we have to set camp so close?"

Philip scarcely glanced up. "I read that it's good to camp in the trees. Gives us some protection from horse thieves and robbers."

"Horse thieves?" She turned to be sure that Buttercup was still tied to the back of the wagon.

"Not just horses. Mules, too. Right along with their harnesses. That's one reason why I decided on oxen." He pulled the canvas aside and motioned toward a wooden box. "Best get started on supper."

"'Spect you're right. I'll have enough trouble without worrying about thieves." She collected a bundle of twigs to make a fire, but the starter was sodden. She used a page of her precious diary paper and vowed that she would keep a dry stash of kindling from now on, even if she had to carry it in her pocket. She went to collect a sifter of flour for biscuits, but she tipped the barrel and had to grab it before it rolled off the tailgate and splintered. They could ill afford the loss. "Philip, you packed this wagon for the fit and not the use. It seems like we could have one box of each thing up close, not all three barrels of flour blocking all three boxes of sugar."

She found the flour, saleratus, and lard, mixed up a batch of lumpy dough and laid the clumps side-by-side in Philip's cast iron kettle then covered it with a heavy lid. After the fire burned to a thick layer of coals, she burrowed the Dutch oven deep into the center and scooped more coals on top. She couldn't see that she did anything different from the two men camped next to her, but her biscuits came out scorched.

"Don't worry about it," Philip consoled her. "If you hadn't come along, I'd be eating burned food every meal. You'll get better. Wait and see."

Having tasted his cooking at the best of times, Mary could only agree. She thought of her mother's cooking and tried to swallow the lump in her throat. To keep from breaking down, she found herself chattering. "I hear the winds out on the prairie will blow your hat clean to Kingdom Come. At least that ugly poke bonnet I brought will stay on my head." Philip sat on a rotted log, wiping salt from his oxen's wooden yokes without speaking. She ducked her head and continued with her chores in silence, pausing only to wipe the tears flooding her cheeks. When she finished scrubbing the pot, she crossed to the stream to draw a bucket of water, fighting the stiff wind all the way to the stream and back.

A woman nearby drew her corncob pipe from her lips and motioned for her to approach. "When you've a few minutes," the woman confided in a low tone so the men wouldn't overhear, "you'd best see to stitching some buckshot into the hems of your skirts or the breeze is going to have you showing more than God intended. I reckon some of them fine Southern gals are going to be leaving their hoops behind or the whole wagon train will be in for a sight!"

The buckshot that Mary stitched into her hem bruised her legs with each step. For the next few days she slogged along in mud-encrusted boots that grew heavier with each step. Sometimes, she gave up and climbed to the wagon seat, but the jarring ride made her teeth jiggle each time the wagon hit a bump. Even when the rain didn't fall, she had mud to contend with.

They passed an over-laden wagon that had slipped off the

track; the harried driver was busy unloading it so the mules could pull it back onto the road. The rest of the group, including a woman and children, huddled in the icy wind and rain, forced to slog along in the muddy ruts, their heads hunkered into their chests, most of them thinly clad in water-logged jackets.

"Folks treat their children like livestock." Philip muttered as they pulled around the family mired down in misery. "Those little ones will be prime targets for influenza and measles. Man could figure out a place for the little ones to ride. He's got a dry place and probably the best of the nightly meal. The children usually get what's left."

Some of the wagons were returning east, their horses limping or sometimes harnessed alongside a milk cow or a steer. One group caught Mary's attention at a moment when her thoughts were on her father and mother. "Oh, Philip, look at the people coming back. They're so grim and defeated. They keep their eyes down so they don't have to see our fresh hopes." One boy reminded her of Toby. Her brother's face seemed so familiar in the young stranger's that she reached out to touch him. The boy's gaze caught hers for a moment, and then, he was gone.

"There're no guarantees, Mary," Philip told her as the boy's family passed. The woman held a limp child in her arms and two grimy children straggled along behind. The horses pulling a homemade wagon were on the verge of collapse, their sides gaunt and heaving. A makeshift pin had been thrust through one wheel so that the wagon wobbled horribly with each revolution. Even the little dog was limping, his coat matted and burred. "Hope they have kin to stay with 'til they get back on their feet. I'll vouch everything they own is tied up in that wagon."

Mary watched until they disappeared around a curve in

the road. "What will become of them?" she whispered.

"Don't let yourself fret, Mary. I know you. You'll give away everything we own."

Mary shook her head. "I've nothing of my own. It's all yours. I own nothing to give away." She wanted him to disagree, but he kept silent.

"The problem with folks who don't make it," he told her, "is that sometimes they ignore the advice of those that do."

"Are you blaming these people for their trouble?"

"Maybe." He spat to the side of the road and wiped his nose with a sodden kerchief. "Half the people we pass today started with the idea that they could hunt and provide for themselves along the way. Eat off the land."

"Is that a bad thing?"

"Live on berries and wild onions? Tell me—you seen much game so far?"

"No, but it's no wonder, with all the braying and shouting going on. At least they have water to drink."

Philip shook his head. "From what I've read, some doctors think it's the bad water and the nightsoil that's causing the cholera."

"What if we get sick?"

"We'll drink boiled coffee. Stay away from other folks. Don't share ladles or whiskey bottles. The book says those things will help. Keep to yourself as much as possible."

Mary glanced up in surprise. "You mean, don't do what Mama did."

He stared across at the swaying backs of his oxen. "I don't mean to be harsh, Mary, but what good came of her helping?"

"She would have done it even if she'd known what was going to happen. She was like that." Mary's voice broke.

"What about Toby? Think she wanted to kill her husband

and her son?" He frowned. "I'm just saying—the risks you take will affect both of us."

"I understand."

• ♥ •

Three weeks passed with the cadence of a slow drumbeat. Gradually the terrain changed from hilly woods to flat grassland, rolling prairie and vast openness. She watched the hawks soar in the bright open sky as she leaned far back on the wagon seat. One day, sleepy and sated, she tracked them through half-closed eyes as they caught a wind current. "Oh, Phil—what it must be like to be so free, to trust the winds to take you where you need to go."

She felt herself becoming one with the land she traveled. Her grief softened into serenity as she experienced freedom from the daily routine she had known since childhood. Each night she captured the essence of that day in her little leather-bound book.

> March 25, 1848. We have experienced no problems, no setbacks, no new grief other than the one that never leaves me. Still, I feel as though I have been reborn, baptized in the beauty of this wonderful country. Already we have seen more than my father ever dreamed. Oh, heart, I shall live, after all.

Philip noticed the change. "Mary-girl, I gave a hard argument for leaving you behind, but you surely brought the sunshine with you. There's a sunray traveling above us this very minute." He pointed up into the cloudless sky. "See, what did I tell you?"

"You could charm the clouds out of the sky. You probably did." She felt her heart lift as she began humming a verse of

"Annie Laurie," her father's favorite song.

At noon, they stopped to rest in a grassy meadow beside a bend in the road. As soon as she had her meal heating, she unbound her freshly washed hair to dry it. Barefoot, she clasped her arms above her head and spun in a circle, her thick curls whipping about her face. At the sound of hoof beats she fell to the ground, dizzy and embarrassed that someone had witnessed her child's play. She expected to see a caravan. Instead, it was a lone horseman driving a string of spirited horses; an olive-skinned man clothed in rough mountain wear, with a black, wide-brimmed hat worn low over thick, black hair that fell across his shoulders. It was his scowl that held her captive.

Unconsciously, she lifted her chin in defiance and waited until the rider disappeared around the next bend.

Chapter Four

April 12, 1848. We are in Independence, itching to begin. The atmosphere here is that of a fair. We all have grand hopes for our journey. Old-timers warn us otherwise, but we cannot help but feel hopeful. It seems that Mother and Father are with us. Provisions are costly, but we are prepared.

INDEPENDENCE, MISSOURI BUSTLED with life and energy, a prairie town full of piss and vinegar. People had been arriving with their wagons and their animals; some had even wintered here, waiting for relatives to catch up. The sprawling town served as the last outpost for buying and selling horses, mules and oxen; the corrals on the outskirts of town held every variety of livestock, with the sounds of cursing muleskinners and horse traders going on all day and long into the night.

Wagon trains began forming on the edges of the town, a few leaving each day, rain or shine. The folks just arriving eagerly lined up to hear the various train companies sell their services. *Westering,* an Eastern newspaper had termed it, and the name had stuck. Some families that couldn't afford a guide or were too anxious to bother waiting, took off alone, planning to hook up with a train when they hit Indian country.

Philip hobbled his team at the edge of town near a man named Murphy who promised to keep an eye on their gear while they saw to their reservations. Mary wanted to change into something that didn't carry the stain of trail mud and she rummaged among boxes and crates until she reached her trunk. With one elbow bracing the lid, she pulled out a buttercup yellow shirtwaist and a black serge skirt and dropped the lid with a *thunk*. Philip kept watch so that she could crouch beneath the canvas cover and struggle out of her mud-splattered prairie dress, but the space was so tight that her heart was pounding by the time she fastened the last button.

Careful of the slippery wagon box, she jumped to the ground. She shook her hair loose, gave it a thorough brushing and tied her thick curls back with a yellow ribbon. The feel of fresh clothing made her skin feel gritty, but Philip wouldn't allow her time to do more than scrub with a ladle of tepid water and a scrap of flannel toweling.

"Maybe we can find a bathhouse. One last bath to last me half a year." She glanced from Philip's dusty hair to her own, tangled and wind-tossed, stiff with trail dust. Her skin was still soft, owing in no small part to the ugly sunbonnet.

"If one is to be found, Mary-girl, consider it done." Even Philip seemed affected by the carnival atmosphere. If Mary had a nosegay she would have pinned it to his lapel, so jaunty was his mood now that they had reached the jumping-off point.

A crisp breeze fluttered her ribbons and she remembered what it felt like to be happy. As they walked toward town she noticed admiring looks from three grizzled men who looked as wild as the beasts whose hides festooned their backs. Other trappers rode past on compact Indian ponies, their disheveled gray beards seeming to have never made the acquaintance of a straight razor or strop, but the men rode with the agility of men half their age, sitting their ponies bareback with just their knees to guide their mounts.

Philip teased, "Maybe I better leave you back at the wagon."

"You could try, but I have my defenders—three of them." She turned and indicated the three mountain men who were grinning at her like she was fresh cream on strawberries. She was relieved when they returned to their conversation.

"They probably like that dirt mustache you've been wearing for the last few days." He crooked his finger above his own lip and grinned.

They made their way down the sidewalk, a haphazard affair of wooden planks thrown down to keep the ladies from the worst of the mud. They passed a bathhouse with crude signs denoting "Ladies" and "Fellers".

"I'll be back here, for sure." Mary was torn between halting on the spot and seeing the rest of the town. The noise and excitement won out.

Next to the bathhouse, a huge, dark woman was operating a laundry with huge vats of steaming water heating over low fires. Several clotheslines held rows of men's red woolen underwear: some bright red, others neatly patched and faded to a dull pink. The lines also held rows of woolen trousers, red plaid shirts, even the occasional ladies cotton unmentionable, sweeping the breeze alongside linsey-jersey shirtwaists.

On the other side of the street a blacksmith sweated in the chill air as he pounded on his anvil under a cottonwood. The *clang clang* of hammer against hot iron seemed deafening after the silence of the past month.

Nearby, a pile of waiting projects attested to the fact that the blacksmith was well on his way to making his fortune, without ever traveling to the Oregon Territory. Apparently, not every emigrant arrived ready for the trail. A red glow of coals bathed the smithy's face in a ruddy countenance that, from a distance, reminded Mary of her father. When she could no longer bear the pain of remembering, she moved on.

Their first stop was at a store whose sign read, simply, *Mercantile*. Built of wide, hand-hewn cottonwood planks, it seemed more durable than most of the surrounding buildings, some of which were merely canvas tents. Inside, Mary was greeted with a blast of warmth from a wood stove. She moved closer and indulged herself until her cheeks took on the ruddy color of the flannel shirts displayed on the store's counter. When she was sated she stepped away to make room for two girls her own age, also Oregon-bound judging by the way they kept their purses closed to temptation.

She began shopping among great sacks of flour set on rough flooring, along with crackers in barrels, burlap sacks of sugar, and boxes of bacon and salt-pork.

The store plainly catered to hungry travelers and not genteel womenfolk like those of her hometown. She saw rifles, but no toys; lead and seed, but not many laces or ribbons. Nowhere did she see cake molds or fancy dishes, or fabric, or any of the fine bric-a-brac favored by the ladies back home, only basic staples at prices that made her cringe. Shoes were sturdy, plain, and three times the cost. For that matter, everything was. At home, a hundred pounds of sugar cost less than five dollars while here in Independence—where a person had the option of paying the price or doing without—sugar cost twelve cents a pound.

She waited until she reached the boardwalk before she exploded at Philip. "Did you see those prices? It would have cost me the whole farm had we waited to supply here."

"Can't eat money where we're going," Philip answered. Nearby, a tent building served as a harness shop with racks of ready-made harness. "I feel sorry for the folks who had to winter over here."

They slogged through the mud, dodging high-strung horses and herds of long-horn cattle bound for corrals on the other side of town. An occasional gunshot rang out from saloons that seemed to be doing a booming business even at this time of the afternoon. From one, the tinkling keys of a piano blended with raucous laughter. A string of curses shook the air, along with a string of language that turned Mary's ears pink. She recognized female voices blending with the laughter and she gawked at the skimpily dressed women entertaining the men. The double doors swung open and a drunken frontiersman lurched forward, so close that she could smell the sweat on his rancid leather jerkin when he landed unceremoniously in the mud.

At the open door, a burly mountain man raised his mug in salute and called, "Little lady, come on in. I'll give you a look-see."

Mary willed herself to turn away and hurried ahead, kilting her skirt in both hands, but she couldn't help herself from glancing back, and when she did the man was enjoying a knee-slapping guffaw at her expense. She was still quailing when Philip hailed a grizzled looking old-timer in a filthy deerskin shirt with enormous red suspenders attached to canvas britches.

"If looks are any indication," he whispered to Mary, "That man knows his way around the frontier." He approached the man with a cautious regard. "Begging your pardon, old timer, but could you advise us of a good wagon company?" The man hesitated and took a swig from a jug without speaking.

Philip seemed loath to continue the conversation, but it seemed that he was already engaged. "Some seem better than others. A stranger might need advice since there seem to be some shady ones…"

Mary stood back, trying to extricate herself from the stench drifting off the man, a mixture that seemed to be part animal, part rancid grease and sweat. Hastily, she grabbed for her handkerchief and affected a sneeze while she managed to back off a few paces.

The old timer paused with a keen eye on Mary while he answered Philip's questions. "Yep. And getting rich right along with them what knows the trail, I reckon. Leastwise, 'til they meet their first dried-up water hole or Injun. Money don't mean much to a dead man." He gaped a toothless grin for Mary's benefit and announced, "Son, ya come to the right man. I'll pardner ya up with the finest hide around. He's hard. Ya might even say ornery, but he'll get ya there safe and sound, with yer hair still in place. Somethin' to be said for that!"

Relief showed in Philip's face. "We're much obliged."

The old-timer grinned while Mary kept her eyes glued to the horse rail in front of her. There was no way that she wanted him to think she was flirting with him. He looked as if he fought grizzlies barehanded for sport.

"Name's 'Mean Bill'. Ain't used a last name in so long, ain't sure I still got one. Speaking of, I was privileged to do some trapping with the young fellow's father that I'm taking you to. He's a square lad, for sure." He bit a plug from a wad of pocket tobacco. A minute later he spit a long stream at the boot of a tenderfoot, who jumped back in surprise.

Mary shut her eyes as a wave of nausea roiled her stomach.

"You all right?" Philip whispered.

She nodded, concentrating only on the muddy path before her. "I didn't expect quite so much local color."

"Well, I don't imagine they come more colorful than Bill. But he may end up saving our lives." Philip took the lead and Mary followed, gripping her skirts in both hands while she dodged wagon ruts. She was winded by the time they stopped outside a building that proved to be as haphazard as the rest of the town.

"Don't need frills to do this business," Bill hollered to Philip. A moment later, he apparently forgot all about them as he hailed the wagonmaster and began a long-winded story punctuated with hearty backslaps and a goodly amount of cursing.

At the sign-up area, a slightly built, bespectacled young man sat at a table constructed of crude pine boards laid across four unfinished tree limbs that read: Columbia/Ft. Boise Route. He appeared to be the clerk for the company and his office equipment consisted of a ledger, a pen and bottle of ink, and a small moneybox that he kept locked until he needed to make a deposit.

"What's the difference between routes?" Mary asked.

Philip lowered his head and murmured, "There's a new bypass into Oregon by the southern route, they call the 'Applegate Trail'. 'Sposed to be easier, but the rumors are that it was a hard push for those who got talked into taking it last year. Worse the year before. It may be a fine trail by now, hard to tell. But I'm taking the Columbia route."

Mary joined Philip behind a giant hunk of a man and his petite wife who held the hands of two little boys who appeared to be no older than five. *Favors the mother*, Mary thought, as she watched the family.

"Howdy. Name's George Tate. Hail from Missouri. We're heading out for the Oregon country, where I hear the trees tower like giants from the mountains clean to the Pacific. Paradise on earth! Where the snow feeds the rivers, the fish jump into your net and the grass grows sweet in the valleys. I plan to cut timber so thick, I'll have to hire men to help harvest it ever' summer." He seemed like a man who loved an audience. Expansive and garrulous, he gestured in huge sweeping motions. "Built my wagon with my bare hands. Took me some osage and planed those boards till they be smooth as a baby's bottom. Coated it with pitch tar so's it'll float like a boat when the time comes for crossing rivers."

"Glad to meet you, Mr. Tate. Our name is Rodgers. Philip and Mary." To Mary's mind, Philip sounded nervous.

"Mr. Tate was my father. I'm just George." George Tate laughed at his little joke and continued. "This here's the little wife, Bethellen. I'd have struck out on my own, 'cept she wouldn't hear of it. Afore I knew it we was all packed up, no two ways about it."

Turning to greet Mrs. Tate, Mary noticed the woman's loose dress hid a swollen belly. *Poor dear, no bigger than a minute. And with child, besides.* She hid her thoughts behind a bright smile. It seemed that Bethellen didn't seem overly concerned at the prospect of an uncertain birth on the trail. The young wife obviously felt the sun rose and set on her strapping man and that she would do her part when the time came.

"George is determined our boys get a better life than us, and he says 'twill be the early ones get the best pickings. We ain't ever been first in anything, so we figure to hurry on out and pick us a good piece of land. He figures to raise a few horses for the army that'll be following. We brought us a good start in livestock."

Mary nodded in agreement. "That's the way Philip sees it. We intend to homestead in Oregon, on land that's fed by a river."

"You seem so young, Miz Rodgers." Bethellen was probably only a couple of years older, but the two children gave her an air of added maturity. "How long you been married?"

Mary panicked at the question. She figured it would come up, sooner or later, but not from the very first people she met. "Uh, why we, er—we got married for the trip." That was pretty close to the truth.

"Goodness. Just newlyweds. Can't have been married more than a month."

"Not even that." There, that was no lie.

Bethellen patted her belly where the baby took up more than its fair share. "Well, you're bound to be in a family way soon, just like me. Seems I hardly get one weaned, got myself 'nother coming along. Makes me happy, though. You'll see when your time comes."

Mary thought her face must be the hue of a wild rose. She was not sure just what was required of her in this odd conversation, but in spite of herself she had an instant liking for Bethellen. "I hope when my time comes I will be half as good a mother as you seem to be." There, that wasn't lying.

The line moved along until it was the Tates' turn to register. They signed up, paid, and moved away from the table after promising to look Mary and Philip up when the wagon train got underway. "Nice talking with you, Mary. I know we're bound to be friends in no time." Gathering her little brood, Bethellen followed her husband off into the crowd.

Philip registered his livestock, noted the number in the party and paid the fee to the young man, who put their money into the rapidly filling strongbox.

"Next train's leaving tomorrow, first light. Line forms out on the prairie. If you're not there you'll get left behind. There's a meeting beforehand. Be sure you allow plenty of time. Wagonmaster will answer all your questions then. If he don't approve of your set-up you'll have to change it and take the next train out two days hence." The man was curt and to the point, but he had a lot of folks to register.

He was likely right. They would have their questions answered soon enough.

Most of the settlers had children along. It seemed as though every woman on the train except herself was either with child or already had several. None of the travelers seemed too well off. They seemed to be trading very little for the promise of Oregon. Mary thought about the farm she had left behind and the offer of marriage, and wondered if she would regret her decision. "Look how downtrodden folks seem, Philip. Is it my imagination, or do you see it too?"

"Sometimes takes having nothing to lose to justify the gamble we're all taking."

"What's next for them?"

"Some'll die on the trail. Some'll die when they get where they're going. Some'll do no better than they did back home, but most will prosper, I suppose."

"And the ends justify the risk?"

"Isn't that what we're thinking? They're no different than us, except we have more to lose than most of them." He glanced from the crowd to her, then back.

"Think I'll come to regret my decision?" Mary stepped into the street, quickly sidestepping to avoid being hit by a trotting horse and its rider.

"Do you?" This time, his gaze lingered.

"Not for a minute. My heart feels full, like I'm on the verge of something bigger than I thought I had in me."

"Won't change your mind when you're walking the desert with little water and no shade, or sleeping in a rainstorm, soaked to the bone?"

"I'll remember that the suffering is temporary, but what

my heart feels is forever. When I am an old lady, I'll tell my grandchildren about this trip and they will know I was one of the pioneers." She paused a moment, then added, "When I buried Mama and Papa I felt like giving up."

"You're not a coward. I've never questioned your grit."

"Speaking of grit, I need a bath." She would concentrate on the things she could change.

Philip sensed her mood and tried to tease. "Funny, I was just going to suggest that very thing."

"You implying I need a bath?" Her effort at levity felt like an effort.

"Meaning if I have to sit next to you at supper, you could have some pity on me." His grin widened as she stopped, her hands balled at her hips like an irate schoolmarm.

Laughing, they started toward the bathhouse. "Now you can get that mustache scrubbed off," he teased. Mary hit him with the only weapon at hand, her tiny handbag with its long silken strap, which she aimed directly at his right ear.

"Stop now, people will think we're newlyweds, you acting so frisky," he whispered. Mary tipped her head back and laughed at the sheer exuberance of being alive.

• ♥ •

Taking a cheroot from his mouth, Lucas Sayer watched as the girl from the inn hauled off and slammed her husband with a totally ineffective little cloth bag. He leaned casually against a scarred wall, his buckskin leggings scratching against the wood. Unhurried, he caught the flash of the girl's yellow ribbons from far down the street and anger settled in his eyes, giving them the sheen of black onyx.

He watched the young woman laugh at something her companion said while the two continued along the rutted street. "Greenhorns," he muttered. Giving her one last probing glance, he spun off into the opposite direction, his errand forgotten.

Chapter Five

April 13, 1848. We are at the crossroads of a nation, all of us with one goal. Never could I have imagined so many diverse languages and means of travel. Regardless from where we hail, from this point forward we are each for Oregon.

MARY LAY BACK in a small tin bathtub filled with hot water. At the farm she had used a hip bath in the kitchen or a sponge bath in the privacy of her room. However, this copper contraption let her sit waist-deep in steaming water, intoxicating her senses with a floral scented bar of soap that was included in the price. She raised her arms in a full stretch that brought her elbows out of the water. Taking a scrap of toweling, she started scrubbing. It was heaven, feeling the sweat, grime and at least a layer of skin disappear along with the tension and stiffness.

"Mercy, if I'm this sore after an easy walk, what will I be feeling in a couple of months?" But that was the future. She would not waste one precious moment worrying.

Finally, when she was sure someone was going to knock on the door to tell her that her time was up, she used the soap to lather her hair. Scrubbing vigorously, she rinsed and lathered again, and rinsed a final time with the bucket of spare water that the man had left for this very purpose. With a sigh of satisfaction she stepped from the tub and rubbed herself dry.

She dressed quickly, glad she had changed into fresh clothing back at the wagon. Fingering her hair into a semblance of style, she glanced in the polished tin mirror and felt satisfied with the results. Her smile matched her spirits when she stepped onto the street and the remaining daylight.

"Whooee!" Philip sounded perky after his bath and shave. "Say, lady, you haven't seen a musty trail wench around, have you? I seem to have lost her. You might've mistaken her for a drover, but she's a little smaller."

Mary flicked her damp strands in the fresh air and turned to study him. "And you? You clean up real good for an ox skinner."

"Watch your words, madam, or you'll miss your chance to have a real pork dinner."

Mary's eyes flew open in surprise. "Oh, Philip. Do you mean it? Oh, I should pin up my hair. Goodness, a real meal that I don't have to cook?"

"You look passable. Now, let's get going before I perish."

They chose a plain eating house that smelled as though the cooks knew their business. Mary's mouth was watering before she even sat down, especially when she passed a pie case loaded with chokeberry and fresh apple pies.

Inside, the room was crowded with people. More prosperous than many of the people wandering around the town, these patrons laughed and toasted and talked while waiters in wide white aprons bustled about with trays of steaks and fixings. She felt as though she were royalty as she sipped water from a real glass and studied a placard with choices so varied as to include buffalo haunch.

Although she was unaware of the effect she made, the dark-eyed man in the corner sharing dinner with two other men was not.

"…What do you think about that, Sayer? Hey, you stubborn cuss, where are you off to? Are you even listening to what I'm saying?"

Luke looked up, blinked, and pulled his attention from the yellow-clad girl and her companion. Returning his gaze to his friends, he apologized and rejoined the conversation.

Philip was sharing his bathhouse trip with Mary. "…so the fellow who was bathing in the tub next to me got into the water wearing nothing but his money belt. He said it'd taken him two years to trap his earnings, and be damned if he was going to take the chance of losing it. Sat there in the tub holding his old muzzle loader and wearing that heavy old belt. Couldn't even enjoy himself for keeping an eye on me." When he finished, she joined his laughter.

"If you'd looked at him crosswise he might have taken you for a highwayman and I'd be a widow," she teased.

"Strangest widow in the history of the West."

As they laughed again, Mary felt a pair of eyes on her, and she glanced across the room to where the dark-haired drover sat watching. He lifted his glass of whiskey to his lips without removing his intense gaze. Her laughter waned and she searched for some thread of conversation to cover her confusion. The stranger's drooping eye seeming to mock her agitation. A scowl lowered the corners of his mustache and her attention was drawn to the line of his upper lip, until she realized that she was staring. She turned away with shame heating her face, but not before the man turned back to his companions with a slight smile. Fortunately, her dinner arrived.

When she finished eating and the effort of ignoring the man became too great, she reluctantly gathered her reticule. "Philip, can we leave now?"

"Sure, but I thought you'd want to linger a bit. Nothing back at the camp but a bedroll."

"A bedroll sounds wonderful. I'm worn out tonight." She rose and followed Philip. At the door, she turned with a sweep of her skirts and caught a breath of sweet, clear air.

Turning to the older man at his side, Luke smoothed his mustache with a casual pinch of his thumb and index finger. "John, you know those two who just left?"

"You mean the pretty little gal with the Texas-rose ribbons in her hair?"

"And the citified man with the light hair? Don't happen to know their names?"

"Saw them signing up for my train earlier today. Name's Rodgers, I think."

"Brother and sister, I suppose." Luke feigned indifference with a long draw on his cheroot.

"Darned if I know. Don't recall that it said Mister and Missus, just the two names. Hers is Mary, I remember. Same as my mother's."

Luke hesitated. "Hm…well, I need to be getting on back. If McCleary is still feeling poorly, I reckon I'll agree to scout this one last time. Same wages as last. You supply the grub and the cook." He stood and stretched, flicking a quick glance at the empty doorway.

"Thanks Luke. Meeting's at sunrise. Appreciate it if you'd say a few words."

"Aren't too many men I'd scout for—any one on your train would be smart to shut their mouths and follow your lead."

"Appreciate your saying so." The two exchanged hand-shakes welcomed of men who hold a deep and time-honed respect for each other. "Luke, I'm sure glad to see you haven't succumbed to the lure of the bottle. I worry about you with neither wife nor family to set you on the straight path."

"You mean because I'm a half-breed?" Luke's eyes narrowed over the cherry red tip of his cheroot.

John Leverenz ignored his young friend. "You ought to give in and marry that little Halsey girl that set her cap for you on the '47 run. She was a pretty little thing. Last I heard, she was still waiting for you to ride back her way. Don't know what she did, chased you off. A good-looking man like you can't escape matrimony forever." He emphasized his words with a mischievous wink.

"My friend, I'm doomed to be an outcast. And crazy for liquor. Isn't that what you whites say about us?"

"Not doomed, just in harm's way. You need a wife." Leverenz's serious manner betrayed him. "'Pears you got a chip on your shoulders the size of Missouri Territory 'bout the way those white girls treat you. Don't 'spect you're ever goin' to trust a gal again with your affections. But it ain't right."

Luke shifted slightly in his chair. "I've heard my people talk of a place beyond the prairie where the trail ends at the big water."

"Out in Oregon Country? Glad to hear that. These risks we take aren't natural. One of these days, they're going to catch up with us. I'll be glad to have you settle on the Willamette with that little Halsey gal, longside Nancy and me."

Luke ignored the first part. "You aim to settle down?"

"Promised Nancy this would be my last trip. Oregon's going to be a state one of these days. Mean to keep my word."

They shook hands again and parted for the night. There would be plenty of opportunity on the trail for conversation. They'd find themselves together a lot, watching the family men eating, laughing and dancing with their wives.

As he walked back to his camp, he thought about John's

words. His friend was closer to the truth than he knew. If the Rodgers woman was married, then there was no sense in stirring anything up. If she wasn't, it made no difference.

Leverenz's mention of Clara Halsey ripped the scab off on old wound. Clara had seemed interested—more than interested—with her saucy looks and the sweet potato pie that she saved on the fire grate until he finished his duties for the night. They'd dabbled at love, even tried lovemaking once— before he felt the heat of the fire he was playing with. Then, he'd called a halt. It was just as well.

When her father heard of his mixed blood, he found better things for his daughter to be doing at night than keeping a plate warm for a half-breed suitor.

John's words surprised him. He had expected Clara to forget him when the first wave of men greeted her wagon train at Oregon City. Thought he'd let her out of her misery before she found out what having a half-breed meant. If she was still waiting, she was a fool. White women married their own kind.

"Damn, how did I get myself into this mettle? I had no intentions of scouting again." He was still scowling as he checked the hobbles on his stallion, a big dun-colored horse with white stockings on all four legs and more common sense than many men he'd met. He figured to set his dun stallion to stud on his breeding operation when he settled in Oregon.

As he spread his bedroll on a piece of sweet grass near his wagon, Luke felt the stars warming the heavens like embers. He heard the murmuring sounds of the plains beyond the noise the greenhorns caused, the steady pounding of black-smiths working through the night to finish needed repairs, people finishing their chores before bedding down, a baby crying in the distance, a fiddle singing a sad refrain, maybe for kinfolk left behind. Not far away a black-haired girl slept under these same stars. He brought her image to his mind with surprising ease since he had not yet seen her up close. His scouting habits had come into good use, first to verify his suspicions of clear, green eyes and then in search of a wedding ring. It had been there.

Sleep didn't come easily, never did for him, tormented as he was by memories. He thought back to his early years in the hunting camps near the rushing rivers of the Blue Mountains. Until his ninth winter he lived with his Umatilla mother and her people, until she died one night in her white husband's arms after a long winter spent coughing.

His mother's people agreed that the boy should learn the ways of his father. At first, he was happy because he thought the two of them could trap side-by-side and he could return to his mother's people to see his uncles and cousins. The following spring his sorrow grew like the mighty thunderclouds when his father led him east to where the paleskins lived. Without ceremony, his father delivered him to his childless white wife and returned to the mountains.

For six years he endured the short haircuts, white schools and the confusion that came of being caught between two worlds. The year he turned fifteen, his father, Ramer Johns Sayer, arrived to winter over at his Ohio home. He recalled listening with a growing heat to his father's account of the Rocky Mountains. He watched his father's eyes as he spun · stories of grizzly, snow-blinded treks through mountain passes and sharing sacred pipe with the chiefs of the Nez Perce. He watched his father try to settle into the starched sheets of his wife's bed, but by the end of the winter, saw him eye each sunset with the longing of a timber wolf.

While his father folded his few possessions into a leather satchel, he watched his father's white wife try to hide her tears. She packed food for her husband's journey, mended the frays in Ramer's city garb, and tried to ignore the buckskin leggings that he stuffed into his satchel. Her farewell kiss was sweet, but the message, in her lilting Scottish brogue, was clear. "Go with God," she whispered, "but don't be thinking you'll be welcome back." He watched her heart break a second time when he followed his father out the door. But, unlike his father, he had twice returned to visit her.

At first, he thought he had returned too late to his own land. The fur trade was collapsing, and Easterners were beginning to trickle into the territory with Bibles, plows, and seed grain. He spent his winters in the camp of his mother's people, remembered the ways of the Umatilla, but he found within himself no calling for a wife among the People.

He traveled down to Mexico, scouted for the Army when it sent men to map the vast wilderness. Finally, he hired out as a guide for people going west. At the age of twenty-five he returned to winter with his father's white wife, finding, instead, that death had visited earlier.

He spent the winter collecting stock and supplies to take west, feeling restless and lonely for something he could not define. It was time, he knew, to settle down—but not with a wife. His father's blood coursed through his veins; he would take no woman to abandon when he felt the need to wander. There was another thing; his years in the white man's settlement had left no doubt as to how they felt about a half-breed. He would remain free.

The winter of '47 was the loneliest of his life. When the snows melted, he looped his herd of hand-picked horses together and set out for Independence. A man in a hurry, he had no patience with the slow-moving wagons of the greenhorns who clogged the trail from Ohio to the setting-off point. He chose his own camps, away from gossiping women and ham-fisted men who tangled their new harnesses in frustration. Gradually, he made his way across Indiana, Illinois, and down into Missouri.

One day, when the spring storms subsided to reveal a clear blue sky, he pushed his herd around a bend in the road. In a grassy meadow to the right, a young couple heated their noon meal over a small fire. The girl spun in a circle, her arms clasped above her head. Her tresses tumbled about her shoulders like an Indian maiden preening for her husband. Her face was wreathed in a smile that included her eyes, her mouth, her very soul.

From his saddle he watched as her arched breasts seared him with longing. With burning envy, he eyed her companion, the one who had sat across from her at the inn, younger than himself, blonde, city polished, the luckiest man alive. When he could not sleep, her image filled his thoughts. Tonight, their paths crossed for the third time—and his feelings had not changed.

Chapter Six

April 14, 1848. I look out from the wagon and imagine a great golden road stretching to the sea. Oregon Territory, here we come. Every day is like a great picnic—never have I had such peace. We women are as children in our freedom.

MARY KNEW THE difference as soon as she opened her eyes; Independence would be the start of a whole new life. She rose to find the camp already bustling. Like a well-matched team, she and Philip went about their duties. She gathered bits of wood and made a fire while he tended the oxen.

Her mornings had a rhythm about them. She baked up enough biscuits for the day in a cast-iron cook pot, sliced bacon and fried it up together with any beans still left in the pot, enough for the noon meal. This morning she boiled a pot of cornmeal into thick porridge. When it was set she would fry slabs in lard until they were golden brown and crusty. The thick syrup and fresh butter that she enjoyed on the farm were luxuries she now did without.

Philip came in for his breakfast carrying a furry critter that smelled musky and foul. He grinned and tossed it on the ground at Mary's feet. "Possum," he grunted unnecessarily. Besides her other chores, she would need to skin and clean the varmint for the stew pot.

She cooked their big meal at night when they had more time to let the beans or meat simmer. Today, she hurried her chores before dawn. She washed the cornmeal from the kettle without using water from the storage barrel, scrubbing it with sand.

At last, they set off for the gathering grounds. They pulled into a front position despite the chaos brought on by one hundred and seventeen greenhorn emigrants and their sixty-one wagons. Sheep and goats ran pell-mell. Flocks became intermingled. Frustrated sheep dogs tried to keep order as they had been trained to do, but even the dedicated herd dogs were having limited success rounding up the terrified animals. Oxen milled and rolled their eyes at the commotion. Mules brayed and backed up as greenhorn teamsters attempted to keep them from bolting while children ran laughing and screaming right under the noses of the frightened animals.

Mary smiled at the children, who acted as though this was the adventure of their lives. It was at that, she realized. For every one of them, the making of history. *Every night we will write our experiences in a hundred diaries. How differently we will probably see the same events.*

Next to her, Philip set his brake in readiness for the meeting. "No sense starting the trip by us running off into the river."

Mary watched another wagon with a run-away team scarcely avoid hitting another wagon. "Will it be like this every morning?"

"Well, remember how confused we were the first few nights—what with open cooking and sleeping under the stars? It'll be the same for the wagon train. We'll all learn. And we'll be in harmony soon enough."

Finally, a shot was fired, signaling that the meeting was about to begin. Everyone rushed to the front, hoping to see and hear the man who held their lives in his hands.

"Give a listen, folks. I'm John Leverenz, your wagonmaster." Mary recognized him from the restaurant. "My job will be to get us through the next two-thousand miles. We'll face rain so thick you won't be able to see the tail end of the animals pulling the wagon. Hailstones as big as walnuts. You'll walk through blazing heat of the prairies, through deserts, mountains and snow. We will be hungry, thirsty, and footsore. There will be decisions made along the way—some put to vote at the camp meetings we'll hold at night. But some decisions I decide alone, along with my guide and trapper, Lucas Sayer. Come up here Luke, and let people get a look."

As the man strode to the front of the crowd he passed close to where she stood. He turned in her direction, hesitated and murmured in a low voice that scarcely carried to her ear, "I was right, they are green." Turning, he continued toward the front and Mary felt herself grow hot.

The stranger took his time as he sauntered past curious ladies to the front of the crowd. He ignored the outstretched hands of a half-dozen children and halted at the wagonmaster's side.

"Luke, here, is the guide. He'll find waterholes, shortcuts, bad spots in the trail. He'll locate the hostiles, open trade with the willing tribes, and his word will be final. If he says we don't drink from the only waterhole in ten miles, we don't drink. When he's not saving our hides, he'll be tracking fresh game. You'll be plumb grateful when he comes riding into camp with an antelope slung over his saddle. Might think about having him over to your stewpot some night. He's a bachelor, and a fair companion, at that."

Distracted by the smattering of laughter, Mary found her-

self looking into the amused eyes of Mr. Lucas Sayer. She
fidgeted with her bonnet strings and waited for the wagonmaster to continue.

"It's my thinking to get you there in six months. If the
journey is well provisioned and the animals sound, God willing, we may do it in less, but I've never taken longer. You
may squabble with the pace we set, but when you see the
snow pack on the mountain range, you'll be grateful. I war-
rant it.

"My wagons don't stop to honor the Lord's Day. Now,
I'm as God-fearing as the next man, and so's Luke, here."
Mary's eyes flashed to the man in question. "But we'll do our
praying and our reading in private, or at the end of the day.
No disrespect intended, but we got a long journey ahead of
us. The Lord'll be riding along too, so, if you have need to
talk with Him, He'll be close by."

A ripple of murmuring followed his words, along with
some fervent "Amens." But a hum of dismay seemed to
drown out the agreement.

"If this is not to your liking, then you wait and take some
other train. Not all the leaders feel as I do. Some will put the
matter to a vote." He paused and Mary watched the crowd.
This issue was the one that divided folks. Probably that was
his reason for bringing it up, first thing. Already, a group
had pulled to the side and their voices rose and fell, female
and male alike. Apparently, even families were divided on
the subject.

Mr. Leverenz waited only seconds before he continued,
probably not wanting the group to think he was weak in his
resolve. "We aim to keep moving. You break a wheel, move
aside. You lack the tools to fix it, you better pray that someone else does. Keep an eye out for anything you might need
on the trail. You can find most anything you need laying out

there among the abandoned wagons. Just take care that yours isn't one of them. I ain't gonna spell no one what ain't fixed fer the trip."

Someone shouted over the hubbub. "My name's Bill Weems, and I'm givin' fair notice. Ain't takin' orders from no half-breed."

Leverenz ignored the man while he glanced toward the sunrise, already a delicate rose hue in the east. His words were rushed. "If you've got sickness in the wagon, drop to the rear and camp a ways off from the rest of the folks. Missouri's full of malaria. The East is seeing diphtheria and cholera. Measles is everywhere. Influenza. No telling what you might be carrying. Hope you all brought medicines, 'cause there won't be a doctor on the train.

"Some of you women will have to act as midwives before the trip is over. I see a number of women who are going to be in need of your services." Against her will, Mary looked up to see the scout scowling at her as if he'd just eaten a green persimmon.

"If someone in your party dies, wait out of the train until you see if anyone else comes down with it. Cholera is a strange disease. You can be up and eating breakfast at dawn, have a little fever by high noon, and be dead by four o'clock. If this happens, bury your dead in his clothes and bedding. Don't wash him or prepare him for burial. Just get him into the ground, wash yourselves and everything you touched, and pray you aren't the next to fall."

Shudders went through the crowd.

"If you're packing house furnishings and gewgaws—anything that ain't needed to make a living—best sell it right here in Independence. It's going to get dumped out on the prairie someplace about the time your animals start dying from thirst. Those critters are the difference between life and death to you, so sell Granny's rocker for ten cents on the dollar to the bartering man over there and be done with it. Otherwise, you'll add it to the pile of furniture that's already scattered out there on the prairie doing nobody any good."

The women murmured their disagreement and vowed to carry the stuff on their backs. "Too bad," Mary heard the wagonmaster mutter to his scout. "Guess they'll have to find out for themselves."

He continued in a loud voice that carried over the crowd. "Likewise, you men. I won't accept any wagons pulled by fancy riding horses. I know some of you've used them to pull you here from wherever you hail, but the roads were good and the weather, fair to middling. It's going to take guts and strength to get where we're going—and farm horses have got neither. A mule is stubborn and will go all day. An ox is strong and dumb, and doesn't know when to stop, but a horse don't have the heart.

"If you plan to take horses for riding and hunting, I say fine. If you're using them to pull a loaded wagon, then find another train, because I won't have you. I see one rig pulled by fancy Kentucky thoroughbreds. Either exchange your horses for mules, or stay back. The man who signed you up told you the same thing. Sentimentality's a good thing, but you'll end up watching them die, and your family right along with them. I won't be responsible. Luke, got anything to add?"

Suddenly, a new voice spoke, a deep, melodious voice with a timbre that resonated through Mary like a lightning rod. The scowling scout was speaking.

"Each wagon needs at least two long guns and a couple of pairs of pistols. If we meet up with hostiles, you'll have time to shoot first and reload later. Guns can come to a sad end. They sink during river crossings and you'll pay a dear price if you have to barter a replacement at the forts or trading posts we'll be coming to. If you ladies know how to reload and shoot, so much the better." He looked directly at Mary and added, "If you intend to keep your hands lily-white and not handle the black powder and buckshot, best have a man along to protect you."

Mary felt a blush claiming her face. She made a vow to show him that she could shoot as well as any man. Lily-white, indeed!

Finally, the meeting was over and the crowds sidled back toward their wagons. Once they began rolling, Leverenz rode out front while Luke busied himself trying to keep the unfamiliar mix of herd animals bunched.

The wagonmaster's wagon was first in line, driven by their cook. Luke's rig came next. He had brought two wagons full of farming implements and ranch supplies, driven by boys who were traveling with their large families and were willing to handle the oxen in exchange for being able to throw their food and personal items in the back.

The rest of the train was open to the other travelers. Families with livestock tended to ride near the center where the herded animals would be kept, and each family with livestock took turns herding them and chasing strays.

Philip was already near the head of the column, walking beside his oxen when Mary caught up with him. "The wagonmaster has a good idea. Folks line up in order of their arrival every morning. An hour saved in the morning might save a couple in the afternoon when the animals are worn out." He flicked his quirt in the air above the lead ox and the team lumbered to a start. "Wagonmaster seems like a good man. They both do." He squinted at the rising sun. "Didn't we see them at the eating house last night?"

She ignored the question. "The guide seems a tad surly to

me."

His eyes widened in surprise. "Now, Mary-girl, you didn't get that from his little talk up there. Would there be more to this than shows?" He studied her tight-lipped expression and her efforts to appear nonchalant until Mary's honesty got the better of her pique.

"Every time I look up, he's staring at me."

"Every time? How often have you run into him?"

"Well, four." She waited for effect. "Isn't that enough?"

"Enough for what?" he teased.

"Oh, you are a reprobate. He undoubtedly chooses a new girl on every trip to shower his attentions upon. That way, he has something to occupy his time."

"What's wrong with that? Trouble with you, Mary, you never choose *anybody*. Acted like you were needed on the farm whenever any man came calling on you. You scared 'em off with your independence. At this rate, you'll never find a husband."

She examined the petals of a cornflower she'd picked back at the camp. Giving him a sideways glance, she murmured, "But, dear, I'm already married."

She watched his ears turn red before he lowered his voice to a growl. "Drat it, Mary, you know what I mean. We get to Oregon Country, I'm going to set up housekeeping with Laurel. It won't be fair to her if you're thrown in on the deal. You need to think about finding yourself a man and settling down." He paused, then added, "Just don't forget our arrangement. You better not set your cap for anyone on this trip."

Mary thought over what he had just said. In some respects, he was right. Some of her closest friends were already settled down with husbands and homes. Maybe she *was* being too particular. But Lucas Sayer was not her idea of a husband.

"I've seen girls married off to the highest bidder. I want a man I can truly love and honor, not marry because his land adjoins mine." She stared out at the rolling land. "Think of all the years you'll spend with Laurel. And I watched Mama and Papa. You know what I mean?" She stopped, flustered at speaking of such a matter with Philip. But that was the problem. She thought of him as a confidant.

"Mary, I understand. I'm just worried about what Laurel will think about this arrangement. Reckon it's making me selfish."

"Maybe if we'd taken more time, we could have come up with a better solution." She felt the wagon jostle as it moved across the grass and onto the track. "At any rate, let's not concern ourselves about it now. I'm sure we'll have enough worries to occupy us."

She'd been so intent on their conversation that she hadn't paid much attention to the ground they covered. Now, the sun had risen on the plain behind them and the grass had a dewy, satisfied look. The air was crisp and laden with moisture from the recent storms, and clouds still dotted the sky in lazy patches.

To the southwest, the Missouri River was a reassuring tangent against the dry days ahead; as long as they traveled alongside a river, they would be safe. The wagon bounced along at the lumbering pace set by the oxen. Already, a gap was forming between the faster paced mules and the slower, oxen-pulled wagons, with the herded animals crowding between the two factions. Mary mentioned this to Philip.

"Lots of folks prefer mules, but they'll be more prone to stampeding when we get into thunder and lightning. There are those who say a mule would rather drown than swim. They spook on a regular basis. My oxen cost me two hundred dollars each, but they're a steady lot. Only two of them came with names. Now, if we can find out which is named Rankle and which is Lucky, we'll be set."

Mary tried his suggestion, "Ho, Lucky…here, boy." No response. "Rankle, here, Rankle. Suey, suey."

"Suey?"

"That's how you call a pig, city boy. At least you can eat a pig. What else are your oxen good for?" She knew he'd read every book he could find on the subject. Book smart, his father had called him.

"They can travel long distances better than any animal on earth, except maybe a camel."

"Then why not get camels?"

"Because then you wouldn't have anything to complain about." He guided the oxen around a box that had fallen from someone's wagon. "Set of mules costs about six hundred dollars. Lots of folks brought them because they were already using them on their farms and only had to buy a couple more. Easier if a fellow and his team are used to each other."

She glanced up at the wagon and considered riding, but the wooden wagon seat was as hard as the ground they slept on. She could take only a few hours of riding before she was ready to walk.

One of the first problems she had to master was jumping down from the wagon as it rolled along. The oxen would walk all day, but once they stopped, their work was finished. Time and again, in those first few days, Philip had to pull around some poor teamster who sat cursing and flailing on a team of sublimely unconcerned oxen standing with eyes half-closed in the noonday sun, swishing their tails at the blowflies and chewing their cud. The driver would try pushing, pulling and threatening, but the oxen wouldn't move until they felt like it. As a last resort, the driver might go into the wagon and get a wooden bucket with some of his precious seed grain and sprinkle a few seeds onto the ground, or hold it in his palm as he backed his way, slowly, toward Oregon. By the time he managed to get the oxen back on the track, the rest of the wagon train would be far ahead. The teamster and his family would be late getting into camp that night, generally in a foul mood.

Out of fear of the same consequences, Mary learned to gather her skirts in her hand and to jump clear of the moving wheels and the brake levers. She generally landed on her feet, but more than once, she met the ground on more intimate terms. Today, she strode off in glad spirits. Nearly every wagon had children walking alongside. She hurried her steps to catch up with a solitary woman.

"Hello. I'm Mary Rodgers, late of Illinois. Now I think I'm from Missouri, and pretty soon I'll have to say I hail from the Nebraska."

The woman gave a sweet, lilting laugh that reminded Mary of her mother. "Howdy, I'm Lillian Stoberson, from Missouri, and still in Missouri." Two girls slowed to walk alongside. "This is Nellie and Virginie. Nellie's fourteen, and quite the cook. Virginie's sixteen, and set to marry, once we get to Oregon. Her young man went on ahead last year. Couldn't wait to claim his land."

"Oh, that's what my cousin's...my cousin Laurel did. She's out in Oregon now, waiting for her intended." *Mary, Mary, keep your story straight.* She'd come perilously close to blurting out her secret.

Mrs. Stoberson didn't seem to notice. "Don't it make a body glad to be underway? We've been packed and ready ever since last fall. Just been biding our time."

"Why so long?" Mary asked, treading carefully over a

mule pie still steaming in the morning grass.

"Folks back home come down with the malaria from the heavy rains we had the last few years. Price of grain weren't hardly worth the planting of it and my Orville, he couldn't get himself a cash job come hell nor high water, which we had plenty of. We was just floating down the river of despair."

"So you headed west."

"We figure out there we got the same chance as everyone else. Leastways, we won't be sitting around waiting for the wolf to come to the door, or for one of the young'uns to come down with the fever. How 'bout yerself?"

Mary offered the barest explanation. "I lost my entire family. Philip was an old family friend." She'd known Philip her whole life, that part was true. "We plan to make ourselves new lives." *Just not together.*

"Poor dear, at least you got age and health on your side. You don't look to be above eighteen, and right pretty, at that. It's a good thing you got yourself hitched before you came, or all those fellows would be wasting their energy trying to woo you after their day's work was finished. "

Lillian was plain speaking. There would be no hiding anything from this woman, because she clearly had an ability to see beyond what was being said. Mary searched for something that would satisfy her. "We wanted to do the respectable thing, so here we are."

Lillian's smile was filled with wistfulness. "I'm not so lucky, myself. I'm on the downhill side of forty, with a brood of eight children. My oldest is twenty-three, and the youngest is seven. I don't suppose I have any business making this trip, but even if I don't make it all the way, the young'uns and Orv'll get a good start. Sometimes it's me that has to get things rolling. You know how it is with men. They can talk up a storm, but if the woman ain't willing, some things just never come to be. Orv, he talked a good bit about this here trip, but it wasn't till I loaded us up and said we was going, that things got taken for serious."

Mary smiled at the heavy-set, jovial woman with a drooping poke bonnet shadowing her face. Lillian spoke the truth in one respect; it was often the men who were dreamers and planners, but the woman who set the plan to rights by seeing that they had savings set aside and the loose ends tied up.

"After you get supper set out for your man, come on over to our wagon and meet the whole brood. Reckon if you're going to eat our dust all day, you might as well see what we look like." Lillian stopped to check her shoe. "Say, here comes that nice Mr. Sayer. Bet he's going to tell us to make camp and rest ourselves a spell."

Nice? Mary wondered if there were two men with the same last name.

"Afternoon, ma'am." His greeting was genial, but his eyes rested on Mary while she suddenly found the detail in Lillian's bonnet fascinating. "We'll be resting up ahead. Pull to the side so the animals can graze. And eat up, even if you're not hungry. You'll be needing your strength." He tipped his hat and nodded before starting on down the line.

Against her will, Mary watched him leave.

Chapter Seven

April 15, 1848. Our fellow travelers are diverse in character. Some are strange in their ways. Others, I have grown fond of almost at once. Mr. Leverenz says we will depend on each other for our very lives. How strange that seems.

THE AFTERNOON SUN was setting when the train slowed for the evening encampment. The emigrants had been told that they didn't need to fear the Indians except for their stealing of the sheep, cattle, horses, and mules.

In cases of storms, or when they were in Indian country, Leverenz had already said he would order the wagons to close into a circle, penning the animals inside the encampment. When no threat was present, the families were free to camp in small clusters, keeping near for communication purposes.

On this first day, Leverenz sent a command down the line for all wagons to form a circle, to ease the herding of the skittish animals. This way, the drovers would get some practice for the time when danger threatened and they had to make camp in a hurry.

The cursing drovers worked to form a crude oval with their balking mules and stubborn oxen. Lillian Stoberson stood next to Mary, watching. "Indians could just sashay in, hand-pick their mounts and pick through the wagons for what they need and nobody would notice in the confusion," she confided in a low voice. Mary laughed and agreed.

Finally, Leverenz declared that the circle was near enough to round that the men could unhitch the animals and turn them loose to graze. It was important that the train be camped early enough in the day. The animals grazed with the sun; when darkness came, they bunched together in an instinctive defense against wolves, coyotes and bears that hunted in the dark. It was easier on the sheep and goats. They were grazers and cropped grass all day long, but the animals pulling the loads—the wagon stock, Leverenz called them—could not eat until they were unharnessed or released from their heavy wooden yokes. They relied on the evening and the early morning to eat their fill for the day. Leverenz had already warned them that some days would be devoted to letting the animals rest and feed.

Nellie Stoberson approached on her way to gather firewood. "Howdy, Mrs. Rodgers."

"Call me Mary. We're too much the same age for you to be calling me Mrs. Rodgers. I won't even know who you are talking to."

"I'd like that. Back home we didn't have hardly no time to meet new people. You're lucky. Philip's handsome."

"Yes, he is. And I have an idea that you and I will become good friends." Mary took the younger girl's hand and led her toward a low hillside in search of downed limbs and bark. "We have to stay in sight of the wagons."

"I had to leave my best friend behind in Missouri. We been friends for so long. We made matching corncob dolls and we used to play with them under the willow trees. It made such a good hiding place from my brothers, down by the river. Most of the time, they didn't even know we were there. Once, we were under the willow and my brother came along with his girl, Regina. He was spooning her and talking real silly. We wanted to giggle right out loud, but we knew he'd box our ears if he caught us, so we sat real still and let him make a fool out of himself."

Mary smiled. "Did Regina think he was making a fool out of himself?"

"Oh, no, she acted all swoony. Beats me how she can even stand him, he's so clumsy. Even his feet are big. Pa used to say he was like a hound dog pup—all feet and paws—and if he ever grew into them he'd be a giant."

"Well, did he?"

"I reckon. The girls seem to think he's something wonderful. Leastwise, Regina does." Nellie's expression indicated that she did not share the girls' opinion of her brother.

"Did Regina come, too?"

Nellie nodded and pointed to a wagon pulling up just behind the three wagons that the Stobersons were hauling. "Her parents pulled up stakes and came along 'cause Billy let it be known he wasn't coming without her. 'Sides, they was just as poor as us, and they're fixing to get them a homestead same as us."

"Did Billy and Regina get married yet?"

"No. The wagons was too full for them to have one of their own, so Regina's sleeping in with her folks and Billy's driving one of the supply wagons. But when they get to Oregon Country they're going to get hitched up and homestead their own place."

"A wedding on the trail would be lovely, but first I have to meet the bride and groom or I won't be invited. I'll have to sit by myself in my wagon while you dance with all the handsome boys."

"Oh, no, we'd be sure to invite you. You could wear your

best gown."

"And my satin pumps with the tiny heels that let me dance like a fairy. And I would have my lady's maid fix my hair into curls all around my face."

"And we could pick more wildflowers and put them into your hair like a wreath." Nellie's admiration was obvious. "Missus...um, Mary, do you think when I grow up and lose my baby looks, I'll be as pretty as you?"

"I should say so! We're different kind of pretty. You have hair like spun gold and mine is the color of midnight. Your skin is the color of pink rose petals, and lots of boys like that. Boy's will be reciting love poems in the dark about your pretty skin. Mine is the color of peach skin, and peaches get all squishy in the sun."

They both broke into giggles.

"Mary, I think you're the prettiest lady I've ever seen. My friend Josie would say so, too." The happy lilt left her voice. "Anyway, I can't think about playing with Josie anymore. Ma says I'm nearly grown."

"Look around you, Nellie. There are all sorts of girls your age. I'll bet they had to leave their best friends behind, too."

"Pa says we have to stay serious and work hard to get to Oregon. We won't have any time for getting friendly." Nellie lowered her lips into a pout even as she glanced hopefully at Mary.

"Oh, you'll find a way. Time will pass faster and the miles will seem a lot shorter if you're walking with someone. Wait and see. Now, let's get this wood over to your Mama and see to our suppers."

Philip was already unhitching the oxen when she arrived in camp. Impassive as always, Rankle and Lucky grazed nearby. "It doesn't seem like they care one way or the other, what they do. If you lead them to feed, they'll eat. Otherwise they won't. Are they always like that?" Mary asked.

"I'm thinking so. Remember the wooden crate I had to pull around today? Well, if I hadn't tugged them to the side they would have gone right over the top of it. Doesn't seem as though anything's going to rile them. In a way, that's reassuring. Don't want a team of high-strung animals running off with my life's savings."

"Running off? Tomorrow they might not even walk. You might be the one in the trail shouting and wearing yourself into a lather." By now, Mary had crawled into the wagon and was sorting through the bins and boxes. "What do you say to rice and fried potatoes, grilled rattlesnake and dessert of poached apple slices?" she teased.

"Sounds good to me." He was too tired to joke. "Whatever you fix, you're going to be doing it under lamplight. I left the lard lantern hanging on the edge of the wagon staves." He finished unyoking the second team and watched as they wandered off to eat.

As she started the meal, Mary hummed a song her mother had loved to sing. Banging pans and mixing biscuit dough with quick, efficient movements, she dropped the clumps onto the hot lard and watched as they bubbled and splattered in the fat. The firelight made patches of light that danced across the darkened camp and she smiled at the pattern. Suddenly, she sensed a scent that she recalled yet couldn't place. Whirling about, she stammered, "You frightened me!"

Mr. Sayer drew a long drag from his cheroot and slowly exhaled, making smoke rings that blended with the campfire's smoke. Mary watched, entranced. Suddenly, she spun about to tend the meal, fussing with inconsequential tasks to cover her confusion. "Did you need something?" she asked.

His actions seemed innocent enough. "No, I'm just checking on folks. My cook's back at the wagon fixing the rabbit I shot today. Should be real tasty with the wild onions I found."

Mary couldn't control her eagerness. "Wild onions out here? Where? How? Can you show me what they look like?" She stopped, embarrassed at her childlike eagerness.

Luke hesitated longer than was polite while Mary wished that the camp smoke could swallow her words like it did his cigar smoke. Finally, he spoke. "There's a patch not far from here. Cooking's plain enough on the trail. You'll need all the help you can get. Tomorrow morning? On that horse I saw tied to your wagon?"

Straightening from the skillet, Mary wiped her hands on her apron and ventured a timid smile. "Thank you. I would appreciate that, truly. I'm Mary Rodgers, late of Illinois."

"I'm pleased to meet you, Mrs. Rodgers." He spoke her name with a roll to the 'r' that made her think she'd never before heard her name pronounced correctly. Realizing that she was gawking, she lowered her eyes, glad for the darkness that hid her blush.

"Mrs. Rodgers…"

His words jolted her from her musing. "Yes?"

"Your biscuits are burning."

"Oh, darn. I mean posh. Oh, bother." Totally flustered, she grabbed the pan with her bare hand, yelped, and let go.

"Here, let me." Luke grabbed at the front of her dress while she watched in horror. But he only snatched a corner of the apron and moved the heavy pan to a safe corner of the grill. After deftly turning the biscuits with a fork, he casually straightened and backed into the shadows with his cigar firmly in his mouth. "Sorry I interrupted your work. I'll leave you to your tasks."

"Thank you, Mr. Sayer. For everything."

"Be sure to put some ointment on that burn, Mrs. Rodgers. Goodnight."

Mary stood holding her burned hand while he passed into the darkness. *Mrs. Rodgers,* he had called her, and had acted in a perfectly respectful manner. Still, as she turned toward the wagon and the medicine box she no longer hummed.

Philip came back with the last of the yokes and poured a basin of warm water. He scrubbed vigorously while managing a steady stream of conversation. "I smell cigar smoke. You got a vice you're hiding?" He reached for the toweling and dried himself.

"Mr. Sayer was by. He's going to show me how to find wild roots tomorrow so we can liven up our meals."

"Suits me. You taking a more tender turn toward the man?"

She ignored his question. "Since I have a horse, he's asked me to show the others. It would save him the trouble of taking everybody out."

"Just watch yourself—you know what I'm saying. Maybe you could take the Hawken and shoot us a rabbit for our stew pot. I could do with a change."

"I was thinking, Philip. I'm going to need to learn to handle the oxen. It's silly for me to be running about picking wildflowers and visiting with the ladies while you work everyday."

"I don't think your arms are strong enough."

Mary persisted. "I could help on flat ground. If you saw a big crossing coming up, you could take over."

"Well, it would be nice to get spelled now and again. Let me get the animals in working form first, though."

Mary filled the lamp with a glob of lard. "I hear we'll be in buffalo country soon. I can burn buffalo fat and keep the good lard for cooking." She struck the flint to the wick and hung it in the corner of the wagon. "There. Much better."

"You're doing a fine job, Mary." Coming from her cousin, that was high praise, indeed. Mary was touched. She had learned a lot from her mother and counted herself well prepared for a life of domesticity. But this trail survival was another matter and it had been by trial and error that she discovered cooking times, amount of wood, and how to clean up with very little water. Up to now, Philip had said little, one way or the other.

After supper, she cleaned the dishes while all around camp men tended to their harnesses. Leather would be a hard commodity to come across and they dare not risk them rotting from the mule's sweat. Oxen yoke was easier to maintain, but mule or ox, every man had to check his animals' hooves every night. A smart drover would check his wheels every night as well for hairline cracks and signs of stressing.

Philip rose to refill the water barrel. As long as they followed the river, most of the men left all but one barrel empty, or with just enough water sloshing around inside to keep the staves from shrinking. They planned to fill them when they headed for dry ground. After supper was packed away, Mary saw to the bedrolls in the space under the wagon. Here again, she was more fortunate than the women with children. If she didn't care about the privacy the tent afforded, she could, as she did tonight, stretch a piece of tarp under the wheels and use the wagon as a lean-to.

She knelt to smooth the ground cloth and a rapid movement startled her out of her lethargy. Two feet from her left hand a small rattler lay coiled and ready to strike. She tried to back out of the enclosure, but her movements seemed wooden. The snake struck and found its target in the tarp that covered her arm. Mary felt the pressure. She pulled her arm back and the snake hurtled harmlessly aside, but she saw blood trickling from a small wound.

"Philip!" she screamed.

From the darkness, Lucas Sayer appeared. He ground his heel against the snake and Mary watched it writhe. When it stilled, Luke turned to Mary. "Are you bit?"

"It glanced me." She brought her arm closer to the lantern. Luke ran his fingers over the area, but he could find no sign of fang marks in the blood trickling from the broken skin. "I must have banged it on the wagon." Unmindful of her protest, he peeled back the cuff of her long sleeve and probed her tender flesh, searching in the dusky light for any sign he might have missed. She stood still while his callused thumb traveled upward. When he reached her elbow he ceased his exploration, a question in his eyes. At the sound of his voice, Mary shook herself from the shock of the past sixty seconds.

"The snakes are just coming out of their dens and they're sluggish, yet. That probably saved you from a nasty bite." His words were soft while his thumb burned like a coal brand. "You want that rattler for breakfast, ma'am?" His fingers lingered as he waited for her answer.

Mary's laugh was shaky. "I'd as soon chew harness straps. Give it to someone who will appreciate it."

"Suit yourself. You don't know what you're missing." He picked up the snake and held it at arm's length in front of her.

Mary felt her tension ebb. "Mr. Sayer, you're close to being a schoolhouse bully."

Luke's eyes shone in the lantern's light. "Is that so, ma'am?"

"Yes." The word seemed a contradiction to her thoughts. He had saved her life; or, at least, prevented a painful injury. They were unaware that a crowd had gathered until someone volunteered to skin the snake for their own stewpot. Without another word to Mary, Luke handed it over and stepped out of the firelight's glow.

Mary decided it was a night for the tent. A bed in the wagon had never sounded better, but there was no space. She heard Philip voicing his thanks to Luke Sayer as the two walked out of sight. In the silence, she had time to put the events in perspective. Why hadn't Philip been there the one time she needed him? Why did it have to be Mr. Sayer who found the snake? The fact that she was safe suddenly seemed less important than the fact that she was indebted to a man whose fascination unsettled her. She tried to discipline her thoughts. *He was just doing his job. That's what we're paying him for.*

Chapter Eight

April 16, 1848. A pleasant outlook seems to be the most valuable commodity we bring with us, the ointment that soothes the strains of daily travel. The men think their way is best, but for the most part, they rely greatly on their women.

THE SNAKE POSTPONED Mary's desire for sleep so she joined Philip for a stroll. The campfires were strung about the plain, giving it the air of an army encampment. Everywhere, people laughed and talked in subdued tones: a mother entreated a cranky child to eat his supper and leave his brother alone; a fiddler sang a rollicking tune celebrating his gladness at being underway. The camp exuded vitality as folks expressed their eagerness for the coming adventure. It wasn't hard to locate the camp of Lillian Stoberson and her brood.

"Hello, Lillian. We stopped by to meet our neighbors. This is Mr. Rodgers—Philip." Mary rightly figured the woman would assume the connection, and she didn't want to do any more fabricating than was necessary.

"Well, pull up a stump. Young'uns, make way for our new friends. My Orville's over yonder if he ain't run off down to the river."

From the darkness, a grinning bear of a man approached,

his red suspenders stretched over a well-worn flannel shirt with its tails hanging over his trousers as if he was fresh from a call of nature. He tossed a couple of limbs into the fire, used another to light his corncob pipe and extended his hand.

Side-by-side, Lillian and her man reminded Mary of Lucky and Rankle, a well-matched pair that could withstand any calamity. Although Orv added a word now and then, Lillian did the talking. "Orv and me was just discussin' the good fortune we've had so far. I've a hopefulness I ain't felt in some time."

Mary knew what she meant. The atmosphere of the camp echoed in the songs the women sang, the tunes of the fiddlers, the wildflowers that adorned supper tables. Whatever might happen later tonight was a night of hope.

Orv spoke from the shadows. "Mr. Rodgers, would you be up for a little fishing come sunup? Saw some catfish jumping, tonight. Be partial to some, pan-fried, come morning."

"Sounds good. We're ready for fresh fodder. Mary's been doing a fine job with the meals, but I figure it's my job to keep her supplied.

"We'll get our share while the boys hitch up the teams." Orv was lucky in that he had three strapping boys to share the workload.

"Speaking of eating, Mr. Sayer has offered to show me where I might pick some wild herbs. I'm craving a pot of fresh greens." Mary was familiar with all the domestic vegetables from the large garden her mother had kept back home, but knowing what to eat in the wilderness was something she would prefer to learn from an experienced hand. "I'll share my bounty with you tomorrow."

"Well, ma'am, I reckon we'll be in for some good eating,

come suppertime."

Lillian's gusto showed her to be a woman who loved her food. *Loves her living, for that matter,* Mary thought. Lillian was quick to make a joke at one of the children's expense, but equally quick to praise their accomplishments. Mary marveled the way she handled her big brood. She had enough love and energy for all of them, and it showed. Something about Lillian brought a tug of longing. When Mary mentioned her mother's fate, it seemed as though Lillian opened her arms and gathered her in like she was one of her own. Whatever the reason, Mary was grateful. *We're going to be great friends.*

"How far do you think we came today?" Philip asked.

Orv shifted toward the fire as he answered. "I heard Leverenz say we'll be doing thirty miles some days, pushing ourselves hard while the going's easy and the weather holds. Later on, we'll be glad for the effort."

"I hope the trip goes this smooth, the whole way. To hear tell, not all the wagons have a rough time of it. A lot depends on fate, how things go. Fate's a funny thing, ain't it?" Lillian was philosophical over her cup of coffee while she stared into the dying embers.

The children began straggling off toward bed and the entire camp began the process of settling down for the night. Philip yawned and stretched, twisting to ease his muscles. "Well, reckon we'll take our leave. See you in the morning for those fish."

"Night, Mary," Lillian called as they moved off into the night. Mary heard her add, "Oh, Orv, remember being so young and fresh in love?"

"Still am, Lilly," Orv replied. Mary turned at her wagon to see him give his wife a pat on her shoulder. "What say we find ourselves a quiet spot to bed down? No sense us crowding all together." He gave his wife a wink that meant sleep would come a little later that night.

Dawn saw the fishermen at the river with their home-made lines and lures—a switch of willow with a bit of twine and a hook—carried in the supply wagon for just this pur-pose. The worms and crickets were plentiful and the fish were hungry in the early morning light.

Philip soon found himself with more than they could eat, even allowing extra for the noon meal. On the way back to his wagon, he met Sazie Murdock fresh from milking her cow. "Nice catch there, neighbor," she greeted him. "You wouldn't consider trading a couple of those for fresh milk? We got more than'll keep. Yer welcome to it."

Philip made the swap under the willow tree, with Sazie making him the loan of a little pot she hung from her bucket. "Much obliged, ma'am. I'll send Mary back with it so she can tell you, herself, how welcome this is."

"There's more than enough nearly every morning. Night time, the milk's a little sparser cause she ain't had time to eat, but long as there's plenty for my young' uns, you're wel-come to the spare."

Mary was delighted. They had a quick breakfast of fresh catfish fried in bacon grease, biscuits, and coffee with real cream. She set the rest of the milk in a crock and covered it with a damp cloth to let the cream rise. They could have the rest of the milk at noon, and if she had enough cream she would make a tiny bit of fresh butter for their supper bis-cuits.

Hurrying through the chores, she scrubbed the skillet and returned the pot to Sazie Murdock before Philip had the rest of the oxen yoked. She had dressed early in a cocoa brown riding skirt that just covered her boy's boots and a clean lin-en shirtwaist that revealed her tiny waist. She tied her waist-length hair tied back in a ribbon that matched her skirt and fastened her riding hat with its little pheasant feather that waved saucily in the breeze. Humming a pleasured tune, she walked to where Buttercup was hobbled in the grass.

It seemed to her that the wagons dallied this morning. Leverenz was firm on the starting time, six-thirty sharp; although he wanted to start at six, some of the larger families needed the extra time. For the women, mornings were particularly hard, even with the later start. Before the wagons set off they had to see to collecting the wood, cooking the big meal of the day, hauling water, milking, tending the children, putting the bedding away, getting the food out then repacking it, making sure everything was properly strapped down.

There was also the feeding and dressing of the little ones, washing out the soiled diapers, washing up the dishes and keeping the little ones out of harm's way while the animals milled around them. If a woman was lucky enough to have a daughter, she had some help; otherwise the chores fell on her.

Most women had little time to chat. Often the women had to contend with the burdens of pregnancy while attending to all her other duties, and woe to the woman who held her husband up from getting a good position in line. She often felt the sting of his words on the trail that day.

Mary felt guilty as she watched the young mothers rushing about with last-minute chores. It seemed that the husbands were limited in what they were willing to help out with, although it was only the women from Missouri who had to do their own milking. Most of the Yankee families enjoyed a far more equitable division of chores. It would be interesting to see if things got better for the Missourians as the trip progressed. On the other hand, she might find herself milking a cow before the trip was over. *Never. My mother would shift in her grave at the thought.*

When the wagon train finally started, it went smoothly. Mary watched from astride Buttercup and it seemed that both animals and drovers seemed to be getting used to the routine. Some of the women were already walking beside their wagons, nursing babies and stopping to change a diaper and fill it with grass. For the small ones who didn't walk yet, a mother was the means of necessity. Some of the children had a small space in the front of the wagon where they could nap, but the mothers kept constant vigil. Even allowing the little ones to ride alongside their fathers on the wagon seat was fraught with danger. The men were often so intent on the animals that they paid little attention. Already, one small boy had fallen from his wagon and narrowly escaped having his arm crushed by the rolling wheel.

The older children, freed from their farm chores, were having the time of their lives. They had paired off into twos and threes, skipping, singing little ditties and telling each other stories. The smaller boys wrestled in the grass, pulling up dirt clods for a rousing grass fight. Others spent their boundless energy running alongside their families' wagons.

Mary thought of her brother Toby, and her eyes filled with tears.

Chapter Nine

April 17, 1848. My friends have become as sisters.
We rely on each other for so much, I would be
lost without them. Nothing we endure is impossible as long as we are not alone.

MARY SAW A familiar dun horse approaching. The sight of
the tall stallion seemed to quicken her blood, but she dis-
missed the idea as merely anticipation of riding astride instead of the bone-jarring pace set by clumsy oxen that moved
with the grace of pigs.

"Morning, ma'am. Ready for that ride?"

Luke formed a slow smile that made Mary forget his
question. His shirt was not the familiar red flannel of the
other men, but a dusky cream doeskin, fringed at the arms
and laced up the front with rawhide cords. He seemed different today, rugged and dangerous in a way that she
couldn't define, but he looked as if he lived in the type of
garb he was wearing; hadn't chosen it to enhance his mascu-
linity, but rather the other way around.

"Ready and looking forward to it, Mr. Sayer." She felt
suddenly shy in his company and found herself studying his
moccasins where they rested in his stirrups.

Her formality brought a chuckle. "Better get used to calling me Luke. Everyone else will by the time the trip is

through."

"I'm not sure I should do that, Mr. Sayer. My mother would heartily disapprove." Her smile belied her words.

"Do you always do everything your mother says?" Luke ventured a sideways glance. Her outfit revealed her smooth lines in a way that the serviceable dresses she wore did not. Her hair was unfurled in the manner of an Indian maiden and he had the sudden thought that maybe she wore it that way for him.

Mary's faint blush was the only evidence of her discomfort. She glanced down at her reins, twisting them in her gloved hands while she wondered what was expected of her. Indeed, the man didn't seem to notice that he was taking liberties. No gentleman stared this long or this openly at a lady. He seemed to be memorizing her very features and it was disconcerting, as though he studied a peach before taking a bite. Like a piece of fruit she felt herself ripening under his regard. "My mother was a very proper lady."

The expression in his eyes caused her to drop her lashes. She was no great judge of men, but it seemed he was uncomfortable around women. He had clearly never taken anyone else onion hunting. He'd probably shared a few dances at the nightly celebrations, maybe exchanged furtive kisses in the dark with eager young misses who wanted to brag to their girl friends. She could imagine that he would be all too happy to oblige, but surely he wouldn't want to incur the wrath of a vigilant father who thought he was making light of a tender young daughter. She tried to picture him with a wife, but the image faded when she remembered that a trail scout had no need of a wife.

"Yes, ma'am. I'm sure she was." Luke studied the ground in front of him, trying not to think about the dark-eyed beauty with a husband and a smile that did things to his insides and made him forget the blood that ran through his veins. Made him feel like throwing caution to the winds. He hid his confusion in a question that he regretted as soon as it was out. "You say she was?"

"My mother is no longer with us. She died several weeks ago, back home. Of a fever she caught from strangers. I was so angry with her. I guess I still am." Mary found herself confessing a truth that she hadn't admitted even to herself. "She was worth the lot of them and now she's gone, and for what?" Without warning, tears began forming.

Luke was beside her, his voice sounding low and strangled. "Do you think she meant to catch the fever and die? To leave you behind?"

Mary replied before she had time to think. "No. She loved life—all of it. She was the first to notice the newly hatched sparrows, to see the new blossoms on the apple tree. She noticed things going on around her and that's what killed her. She saw the wagon parked in the trees and went over to see if she could help."

"Mrs. Rodgers, it wasn't anyone's fault. The folks she helped, they were victims, too."

"I know."

"What about the rest of your family?" His concern was an invitation and she found herself revealing her story. When she finished, Luke shook his head in disbelief. "Are you saying you lost your family in the last six weeks?" Mary nodded, unable to speak. "And you got married and started out on the trail to make a new start?" Again she nodded.

Mary searched for a handkerchief, but found none in the pocket of her skirt. Luke offered her a large crumpled kerchief and she blew her nose, not caring that he watched. She finished and started to hand it to him, realized her mistake and pulled it back with a blush.

"I'll see this laundered."

"Don't bother. You ready to ride?" He sounded angry, whether at her or himself she couldn't tell. He sat in silence, frowning while his horse stamped at a fly. Finally, she nodded and reined her horse in behind him.

The onions were located in the draws. She had brought saddlebags and Luke pointed out the edible plants: sage that Indians used while hunting to mask human odors, wild garlic, leaves that could be eaten as fresh greens or steeped to bring down swelling of a sprain. He pointed out mushrooms, both edible and poisonous.

"Don't try this alone," he said. She glanced up, surprised at the seriousness in his tone. "Take care to keep the wagons in sight." His gaze skittered to her neck.

Mary followed him across the uneven terrain with a bundle of dirty roots clutched to her bosom. She was unaware that her blouse was brushed with dirt, or that her cheeks were in danger of bronzing because she had lost her hat in the breeze. She shaded her eyes, noting the position of the sun, which was straight up in the sky. "I should be getting back to fix Philip's meal."

At the reminder of a husband, Luke dismounted to retrieve her hat and stood watching as she pinned it in place. When their eyes met, he turned away, suddenly unsure what he was doing here with this woman—girl, really—with her windblown hair and tear-softened eyes, and her bosom that needed brushing. In a sudden, deliberate motion, he strode toward his horse.

Mary hurried to catch up, laughing at the sight of the two horses. "Looks like Buttercup has found a friend." The big stallion was standing alongside, nipping at the filly's cheek. The filly shook her head, her mane wafting in the soft breeze as she leveled an ineffective kick at the nuzzling stallion. "I think she likes your horse."

Luke's hands lost their purchase on the saddle cinch. He tried again, fumbling blindly while he watched the two horses.

On the way back to the train, Luke showed her signs of recent Indian movement in the grass. "They follow the buffalo. Soon, we will eat well."

"Speaking of hunting, I brought my rifle to shoot us a stewpot for supper," Mary remembered.

He nodded toward the Hawken. "You plan on firing that?"

"As a matter of fact, I do. And my lily-white hands can reload, too."

Luke's face took on a shading of color. He turned away and spotted a rabbit in the grass. "See if your words ring true."

Mary quickly untied the scabbard and brought the rifle to her shoulder, pulled the lever back and waited until she had the rabbit in her sights. Leaning, she pulled the trigger, careful not to jerk. A flash of fire emerged from the barrel; the rabbit jumped and was still. "One shot, one dinner," she remarked as she started for the animal.

Luke watched as she field-dressed the critter and tied it onto the back of her saddle. "You would make an Indian woman," he said quietly. Her actions reminded him of his mother, of their home in the Blue Mountains, of soft hands. He turned toward the west and heaved a sigh.

"An Indian? If you wish, you may come for supper tonight and see if I cook like one."

He winced at the reminder of the differences between them. "You have a man to cook for. There is no need to feed me." He sensed the direction of the sun and turned toward his horse. "It is time to start back."

The ride back was made in silence. During the noon rest-Mary passed out herbs and greens to Lillian, Sazie Murdock, and the other women. She scarcely had time to eat before it was time to start out again.

Bethellen, with her two little boys and a third baby on the way, never complained, carrying first one child and then the other when they tired of walking. She sang songs and pointed out the yellow-breasted meadowlark hiding its nest from the coyotes and snakes. The mother meadowlark squawked when they approached, acting like her wing was broken while she led them away from her nest. Bethellen instructed the boys not to touch; they soon left the bird to her eggs and ran off to collect a bouquet of wildflowers for their mother.

"How good you are with the boys," Mary told her. "You make the day more than just an endless march. With you, everything seems so special, even if you are worn to the bone. Here, let me carry Nathan for awhile."

"It's hard, but what are my choices? I've heard of children falling off the crosstree or getting trampled by the oxen. I don't aim to have my babies fall victim to some carelessness on my part. It's about the only thing I can control." She handed the child to Mary with a sigh, placed both hands on the small of her back and stretched her cramped muscles.

Mary swung Nathan onto her shoulders and started galloping. She neighed and pawed while the giggling boy held on. He had already knocked her hat to the ground; now he pulled her hair free from its ribbon so that it cascaded with each shake of her head. He squealed in excitement while his brother came running up for a turn. Panting, Mary lowered a protesting Nathan to the ground and picked up Aron. Then it was time for Nathan another turn. Finally, the three of them fell laughing into the grass. "Are you going to be a farmer when you reach Oregon?"

Nathan shook his head. "I wanna be a guide like Luke."

"Luke?" Mary was puzzled. "Oh, you mean Mr. Sayer."

Nathan nodded. "He's going to show me how to shoot when I get bigger. He said."

"Well, Nathan," Mary ruffled his hair. "There's more to being a top guide than just shooting."

"Like what?"

"You have to be big and brave, and honest, and good to your horse, and kind to ladies, and all kinds of things—" She halted in mid-sentence to see whose shadow was laid across the ground before her. Turning, she found herself face to face with Luke Sayer. It was obvious from his amusement that he had overheard.

"Many things a man must consider. You will discourage the boy."

Mary blushed crimson.

After a prolonged pause, he added, "Ma'am, we'll be leaving the river tomorrow. Best see to your washing. Some of the water holes ahead will be wanting. Some are down-right undrinkable. Keep a watch for the tribes. Unless you're prepared to barter all your goods to ransom your child, I suggest you keep a tight eye on your children. We will soon merge with another wagon train. Keep your party together so no one gets separated. Same goes for your animals. It's easy to lose your cattle when the two herds get mingled."

None of the women spoke. They were scanning the area for their children.

"Well, I'll be going." With a tip of his hat, he was gone.

"That sure is a fine man." Nellie Stoberson's eyes followed him with lingering curiosity. "He's shy-like, don't you think? I'll bet he can dance fine. Don't you think so, Mary?"

Mary tried to sound nonchalant. "We need a dance so you can find out. Maybe tonight?"

The young girl glanced quickly at her mother and her face colored like a beet from the garden. "Ma likes me to stick close to the wagon at night."

Mary clapped her hands enthusiastically. "Philip plays the fiddle, Mr. Murdock has a harmonica. I'll bet there's plenty of others."

Nellie was already on her feet. "I'll spread the word. It'll take us 'til sundown to shake the dust from our hair."

"That was handled real nice, Mary," Lillian commented when her daughter was out of hearing. "She's been trying to figure out how to spend more time with the Landers boy, but his father keeps him pretty busy. Fact is, this'll do us all good." She paused. "Will you dance with Mr. Sayer if he asks you, Mary?"

Mary tried to study the horizon. "Women are scarcer than hen's teeth here on this wagon train. We'll likely be pressed into every dance." She paused. "Why do you ask?"

"Oh, I don't know, just the way he studies you. He seems a decent sort. If my suspicions are true, then I feel pity for him."

"Lillian—I've done nothing to encourage him. He's just friendly."

"Seems more than that. Sometimes you meet a fellow traveler on a similar path. Call it fate that brings people together. Some folks'll risk everything to follow it."

"And you think I'm that kind?" Mary was concerned about Lillian's opinion. Her friend was just stating an age-old fact that Mary knew to be true. Philip and Laurel had it. He could find her in a snowstorm, they were so connected. She recalled watching his face when Laurel and her family pulled out the previous April. His look of pain was a cry from his soul, the kind a wolf gives when he finds his mate dead in a trap. But why would Lillian connect this primal connection with her and Lucas Sayer? "You think there is more than one right person for a person?"

"There's no telling." Lillian sounded casual, her answer innocent, but Mary felt a need to escape. With a feeling of relief, she headed toward her own wagon.

Chapter Ten

April 25, 1848. The prairie has opened to a vastness that unnerves me. How I long for the comfort of a roof over my head. Sometimes I sleep
under the wagon just to feel a canopy above me.

MARY SKINNED HER rabbit seated on the buckboard of her
wagon and hung it on a peg to season. Then she carefully
separated the cream from the milk and placed it in a crock
with the hope that the moving wagon would shake it into
butter. They drank the skimmed milk in their coffee at the
noon break.

By the time Leverenz called the day's halt, she had managed to find a few broken limbs and twigs for the supper
meal. Fire starter had become scarcer as they approached the
open plains. Soon, they would be cooking with buffalo chips.
The women were nearly all in accord; given the choice between the dried chips and a cold meal, they would manage
with the dried dung chips.

She broke the rabbit into pieces, dredged each in flour and
simmered them in a hot skillet with lard, wild onions and
plenty of salt and pepper. To the skillet, she added water,
wild tubers, and the herbs she and Luke had gathered, and
let the stew simmer. An hour later, she dropped mounds of
dumplings on top of the thickened broth and closed the lid

again. While her biscuits baked, she checked the cream crock. Sure enough, butter globules floated to the top of the buttermilk. Scooping them into a crock of cold water, she worked it with her fingers, a poor substitute for the wooden butter paddle she'd packed away. Then, she pressed it into a clean kerchief and squeezed until the mound was firm, added a pinch of salt and formed it into a ball. She set the buttermilk on the buckboard for supper.

As she turned to call him, Philip came strolling into camp with Luke Sayer.

"I convinced Luke to see that rabbit through to the end." Philip smiled, but she kept her gaze lowered as she finished the meal preparations. Apparently, he sensed her mood, because he kept up a steady stream of conversation for Luke's sake. "That's how her Pa taught her. Lived by the rule himself." Philip's eyes lost their gaiety as he reminisced. "He was a good man." She looked up, surprised. It seemed he missed her father almost as much as she did. "Her Pa taught her to shoot her supper and her Ma taught her to cook as fine as any," he finished.

"Let us thank the rabbit for the sacrifice it makes that we might live," Luke said. "It is a good thing for us, because my belly is hungry."

The men ate in silence, their attention focused on their food, while Mary tried to think of something to say. "We were talking today about what we miss most. Lillian misses her Twelve Egg Cake. Orv misses his cracklings. Philip craves sweets. What's your secret desire, Mr. Sayer?"

Luke pulled a toothpick from his pocket and slipped it between his teeth. In the fire's glow his dark eyes appeared half-closed as he studied her beneath his lashes while the seconds ticked past. Finally, he removed the toothpick and without taking his eyes from her, said simply, "Pie."

Mary could feel her breath expelling. *Pie!*

Philip looked back and forth between the two of them as if he were missing something. "You haven't lived until you've tasted Mary's dried apple pie. I thought for sure it was going to get her a husband." He looked up and saw that both of them were watching him. "I mean, that's why I proposed," he hastily amended.

In the tension that followed, Luke rose and stretched. "I'm expected to make the rounds, see how the livestock is settled in. Can I carry water for you, ma'am? Least I can do after that fine meal."

Philip disappeared into the wagon to search for his fiddle.

In his absence, Mary felt nervous in Luke's presence. "I would think you would have better things to do with your evenings, Mr. Sayer." Mary grabbed the bucket and started forward. "You'll no doubt want the extra time to ready yourself for the dancing. Philip will be there soon with his fiddle and you'll want to look your best."

Luke followed her to the river and back again. He had to twist out of her way when she grabbed a handful of sand and started scrubbing the skillet. Finally, he touched a hand to his hat. "I'll be going, then. Supper was as fine as I've had." He disappeared into the dark.

Mary worked out her frustration on the cast iron skillet without fully understanding why she was annoyed. Her spirits rebounded after she donned a fresh green cotton dress with sprigs of lace and a tiny nosegay of fresh flowers pinned at the center—the lace-trimmed bodice dipping just enough that her mother had fussed about it when Mary sewed the dress. She looked down, remembering when she wore it to her first grown-up event with her mother and father. She had chosen the fabric for its color; it was the same shade as her eyes.

The first reel had begun by the time she arrived. Out on the floor, Lillian and Orv were wheeling down the center like a pair of spring fawns. The young man who drove the wagon had overcome his shyness, because he and Nellie were doing the Virginia Reel. Even John Leverenz was stomping down the line with one of the wives Mary had yet to meet. More couples appeared until it seemed like everyone on the train was there. Looking around, Mary spied the Tates. George was tapping his toes to the beat while Bethellen held Nathan.

"Here, let me," Mary offered, "I have no partner." Bethellen protested that she hadn't an extra ounce of energy for dancing, so George found a crate for her and the youngest child. With his wife's blessing he grabbed Mary and stomped out into the circle of dancers.

What he lacked in style he more than made up for in enthusiasm. Mary was twirled across the dirt, her feet not always touching the ground while George's big arm clamped her waist with a force that threatened to bruise her ribs. Two dances later she pleaded off with the excuse that she needed to catch her breath, but before she could make it off the dirt circle, one of the Stoberson sons claimed her.

In short order, nearly every man in the train asked; even a very young boy who gazed up at her shyly while he led her in stiff box steps—while his older brothers watched with ill-concealed envy. Finally, holding a stitch in her side, she eased out of the circle.

She found a spot near the river that featured an inviting bench of flat rocks where she removed her lace-up shoes and dangled her toes in the water. Remembering Luke's warning that this would be the last night at the river, she closed her eyes and leaned back to feel the breeze on her bare throat. She opened her eyes in time to see the moon peep through a cloud. How neat the stars looked. Luke had said the Indians imitated the calls of animals to communicate with each other, and she shivered at the thought.

"Cold, Mrs. Rodgers?" There was the deep, timorous voice that seemed to follow her thoughts. On a rock, not ten feet away, Luke Sayer sat smoking his cheroot and waiting. "I saw you shiver. Are you cold?"

"No," she managed. "Just a little lost on this prairie." She turned back toward the water but she felt his eyes. His Adam's apple bobbed and she realized he was assessing her profile against the darkening sky.

"We're not lost, ma'am. Just small and unimportant. There's a difference."

She kept her face trained on the stars, waiting for him to continue. When he did not, she asked, "What's the difference?" She smelled the smoke of his cigar and his muffled voice sounded as though he, too, faced the water.

"Lost is where your soul is hidden and you can't find it. I won't get you lost, ma'am." To her ears, his words sounded like a poem.

"We're on the Promise Road. That's how I think of it."

He nodded. "You walk toward a promise. This is good. Do not let the trail be a killer of dreams. " Crickets chirped in the background while they listened.

"Why have you never married, Mr. Sayer?"

A long silence before he said, "Maybe my spirit lives in two worlds."

"Two worlds? You mean between two shores? You attended school in the east."

"Two worlds—rock and hard place—the People and the whites."

Mary fought the stirrings inside her with a nervous laugh. "Are *you* lost, Mr. Sayer?"

"You say I should take my own counsel? Find my way between the rocks? My friend Leverenz tells me the same."

"Maybe he's right."

"This may be. I will give your words some thought. And maybe one day I will taste your dried apple pie."

This time, her laughter was not nervous. "You are easily pleased, Mr. Sayer. If Philip were as susceptible to my pies, he would have filled his wagon with apples."

"It is not his lack of provisions that worries me."

"He has a brave heart. He will get us through to the Oregon Country or—"

"Or die trying? You speak the words lightly. With so much waiting ahead, you wish to die on the trail?"

Mary heard his frustration. "If you feel that strongly about us greenhorns traveling into danger, Mr. Sayer, why do you agree to help us?"

He ignored her question. "I am a simple man of horses and mountains. Call me Luke."

First name basis with a stranger? Her mother would have abhorred such casual manners, especially in this private spot, with her "husband" busy entertaining the people who had accepted their relationship as they stated it to be.

Seeking something to strengthen her resolve, she took refuge in anger. "One of the reasons the women and their greenhorn husbands are going west is because they have no other choice. The time is coming that men will be caught up in a war. That's why Philip is leaving. I'm fortunate because I want to go with him, but some women aren't. Some are burdened with too many children, their health is broken, their youth gone before they have weaned their last child. Look at that dance. There are a lot of old men dancing with young girls, but many of the women can't spare the time. They're still hard at work at their camp. A wife's life is lonely and exhausting. Can you argue that I am wrong?"

"No, ma'am, I can't. A decent man values his woman."

Mary felt her anger dissolve. "Everything isn't as bleak as I describe. Some couples rely on each other, live for each other. This is what I want for my marriage."

"Do you have it?"

"Have what?"

"What you want. Do you have that with your husband?" He watched her closely, waiting for her answer, even though the night was so dark that the truth could be revealed only in her voice.

"Philip is the best men I have ever met."

"You didn't answer."

"I have loved him since I was a child."

"You still don't answer me."

"Why do you ask me these questions? Can't you see that we care for each other?" To her ears she sounded breathless.

"Like a brother, but like a woman loves her man? No, I don't think you do."

Mary's heart pounded. "How dare you? You have no wife. How can you speak to me like this?"

"Ma'am, I see the way you search for wildflowers. You find the bird nest in the grass and you do not touch because you understand the heart of the small hen. You are not a woman for half measures."

She said nothing for a long while, thinking on his words. "Lillian said the same thing today."

"About you and your husband?"

"No."

"About you?"

"Yes." She hesitated too long to sound convincing. He guessed.

"About us—you and me?"

Again, a long hesitation. Then slowly, regretfully, "Yes."

She heard him inhale a long, slow breath. Her single word hung in the air and something changed between them while he dragged at his cheroot.

Mary watched the tip glow red. He was not a conventional man, and he tended to get straight to whatever was on his mind. Apparently, tonight, *she* was. She waited in silence, knowing she should go back to the dance, but unable to convince her limbs to carry her there.

"Ma'am, are you a brave woman?"

"I have never backed off from anything in my life"

"That is good. You will need courage before this journey is over."

"You said you'd never let me lose my way. What did you mean?"

"In time you must face the truth, even if it causes pain. Keep your courage."

"Mr. Sayer, there are things you don't understand." She came as close to telling him as she could, but the secret would stand between them. It would be Philip's place to admit the truth, if the time ever came, for she had given her word. Afraid of where the conversation was heading, she rose and prepared to return to the dance.

"Ma'am?" His low pleading was nearly her undoing.

"I have to go. Philip will be wondering where I am." Turning, she picked her way across the rounded rocks, lifting her skirts to keep them from the mud and moss at the water's edge while she made her way into the light of the campfire.

Philip nodded in greeting. He was playing the last of a robust hill song that had the Missourians stomping and frolicking inside the circle. Mary marveled at how they could still move after the vigorous pace the wagonmaster had set for them today.

The next song began. Slower-paced, it required more touching of partners. A couple of young men started toward her. She waited, not sure what she should do until, at the last moment, a hand on her shoulder spun her around.

"Ma'am, I believe this is my dance." Luke glared at the youngsters, who had no wish to butt heads with the guide. Beauty or no, they decided to look elsewhere for partners. Luke gripped Mary as close as was acceptable and they settled into the music. His feet led in a smooth circle that made her feel like she was soaring. Around and around they twirled, saying nothing, enjoying the feel of each other in the dark. She looked up to find his eyes impaling her with an intensity that made her lightheaded. She faltered and he strengthened his grip, pulling her against him with a force that was unseemly for two strangers at a public dance.

Her face flushed with more than exertion by the time the dance ended. With a final squeeze of his hand on her shoulder and the bitter hint of a smile, Luke turned and disappeared in the direction of the river. Mary watched him go, confused at the suddenness of his departure. Suddenly, she was tired of it all. Waving to Philip, she gathered her skirts and left the circle in the opposite direction, making her way back to the wagon.

When Philip finally came in, he shuffled in the darkness as he removed his boots. "Where did you disappear to tonight?" His question was more a growl, as though he already had his answer. "It ain't seemly. I noticed that Luke Sayer was gone, too. I'm warning you, Mary, people will notice every single time you say hello to him—or any other man. You can't be acting like a single gal if you're trying to pass for married. I suggest you spend your time knitting with the married gals. Keep you out of trouble." He made a whacking sound on his bedroll, climbed inside, and was still.

Mary feigned sleep because she needed time to understand her feelings. But sleep—and understanding—were a long time coming.

Chapter Eleven

April 30, 1948. Our wagons are no longer fresh
and new. Neither are the hopes we carry. The
trail is like life itself, full of both hope and despair. Oh, but how much harder the despair.

THE NEXT MORNING Mary noticed the other women,
young and old alike, seemed in high spirits. "Morning, Lillian, how are things this morning?" she called.

Lillian laughed and stopped to pick a bunch of buttercups
for her graying hair. She had the look of a woman whose
husband had nipped on corn liquor the night before and had
come to bed in a randy mood. Her cheeks glowed with a
softness that Mary found charming. Was that what love did
to a woman? If so, Lillian was lucky. She had a good man,
wonderful children and the sense to recognize her good fortune. She was a breath of fresh air to everyone who knew her
and whenever the wagon train started out on the track, Mary
always tried to find her and her girls to walk beside. Many
days she even gave up riding Buttercup, just to enjoy the
Stobersons' company. She liked Lillian's cheerfulness and
airy practicality that minimized the discomforts of the trip
and made everything seem temporary and minor.

Mary longed to confide her dilemma to her friend, but
this was what Philip had warned against, the letting down of

her guard. Biting her tongue, she allowed the secret to stand.

"Lillian, does your husband drink whiskey?" Mary's own father had not been a drinking man, except for the wine he made from his prized vineyard each fall. The image of Lucas in the eating house, obviously comfortable with the glass of whiskey he held, kept coming back to her, along with her mother's warnings about drinking men. There had been a bottle on the table between the three men. She'd seen enough of the woes that some wives suffered, and she wondered if that would include Luke's.

Lillian's words penetrated Mary's thoughts. "Orv likes his nip as well as the next feller, but he's a hard worker. Saves his good times for when the work's done." Lillian wasn't the type to put up with such a fundamental flaw in her man, Mary decided while she continued. "Some men let drink cloud their minds of what needs doing and their family suffers for it. 'Sides, most fellers control the money. When you combine a love of corn likker with a pocketful of cash, you've got a feller forgetting about the little ones at home doin' without. I've seen women plumb shrivel up and die for the lack of caring that their drinking men give them."

Lillian paused to tousle her youngest's hair then watch as he bounded off to join a group of boys tumbling on the grass. "Men're weak-minded to let their cravings get the better of them, but that's a far cry from having a nip when they're feeling good. My Orv keeps a jug under the wagon seat. Thinks I don't know it's there and I don't say nothin'. A man's got to have something of his own, same as a woman. You got any secrets from your man?"

Lillian watched from the corner of her eye while Mary shifted uncomfortably. She wasn't blind. Camping next to the Rodgers as often as they did, she would notice how many nights Luke Sayer had dropped by with a need to speak to

Philip. Lillian might watch, but if she suspected anything she was waiting until Mary came to her for advice.

Mary finally mustered her nerve to speak. "Do you think if someone seems comfortable with a bottle of whiskey at an eating house it could spell a problem?" She remembered Luke's suave salute and how she had felt it was not his first night in a saloon.

"Well, I don't think either Philip nor, for that matter, that nice Luke Sayer have any problems with the drink. You can tell about those things. Both of them hold themselves in high regard—too much so to waste their lives on likker."

Mary started in surprise. How did Lucas Sayer's name get into the conversation? She ventured a peek. Lillian was twirling a buttercup nonchalantly between her fingers. Now would be the time to tell, if only she could. Instead, she said, "My father drank only wine. Did your father drink?"

Lillian smiled at the memory. "I only saw my father drunk once. Ma had taken us all out berry picking on a Sunday afternoon and Pa was going over to help a neighbor mend fence. When he got there, the neighbor couldn't do it that day, and Pa found himself with a day off and no one at home. When we returned, we looked all over for him, finally found him passed out in the corn barn. We had us this fine big barn where we stored the corn and the potatoes and the grain. It had this big walkway between the compartments, and there he lay, dead-to-the-world drunk and passed out.

"'Children', Ma said, 'You get yourselves some ears of corn and start to shucking.' We done what she said, though we didn't know what for. But no one crossed Ma. After a spell, she told us to throw the corn down on Pa. We done that and the corn went in his pockets and between his legs and ever-place. Then she told my brother to let the ducks out.

"Now, we had forty-eight ducks and they come flying for that corn. Like to have pecked my pa to death afore he got himself sobered up enough to stagger out of that barn and into the house. I never saw him drunk again. And, come to think of it, my brothers, neither." Lillian laughed loud and hard at the memory. "None of my brothers ever took to drink because they used to laugh at the consequences if Ma found out."

Mary had to wipe her eyes with the corner of her apron as the tears streamed down her face. "Oh, Lil...Lil...ian. Your girls are so...oo lucky to have a m...mother like you." Her hysterics set them both laughing again, until the other women around them were all laughing too, even though they were not sure what the joke was. When Mary could breathe again, she remembered her errand. "Lillian, we're traveling on flat ground now and there's precious few trees around. I'm thinking about our um, personal needs. What are we going to do when we get out on the flats and there's no cover at all?"

"Honey, we'll three or four of us walk out aways. Three of us will hold our skirts out full while the other attends to her needs. Then we'll take a step to the side, and the next one can take a turn. We'll get through that problem just fine. We'll all be in the same fix, so there'll be no reason to feel shy."

Sure enough, when the need came an hour later, Lillian's idea worked fine, and the problem took care of itself.

Mary had worried about her privacy with Philip, as well, but he allowed her to get ready for bed in the darkness while he tended to his own needs out in the flats. She had become an expert at wiggling into fresh clothing in the privacy of her bedroll, and she gladly dispensed with many of the conventions that the ladies back home would consider essential. She had joined Lillian in tossing their corsets into a campfire, early on, and she and Nellie traded braiding each other's hair when they had a spare minute. Gone were the elaborate hair arrangements that her mother had favored. Although Mary tried to maintain her starchy white aprons as a token of civility, practicality gave in to form on this wide-open plain. Some of the women had dyed their aprons black. The rest of them decided that dingy-clean was good enough; they would boil their whites again when they reached Oregon.

One day, Luke saw Mary change a diaper on one of Bethellen's little boys and noticed that she wrestled with what to do with the soiled cloth. The next morning he rode over with a bundle of fur tied into a small ball. "Here, ma'am, this is what my mother used." He tossed her the bundle then sat astride his horse and watched her open it.

"What is it? It's so soft!" She put the skin to her face and rubbed, feeling the fur on her cheek and lips.

"The tribes raise pups to eat and they use the skins for diapers. They use doe skin, too. They'll fill them with moss or grass or anything they've got. Then they just toss the grass out when it's soiled and replace it. I traded a tribe south of here. See how it works."

The women declared that the skin worked well. But new pups were highly coveted and Bethellen had to continue using her flannel diaper squares as well.

Luke held the attention at the campfire one evening. He explained that the Sioux, Pawnee, and Northern Cheyenne were growing leery of the steady horde of settlers coming across their hunting grounds. Everywhere the whites went, disease and waste followed.

"You fall sick, take your wagon to the rear. Don't trade with the tribes if you have tainted clothing or food. Some of the diseases we get aren't so deadly to us, but the Indians take it hard." He paused as a murmur swept among the travelers.

"Ain't gonna trade my life fer one of those damn red-skins." As usual, Bill Weems led the dissent.

Luke fixed a hard look on him. "The devil take you, you varmint."

Leverenz stepped in. "If someone in your party dies, bury them at night, in the middle of the trail. The next morning the entire train will drive over them. If this doesn't meet your fancy, try to hide the grave in some fashion so the coyotes and wolves don't find it, even if the Indians leave it alone. On our last trip through, a man died of cholera and we buried him on the plains not far from here. The next day, Indians attacked the wagon train. We saw one brave galloping by, wearing the dead man's clothes. Now, it's a sure bet he took that cholera back to his whole tribe. Keep it up and their war chiefs will call for attacking and burning the trains to rid themselves of the bad spirits."

The group at the campfire was silent. They were passing burial sights all day long now. Most had markers; on some, loved ones had carefully recorded the names and date of death. Sometimes, whole families were buried, the markers made from board torn from their wagons, their names scratched on the wood with the point of a knife. "We have to get over the idea that we're just passing through, that none of this matters. This is the tribes' home and they have to live with what we leave behind."

Luke listened to Leverenz, but his heart knew the words would do no good. The settlers had their minds set on Oregon. Nothing else mattered.

After the meeting broke up, Luke walked Philip and Mary back to their wagon. Philip captured Mary's arm in a proprietary grip that forced Luke to walk on his other side.

Mary tried to keep up the conversation. "Is the problem

with the Indians really that bad? We've seen nothing but friendship on their part."

Luke thought a moment before he responded. "Right now your people are just passing through, but in five or ten years, they'll claim this land for their own use—stage stops, military outposts and the farms to supply them. The range will open up with free land for settlers, just like Oregon Territory. The tribes will be drawn into wars that they don't want to fight. Some of the chiefs realize this, now. They want to stop us while the travel is still a trickle."

Philip tugged at his mustache, as he did when he was worried. "Strange that we never read about this in the newspapers back home."

"Telling the truth doesn't serve the money interests. Their profits come from exaggerating and lies."

"Mr. Sayer, did you mean what you said about the Indians digging up the dead?"

"Ma'am, they seem uncivilized to you. It's easy to see them as hostiles, primitive. But their traditions serve them well."

"It sounds as though you side with them." Philip sounded surprised.

Luke seemed to hesitate. "My mother was Umatilla." He paused, waiting for Mary's reaction. "I am of the People."

"You're a half-blood?" Mary couldn't mask her surprise.

"Yes ma'am." Luke's dark eyes challenged hers. He stood tensed while his mistrust crackled in the air.

Mary felt his conflict. She had said something to offend him, but everyone used the words like squaw and redskin. "Are you on the warpath, too?" she teased.

Luke scowled at her until he was sure she meant no insult. "No warpath, ma'am. My father was Welsh. He had another wife, a Scottish woman who reared me in the East."

"You regret this?" Philip asked.

"Ever see an Indian child in a white man's school?" He waited for Mary to shake her head before he continued. "Doesn't take long to figure out where you fit in."

"Is that why you're going to Oregon? To be free?"

"Free?" He laughed. "I was born free. I'm just trying to find out where I belong."

"Have you?"

"Found out where I *don't* belong. And there's others who feel as out of place as me. Mormons burned out of Missouri end up giving travelers supplies if they can't afford to pay. Half-breeds of every color hounded by folks who think they have the right. People ought to be judged on how they come to grips with this new land, not on their skin." His voice rose across the camp.

Beside them, Philip coughed. "Noble words. I'll try to live up to them." He tightened his grip on Mary's arm. "In the meantime, reckon we best head to bed. Come on, Mary. It's getting late."

After they parted for the night, Mary thought of what Luke had said. He was willing to stand up for his beliefs. She had never seen him treat anyone except with the utmost respect—and that included the folks at the back of the train who were suffering from sickness and breakdowns.

He had a soft spot in his heart for the escaped slaves that rode with one eye out for the bounty hunters that searched the wagon trains. She had watched him help one escape discovery by a slave hunter who had approached on a late afternoon from the east, riding a lathered, wheezing gelding. She was standing alongside the oxen with Philip when Luke rode in at a gallop and crossed to his own wagon. Without halting, he lifted a young Negro boy onto the seat and Mary saw that his leg was a bloody mass that looked as though a bullet or a whip had torn the flesh from the bone. Within seconds, the boy disappeared into the back and closed the canvas covering. When the lone rider reached the lead wagons, Luke was riding alongside Leverenz, calmly discussing something with no regard to the visitor.

Mary heard the stranger's voice raised in anger. "I know he's here. Heard a report that someone picked him up on the prairie. Leg's stoved up. Probably useless. But he run off and it's my job to find him."

Luke must have said something, because the man shouted, "And I say you're lying." He turned toward Leverenz. "I get paid by the head, same as you. No difference between my job and a trapper's." Mary heard his coarse laughter. "'Cept I have to bring my black pelt back alive before I get paid."

She saw Luke stiffen and Leverenz motion for him to back off. Leverenz's voice was so faint that she had to strain to hear his reply. "I don't recognize any law says you can take prisoners from a free territory. I'm the law here, and you ain't plowin' through these folks' belongings on any wild goose chase."

"Oregon will be white territory, wait and see. They won't let blacks own land out there, nor stand in line for the free land that's being offered. Might as well stop them before they reach the borders." The bounty hunter jerked his horse back in the direction he'd come.

He rode past her, examining the faces of the emigrants with hard, practiced calculation. At the last wagon he leaped to the ground and climbed over the box of a dilapidated wagon driven by a young Negro couple. Luke had told her that Leverenz let them tag along because practically the only thing of value they owned were their free papers, which they kept in a beaver skin pouch that an Indian had traded them.

The black man jumped to his feet from the seat and faced the intruder. Without warning, the slave hunter fired a ball from his revolver, creasing the black man's neck. When the man toppled from his wagon seat, the woman screamed. Within seconds, the stranger began throwing their goods onto the ground. He pulled a frightened child by the arm and shook it like a rag doll, ignoring the child's cry of pain. When he saw that it was a girl child, he shoved her out of his way and continued his search. He pitched a barrel of flour onto the dirt and it exploded in a cloud of white.

By now, the owner of the wagon had raised himself from the ground, wiped the blood from his wound and dropped into a crouch with a small, sharpened bone-knife in his hand. Above him the slave hunter raised his revolver. Mary heard herself scream. In a heart's beat Luke was upon the bounty hunter, grappling for the gun. He twisted the angry, flailing man until his upper body extended off the wagon seat. With a fluid motion he pulled his own knife and held it to the man's throat.

"Please, mister! Don't do it." The Negro woman stood beside her husband, eyes round in horror at what Luke was planning to do. "We'll all suffer for it. Please don't."

Her words seemed to penetrate Luke's consciousness because he slowly lowered the knife. With an angry twist, the bounty hunter lunged to his feet, shrugged his shirt back into order and climbed from the wagon. "I'll be back with more guns."

It had been over a week, and they had seen no sign of the slaver. Luke had taken a supply of his flour and coffee to the couple. When Mary appeared with her healing box and a needle and thread to stitch the boy, Luke had waved her away saying that he would take responsibility in case there was any lawman to answer to. The next day, the boy's leg was stitched up and he smelled like pungent healing salve. She had seen the boy once since then. The slave hunter was right about one thing; he would walk crippled.

Mary recalled other kindnesses that Luke had done, like the puppy skin, and she realized that the womanizing, drinking man she had thought beneath her regard had vanished, along with a lot of her other misconceptions in the last couple months. Or, maybe she was growing up.

Philip's voice interrupted her thoughts. "You know, Mary, people are noticing how much time Sayer spends at our camp—just like I warned. You better spend more time talking to the women."

Mary made no reply.

Chapter Twelve

May 4, 1848. We pass tribes of Indians who seem quite friendly and accustomed to trade. We grow used to having fresh corn, squash and fish, in trade for flannel shirts, needles and knives, especially those made by Mr. Bowie. How fortuitous that the guide books advised us to bring trading items, for the barter is advantageous to all concerned.

THE WAGON TRAIN had stopped at the Big Blue River crossing while they waited for the water to recede. True to Mr. Leverenz's warning, the folks did their churching and praying on the days they halted, not the other way around.

Lillian was beside herself as she joined Mary the next afternoon. "Oh, what a day! I been holding the Johnson baby. He's a might fussy with the storm coming. His ma's got a touch of the heat prostrate. It's no wonder—it must be near a hundred today, and muggy to beat all. If I had an egg, I told Orv I'd cook it right atop his bald head. He'd probably eat it too, much as he loves fried eggs."

She gave her husband a fond look and a wave, which he returned with a "Howdy, there, Sweetcakes."

"That baby was fussin', so I thought I'd have a turn at him. Not much I can't remember about gettin' a baby over what ails him. Anyway, the baby upchucked his dinner all over me and I had to give him back to his father while I climbed up and changed."

Mary's heart sank. No! It couldn't be. It wouldn't be fair! In a trembling voice she demanded, "Did you wash up good after handling the baby?"

"Why are you asking that, honey?" Lillian turned to Mary with a look of dread. Almost like she knew what was coming next, she asked again, "Why, Mary?"

"Mrs. Johnson died a few minutes ago of cholera. The baby is sick and fading fast. Mr. Johnson is with them now, alone in the wagon. Oh, Lillian, what will we do?"

Lillian stood ramrod straight, facing the sunset as the last rays of the fading day shone red on her fine face and slipped behind the western horizon. Her face reflected fear. At last she turned, and in doing so, seemed a different woman. The fear was gone, along with the panic. She seemed in control — even tranquil. "*We* do nothing, Miss Mary. You get on back to my young'uns and see to their supper. Say nothin' to no one. I got troubles enough without anyone interfering."

"Lillian, I want to help."

"Then, girl, do as I say. Keep the young'uns away 'til we see if I come down with it. You can do that much for me, and maybe save my family in the bargain. If you don't think that would be a blessing to me, it's 'cause you haven't got no child of your own. I'd die a death for every one of mine."

Mary left Lillian sitting on the riverbank looking far more composed than she, herself, felt. She approached the wagons with a hope that she could control her fear. "Hello there, Virginie and Nellie. Your mama asked that I fix supper with you tonight. Let's combine our efforts. Won't that be a nice change?"

"Where's Ma? Wasn't she with you?" Nellie started in the

direction of the river. "I'll find her. We can have a campfire and pop us some corn. Pa might dance a jig, 'specially if he has a nip from the jug he keeps under the seat, where he thinks Ma don't know."

Mary called, "Wait, Nellie. Your Ma said to tell you she's bone-tired and just wants to soak her feet in the cool water and be alone."

"Is she sick?" Nellie glanced up at Mary.

Drawing both girls to the side, she improvised. "Actually, from what she's been telling me, I think she is having a touch of the change of life. She says she gets touchy over nothing and just wants to be alone sometimes. Let's give her a little time. It must be hard, all of us crowded together like we are." *I should be an actress like that Mrs. Siddons in New York City. She probably never played such a difficult role in her whole life.*

Virginie pulled her sister back. "Mary's right. Let's leave Ma alone. We're always needing her for something. It's her turn."

Dinner went off more or less without a hitch until Nellie lost her balance near the campfire and caught the hem of her dress on fire. Ned stomped the flame out with his big boot and tore the waist, so Nellie hauled off and smacked him. Virginie tripped on Ned's other foot and nearly spilled the big pan of fried potatoes she was carrying, but the fried fish and beans and dried apple cobbler were finally ready.

"Save a plate for Ma. She'll be along soon."

The absence of Ma Stoberson was an event to remember. She had never missed a meal in her own home except for the birth of each of her children, and even then, she hollered instructions from her little room so the children knew she was still in charge. But she had done a good job; both the girls were fine cooks and homemakers.

Long after the younger children were asleep, Lillian appeared at the edge of the camp, careful to keep her distance. "My stars, but somethin' smells good, even if I left my appetite for vittles out there on the prairie. I had myself a little nap, but I swear I'm as surly as a bear. I'll thank you all to just leave me be." She moved closer to the fire, holding the soiled dress she had changed out of after holding the Johnson child. She let a corner of it trail into the fire, and in an exaggerated attempt to retrieve it, pushed more of it in until the whole dress was aflame. "Lordy, just look what I've done. I'll be hard-pressed to get to Oregon if I don't keep my wits about me better than that. What a shame."

Her daughters stared as if they had been turned to stone. Their ma had made a mistake, especially one as wasteful as that? Their ma had never made a misstep in all the years they had been copying her actions, but since Nellie had just nearly fallen into the fire herself, her mother's clumsiness didn't seem nearly so impossible.

"Mary, would you fetch my bedroll?" Lillian asked in a casual tone. "I got a hankering to sleep out by myself like you do. Thought tonight would be the night. Just look at all them stars."

"Oh, Ma, can we sleep out with you?"

"Well, then I wouldn't be alone, would I?" Lillian gave a slight shake of her head and turned away.

Mary exchanged glances with Virginie. "Remember what I told you about your ma's condition? I'll bet with the change of life, she's also feeling some hot flashes and having trouble sleeping in that stuffy tent. You girls know what I'm talking about, don't you? Best get yourselves to bed and let her have her time." Mary gave them a pointed woman-to-woman look.

After Lillian disappeared into the night, Mary continued to sit at the fireside. How long would it take—a day, two days—before they would know? It had already been twelve scorching hours since Lillian had held the Johnson baby. How many times had she kissed the baby, brushed his tears away with her lips, wiped his nose, and did all the things a loving woman does for a fussy little one? The baby had seemed so normal. He played with Lillian's bonnet strings, with her face. They even shared a drink of water from a tin cup, the same one that the Turlock family had used. And the Johnsons. Weary and discouraged, Mary made her own way to bed, glad that Philip was occupied elsewhere. Tomorrow would be a long day for them all.

In the morning, Lillian declined the bite of the dinner her daughters had saved from the night before. After taking a long draught from the tin cup, she instructed Mary to leave it with her. "Best you boil the drinking water from now on, Mary, and tell the girls to do the same. I brought some ginger tea. Have them drink that. We can't be too careful, and Mary, don't come around me."

By noon, Lillian was twisting in agony. Mary examined the older woman from a distance and blanched at what she saw; Lillian's cheeks were flushed and her eyes held the glassy look of fever. Mary searched under the wagon seat, found Orville's jug and brought her a drink of whiskey that temporarily soothed her, but soon her pain became excruciating. She began vomiting black bile and her eyes expressed the despair she had tried to hold back. Mary soaked a rag with more whiskey and applied it to her friend's belly. There was little else she knew to do.

"Go away, Mary. See that none of my family comes around. When I'm gone, bury the beddin' with me. Please, don't let none of my babies die."

As Mary walked back to her own wagon, she understood the greatness in her mother that compelled her to aid strangers who had no one else. In her hour of compassion for Lillian, Mary forgave her mother for dying. From the left, a horse approached at a gallop. Through her tears, Mary tried to see which rider blocked her path to the Stoberson camp.

Lucas studied the dark smudges around Mary's eyes and the tears streaming down her cheeks. When her dull eyes met his, the color in his face faded. "Trouble here?" he asked. Jumping from the stallion with a force that caused the horse to shy away, he grasped her shoulders. "Mrs. Rodgers, talk to me."

Her voice quivered. "It's Lillian. She's got the cholera."

"That's trouble, for sure. You weren't with her, were you?" He glanced closer and scowled. "Dammit, woman. Why?"

"'Cause she's my f-friend. And my mother died and I was…angry. Oh, Lucas, I'm so sorry."

He gripped her in both hands and made a desperate inspection of her face as though he could read the answers there. "Did you touch her body fluids?"

She nodded. "Yes. No." He squeezed his eyes closed and she added, "She wouldn't let me come close. She wants to end it with her."

His eyes opened with a shadow of relief and his tone softened. "Maybe there's a chance. My mother used a plant that grows a half-day's ride south of here. It might help. I'll be back by evening. Stay away. You can't help her."

"A wild root can't help me. Only God can do that."

He acted as though he didn't hear her. "Have some water boiling when I return tonight. Promise me, Mary."

"I will be careful," she promised, but only that.

Gathering the reins, Luke circled south and started off at a run.

It was late when he rode back into camp, exhausted and

caked with dust. Hastily rubbing down his horse, he hobbled it in the tall grass and made his way to the camp where John Leverenz was preparing his bedroll. "Rode down to where the hostiles were camped last time we came through. No sign of them." He poured a cup of coffee and waited for a response. When it didn't come he gulped the contents and filled the cup with boiled water and some of the crushed stems he carried. "I'll be back." Picking up the mug, Luke hurried through the camp, past the Stobersons' wagon where the girls were standing at the fire, silently waiting. At the Rodgers' camp he greeted a sober Philip in the half-gloom of a hastily built fire. "Where is she?" he asked, looking around.

"Not sure. Maybe she's over with Lillian."

"You mean she went on back after I warned her? Damn it, man, I thought you had more sense!" Luke heard himself raving, but he didn't care. His head threatened to explode as he paced with the steaming cup of potion forgotten in his hand.

"Calm down, Luke. I haven't been back but a half-hour myself. I went hunting. Time I returned and skinned out my antelope, she'd been with Lillian most of the day."

"I left word she was to stay away. She didn't listen?"

"Don't know what to say. You know yourself she's a stubborn woman. Takes after her mother. At any rate, the damage is done."

Luke set the cup down. "Fetch the biggest tub of water you have and set it to boiling. Get out your strongest soap. We'll need some toweling. Rig your tent so she can clean up in privacy. She'll need a fresh set of clothing, from the skin out. We'll have to burn everything she's wearing and maybe she'll have a chance."

"You figuring to do the honors?" Philip stood unconsciously clenching and unclenching his fists.

Luke looked up with a scowl. "Won't ask any of the family women. You up to the task?"

"Well…I reckon not. I need to check on the oxen. You go ahead, but keep your voice down. I don't want our neighbors knowing. Already hell to pay—and hear tell, the worst is still ahead."

Philip gathered the supplies and started heating the water before he strode off in the direction of the makeshift corral. Out of the dark, Luke noticed a dark form approaching. It was Mary, head bent, her body sagging as she made her way back from the little camp in the buffalo grass where Lillian Stoberson must have just succumbed, because she untied a scarf from her face, wadded it into a ball and dropped it into the fire. She started toward her wagon without looking up. She was almost upon him when he took her arms in his hands and gave her shoulders a shake. "You little fool. I won't let you die."

She looked up and her eyes registered confusion. He drew her to the dark side of the tent. With fingers that seemed to have lost their sense of feel, he tore the bodice to the hemline and freed her from her petticoat before he tossed both onto the ground. A moment later, he began scrubbing. She was too exhausted to realize that she was sitting alongside the wash pot, being rubbed down with rough strokes that showed little sympathy for her dignity. When the chill pervaded her consciousness and she felt her hair being doused with cold water, she wrinkled her nose at the lye soap burning her neck. "Stop," she protested. "That hurts."

"I'm sorry for insulting you like this. But dammit, you're not going to die." Luke continued to scrub her with an impersonal touch. Angry at himself, he dried her reddened skin with as much haste as he could manage. He rummaged inside her trunk for a clean dress, abandoned the search with an impatient curse and pulled the folds of her bedroll around her. Before she could escape into sleep, he tipped the mug of water to her lips. She took a sip, grimaced and turned her face away.

"Drink it, dammit, all of it." He poured the brew into her mouth, forcing her to swallow until she finished. Only then did he release her.

While she slept, he scrubbed the tub with the same soap. He saw to the burying of Mrs. Stoberson and the burning of her bedding, insisting that Orv and the children remain at a distance. When he was satisfied, he made himself a cup of the bitter brew and swallowed it. Finally, he crawled into his own bedroll and slept.

The camp was just beginning to wake when he rolled out of bed and made his way to the pot of coffee hanging above a struggling fire his cook had started. He tossed down a cup without tasting it and headed for Mary and Philip's camp. It would be too early to tell, he knew, but he had to see her. Philip was already stirring in the silent camp and they greeted each other cautiously.

"Listen. That was a fool thing I did last night. I insulted your wife. Take it out on my hide if you want to. I won't stand against you."

Philip fidgeted with his coffee pot, his face red to his ears. "Probably should tell you I bear you no grudge. You did what needed to be done and I'm in your debt. Let's put this behind us. For Mary's sake."

Luke nodded, but it occurred that the husband acted relieved at having escaped the duty himself. "She's strong and determined. I'll put my money on her making it."

Mary woke with the taste of poison in her mouth. She vaguely recalled someone handing her a drink the night before and forcing her to drink. Philip? She remembered hands helping her, hurting her, being unbearably cold and tired before she was allowed to sleep. An image of Lillian filled her memory. She had failed to save her, just as she failed her own mother. An aching sense of loss weighted her limbs and she gave in to wracking sobs.

Finally, she rose to her feet and tied her bedroll with tight, angry motions, determined that neither her mother's nor Lillian's memory would be besmirched by wallowing in grief. She glanced down at herself and realized that she was naked. Her skin felt tight and smelled faintly of lye. The dress she had worn the previous day was nowhere to be seen. Defiantly, she donned her yellow calico shirtwaist with its short, puffy sleeves, and after fastening the hooks, slipped her hands along her ribcage and felt the strong beating of her heart. Yes, she was alive. She would wear her prettiest dress in memory of Lillian. As an afterthought she combed her hair and added bright yellow ribbons. "Lillian would want me to celebrate her life, not the ending of it," she whispered before bending to slip through the opening of the tent.

Straightening to her full five-feet-two inches, she looked around for Philip, and rounding the corner of the tent, found him deep in conversation. "Oh, good morning, Mr. Sayer. Did you hear the sad news about Lillian Stoberson?"

Luke's discussion with Philip trailed off when he saw her standing with the glow of the cookfire illuminating her bright yellow dress, her soft peach skin ripening in the sunrise. He gulped and stumbled for something to say while he tried to press her vision into his memory. Suddenly, he was struck by the realization that he was hopelessly in love with a girl who might die today. Fear flooded his brain and he reacted with a tight, angry scowl that drew his eyes into narrow slits. Unwilling for Mary to witness his confusion, he tipped his hat in a hasty salute and fled in the direction of his own camp.

As the silence grew, Philip glanced at Mary. "How are you feeling?"

"Strange. I dreamed I drank a potion last night that caused me to sleep like a log. I didn't even feel the ground."

"So you don't remember anything?"

"I recall sitting with Lillian until the end." She turned to watch the fire. "She had a hard death. She suffered so, and yet she never complained except to make me promise to keep her family away. I'm so angry. Now, I have to wait to see what fate holds for me. What kind of world is this?"

"No more talk of dying, Mary. Get something to eat and go share with her family what you can about her last hours. It'll be a comfort to them." He gave her a weak smile and pointed toward the neighbor's wagon. "They need you."

Mary glanced toward the Stoberson wagons. Silence had replaced the sounds of breakfast at their camp this morning. "I'll go over and see if I can help."

"Best keep a distance, just in case—"

"I know."

At the Stoberson camp, Nellie and Virginie sat weeping next to Orv, who looked as if his wind had been knocked out of him. His mason jar of corn liquor set near his feet, empty. Dying embers in the fire pit indicated that they had made no provisions for a meal before the wagons headed out. Mary picked up a tin plate from the dirt. "Virginie...we need to get some food started."

"Oh, Mary." Nellie rose and started toward Mary, arms outstretched.

Mary turned away. "It's best I don't touch you." Orv looked up, blinked, and seemed to notice her for the first time. He lurched to his feet, his arms clumsily at his side and ambled off to gather some firewood. Mary turned to tend the fire.

In his camp, Luke took a plate of food, but his thoughts were on a girl in a yellow dress and there was no room for thinking about anything else. His throat had a lump the size of a goose egg and he struggled to swallow the last of his coffee.

"You all right?" John Leverenz interrupted his thoughts while Luke leaned against a wagon wheel and tried to keep his head from spinning. Stirring his plate, he grunted and dabbed his gravy-coated fork into his coffee. Without thinking, he tipped his plate toward the fire, spilling grits onto his moccasins.

"You know, Sayer—you better get your mind back to what you're doing. You hired on to look out for the whole train. Mrs. Stoberson's death was bad, but if we don't look out, the cholera'll spread to the whole clan. We've had three deaths in as many days. Some illness, others just bad luck." Luke glanced up frowning as Leverenz continued. "Yesterday you took off and I lost a day's march. I got a lot of folks who paid their last dime to make sure they get their families across. You better pull yourself together and see they do. Get my drift? Anything you ain't clear on, you let me know."

Luke set his mug on the wagon wheel and stalked off toward his horse.

Chapter Thirteen

> May 10, 1848. Our leaders advise us that the Indians rarely molest the trains, and then only to steal supplies. We are warned against struggling, and are cautioned to travel in a pack.

LUKE CAUGHT A glimpse of Mary a half-mile from the train and heading away through the tall grass. He kicked his horse into a full run to intercept her. "Whoa, there, ma'am, you can't be riding off by yourself. The braves in these parts would haul you off for their troubles."

Mary looked up, her eyes widening as she became aware of her surroundings. "Sorry, I guess I was woolgathering. I needed to get away for a while." She leaned in to hug her horse's neck as it danced away from the stallion's attentions.

Luke glanced up to see that the wagons were close enough for the gossips to get an eye-full. Wariness warred with the wanting in his gut until the latter won out. "Mrs. Rodgers, do you take me for a reasonable man?"

"Yes—"

"Maybe even a friend?"

Her eyes darkened. "I'd say so."

"Then slide off."

Despite her misgivings, she slipped slowly to the ground. Luke dismounted with an easy leap. In the space of a heartbeat, he pulled his horse around so that it sheltered them from curious eyes. He glanced at the slowly moving wagons and back to Mary—who watched him with wide eyes. He turned her so that they faced west where the sun would set in a few hours.

"What do you see out there?"

"Nothing."

"Look harder."

"Grass. For as far as I can see, just clumps of grass. I don't think it will ever end. Lillian died in this prairie, and she's lost to us. I fear this place."

"Look harder. People have lived on this prairie for as long as the sun has risen and set. They live and they birth babies and they die. Would you change that? We die the way we live, noble and brave or filled with fear and anger. Do you want that for your friend?

"She died bravely."

"The way she lived. She could ask for no more." He pointed to where the sun was beginning its downward arc. "Look with your heart. You will see that nothing can hold back the sun. My mother's people say it dies so that it can be reborn tomorrow and all other tomorrows until the last sunset dies and the winds are no more."

The wind billowed her skirts and tore her hair loose from its pins while she considered what he was telling her. When the silence grew weighted, she turned away. "Thank you. That helped more than you can know." She blinked back her tears and saw his cheek twitch as he tried to swallow.

He turned and remounted as though he were angry with himself. Below, a shout covered the distance and he turned to ride back. "Mrs. Rodgers, you're used to doing for yourself—you could be drowning and no one would notice. When that happens, come find me. Will you make that promise?"

"If I can." She managed a weak smile. "But when will the dying end?"

"I can't say, ma'am. No one can. When we've taken other settlers across, not everyone gets through."

"Why?"

"Lots of reasons. Sickness, childbirth, accidents, thirst, starvation, nervous attacks. Sometimes people just lack the will to go on. I've seen folks get to Oregon City at the end of the journey, pick up a handful of dirt and keel over dead."

"Mr. Sayer, you're making that up. No one would get that far and then die."

"I think they died a lot sooner, but they had to finish what they started. Or they wanted to get somewhere worth dying for. And when they do, they can let go."

"*Are* there things worth dying for?"

He looked down at her earnest face, her ribbons flowing in the morning breeze. A few days ago he might not have had an answer. Now, he managed a wry smile. "Yes, ma'am, there are."

"Then I must find mine. Just like Lillian."

Luke turned so that one side of his face was shaded by the afternoon sun. "Take care, Mrs. Rodgers. Don't get careless and rob yourself of whatever's in store."

Mary heard pain behind his words. Suddenly, she remembered Philip's warning about playing her role as a wife. It was time to return. Remounting, she bid him farewell and rode off toward the last of the wagons. At the top of a knoll she turned in her saddle and started to wave, but he stood like a statue facing the west, only his wind-tossed hair making him seem real in the tall grass. Finally, as she topped the rise, he raised his flat-brimmed hat in a salute. A moment later, he disappeared from sight.

Riding back toward the train, Mary was suddenly stricken by a low belly pain, probably from the sun-ripened antelope that one of the men had shot in the early hours and carried, slung over his saddle until evening. Some of the women complained about the provisions they were expected to serve, but no one could afford to turn down the offer of fresh meat. Several minutes later, the pain occurred again, sharper, more intense this time. She felt herself getting nauseous and she knew she had to dismount. Easing from the saddle, she tied the reins to the horn and tied to stand, but when another cramp gripped her, the intensity took her breath away and she folded into the grass. She couldn't open her eyes. When the next one hit it was all she could do to pant in shallow breaths until it passed. The next pains were low in her belly. Her mouth was parched and her skin felt clammy and irritated, the same symptoms that Lillian had complained about; heated face, thirst, cramping, nausea.

With a vague sense of panic, she realized she couldn't make it back to camp. Maybe it was providence that she didn't have strength enough to mount; if she were stricken, at least she could spare the men. She didn't want Philip to feel an obligation to her; his destiny was with Laurel. Luke Sayer would probably have some misguided idea that she was his responsibility. She recalled the single-mindedness that had driven Lillian. Luke's words came back to her: It was something worth dying for—the sparing of those you love.

She found a comfortable space between clumps of tall grass and tried to prepare for the coming hours. The sun beat down and she covered her face with a hand, but the effort was futile; she closed her eyes again and saw her mother, her father and Toby as they had been in the happy days. Images of her mother, her father and Lillian came and went. Between spasms she recited snatches of her mother's favorite psalm. "The Lord is my shepherd, I shall not want. He maketh me to lie down in green pastures." The green pasture in her prayer was her father's farm. His breeding mares played with their foals, their tails held aloft as they chased each other around the paddock. Eventually, she drifted asleep.

Evening came, and she awoke, surprised to find herself alive and feeling infinitely better. Looking around, she saw Buttercup grazing nearby. She was weak, and her stomach roiled with hunger. Her back was aching just like—she glanced down and saw the crimson patch staining her riding skirt and her sense of foreboding gave way to a giddy sense of relief. *I'm not dying from cholera.* The thought echoed in her brain until she wanted to sing it aloud. Her belly felt tender and sore to the touch, but the cramping had passed, along with the lightheadedness that marked the start of her monthly flux. Waving her arms, she arched her back and twirled in a circle. "I'm not going to die! I'm not going to die!" Never had she been so grateful for her monthly annoyance. Still laughing, she mounted Buttercup and started toward.

She rode to the top of the knoll where the sun had long ago tipped down behind the flat expanse of land. The prairie was empty. She saw nothing but clots of thick tall buffalo grass forming shadows in the gathering darkness. She gripped her reins and turned Buttercup in a semi-circle, but the horse balked and fought for control. She lashed it with the tip of her rein and muttered a command that had little effect except to remind her that she was utterly alone. She tried to remember where she had seen the wagon earlier that day, but north seemed like south, and east could be as likely west.

Suddenly, she remembered standing next to Luke, anticipating where the sun would set. She saw the spot where she had laid and the direction the sun had taken. Buttercup took a few tentative steps forward and she imagined she could see a faint rim of light tipping the far horizon. Soon, the mare was picking its way between the grass, and she gave it the rein because anything was better than standing still in the gathering darkness. Horses had night vision—her father had taught her that. But the train had at least a five hour lead; she would be lucky to find it by midnight if she managed to come upon the tracks.

The horse continued to walk while she sat hunched in the saddle, knuckles clenched and knees gripping so tight that she felt her legs stiffen in the stirrups. With each step she waited for the horse to fall into a varmint hole and break its leg, until dread anticipation caused her head to ache with tension. After an hour of riding she felt the mare lift its head. She turned, expecting to see an Indian or a wild animal watching with yellow eyes, but when it whinnied, she lifted her head and smelled manure mixed into fine powder. She was almost giddy when she realized the grass underneath her horse had been trampled into dust. They had found the wagon track. Now she only had to worry about ruts and dead animals or fallen goods clogging the trail. But at least she wouldn't die in the wilderness.

The moon had not risen yet, and in the terrifying darkness her mare gave a hoarse rasp that made the hair on the back of her neck stand up. She kept looking over her shoulder, but the darkness cocooned her until she felt like she would smother with terror. It took courage not to kick her horse into a run and take her chances. Hours passed; her throat swelled with thirst. Buttercup's head dipped in exhaustion and she felt the horse stumble. She was woozy with exhaustion, and the dull rasping in her mare's throat kept her nerves constantly on edge. She tried to keep from dozing, but she jerked awake when Buttercup stumbled. She caught herself just before she fell from her saddle.

Her eyes began playing tricks on her. She imagined a thin ribbon of light bobbing in the distance, and sounds of mooing and bellowing, stamping of hooves and the tinkle of bells. When she woke from a half-stupor, she realized it was not her imagination.

Luke found her just before she pitched to the ground. His arms grasped her and she felt herself sliding from her saddle. A moment later, he pressed a drink of water to her mouth. He sounded as though he had rehearsed his lecture a dozen times already. "Where were you? I thought you were heading back for the train. When I rode in at sunset, your husband told me you hadn't been back all day."

"I was so scared. I didn't mean to make anyone worry."

"I didn't know if you'd been thrown from your horse or taken prisoner—or if you were lying somewhere dying of the—" He began again, softer. "Mrs. Rodgers, where were you? What happened?"

Mary's face flushed with embarrassment. "I'd rather not discuss it."

"Are you hurt?" He studied her face in the meager light. "Let's get you laid down." He helped her to her bedroll and knelt over her with dark, worried eyes. He straightened and looked around for someone to help him, but the camp was long asleep. Left with no choice, he set off to fetch Mrs. Murdock from her bed.

Sazie Murdock was still adjusting her clothes when she arrived out of the darkness, whispering questions before she reached the bedroll. "Mr. Sayer claims it looks bad, maybe the cholera, Mary? Lordy, are you able to talk? Let me take a look." She shooed Luke away and waved Philip back when he appeared in time to hear the word 'cholera'. The men back off to stoke the fire, their faces pinched with concern. A couple of questions later she let out a whoop that brought both men running. "You men don't have the sense of a mule. She's no more got cholera than I do. Leave her alone to tend herself and get to your business."

The two men stared at each other in perplexed silence. Suddenly, Luke threw his hat on the ground and snorted, "Women!" and stalked off to tell the wagonmaster that the lost had been found.

Chapter Fourteen

May 15, 1848. We have now been made aware of the true powers of Nature by storms worse than any we have seen. Last night, we had thunder cross the sky in huge claps; rain and winds that blew the covers off the wagons and hailstones that knocked the horses to their knees as we struggled to continue. There is no recourse from the rain. Everything is wet. Fortunately, we will halt to repair.

NATHAN TATE CAME running up while Mary paused at her camp to watch the sun slip down the distant horizon. They were traveling the flat land now. The days were long and the travel harder because they had to stay on Leverenz's schedule. It was just as he had warned; they walked every daylight hour and rested when they found a water hole. Tonight they had found one, and Mary was hoping for a quick bath when she finished her chores. Her hope came to a quick end when the child ran up, panting, "Hurry, Mrs. Rodgers. Mama says come quick. The baby's coming."

Mary handed her kettle to Philip and went running after the boy, thinking that surely Bethellen could find someone more qualified. She said as much to the young mother who lay sweating in the airless wagon, her hands clutching the wagon staves while an intense cramp gripped her midsection.

"I want you, Mary. I know what to do. I'll learn you what you need. You'll...do just...fine. Whew! That was a fine cramp. Shouldn't be but two more hours if this baby comes same as the others."

"But, Bethellen, your other children were born in a house, with a midwife nearby if anything went wrong."

"But nothin' ever did. 'Sides, it gets easier every time. Start some water boiling and feed the boys their supper. It's all laid out. When they're finished we'll send them to take a look at the livestock. They love that. We should be done by bedtime."

Mary finished frying the venison steaks and boiled rice and coffee while George Tate came walking up with a wooden bucket half-filled with frothy goat's milk. She poured two cups for the boys, then one for herself. Bethellen had explained that they brought a goat along in case anything happened to her, or in case her milk supply wasn't ample after the baby came. Goat's milk was easy for a baby to digest and good insurance all the way around. A goat was also an easy grazer for the days when the grasses petered out.

"Wash up now, supper's ready," Mary called, and turned back to the wagon where, from the sounds, Bethellen was having hard labor.

A nervous George Tate hurried his children through the meal before he led them off to see the horses grazing in the tall grass. Mary finished her last swig of milk and looked around for something to feed Philip for supper. The Tate's meager supper wouldn't support another mouth, and Bethellen would want a plate afterward. Philip could see to his own supper.

• ♥ •

Philip strolled over to Luke's campfire just as the cook was dishing out the grub. "Can you spare a plate? Mary's over with the Tates, tending the birthing. Looks as though she may be there for a while, and I'm fending for myself."

"Sure," Luke agreed. "Pull up a barrel. Venison's tender, coffee's strong, and the whiskey will soften the ground tonight. Seems like you do more fending for yourself than any married man on this train." Philip joined the good-natured laughter.

After the meal, they sat staring into the flames while the cook cleaned the plates. A splash of whiskey eased their weary bones and muscles while the talk turned more personal. "Mary's always the first to offer her aid to anyone who needs it," Philip mused into the firelight.

"Yep, and it almost got her killed with the Stoberson woman." Luke shifted his leg, remembering the night. He offered Philip a cigar and settled back on the ground with his back against a wagon wheel.

"It did kill her mother, and Mary's a lot like her. They share the same nature." Philip described Mary's family, filling in answers to questions Luke had wondered about. "They were a fine family. House had a good feel about it, the minute you walked in the door. Mary thinks a lot of that mare of hers. She had a good-sized farm, back east, but when the family passed on, she figured she had to put down roots someplace else. She wants to have a family. She'll be good, too, when the time comes." Philip spoke impersonally, not realizing the lump his words were causing in Luke's throat.

Luke listened with panic building until he could hardly speak. Was Philip trying to tell him that Mary planned a birthing out here on this prairie without a doctor, and for the first time? White women didn't take to birthing as easily as Indian women. He tried to sound casual as he gave advice on a subject that was absolutely none of his business. "There's one thing I can't figure out about men. They bring their wives on this trail and the women suffer. Seems they could use a little caution and spare her yet another burden, at least until they arrived somewhere safe." He watched Philip out of the corner of his eye, trying to see if his words hit any nerve.

Philip reddened under his scrutiny. "If it'll put your mind to ease," he replied, the unfamiliar whiskey loosening his tongue and his judgment, "I promised Mary I'd wait 'til I got to Oregon before taking anyone to my bed. Mean to keep my word."

Luke straightened, his cigar bobbing with surprise. A girl like Mary, and Philip had the restraint to keep away? He tried to hide his surprise at the impact of his friend's words. For whatever reason, they hadn't consummated their marriage. The fact kept running through his mind while he tried to find words to strengthen the husband's resolve. "Real rough crossing, the last half of the trip. You're a wise man not to put her in jeopardy so she can make the trip safer."

He leaned back, weak with the thoughts that were running through his head. That would account for Mary's blushes and starts when he brushed up against her, the questioning look in her eyes when they danced, the way she avoided answering some of his more pointed questions. She was still a virgin. *Well, shut my mouth,* he thought, halfway wishing he could walk out into the dark to digest this news. Finally, feigning weariness, he stretched and yawned. When Philip took the hint and started toward his wagon, Luke made his escape into the darkness where he could think.

He had always had the highest regard for women, even the fancy women in the dance halls. He figured he couldn't have one standard for some and another for the rest. They were all somebody's sisters, someone's daughters, and he respected them all—all except the ones who treated him like some uncivilized half-breed. But married women were off limits. On the trail he danced with them, answered their questions with courtesy, even supplied game to the new widows when their husbands got themselves killed out of stupidity or accident, but he gave wide berth to the man-hunters who would have been glad for the offer of a strong arm—or more. Or, at least, he had until he met Clara. *What kind of a man marries his childhood friend and then doesn't feel the need to bed her?* Maybe his friend was truly considerate of Mary.

Disgusted by his ramblings, tired and frustrated, he made one last loop past the Tates' wagon on his way back to bed. Inside, he heard a baby squalling. He paused and heard Mary murmur something soothing just as the father came walking up, carrying two tired boys on his shoulders.

"Another hand for that farm you're planning," Luke said. He pumped George Tate's hand, careful that his smile didn't betray his thoughts. Best he show a little enthusiasm now, for they would be burying it soon enough, what with the diseases, the heat, the thirst and the long road ahead. Poor little thing.

"Hope so." The father's eyes reflected an unease that matched his tone. "I wanted to spare the Missus this, but last year we delayed makin' a start 'cause she was with child. Then, she lost it. Figured we couldn't wait no longer. I want you to know it wasn't just my decision. To come, I mean."

Luke glanced, surprised at the anguish in Tate's voice as he stood bareheaded with his two young ones asleep on his shoulders, his eyes filled with concern over what Luke thought of him. The thought occurred, that maybe he'd been looking at this like a man who didn't have to make any hard choices. And just maybe he was wrong. He reached over to take one of the little boys from the father's shoulder and he was surprised at how light and warm a sleeping child felt in a man's arms. Looking up, he saw Mary watching from the edge of the wagon, waiting to take the children into their bedrolls.

"It was Bethellen," George told the two of them, "who had insisted on bringing the goat. I raged against the idea. Bad omen, it seemed to me."

Pushing away from the wagon, Mary said simply, "Bedtime, boys."

Luke watched her soothe their fidgeting with a soft tune that he'd never heard. In the lamp's glow he studied cherry-red cheeks against baby-fine, wispy hair that resembled two dandelion puffballs ready to blow.

Mary stood, straightening her back to ease the strain of the evening, and prepared to leave. As she started back toward her wagon, Luke fell in beside her on the outside of the wagon ring where the air was devoid of camp smoke and there were fewer distractions. He watched her out of the corner of his eye as she closed her eyes and took a deep breath.

Suddenly, she gave voice to her fears. "I was so scared. What if something had gone wrong?"

In the glow of his earlier whiskey, Luke forgot that he and white women didn't mix. "You did fine. You have more spunk than most women I've seen. A lot of men, too, for that matter."

"I was surprised when she asked me, but what choice did I have?" Mary kept a low voice because the camp had settled down for the night.

"Your spirit is strong. You have a brave heart."

They had reached the Rodgers camp and he felt a quick stab of relief at not seeing Philip near the wagon. Every stolen moment with Mary occupied his mind during the long hours until he could see her again.

Mary turned to say goodnight and saw his shadowed profile outlined in their neighbor's campfire. Distracted, she forgot to keep a sharp eye out for wheel ruts until she stepped in one. She grabbed at his arm, clenching her teeth as a sharp pain shot through her leg. With a low groan she clung to him for support while she tested her foot. "No real harm done, I think. It just hurts. It should be fine by morning."

Luke's voice was concerned. "Here, lean on me until the pain eases." She kept her gaze trained on the shadows. Lately, it seemed that she found herself alone with him, facing temptations she did not consider seemly. He spoke close, keeping his voice low, and when he continued she felt his breath on her cheek. "Don't be afraid to let me help you. That is all I ask. No more."

A frightening intimacy had sprung between them. Mary gave a short laugh and pulled away. "Seems you spend a good amount of your time helping me."

"Just doing my job. I know the rules we live under." Their eyes met and tension threatened to burst the fragile dam they had created between them. Luke added in a voice loud enough to be heard by the neighboring camp; "I'm glad to be of service, ma'am."

Mary's foot had ceased its throbbing and she limped to her wagon in silence while she struggled for something to say. "I promise to take a lantern next time." Luke's chuckle had a tender sound to it. In a nearby camp, someone stirred. There was nothing more to be wrung from this night so she whispered "Goodnight." With a light wave she disappeared into the darkness.

Unnoticed, Philip watched from the darkness.

Chapter Fifteen

May 21, 1848. We continue to see signs of those who have gone before. Graves, furnishings, dreams, and hopes. They lie alongside the track, the story as clear as if an orator was telling the tale. We shudder and say, "There but for the grace of God, go we."

WEDNESDAY DAWNED CLEAR and bright. The days grew warmer, with humidity that sapped the strength from man and animal alike. Luke rode through the train advising the women, "We will halt up ahead to repair the wagons. Windlass Hill was a hard climb and the animals need to rest." He motioned toward one of the more severely damaged wagons that had lost an axle on a stump and had overturned, breaking a sideboard and popping rivets when it landed hard on its side. The wagon's contents bulged against its canvas covering, making it look like a floundered tall ship in an ocean of brown and green grass. Irritated at the loss of time, he shook off his impatience and tried to make use of the delay. "Tell the women that the river is close. It will save time for them to ride ahead and do their washing while the repairs are made. Once the train catches up the animals will churn the water to mud."

According to Luke, the North Platte lay to the north. Mary

and the Stoberson girls joined the other women and older girls while the younger girls stayed behind to tend the children. Mary collected Philip's dirty clothing and added it to her own, tied to the back of her horse. Two men would ride along as escort to the supply wagon, to watch for Indians and refill the water barrels while the women did their washing. The rest of the train would join them as quickly as they could.

Mary's friends piled in with their laundry and washboards; Bethellen carried her baby tied into a shawl against her breast, and Nellie and Virginie, who now had the burden of their family's chores. The wagon resembled a nosegay of colored bonnets bobbing in the sun while Mary rode alongside, listening halfheartedly to the chatter. It would have been simpler to climb in with them, but there wasn't enough room with all the laundry.

She urged her horse into a trot. The women's chatter grew silent as she outpaced them with a feeling of delicious freedom; she even abandoned any thought of danger. The two men were riding on the wagon with their rifles across their knees, even though Luke had said this wasn't hostile Indian country.

She rode over a rise and saw a wide stripe of muddy water across the flattened landscape, broken by a verdant strip of trees and bushes. Mary urged her horse ahead in hopes that she could enjoy the river before the others arrived and found a place on the flat sand banks where she could have some privacy. Around the bend, just a hundred yards off, stood a small stand of sycamores, not thick, but offering enough cover that she would be out of sight of the men. With only laundry for her and Philip, she would be finished long before the others, and their chatter would provide plenty of warning when they were ready to leave.

She was already stripped of stockings and boots when Nellie came running up with her stack of soiled things.

"Mary, let's do ours together. It'll be more fun that way."

"Well…can you keep a secret, Nellie?"

"You know I can. I'm practically grown up now." The girl stuck out her tongue and Mary hid her smile, remembering how it felt to be fourteen.

"If we wash our things really fast, we can shuck our dresses and swim like otters. Want to?"

"Oh, you know I do."

They scrubbed and soaked their clothing in record time, tossed the garments on bushes and trees to dry then stripped down to their bloomers and camisoles. The shallow water felt wonderful. Nellie dove as if she were a bottom fish, coming up only to breathe while Mary floated out with her hair flowing about her like a sheet. She closed her eyes and floated on her back, enjoying the silvery feel of water on her skin. Downstream, the women's voices reminded them that the men and mules would be arriving soon.

When it seemed they had dallied long enough, Mary reminded Nellie that they needed to turn back. They reached the bank just in time to hear the report of a gun being fired. "I thought we were staying until the wagon trail arrived. I wonder what happened? We better hurry, Nellie."

Nellie donned her dress and began thrusting her damp laundry into her mother's old petticoat. Suddenly, they heard a shout and more rapid firing. From upstream a trio of Indians appeared, riding straight for the wagon. Utes, from Luke's description. She watched in horror as the wagon driver took off at a run. The mules managed to hold the lead for several hundred yards, but they were pulling a load and the Utes began narrowing the lead until a well-placed shot from the wagon pierced one warrior's arm. The others fell back, apparently deciding the spoils were not worth the risk.

Mary stood frozen as the wagon raced back toward the wagon train. Slowly, the three braves started toward the clothing she had hung on bushes and limbs. The braves crossed the river at a run and rode straight toward them. One of them gave a howl of excitement when he sighted Buttercup.

"Nellie—they're coming! Get on." She pushed Nellie into the saddle and slapped the mare hard on the flank. "Get Luke. Tell him what happened. Go."

The girl kicked the horse into a gallop with the mounted braves in pursuit, shouting and brandishing their bows in the air as they closed the gap. One of the emigrant guards in the wagon fired a shot from his rifle that landed close enough that they backed off, changed course and headed back to the river. Mary realized they were heading directly toward her. She crouched under a thicket and hoped the tangle of branches would hide her until Luke arrived.

From her hiding place, she watched them dismount and begin flinging her laundry to the sand. One brave, his hair greased into slick horns on either side of his head, picked up her spare petticoat and slipped it over his shoulders, dancing for the others while they hooted in delight. They tried on Philip's red shirts and stuffed whatever else they wanted into a pack. They seemed to take forever, as though time had no importance, while her heart thudded in her chest and her head ached with a band of tension. Finally, they remounted and started back in the direction they had come. She counted slowly to ten before she slowly expelled her breath and raised her head to peek through a limb. Too late, she realized that they had tricked her into revealing her position. With menacing whoops and war shouts they turned and rode straight toward her, leaping the bushes in their path until she felt as trapped as a rabbit in a bramble row.

She stood up and began running in a zigzag pattern away from the water, trying to avoid the pebbles and twigs. The sand and rocks cut her bare feet, but she ignored the pain and concentrated on the fact that every step took her closer to the wagon trail. But as the thunder of hooves sounded in her ears, she had no illusions that she was doing anything but prolonging the chase for the enjoyment of the whooping, laughing men behind her. She ventured a quick glance behind her and saw that they were gaining on her.

Suddenly, one of the braves jerked her onto his horse. She struggled to right herself, but an iron hand forced her down and she felt the air whooshing out of her lungs. Her last thought before she blacked out was that she was going to die.

When she opened her eyes, the ground was racing beneath her and her shoulder ached from being draped over the horse's shoulders like a feed sack. It took all her discipline not to struggle; if her captor lost his grip she would slip beneath the flying hooves and death would be immediate. *Hurry, Luke.* The single thought reverberated in her mind to the rhythm of the horse's gallop. *Hurry, Luke.* At some point, blackness invaded her fear and she fainted again.

When she regained consciousness, she was in the same position, stiff and bruised. They had been riding for some time because the sun was high overhead. Her flesh burned like fire on the thin strip of skin where her camisole had slipped up her backside. She imagined the view that the brave must be enjoying, and regretted her hasty decision to remove her dress, until she realized that vanity was the least of her concerns.

Finally, her captor halted. She was thrust roughly to the ground and allowed to drink from a small stream, but only after he and the other men had taken their fill and watered the horses. With a rough gesture, he indicated that she was to ride behind him for the rest of the trip. She scrambled to do his bidding, grateful for small favors, while the three argued over a piece of rawhide thong that the others wanted to attach to her hands. Her captor pointed to her tender, uncalloused feet and said something that made the others laugh. She kept her head lowered and her face hidden in her tangled hair, in hopes that they wouldn't see her fear.

At sundown, they rode into what appeared to be a summer camp judging by the corn that grew in nearby fields and the skins and baskets of berries and roots setting about. While the tribe looked on, the brave jerked her off the horse with a quick movement that left her sprawled on the ground. Without ceremony, he grabbed her arm and half-dragged her toward an enclosure, and shoved her inside a teepee made of hides similar to those she had seen while on a ride with Luke.

She collapsed onto a buffalo skin and looked up to see a silent Indian girl no older than herself, who didn't appear overjoyed at the guest her husband had brought home. Scowling, the girl obeyed her husband's command and held out a gourd that contained a pint of tepid water. Mary grabbed it and gulped before anyone could change their mind. When she finished, the wife took it back with a disdainful glare and waited for her husband to leave before she aimed a moccasin at Mary's shin and sat down to stare fixedly at her prisoner.

Mary wrinkled her nose against the pungent, oily smell of the hides beneath her, but she realized the folly of insulting her hostess and quickly looked away. She willed herself to be calm and tried to quell the roiling of her stomach while she prayed for her rescue.

• ♥ •

Nellie slumped against Buttercup's neck and let the horse fly across the prairie. She looked up to see the bouncing wagon filled with women, their damp clothing dropping over the sideboards with every bump. Just beyond, she saw Luke Sayer at the edge of the wagon train. She reined in and tried to catch her breath as he came to a halt beside her.

"Mr. Sayer...we saw...Indians. No time for Mary. Said...ride. Get you. Hurry." She was wheezing so hard that her words came in spurts. When Luke leaped from his horse and helped her to the ground, her legs buckled beneath her.

"Slow down, Nellie. It's all right. Now, where's Mary?" Luke listened with fire building in his eyes. The screams of the arriving women created more chaos and his grip on Nellie's arm tightened. "Nellie, where's Mary?"

By now, Nellie had caught her breath. "Mary made me get on the horse 'cause the wagon went off and left me. She's out there alone with the Indians." She was still explaining but he had already remounted and was headed away.

Inside his supply wagon, he filled his hands with spare cartridges and tossed them into the saddle bag along with a canteen, a handful of jerky and some cold biscuits.

Philip came running up. "Man says they got Mary. I'm going with you."

Luke acted unconcerned while he pulled his Hawken .54 from its scabbard and chambered a quick round. When Philip repeated himself, Luke slammed the rifle back into the scabbard and turned away. "The hell you are."

Bill Weems spat his tobacco as Luke strode past, dragging his horse with a taut rein while the horse side-stepped. "Hey, squawman—you planning a swap to yer relation for Miz Rodgers? Maybe you was in on the deal from the start. Maybe our women ain't safe with you around."

Philip followed a few steps back, his face blazing. "I said I'm going with you."

"Maybe the squawman got his own ideas about Miz Rodgers."

"Shut up, Weems. Rodgers…you ain't going."

"Sayer—you aren't her husband."

"You tell the squawman, Rodgers."

Philip took the first swing, landing a hard right to Luke's chin. Luke reciprocated with a head butt that sent them both sprawling. Dust kicked up around the horses' hooves as they rolled across the ground, their punches filled with mindless fury. Luke sprang to his feet first. When Philip gained his feet, Luke was waiting with a blow that knocked Philip's air out. He sagged, gripped his belly and moaned.

A group of men booed and Bill Weems shouted, "Give it to him, Rodgers. Don't let that redskin tell you how to treat your wife."

At the words, Luke swung on Weems and landed a solid jab to his jaw. Weems lunged, a belly sticker in his hand. Luke ducked the knife swipe, hesitated a second, and brought his fist down onto Weems's forearm hard enough to force the knife from his hand. With a scream of pain, Weems dropped to his knees, clutching his arm.

John Leverenz approached, his face a mottled map of disgust. "Sweet Jesus, we don't have enough problems, we got to make our own? Weems—get your arm tended. It don't look to be broken. Luke, I want to see you. Alone."

Philip reached for his hat, shook the dust from the brim and settled it on his head. He panted his words. "Sayer, we got some words need to be said. But this isn't the time—or the place."

Luke licked a drop of blood from his knuckle and stared at his friend. "'Spect we do. But you want to see her alive, you better let me go alone. I've got some acquaintance with this tribe, and I may be able to get her back. Either that, or they'll kill us both. Stay here." He strode off to the mutterings of the half-dozen men who surrounded Philip.

Leverenz was waiting at his wagon, and his face reflected his anger. "Luke—you go find Missus Rodgers. Bring her back here, and then you stay out of camp for a few days. Make yourself scarce until tempers calm down."

Luke started to speak, thought better of it, and stalked off. In a single motion he slung his saddlebags over his horse, mounted, and started off at a gallop.

The ride served to cool him down. He slowly channeled the anger that was creating havoc with his common sense, reminding himself that he would need all of his faculties to find Mary. None of the men at camp were worth jeopardizing his search. He began recounting the facts that the victims had related to him. The driver of the wagon had seen only three Indians and they were not wearing war paint or markings, so they were probably a hunting party that got lucky. Probably from the tribe's summer camp a day's journey off. Maybe he'd be lucky. If they hadn't had a lot of contact with the wagons, maybe they wouldn't have an axe to grind, he thought. Maybe.

He rode to the river and saw the events laid out in the tracks: the spot where Mary had run, and where she was caught—barefoot. He saw the dress she had been wearing, lying crumpled in the sand, and he felt his blood chill. He picked up the trail leading north and settled into the ride.

The sun was low in the sky by the time he reached the Indian's camp. It wasn't well guarded, so he reckoned the driver was right in thinking they weren't a war party. Women and children abounded—another good sign. Drawing a breath, he rode straight into the camp.

An Indian appeared from inside a teepee. Luke remained astride, his face an impassive mask while the man stood for a moment then disappeared into a neighboring enclosure before reappearing with a man who appeared to be the chief. When the leader indicated he was to dismount, Luke slid from his horse and landed with an easy motion that brought a hum of approval from the women. He followed the chief back into his teepee.

Once inside, he waited while the formalities were dispensed with, but the tobacco tasted foul in his throat and the endless delays played havoc with his nerves, even though he understood the importance of the pipe ceremony to the negotiations. Finally, he was invited to speak.

"Your braves are good hunters to capture such a fine rabbit. But she is not tasty game."

"What right do you have to this fine rabbit?"

Luke kept his face impassive. The chief's sense of justice was simple. He would hear the answer and decide who had the stronger claim. If allowed, Leaning Feather, the man who had captured her, would have a slave for his household. They were not at war, so each man had equal rights. But he knew there could be only one answer that would satisfy the chief.

"She is my woman," he answered in a loud voice.

There was a gasp among the crowd, for Luke was known to the tribe. It was known, too that his half-brother was a mighty warrior of the Umatilla tribe.

The chief, Old Dog, considered this. Finally, he spoke. "If what you say is true, then she will go with you."

Leaning Feather raised a fist and Luke understood his frustration. The brave did not want to lose his prize so easily. She was spirited, and looked to be much fun to tame.

Old Dog continued, "She will be tested to see if you speak

the truth. If she comes to you like a white man's wife, then you will both be free to go. If she shies from you like an un-broken colt, then you will be flogged by Leaning Feather."

Luke nodded. Outside, the sun was rising in the east and the tribe stood silently, waiting. He was glad to see that they did not appear hostile. Many among them probably hoped that the white woman would disappear in the direction she had come. Even now, they scowled as Leaning Feather's wife emerged from her teepee, keeping a firm hand on her pris-oner as Mary limped barefoot across the broken ground.

The setting sun caught Mary square in the eyes. The tee-pee had been dark, and her eyes had no chance to adjust to the light before she was shoved forward. At the opening she paused in confusion and earned a kick from the girl. Straightening, she shook her head. Her vision cleared, and she saw Luke standing near her captor. He was angry, she could tell. The corner of his cheek pulsed with a tiny tic, as it did when he was annoyed. "Lucas," she implored, but he made no response. He must be furious, she decided, not to offer so much as a token of comfort. Didn't he realize how frightened she was? Maybe he faced danger by coming here; she hadn't thought of that. In a voice that trembled, she tried again, louder this time. "Lucas?"

Still he stood, arms folded across his chest, his face in a scowl, not moving so much as a muscle while everyone waited. Suddenly, she knew that if she didn't reach his arms she would collapse. With a wild cry, she ran for him with the single thought that if they were to die, they would do so to-gether. Flinging her arms around his neck, she pressed her-self against him and sobbed, "Lucas, you came."

Slowly, Luke unfolded his arms and wrapped her in a strong embrace, his body trembling as he nuzzled her neck and hair. "Are you all right, little one?" he whispered.

She felt warmed by his embrace and realized she was shivering. "Now, I am. Luke, I was so scared."

"Shush…not now. Later." He let his lips rove over her face, giving the crowd a good show. The women nodded in approval; even the men seemed satisfied, all except Leaning Feather, who spat at Luke's feet and stalked off to his teepee with his wife close behind.

Old Dog called for silence. "You have proved you speak true. You may go in peace."

From his stock of trading goods, Luke selected a curved Bowie knife for Old Dog that brought a shout of approval from the watching braves. To each of Old Dog's three wives, Luke gave steel needles to sew their hides, and ribbons for their braids, which he held out with a grave face while they reached gingerly for their gifts. The other gifts he left for Leaning Feather, as payment for his lost slave.

Old Dog nodded in approval. "We will smoke another pipe before you go."

It was many hours before Luke returned to find Mary surrounded by a handful of women who had taken interest in the ruffles and ribbons of her pantaloons. She smiled with relief and rose to greet him, expecting that they would walk side by side to his horse. Instead, he picked her up like a sack of flour and hoisted her over his saddle much as the warrior had done at the river. Mounting his horse, he placed a hand on her rump where it bobbed above the saddle horn. "Keep still, woman," he growled. The tribe roared its approval as he rode out.

When they were no longer in danger of being seen, Luke reined in. "Are you hurt?" His tone underscored his relief, now that the danger had passed.

His words were as soothing to Mary as a red flag to a raging bull. She came up kicking and flailing. "Why bother asking? You're no better than that…that *Indian*. Yes, I'm hurt." She pushed off and landed unsteadily on her bare feet. "I've been out here all day. I'm sunburned. I'm wearing my underclothes. Go on, have a good laugh. I'm sure I must look a sight." Her eyes misted, and she began to tremble.

It would not be a prudent man who smiled at this moment. Luke's expression was grave; he did a good job of hiding the tremor of amusement behind his lips. "I'm sorry for hoisting you up, ma'am. But I had to give them what they expected."

His words contained a ring of truth. Mary felt her face heat. "Oh, Luke, I think you saved my life. I keep getting myself in trouble. You must be so tired of me." She wasn't sure that she was making herself clear.

"All in a day's work, ma'am."

"Why did they let me go? What did you tell them?" She searched his face for an answer.

Luke sat motionless, his jaw clenched, his eyes inscrutable. "We'd better be getting back to the wagons. People are worried for you." He slid far back in the saddle and braced himself against the low cantle, leaving room for Mary to settle in front. The rocking motion of the stallion lulled her into exhausted stupor and her head fell against his shoulder. When his horse stumbled on a rough spot in the trail, he tightened his grip. "The horse knows what he's doing. Don't worry. Just sleep."

"I wasn't worrying, Lucas. I was just thinking of all you've done for us."

Luke closed his eyes at the inclusion of Philip, while the scent of her hair wafted in his nostrils. The night breeze blew a strand against his taut cheek, the contact an intimate gift from a woman with a grateful husband named Philip. He tightened his grip and prepared for the long ride, alert to danger, but the only sounds he heard were his horse's hooves and Mary's breathing.

Day was dawning when they rode into camp. From a distance Luke could see Philip already up, his fire the only sentry in the darkened camp. He dismounted with Mary still asleep in his arms. As he laid her on the waiting bedroll, she stirred enough to murmur, "Thank you, Luke…for everything," before she fell back in exhausted slumber.

Observing her half-dressed state, Philip's eyes turned questioning. He swung to face Luke, his hours of frustration giving vent to the suspicions he no longer tried to conceal. "What went on out there, friend?" The word seemed to take on an ominous weight in the darkness. "What kind of hell has she been through today?"

"Nothing happened. She's safe and—unharmed."

"She gonna tell me the same? I'm not sure I know who the enemy is any more."

Luke shook his head and extended a hand as if to ward off suspicion. "Look man, I know it looks like I'm always seeing your wife in a compromising condition. Don't hold this one against me, though. That's how I found her. She's not hurt." Half angry and not sure why, Luke made Philip wait while he poured himself a cup of Philip's freshly brewed coffee. "Seems one of the braves thought he's found himself a second wife. He was pretty sore about losing her so I'm going to suggest a second guard until we're out of the area."

Philip started to speak, hesitated, and seemed to accept the explanation. "Think the tribe will attack?"

"No. I know them. But some of the renegades have teamed up to harass the wagons, and by the looks of that brave, I wouldn't put it past him to join them."

"Will they come after Mary again?"

"Her or one of the other women. Don't let her out of your

sight. And don't let her ride that horse of hers until we get through this territory." Luke was thinking he would need to warn the wagon trains that were coming up in the rear. That was often the result. Another train would pay for the trouble he had caused.

As Luke turned to go, Philip said, "I suspect there's more to the story than you're telling, but we got Mary back, and I'm grateful."

Luke nodded. There was no point in telling Philip that he'd gotten Mary back because she passed for his own wife well enough to fool the chief. Less said the better. Her clothes were still strung out all over the river. He'd ride back in the morning and collect them.

The train was agog with news of Mary's rescue so that she could hardly get her chores done for the interruptions of the women. The men, too, seemed curious to know the details. Some of the older women looked speculatively at her. Mary knew the reason for their curiosity and was determined to keep up a casual front. She was stiff from the long hours in the saddle and sunburned in places that would be hard to explain, so she mentioned neither. When Sazie Murduck offered her a glass of cool buttermilk, Mary drank part of it and applied the rest to the strip between her camisole and pantaloons where the sun had done its worst.

Luke was gone by the time she woke. He'd ridden out early and returned with the rest of her things, as well as Nellie's, so no one realized she'd taken her adventure in her undergarments. Except for Philip's missing shirts, nothing was the worse for a night on the bushes.

In the shadow of his wagon, Leverenz watched Luke ride off, concern furrowing his forehead. Luke couldn't have chosen a worse time to ruffle feathers. People were already divided on more issues than they agreed on; they didn't need to be taking sides about their guide. Some thought Luke could conjure up water in a pile of sand. Others wanted to send him packing back to his brother's tribe and be rid of him. One man he couldn't figure was Philip Rodgers. He had good reason to despise Luke, but he seemed to invite his friendship, even while Luke hankered after his wife. After the fight, he'd seen the two of them talking in low tones like good friends. Leverenz shook his head. There was no accounting for people's actions. He'd seen that often enough to know that good people did bad things and bad people—well, he wasn't even sure anymore what bad was. He knew one thing, though; he'd feel a lot better with Luke watching their flank.

Chapter Sixteen

June 4, 1848. Every waking thought is consumed
by one need—water. We imagine we see it where
we do not. The animals bawl for it night and day.
No one talks now; we trudge on, as dumb as the
oxen we follow.

MARY BRUSHED THE sand from her gingham dress and
inspected the petticoat for signs of damage. She was grateful
that the Indians had left most of her clothing behind, or she
would be borrowing a dress for the rest of the trek. The skirt
had a few snags from the bushes; it would be a rag by the
time she arrived in Oregon City, but she planned to burn
everything when she would afford new. She hummed a few
bars of "Annie Laurie" while she fretted with the soft wisps
of hair that escaped her bun.

Her dress was a mass of wrinkles. She yearned for the
look and feel of a starched apron, but at least all the women
look about the same: limp, mussed and tired, she thought, as
she swiped ineffectively at the wrinkles. With a shake of her
shirt, she decided to be grateful she wasn't wearing buckskin
and cooking breakfast for an Indian brave this morning.

She left the wagon to search for Luke, but he wasn't in
camp. No one knew where he might be, and even Philip was
silent on the matter.

"Philip, I can't find Mr. Sayer. I wanted to thank him properly. I checked with Leverenz and he mumbled something about having to get back to work. Do you know where he is?"

Philip straightened from the cow's hoof he was examining and shook his head before returning to work with intensity that invited no further conversation. He was already weary from lack of sleep, and he was worried about Luke's absence, feeling like it was his fault. For several nights he had taken turns with the other men in watching for Indian sign, even though Luke assured them that Indians didn't attack in the dark. They raided, and that was worse.

Luke's absence left an ominous mood in the camp. John Leverenz sent orders for the night watch and the cattle herders to double up. They began camping in a circle again with the animals inside the compound. During the days, temperatures climbed to a hundred and ten degrees in the airless, tree-starved terrain. Chiggers and wasps plagued everyone during the day, and mosquitoes swarmed into the cook pots when the women tried to prepare meals. Waterholes were stingy and polluted. Dust filled their nostrils and those of their animals, some days so thick that it looked like fog.

During the days they walked, dead on their feet and breathing each other's dust. For most of the journey the wagon drivers had been able to travel side by side rather than behind each other. But Mary's rescue had caused a loss of face for the Indian raiders; they could expect retaliation by the group of renegades. With the Indian threat, Leverenz gave the order for the wagons to bunch up and not travel more than three abreast. Now they breathed each other's dust until it lodged in their clothing, sifted through the boxes to their bacon and beans, ruining the tea and salt.

They were still in Nebraska Territory, an endless monotony of plain where the emigrants could travel for one day or seven and nothing changed. Like a squirrel caught in a cage, some of the more outspoken travelers grouched that they might just as well sit by the side of the road as trudge another day on hollow bellies and sore feet; either way they would have nothing to show for their efforts. The men who had taken steps to shoe their cattle before the trip were happy, but they had to contend with envious griping from those that hadn't bothered.

The women talked less now, unless it was to complain about their men, their children or the lack of facilities for their personal hygiene. Sometimes they ganged up to complain about a woman who wasn't in their immediate company and changed to another woman when the first returned. Toward the end of each day, they clammed up and concentrated on putting one foot in front of the other. The men, it seemed to Mary, disagreed more than the women.

"Have you noticed what the men find to argue about, Bethie?" she commented as they slogged along the track one morning. "I heard those two over there arguing over whose mule made a plop that one of them stepped in." Both girls laughed at the filthy, sweat-encrusted men who bore little resemblance to the fellows who had twirled them about the dance floor a week before. It wasn't just the heat or the expected Indians, but the monotony of the flat land that weighed on them; no matter how far they traveled in a day, it didn't seem to make a difference. The mountains lay somewhere in the distance, maybe a thousand miles off; there was nothing they could do but keep walking.

Nellie appeared one morning, her hair distraught and her dress stained with blood. "Mary, what am I going to do? I haven't been able to wash my women's rags since the last time I flowed, and now I'm bleeding. I started sometime this morning and I didn't realize it. It's all over my dress. What am I going to do?"

Mary glanced down and saw the dress crusted with fresh blood across the back. She met Nellie's eyes and realized the girl was missing her mother. She decided that Lillian Stoberson didn't have a corner on practicality. "Quick, work some dirt into the blood while it's fresh. That way people will think it's just dirty. I'll find rags in my wagon to rip up for you."

She climbed aboard Philip's wagon and rummaged in her trunk. Since the Indians had taken some of her clothing, she had little to spare, and nothing absorbent enough to use as personal rags. Below, on the ground, Nellie was walking in the shadow of the wagon, clutching her soiled skirt in her hand. Slowly, Mary reached in and took two of the sturdy dish towels that her mother had embroidered for her hope chest. She hesitated a moment while she ran her fingers across the fine lace tatting before she steeled herself and brought the finely hemmed end to her mouth. She used her teeth to tear the cloth into four wide strips and folded them into packets. Back on the ground, she handed them to Nellie. "Here, slip one on while I shield you. When we reach water, you can boil them up for next month."

That scorching afternoon, Mary walked beside Philip while the oxen kicked up dust behind them. "Philip…where is Luke? I asked Sazie Murdock the same question, and she looked at me like I had two noses on my face. What's going on? It's not like him to abandon us this way."

Philip scowled without meeting her gaze. "He'll be back. Don't fret about it."

"Don't *fret*? I've been asking you all week, and now you tell me 'don't fret'? You know something I don't." Mary hurried to stay out of the way of the oxen. "Tell me why he's left us to die on this God-forsaken plain."

By the time Philip finished telling her about the fight and his part in it, and why Luke had been banished from their midst like a common thief, Mary wasn't speaking to him. When the day's travel was finished, she served his supper in silence and retired to her bedroll to fight the clog of tears that had been building over the past week. Given the choice, she would have traded her ration of coffee to have Luke back in camp.

The camp was unnaturally quiet during the evenings. The fiddles no longer sang because travel-weary men and women lacked the heart to pick up the bow. Tongues swelled to twice the normal size, making swallowing difficult and appetites jaded. Often, when someone killed fresh game it was the blood that the emigrants fought over, moisture that would slide down parched throats and over swollen tongues.

One evening, after a week of unvarying monotony and dust, Mary heard the crunch of dry grass near her wagon wheel as she mended Philip's threadbare shirt. She looked up and the shirt fell into the dirt. "Lucas..." She felt her mouth go dry at the sight of him standing safe and in the flesh.

"Shhhh." He put a finger to his mouth to silence her. He stood painted in moonlight, with an intense look in his eyes. A thousand thoughts conflicted in her mind, but only one surfaced. *He has returned.* In a low voice, Luke explained, "I rode in to make my nightly report to Leverenz."

"You mean you—every night?"

Luke nodded. Philip had returned in time to hear the question and Luke addressed his conversation to both of them. "I found a water hole. Leverenz will be taking you there tomorrow morning. But I wondered if you want to ride over there to cool off tonight? Just the two of you? It's not a pretty sight, but when the cattle get finished tomorrow, it will be unfit for humans. Some of the men will ride out early to fill barrels tomorrow."

Philip paused in the midst of whittling a dowel pin to hold the curved neck harness onto the ox yoke; the other one had dried in the heat and fallen out, and without it they couldn't continue on. "Maybe you could take Mary. No sense in her missing out because I'm in the middle of this." He returned to his work, whistling as he worked.

Luke stared from Philip to Mary and back again. He swallowed and tried to speak. When his voice came out a hoarse croak, he cleared his throat and began again. "That wouldn't be proper."

Philip replied without looking up from his task, "Can't be improper if I give my consent. Like I said, no sense in both of us missing out." Mary sat silently, her hands and her eyes on the mending in her lap, but her fingers had ceased attempting the tiny stitches. "Go ahead, Mary. Enjoy the water. Bring some back for the horses."

Luke reacted in a stupor. He managed to walk over to Mary's horse and saddle her while Mary rummaged for a small barrel. He tied it on before he turned to help Mary mount. "Set?" he managed. She merely nodded.

They rode out in silence, trying to keep the horses hooves from striking rock. Finally they were far enough to risk conversation.

"Luke, it's so good…" She couldn't get the words past the lump in her throat. Finally, she tried another tack. "What about the Indians?"

"I don't expect trouble after dark." They both gave up talking, and the rest of the trip was made in silence.

In the darkness, the waterhole smelled sweet. Luke beat the weeds for snakes while Mary paused at the edge, shy and unsure of herself now that they were alone. Never in her eighteen years had she experienced anything resembling the situation in which she found herself. Uncertain whether she should remove her shoes or wait, she tarried with her horse's reins and hoped she didn't look as frightened as she felt. She was trusting him with her life as well as her reputation—one as valuable as the other. A shiver of fear ran through her when she thought of the women back at camp, of the price she would pay if she were discovered—she would be traveling the next three months ostracized as a loose woman.

Luke noticed. "I'll attend to the horses."

"You're not coming in?"

"No, ma'am. It's all yours."

She found a clump of sage and hid behind it while she disrobed to her bloomers and camisole. Tiptoeing gingerly to the water's edge, she waded in and gave a moan of pure pleasure. When she could speak, she called, "This feels wonderful. The water is so cool."

She paddled in and made a turn, in no hurry to reach the other end. On her second pass, she collected a mouthful of water. Luke was crouching on his heels near the water, his back to her. She lifted her hand and splashed him.

He half-turned at the impact, but remembering his resolve, he paused. There was no doing anything halfway with this woman. He hadn't brought her out here to tempt them into something they'd regret. A solid week without any sight of her had drawn him to her campsite tonight, a moth to flame. He hadn't known until he spoke, what excuse he would use until the swimming idea cropped into his head. It was a fool plan, bringing her here, but he was a fool in the midst of hostile territory, pretending that he had her best interests at heart instead of his own selfishness. He was angry at himself. "The waterhole's fed from an underground spring. Best not stir it up too much."

"I'll be cautious. I learned to swim when I was a girl." To prove her point she dove under and reappeared on the far side. Backstroking toward him, she closed her eyes while cool water infused her weary body.

Luke heard the splash, half-turned, and caught his breath at the pink patch of skin that winked from above her bloomers. He looked away and tried to quell his racing thoughts when she turned and swam toward him. He heard her climb from the water and begin scrubbing herself with a handful of sand while she hummed a tune that he recognized from an evening at her campsite. From the corner of his eye he saw her run her hand over her shoulders, arms and legs, while sweat beaded his forehead. Soon, he would need to douse himself in the pond. She reached into the water, cupped her hand and emptied it over her skin until he closed his eyes in agony.

Finally, he heard her begin the sounds of dressing.

A new woman seemed to greet him in the moonlight. She had washed her old clothing and held the damp bundle in her hands while she spread them on the warm rocks. Finding a smooth recess, she knelt and began creating order to her tangle of curls that cascaded nearly to her waist. Sectioning her locks, she extracted all the water she could manage then finger-combed the strands, one by one. Lifting the mass above her head, she fanned the nearly-dry strands in the night air.

It gave him pleasure to watch her perform this intimate act, something a woman would do in front of her husband. He watched, saying nothing; not even by the sound of his breath letting her know that he shared this private moment. Something about the way she arched her neck reminded him of her filly when it emerged from the river. It was the same action and yet, on Mary, intensely personal. She had a scent that was hers alone. He first noticed it the night he toweled her dry, then again on the ride back from the Ute camp, with her hair fresh against his cheek. He recalled the scent of her skin, like ripe peaches in the summer harvest. Now, it was here between them, filling his senses and creating a longing deep inside.

He shifted on his heels while she walked to where he sat, not moving, imagining he could feel heat emanating from her body. She took a seat and continued to shake her tresses. Finally, he could stand it no longer. His hand moved toward her and he felt himself stroking her cheek with the backs of his fingers. He heard himself whispering her name for the first time. "Mary." His touch grazed her skin, a butterfly's wing softer than anything he had ever felt. He could live his whole life with this memory to sustain him. He whispered her name again, so close he felt his breath settle on her skin.

Again, he stroked her, moving a finger along her eyebrow. Only his fingertips touched her, but she reacted as if she faced a great storm. He reached to gently tug a curl caught against her, swallowing hard when her tongue appeared to wet her lips.

His hand cupped her chin and he turned her fully into his gaze. "Mary," he whispered, "Why did you settle for him?"

Paralyzed by his touch, Mary sat motionless, barely breathing until he released her. "Lucas, I can't," she whispered while her eyes gave him a different message. "Please, don't ask this of me. I can't."

He heard her words. Thinking she pleaded for her marriage, he gave no argument, only tipped his forehead, touching his nose to hers. Soft ebony hair against coarser, windblown locks, he took every ounce of feeling and let it pulse through him like a bolt of lightning from a prairie storm, until his heart threatened to break through his ribcage. He closed his eyes and breathed deep, seeking her essence, something to take with him this night. Moving his lips over her face, he absorbed the warmth of her skin. When it was too good, he forced himself to stop. "Mary, if you'd waited a few more weeks, I would have found you."

"Oh, Luke, since the day…you have been in my thoughts. Please, give me time. Till this journey is through."

"Mary, I feel I have a right to you. That scares me because there's a very good man between us, and I'm a friend to him, too. What are we going to do, Mary-girl?"

With the use of Philip's nickname for her, Mary began to return to reason. She knew she was hurting him; he needed words that could set him free and she wasn't able to utter them. Until she could, it would be best to keep her distance, because her body was becoming a traitor to her resolve.

She brushed his cheek in a tentative motion and caught the pain in his eyes. "Lucas, sometimes the best has to wait for us to deserve it. You are what took me from my parent's graves into this desert. I have been so selfish, my heart breaks for you."

Luke brushed her fingertips against his lips again. "Not selfish, Mary. Never that. Neither of us planned this. By all that is right, I'll not come between the two of you."

It was time to leave. Mary squeezed her eyes shut, unable to face the longing illuminated in Luke's eyes. Slowly, she backed toward her horse and mounted for the ride back to camp.

Chapter Seventeen

June 10, 1848. Grasshoppers! Everywhere we look. In our food, in the mouths of the children, even in the bedrolls. Sometimes they lie a foot thick, crunching underfoot like frozen snow. It is difficult to imagine going on.

LUKE SPENT A tongue-dragging day on the mesa searching for signs of the renegades he knew were watching. They expected to find easy pickings in the wagon train filled with farmers, women and children. It was late when he stumbled into camp, unsaddled his horse, and rubbed the stallion down with a handful of dried grass. The horse was used to grazing in hobbles close to Luke's bedroll, from their days together in the mountains. Now it did the same, calmly munching on a ration of grain. Limping on worn moccasins, Luke grabbed the coffee pot and poured himself a cup of strong, hot brew.

John Leverenz was already working on his second cup. "Good to see you back, Luke. I was beginning to get worried. See anything?"

"I can feel them...just can't tell when or where. Folks aren't helping much. Look beyond our small train. Travelers strung out along the trail until it's too late in the day to catch up. The renegades attack the lone wagons. The more times they succeed, the easier it is the next. Look out there."

Leverenz nodded. "I been thinking the same. Campfires strung out from here to next Friday. Looks more like a camp meeting than a defense in hostile country. When some of them get killed, they blame all the tribes. Pretty soon the army will be stirring things up, trying to protect them for something that needn't have happened."

Luke drew a swig from his coffee and wiped his mouth with the back of his hand. "Some of these men shoot a pair of single-shot rifles. Nothing more. Now you tell me, what good is that against a bunch of renegades with bounty and scalps on their minds? Hell, it's the whites that gave the tribes the idea of cutting scalps in the first place."

John Leverenz cut him off with a plate of food. "Here, Parson—eat. Save the sermon for tomorrow morning. Camp's settling down for the night and if they hear you ranting, they'll think something's up for sure."

Luke applied himself to the first hot food he'd had all day. "Well, it's not as good as some of the women have been feeding me, but it's pretty good."

Leverenz settled back on his heels, pipe in hand. He slowly poured a wad of tobacco into the bowl, tamped it with his index finger and held the pipe to his mouth. Inhaling, he put a lit twig to the bowl and concentrated on the flicker of flame. After a half-dozen sucks, when the flame caught, he tossed the stick back into the fire and gave a few quiet puffs of satisfaction. When he was ready, he broached the subject. "Speaking of the women, a couple of them paid me a visit tonight."

Luke grinned over the rim of his tin plate. "John, you devil, you."

"Not that way, Sayer, and you know it," Leverenz growled. "This is serious. They're riled 'bout the fight that broke out between you and Weems. They see it as payback for the time you're spending with the Rodgers woman. They claim you and her were seen coming back to camp with the husband nowhere in sight, and Mrs. Rodgers's hair was still damp."

Luke rocked onto the balls of his feet, tense, angry and waiting. His voice was deceptively casual. "What are you saying, John?"

"Just this. You ain't been around some of these woman the way I have. They got themselves a pecking order, just like hens. Now, I ain't saying there's anything going on between you and that little girl. I know you well enough to know, even if you wanted to, you wouldn't press your attentions. But look at this from her point of view. Traveling the plains is pretty lonely and all those women got is each other. They work hard—harder'n men for the most part. They palaver during the day to take the sting out of their trials. Some of them didn't want to make this trip in the first place, and they're feeling a little sour. If they can't vent their spleens to their menfolk then they'll do it at Missus Rodgers. They figure you and her are up to mischief, they'll shut her out of their circle. I've seen it happen."

"Not with Mary, it won't. She's as fine a woman as I've ever met. I'd fight any man who said otherwise."

"That's what I'm saying, Luke. You could fight a man and get him to see things your way. But women got their own ways. I had a lady schoolteacher one time, travel with us. She was single and paid same as the other men who rode. Paid for the supply wagon to take her grub along, rode her horse same as the men. Well, the women on that trail shut her out complete. They never shared so much as a meal or a conversation with her. She rode the whole way atop her horse and cooked her own supper when it came mealtime. I reckon they resented her for riding with the men. Or, maybe it was the fact that she'd chosen her own lot in life that galled them. But they were purely mean to that little gal. Be the same with your Mary if they're given reason."

"She's not my Mary. You saying if I eat any more meals with the Rodgers family, there'll be trouble?"

"You having supper with the family? Or are you having it with the missus? Sometimes folks that ain't so close can see better than those right in the thick of it." Leverenz emptied his pipe into the embers. "I'll be off to bed and let you finish your meal. Night, Luke."

Luke was left with the flickering light of the campfire for company, probably all he was fit for at the moment. He glared into the flames, forming silent arguments against those who accused him, but as his anger cooled he began to see reason. John was a friend. Still, he had joked one night, saying that Luke had only agreed to go on the wagon train after finding out that the Rodgers couple had signed up. And it was true. Luke knew it. He suspected that John did, too. To give up the pleasure of Mary's company was to give in to a bunch of meddling hens. He'd done it for a week, and the effort had nearly driven him crazy—he'd fight Leverenz himself before he'd let that happen again.

His argument with himself gave him no peace; his wanting to bring a smile to her face, to hear her soft words directed at him would put her in danger. Still, nothing had happened that either one of them needed to explain. He'd been so careful. But, as he thought back on the talk by the river, the dance—where his emotions had been an open book—and the ride back from the water hole where anyone could draw the their own conclusions, he realized that his idea of "nothing" might differ from those who might be watching. Maybe it differed from Philip's, too. The last thing he wanted was to get Philip fired up at him again. Funny, being a womanizer was what Mary had accused him of in the first days of the journey—and he had laughed at her.

He stamped out the fire and turned toward bed, still thinking on what could be done. "Damn old biddies ought to mind their own business," he growled as he pounded his coat into a reasonable lump of a pillow.

Morning didn't bring a solution, although he tried not to take his wrath out on anybody who got in his way. Leverenz eyed him cautiously and made a wide berth on his way to saddle up. But he had no quarrel with the man. Leverenz wasn't a meddler. What he'd said needed saying, but he probably hated being the one to do it. Better a friend than a stranger, though. If anyone else had accused him about Mary, the mood he was in, he might have knocked their head off.

Luke spent the morning looking for signs of a buildup of unshod ponies. He tried to keep his mind alert and off the problems back at the wagons, but his thoughts returned to Mary. When he closed his eyes he could feel her stirring his loins.

From the corner of his eye, he saw movement on the ridge where the rising sun tested his ability to discern distance and detail. He scanned the horizon and saw it again, a glimpse of rising smoke. From far-off mesas, answering puffs of smoke disappeared in the clear air. If he hadn't been looking he would have missed them.

He urged his horse toward the wagons. He might not be welcome, but the emigrants would need time to build an adequate defense and he knew how to do that, even if the farmers did not. He was still some ways out when Leverenz caught his signal. By the time he rode in, the first teams were already circling their wagons.

Luke leaped from his saddle and began rapping orders. "Get your families under the wagons. Use your supply barrels for cover. Turn the lighter wagons over and get the canvas covers off. The renegades will shoot flaming arrows to try and burn us out—you can't shoot if you're fighting fire, so try and protect everything that can burn.

"Get out your weapons, along with the ammunition, and load everything that'll shoot. If the women are reloading, have them up front. Otherwise, keep them out of the way. Boys, keep the animals inside. Keep your heads down and talk to the critters so they don't stampede. Keep a bucket of water handy, and as much dirt as you can gather. When a fire starts, use the dirt first.

"Don't shoot until you have them clear in your sights. They'll come rushing in like demons from hell and you'll be pretty scared. That's part of their act—get you to rush before you have a chance to reload. They figure you for a bunch of greenhorn farmers. So be ready and be smart. Above all, don't panic."

He ran through the camp repeating these orders until he came to the Rodgers' wagon. Mary was down on all fours with her skirts tucked into her waistband, loading and positioning Philip's weapons.

Turning, she caught him staring. "Looks as if I'm going to get a chance to soil my lily white hands after all."

He gave her a tight, worried smile before he started off in another direction. "Those of you with pepper guns, keep your six-shooters in reserve. If we get rushed, we'll save a little surprise for them." He saw that many of the men had Patterson Colt .36's that used a cap and ball. Next to them lay a number of Hawken .54 rifles which, although only a single shot, could be deadly, and in the hands of an experienced marksman, could be reloaded in only thirty seconds. Some of the poorer farmers lacked the resources to trade their old flintlocks for modern firepower, but as long as the weather held and their powder stayed dry, their antiques should do a capable job of defense. He'd had seen times where rain dampened the black powder on the powder box so that, when the flint struck the powder, it failed to ignite. But the sun was blazing hot today.

Back at his camp, he saw to his own weapons. He carried a pair of Walker Colts—a huge, matched set he'd purchased on a trip down to Texas to return an escaped prisoner to the Rangers, bought from a Mexican War veteran. He'd learned to depend on them. He could knock out the wedge and slip in another fully loaded six-round cylinder in the time it took to load up a single shell. This had created an element of surprise in several fights and he figured he owed his life to his Colts.

"John, where do you want me?"

Leverenz pondered a moment then pointed to the Rodgers' wagon. "They're undefended on that side. Most of the other wagons got grown boys or hired men to help out, but those two leave a gap. Go fill it." Luke met the man's unfathomable gaze. They'd deal with the issue when the battle was over.

The minutes seemed to drag into hours. Men hollered to their friends across the way, trying to keep their nerves in order. Women hushed children. Older boys carried buckets of dirt and water to strategic spots. Finally, after what seemed an eternity, the first round of renegade braves rode from the gap, their horses seeming to relish the adventure as much as the men. The braves wore full war paint to intimidate and bring favor for their victory while they made the charge with blood-curdling yells that unnerved the defenders waiting at the wagons.

Mary nearly swooned when she saw her first war-painted brave sweep past. The band circled, just out of range, trying to draw fire from the untried farmers, but Luke ran, head down, from wagon to wagon reassuring the men. When they could draw no wild fire the renegades raced out of range and regrouped while the emigrants waited. Luke had told them it was practically unheard of for Indians to attack a circled wagon because there was easier prey around. He was wrong in this case. These renegades showed every sign of meaning business.

Some of the Indians carried muskets and rifles taken on previous raids. Some held army-issue weapons captured from skirmishes or from looting an under-guarded supply train. What the hostiles lacked in firepower, they more than made up in riding ability; some shot a bow and arrow, riding at breakneck speed.

True to Luke's warning, a fired arrow struck a wagon and the women and boys worked to douse the flames. It seemed that the Indians were trying to create panic without risking their own numbers. They fired flaming arrows into the circle, trying to stampede the animals to open ground. Luke gave a signal and the farmers began returning fire. They managed to claim a few casualties. The next charge saw the settlers tiring. They were slower to reload and some of them spent valuable time stomping out flames. If fire destroyed their supplies, they chanced a surer death than by bullet or arrow.

Philip made use of his Colts. As fast as he emptied one, Mary readied the other. It was hot, dangerous work, and she was on the firing line where a bullet or an arrow could strike her as easily as one of the men. She grabbed an empty gun and was in the process of loading it when Philip suddenly rose halfway to his feet, arched back and collapsed. She bit back her scream as she crawled over spent cartridges to see where he had been hit. Using her whole strength to turn his body, she found an arrow stuck tightly between his ribs on the left side, underneath his heart. Blood ran from a wound and he was slumped unconscious, his face ashen.

"No, Philip, no!" she screamed, as if her cries would summon life back into him. His pulse was weak and irregular. With a sigh of relief she noticed movement in the shadow. "Oh, Lucas. Thank God you're here—" she began. Turning, she looked up to see a war-painted intruder enter the small enclosure.

Her limbs hung motionless with fear. The Indian approached with a look of raw hate in his face. He loosened the knife from the sheath at his side and recognition cleared the fog in her brain. It was Leaning Feather, the brave who had carried her off from the river. He had returned to avenge his shame. Without risking a glance, she patted the earth beneath her skirts for the spilled pistol at her side. Praying that it was loaded, she cocked the percussion cap and fired, using both hands to hold the barrel steady. A flash exploded, temporarily blinding her in the shadows, followed by a thunderous roar. She felt, rather than saw, the man falling forward, blocking her escape. With grotesque strangling sounds he clawed his way toward her and she fired again, but she heard a loud click. Terrified, she waited while the brave flopped over to reveal a gaping hole in his chest. He gurgled and lay still.

The smoke slowly cleared while she sat numbly staring. Even the blood pooling the soil in front of her didn't register. She could only think, *in my entire life, I will never be more frightened than this*. She heard a moan and slowly turned toward Philip. He was still alive, and still bleeding. Bright pink blood, she remembered, would mean a lung shot, but there was none of that. She reached for his hand and was immeasurably comforted by his warmth.

She tried to crawl to him, but the dead renegade blocked the crawl space, and she found herself unable to move. Shock traveled down her legs. Her ears rang from the report of her weapon, but from somewhere far off, she heard the sounds of the battle continuing.

Suddenly, it was over and someone was at her side, shaking her shoulder. She turned to find Luke shouting through lips that seemed to make no sound. Finally, she cleared her head and his words began to penetrate. "Mary, let's get you out of here." He pulled at the dead renegade, clearing a path through the barrels and saddles around the base of the wagon wheels. She stayed motionless, unable to follow him through the gore in the grass.

He pulled at the barrels, rolling them from beside the wheel until he had her free. When she remained frozen in shock he shook her gently. "They're all gone, Mary. They won't return. We gave them a good fight and they won't think we're such an easy mark, next time." He paused. "Where's Philip? Were you alone in there?" Mary could only point. Suddenly, Philip groaned. She leaned over and pulled back his shirt, revealing a dark, bloodied gash in his side.

Luke slipped to his knees and grabbed her arm, half-pulling her out of his way. "Move aside, Mary. Let me get that arrow out." He skimmed along the ground on his belly until he was under the wagon, within reach of Philip. Breaking off the end, he drew the arrow through the gaping wound and watched it begin bleeding. "Didn't hit anything he can't live without. It will be the infection we'll have to worry about, most likely."

"Thank God."

"Help me get him into the wagon."

Philip opened his eyes and his voice was a hoarse croak in

172 of ANNE SCHROEDER

the back of his throat. "Luke…take care of Mary. If I don't—"

Luke's voice sounded loud and angry. "Don't worry about Mary. Worry about your own life."

Philip groaned again, pitched forward in a spasm of pain and fainted. Mary began tossing boxes aside, looking for her medicine chest. When she found it she took a length of sewing thread and a needle and set them aside while Luke and another man lifted Philip into the wagon. She rolled up her sleeves and threaded a curved sacking needle with fingers that shook. It seemed as though everything took hours while blood seeped into the scrap of Philip's shirt tail that Luke pressed against the wound. "You need me to do that?" he asked.

"No, I'm not afraid." She cleaned the wound and then stitched the muscle underneath, making stitches tight enough to stem the bleeding but not so tight that they would tear. The silk thread would dissolve in time, she hoped, for she would be unable to remove it once the wound healed. Tying the sutures, she prayed for her mother's hand to guide her. Her face was sweating by the time she was able to tie off the thread. This last part was easier, although Philip would carry the scar for his lifetime.

She tried to finish, but her eyes were blinded by salt. "Luke, can you help me?"

Luke grabbed a corner of his shirt and wiped her brow. "I would want you in my teepee if I ever need tending," he said.

She looked up and managed a smile. There was no point in pointing out that each of her previous patients had died, anyway.

With darkness only an hour away, Leverenz gave the command to make camp. After the wagon fires were extinguished and the losses counted up, the count was three men wounded and one killed, an Ohioan named Jeb Nagy. Two wagons had burned. Their loss meant that two families would have to double-up. Their animals could be used on other wagons, but their supplies would be divided.

Mrs. Nagy, the dead man's widow, would accept no help. She and her husband had started together; she would drive her gear on to the Oregon Country and settle the land as they intended. There was no question of her turning back. Over a bowl of stew that one of the women insisted she eat, she told John Leverenz that her sons would grow up and the family would make a go of it.

Philip sustained the most serious wounds, but during the night his bleeding stopped and Mary began to relax. By morning, he was alert. She found him struggling to get to his feet when she carried his morning mush up to his makeshift bed.

"You just stay in that bed and give yourself time to heal. After the scare you gave me—"

"What about the oxen?"

"If Mrs. Nagy can get her family to Oregon, I'm sure I can take care of things for a few days."

The next evening, Mary unbound the wrapping to inspect the wound and found an angry red inflammation with darker streaks branching along Philip's side. She showed it to Luke when he walked by.

Luke kept his expression guarded, but he was clearly worried. "Blood poisoning. What have you got in the way of medicines?" Mary uncovered the small chest and showed him her supply of herbs and patent-medicines. Some she had used back home and others she had added after reading Philip's book.

Luke snorted with disgust. "That's the trouble with those guidebooks; while they're mostly accurate, they don't cover every situation. Nothing mends an arrow wound as well as the Indian cures. Those braves we shot are probably healing better than our own men. There are cures growing all around if you know what to look for: *Pouip* root, *nopal,* mosses and fungus from trees, yarrow, spider webs, mimosa, berries. A squaw carries her medicines in a bag so she'll be ready after a battle." He studied the prairie, wondering what he could find to draw the bad blood from the wound. His eyes drew down the line of wagons. "Wait here, I have an idea."

On the way down the row of wagons, a niggling thought occurred. If he did nothing, it was a pretty sure bet Mary would be a widow within the next few days. If his plan worked, she would be grateful to him for saving her husband's life. Happiness or honor; whatever he did, he figured he would lose.

Chapter Eighteen

June 17, 1848. The human spirit will triumph in the midst of defeat. Perhaps it is the misery that makes hope shine brighter. I have learned to embrace life the more for its elusiveness.

MARY ROSE TO the sound of a timid voice at the back of the wagon, and opened the rainfly to the quiet Negro girl who traveled at the end of the train with her husband and small daughter. She had seen the young woman many times, the only family of color on the train except for a couple of hired men and the escaped boy that Luke still kept hidden in his wagon. They kept to themselves, as a rule, and usually didn't attend the dances or evening campfires. Now, Mary wondered why the girl had come.

"I'm Matilda. Mister Luke sent me with some wound medicine. He says for me to heal this man for you." She spoke with no hint of vanity, but Mary noticed both the girl's assurance and her strange way of referring to Philip.

"I am obliged. What did you bring?"

The girl climbed into the wagon with a woven willow basket cradled in her arms.

"Salves and potions my mama learn me to make. This man have bad fever. I heal it now."

"Thank you. My name is Mary. This is Philip."

"I know you. I watch you sometimes ride horses with your man."

"I never ride with my husband. He has to manage the team."

"You say otherwise, but this is not your man." She spoke in a soft, calming voice as she busied herself with the unwrapping and the cleansing of the wound. Mary felt her heart drop. What kind of powers did this girl have? More importantly, who else had she told? "We speak of it later, Missus. Come, we heal your friend."

Matilda unwrapped the bindings and applied her salve to the angry red flesh. Mary had smelled the salve once before—on Luke's hands the day he tended the escaped slave boy. Whatever harm had been done to the boy's leg, his wound had healed. Now she knew where Luke had gotten his medicine.

As Matilda worked, she told Mary of the herbs she used, the dried yellow yarrow from a distant plantation, how she mixed it with dew-kissed spider webs that covered the tops of the snake holes and prairie dog hills. When she finished, she gathered her herbs and stood to leave.

"Matilda, thank you." Mary grasped the girl's hands, momentarily distracted by the calluses and scars on a young girl no older than herself. "I've seen you riding back there and I wanted to make your acquaintance. But some of the others…" She paused, hearing her unspoken words. "I'd like for us to be friends."

Matilda nodded, her eyes wary. "Your friend will get better. But you have other worries that need healing. This, I cannot do. God will." She climbed over the wagon gate.

Mary grabbed a flour sack and filled it. "Wait. I have extra coffee."

Matilda reached for a cloth sack, pulled open the drawstring and slowly inhaled. "Coffee. My man will be pleased. Thank you, ma'am."

"Mary," she corrected.

"Ma'am."

In the hours that followed, Philip continued to thrash on the narrow bed Luke fashioned over the top of two wooden barrels while Mary ran back and forth between the oxen and her patient. She tried to make him drink, but he swatted away the cup in the midst of some dream. By nightfall, his thrashing was too powerful for her to handle. Frantic, she looked up to find Luke watching from the tailgate.

"What is going on? I could hear him from across the camp."

"Luke, thank God you're here. He's so restless. Help me tie his hands down. I have some sheeting—" Tears clouded her vision. Suddenly, she sagged against the edge of a barrel.

Luke met Mary's eyes over Philip's blanketed form. "Get some rest, Mary. You look worse than he does. I'll stay with him." He helped her from the wagon. Gripping her trembling shoulders, he said, "Take care of yourself." Minutes later, he heard her slip into her bedroll under the wagon.

During the night, Philip's fever mounted. He thrashed, fighting something or someone, crying out unintelligible sentences. "Tell him…tell him. Let him know. Mary. No lie." Luke leaned near, trying to get him to finish the phrase so he could rest. He seemed to have a secret, something he and Mary shared. Finally, without giving any clue, the patient dropped into an exhausted sleep.

Mary slept, too; her quiet breathing came up to Luke from beneath the wagon, the sound of a sleeping child's. He had promised to wake her when the fever died, but now he didn't have the heart. Instead, he dozed, waiting for the dawn that would decide Philip's fate—as well as his own.

Giving his friend another sip of water, Luke thought of his strange dilemma. He loved them both—wanted them both safe.

Morning was only a promise when Mary came flying from her bed. "Why didn't you wake me? Is he better? Has he eaten?"

"Whoa, there. Which answer do you want first? He's better. You were snoring so loud I was afraid to get too close."

"I was not snoring. You were probably over with your horses. I do not snore!" Mary leaned against the wagon when the sight of Luke, sleepy-eyed and whiskery took her breath away. She hid her confusion in an outburst of impatience. "Move aside. I need to check my patient. You probably didn't even give him water." She turned away, conscious that she sounded peevish. With Philip so sick, she felt shame that she had spent a moment attending to her own looks before she approached the wagon. She climbed into the wagon and waited for Luke to move aside. "Oh, thank God, he's better. The fever has broken. His color is good. Matilda's balm worked."

Luke slumped against the wagon until he could muster the relief that Mary expected to see in him. By the time he joined her, Philip's eyes were open and Mary was already fussing.

"How do you feel?"

"Like I was shot in the side with a poison arrow. You sure there wasn't something on that arrowhead?"

Luke tried for humor. "That arrow was fine till it ran into you. I saved it—a souvenir for your grandchildren." His smile, directed at Mary, did not quite meet his eyes.

After a moment, he broke the awkward silence. "Well, I'll be making my way to breakfast. I'll hitch up your team after we eat. Best you stay down. If Mary can't handle the team,

I'll find someone who can. I will ride out to look for Indian sign today, but I believe they will not bother us again. They will prey on some other train next time."

Mary appeared with a broth of venison and crackers for her patient. Philip complained between sips, "I'll need more than this if I'm going to recover." The fact that he had scarcely the strength to lift his head made her smile at his bluster.

"You heard the man," she teased. "Take a few days off. I can handle the team, and if I can't, there's plenty more who can. Two of the wagons got burned. We'll be doubling up, anyway. You lay there and get well."

Luke arrived with the first of the team and quickly yoked them into place. When he finished, Mary watched him ride off toward the first streaks of light with a frown on his face.

Philip was watching her. "He has powerful feelings for you. I sometimes feel like an intruder in my own camp."

Mary turned with a start. "I gave my word and I intend to keep it." She moved about the wagon, securing the barrels.

"I feel sorry for the man. He's a decent fellow. Must be tearing him up inside to have the kind of feelings he does."

Mary tried to keep her face a blank. How was she to form an opinion when he overwhelmed her ability to be rational? "Do you think he's what Mama used to call a womanizer?"

"You know better than that, Mary-girl. That night at the waterhole, did he try anything?"

She turned on him, her anger flaring. "Of course not. He was a gentleman."

"There's your answer. Way you jump to his defense tells me you know it, too. Maybe you just don't want to trust another person to stick around. Maybe you want to save him from the same fate as your family." As though he just recalled her previous answer, he asked somewhat incredulously, "Mary, have you spoken to him about us?"

In truth, how could she answer that? Slowly, she shook her head. "He feels lower than a dog for having these feelings. He's never kissed me, but it has taken all his resolve not to, I can tell. We danced once. He said he'll not do that again." Her voice lowered to a whisper. "What am I to do?"

"Figured something like this might happen." Philip's voice grew weaker with each word. "I owe the man my life." Exhausted, he leaned back on the pallet and closed his eyes.

Mary panicked until she saw that he was breathing steadily. "We will take this one day at a time, as we planned. There is nothing else to be done. Now rest."

When the wagon train started up, Mary took her position at the head of the oxen, comforted by the slosh of full water barrels on the wagon. Water was more precious than gold now that they had left another river. Whenever they passed abandoned wagons the travelers tried to scavenge water barrels, but unless they were the first on the scene, it was rare that they made this find. Even when wagons were abandoned, the kegs went with their owners.

As the wagon train moved across the prairie, she tried not to fixate on the low horizon that made the daylight seem long. At the noon rest, she hurried to prepare food. For the first time, she realized what a contribution she was making, and she told Philip as much as she scooped beans into a tin plate. "You had me believe you were doing me a favor, taking me along. I don't think my stewed apples and beans have been hurting your feelings too much. Shame on you."

From the back came a weak retort. "I've been found out. You keep doing the cooking and I'll tell you every night how fine your skunk pie tastes."

"You shoot me a skunk and I promise I'll cook it. In the meantime, we'll have to live on buffalo."

The afternoon passed slowly; she was so exhausted that

even walking alongside the oxen was hard work. She heard Philip stirring and called, "How do you keep this up every day?" His voice seemed stronger than it had; he must be feeling better. "You gripe that cooking is the harder job. Make up your mind."

She smiled at his bantering. "I'll stick to the cooking," she called to the wagon. "Tending oxen is unbearable. By the time we get to camp tonight I'll be just two eyes peeping out of a dusty face."

"Try having some ham-handed surgeon stitch you up, then having to ride this twisting wagon all day. I've seen women waiting to deliver their babies in these wagons when the train couldn't take time to stop. Never thought about their pain. Ouch. Mary, you trying to split me open again?"

"Sorry, but there are boulders on the trail that someone should stop and pry out. It doesn't seem right that folks ride over them all day long and no one fixes the trail."

Philip's voice drifted from the bed. "We're all in a hurry and we know we won't be coming this way again. Everyone says, 'let the next fellow do it.' There's a group of Mormons who've taken to building ferries and fixing the road up more permanent. They plan to settle and improve conditions for the next passersby."

"Won't be too soon to suit me."

Philip fell asleep again, leaving Mary to the solitary job of handling the oxen. By late afternoon, her hands were cramped from holding the whip and every muscle sore from fighting the beasts into compliance. At least her posterior wasn't sore from riding the wagon seat. At the end of the day's journey, Luke had a boy come by to unyoke and settle the animals to feeding and she gladly began cooking. Supper was quick and simple with the limited fare they had left: fresh or salted meat and beans, and the last of the loaves of bread she had prepared a few days earlier.

Philip ate with indifferent enthusiasm. He would be on his feet long before he was ready, and he needed to be strong. After the supper pots were scrubbed and a new batch of dough set to baking, Mary looked around for a comfortable place to rest. She was anticipating a short nap, but Virginie and Nellie dropped by to see if she wanted to go to the campfire. Virginie had a serious beau now and wasted no opportunity to sit with him in the moonlight. Apparently, the admirer waiting for her in Oregon was long forgotten.

Nellie had celebrated her fifteenth birthday on the trail and was getting her share of attention. Her mother had once mentioned that her quick wit and sense of humor attracted boys like flies on a watermelon rind. Emigrant girls grew up fast, partly from the responsibilities that were expected of them, and partly because of the uncertainties of the trip. A girl who did a woman's work was thought of as a grown woman—and young men were not slow to make their claim.

Mary tagged along to the campfire. She witnessed the fun that the young people were having and felt a pang of jealousy. As a "married" lady, she was not allowed to enter the bantering and conversation with the young men. She suspected that the ones who stared at her with open admiration would be less shy if they guessed the truth. Instead, she felt an outsider, watching others fall in love while she bridled her emotions and waited. Tonight, she felt old and tired from her day's activities and the night was curiously empty. Signaling Virginie with a wave, she walked back to her wagon.

• ♥ •

Luke rode into camp quietly, hoping to speak to Philip alone. He reined in, for once glad that Mary was nowhere in sight. Philip was in the wagon, listless and uncomfortable in his narrow bed.

"Looks as though we're going to have to put up with you for a few more months, at least. Gave me a fright when I saw that streak of red going up your side. I thought you were a goner."

Philip studied him with an inscrutable expression. "That why you sent for the Negro girl, Matilda? You know, it hasn't escaped my thinking, if you'd left well enough alone, Mary'd be a widow by now."

Luke fidgeted on the barrel of flour where he sat. In his hands his wide brim hat was getting mangled from his white-knuckled clench. "Don't kid yourself. I thought of that myself. But I will not resort to murder to get myself another man's woman. You stand a good chance of making her happy out there in Oregon Country if I can just keep the two of you alive till you get there. If I'd known it was going to be such a full time job, I might not have signed up."

Philip grasped Luke's hand in a weak grip. "I know all you've done for us, and I'm grateful. Even if I am a little touchy about Mary."

"You got the right. If I was in your place, I'd do the same thing. Probably worse."

"Can't eat my supper most nights without some fellow nosing around camp to visit my wife." Philip's smile was weak.

Luke tried to return the smile but his gaze stayed downcast while he studied the floorboards. "I'll be taking my meals with Leverenz from now on," he said quietly. "You won't see me back here until you're up and around again."

"I trust you with my life. You're welcome to stay. And any favor you need—"

Luke glanced up at the sincerity in Philip's voice. He took a breath and heard the words spilling out. "Well, there's one thing—"

"Anything."

"Last night, you were out of your head. Thrashing around, saying something like 'tell him, Mary.' I got the feeling you didn't want to die with something weighing on you. Would you tell me if it's anything I have the right to know?"

Philip paled. Looking steadily at his friend, he filled his lungs and exhaled painfully. Maybe the time had come. He was weary—from lack of sleep, from pain, from fever. Mostly, he was weary of watching his friend dying a day at a time. He began tentatively. "Mary and I aren't married—"

Luke half rose, his face flushed in mottled anger. "What the hell—"

Philip continued. "We traveled out here together because we couldn't think of any other way to do it."

In a low, flat tone, Luke growled, "Who are you that she would travel with you?"

"I'm her first cousin." Philip's words were little more than grunts.

Silence took over the conversation while each man considered thoughts too weighty to be spoken. "Why didn't you just get married? Lots of cousins do that." Luke tried to keep his voice level while he thought his heart could burst.

Philip sensed his strength failing. "Got a girl…out in Oregon. Promised. Means the world to me. We heard your wagonmaster…another couple…over barrel of his shotgun. Was afraid I'd end up saddled to Mary."

Luke sat staring out at the darkness. "I guess you've made me a happy man."

Philip watched the fire in his friend's eyes replace the pained longing. "Luke, I never wanted to hurt you. Just had to take care. For Mary's sake. No way to change horses in the middle of the stream. You know?"

Luke turned and faced him for the first time in several

minutes. "The moon will not rise on my anger for you, my brother. Not tonight, not ever."

"Luke, I could see you had feelings for her. Hell, a blind man would see that." This time, it was Luke who looked chagrined as Philip continued. "It was tearing me up to see you. Last night, I thought I was dying and Mary was sitting next to me."

"Then I should be glad for your poor sight. But my brother, what do we do now?"

Philip shook his head. "I need your word that you'll say nothing about this. To anyone."

Luke nodded slowly. "It will be hard."

Sweat beaded Philip's forehead. He straightened, then collapsed onto his pallet with a groan. "Don't even think about courting Mary. Promise me."

Luke gave a quick glance to see who might be overhearing. Fortunately, no one seemed interested in hearing another argument, but he lowered his voice, just in case. "Take it easy, friend. I will say nothing to Mary, and I want you to do the same. She needs to trust me enough to tell me on her own."

"You forget, man…" It was Philip's turn to be startled. "I swore her to secrecy."

Luke spoke his thoughts aloud. "She needs to trust. That has not happened yet. It will take time."

"You know, Sayer, you're a damn fine man." Philip brushed the corner of his eye with his index finger. "Her father wouldn't have wanted better for her."

Luke's face turned red. "Will you do that for me? Hold off saying anything to her?"

"If you promise not to be spooning in the dark. I've no desire to look like a spurned husband—or a fool."

"No spooning. I make you this promise."

Philip gave a weak chuckle. "Mary'll be disappointed. Can't wait to see how you two work things out. Good luck with her, Luke."

"I will be off before she comes back. And thank you again, my friend."

"Thank you for saving my life. Another man might not have." Philip extended his handshake even though it caused pain to rip through his chest.

Making his way back to the wagon, Luke was filled with peace he could not have fathomed earlier in the day. In the darkness he saw a form coming toward him. It was Mary, walking alone back to the wagon. Behind her the rest of the camp seemed to be paired off at the dance and he could see her tears in the moonlight. Instinctively, he took a step toward her, checked his impulse, and lowered his arms. When he felt calm enough to trust his voice he tipped his hat. "Evening Missus Rodgers."

Mary looked up, surprised. When she spoke, her voice seemed tinged with tears. "Good evening, Lucas. Um, are you off to bed, already?"

"Yes, ma'am. I will stop at the meeting and say hello. It gets lonely riding out all day."

Mary's voice seemed strained. "Wouldn't you care to sit and talk for awhile—maybe back at camp?"

Two of the more outspoken women passed by on their way to their wagons. One glared at Luke with pursed-lip disapproval. He cursed his luck and raised his voice for the ladies' benefit. "I just left your husband. He's doing fine. I'll be off early in the morning—probably be gone for a couple or three days. See you when I get back. Good night." Forcing a tune from his lips, he started toward his camp, his promise to Philip ringing in his ears.

Chapter Nineteen

June 20, 1848. We see buffalo daily now. Great shaggy beasts that pound the ground while we sleep until we think we will be crushed. Luke shot one, and we will feast for days. I have made several fine sketches. The beasts are magnificent, and so bountiful as to be indestructible.

THE NEXT WEEK brought new difficulties. The wagon train wound its way across the last section of the Nebraska flatlands near Wyoming Territory. The early summer columbines and buttercups had long ago given way to buffalo grass that scratched the women and children's legs, but the cattle and horses thrived on the easy pasture. Dried buffalo chips replaced firewood as the only source of fuel, and the women soon settled their squeamishness, collecting chips in their once pristine aprons until they could transfer them to their wagons.

Waterholes were far between and Luke rode endless days searching. Sometimes, he located one only to find it fouled by previous trains when mules and cattle stomped the banks and created mud and manure in the small source. Sometimes a dead animal, left behind because it was ailing or had gotten lost, found its way to the drinking hole and died, rendering the pool undrinkable. Cholera was a constant worry, and

Luke fretted about traces left in the small, stale ponds infecting another batch of travelers.

On the trail, Mary, Bethellen and Virginie stared at the burial markers. Sometimes, they counted as many as ten pounded into the baked soil for every mile they walked, commemorating the spot where a loved one had been left behind. Some markers had been carefully etched with a message of love, but most contained simply the name and date. Some graves had a single occupant, with other family members buried farther on down the road. Some markers contained the names of whole families, often with an abandoned wagon lying nearby. Sometimes the skeletal remains of oxen lay still attached to stiff harnesses. The girls took turns writing down names and dates, hoping to pass the information to folks in Oregon City waiting for relatives and friends who would never arrive.

Mary passed furniture discarded along the edge of the track by husbands desperate to save the flagging strength of the animals. It was just as Leverenz predicted. Better to have sold things back in Independence for ten cents on the dollar than to have it come to this. Having their prized possessions tossed aside was just the latest in a series of indignities most of the women had to suffer. The women compared notes about the painful decisions they made back home; they had all been forced to leave their pretty dishes with relatives or watched them be sold at auction for money to buy supplies. For women who had little to start with, each item in her house was a treasure. Deciding what to bring was difficult, but watching their men toss it off in a fit of anger on the trail filled the women with resentment.

She and Philip passed a wagon that had pulled off the track. The four skinny mules were down on their knees, winded and heaving. In the back of the wagon the man was raging as he tossed out everything within reach. "Damn junk. You had to bring everything in the house. Weren't no use for us to pack this. Everyone told us so. But you had to bring yer ma's plates. What's a body need with China plates on a homestead?"

The woman crouched on the scorched plain, sobbing, clutching the handle of her broken and discarded porcelain pitcher in a tight grip. Mary had to turn away. The couple traveled behind them for two days while Mary watched to see what might become of them. The woman seemed to neither eat nor drink, just sat on the wagon yoke in the evenings, mutely clutching the broken remains of her pitcher while the husband fended for himself. On the third day, when the heat was unbearable and pity eclipsed her better judgment, Mary took a cup of coffee to the husband. "Here you are, sir. You look as though you need a drink. I'll offer some to your wife, next."

The man's eyes were tired. "Thank you kindly." He started to bring the cup to his mouth then glanced at his wife. "She's…she's not right in the head any more. Teched from the hardships, I expect. She ain't spoke in three days."

Mary could see the pain within each of them. She watched as the husband offered the cup to his wife. "Here, wife, you need it worse than I do." The woman raised her eyes and Mary thought she was going to refuse when she suddenly dropped the piece of porcelain and took the cup, clasping it over her husband's hand. When the cup was empty she handed it back with a look that was not quite a smile, but Mary sensed it was a softening. When she saw them later that night, she noticed the woman no longer carried the broken handle.

The next morning Bethellen caught up to walk alongside her. "Land's sake, we could start us a furniture store with the finery people have thrown off. Makes me glad in a way that I never had such goods, because now I ain't having to cast it aside." Mary knew what she meant. Although they bickered about other things, none of them took pleasure in seeing someone else forced to endure loss.

The children became a source of constant irritation. The women had barely the strength for their own needs, and caring for hungry, thirsty and footsore children often seemed the last straw. Sometimes the little ones cried all night, at times from sickness and pain, but often in total despair.

Philip had been right about the oxen; the team plodded all day with the same steady gait. The team was mostly gaunt muscle and sinew—a walking ripple of loose skin covering their ribs. In their misery, the cattle and mules bawled throughout the night. There was little the men could do to relieve their misery. Their helplessness went against the grain for farmers taught since birth to put the needs of their animals before their own.

Late one night when most of the camp lay awake in the dusty, stifling heat, the Murdock's prize mare milled restlessly, neighing with a hoarse croak that only underscored the need to find water. Above the din of cattle and mules, the sound came again and again. Philip tried to block the noise, but the animal continued with a restless vigor that made morning seem long in coming. He heard his friend Murdock stroking the animal, pleading with it to get to its feet. An hour passed before Murdock gave up and returned to his bed. As he passed by their wagon, Philip wanted to say something, but he held his peace when he saw the grizzled Missourian wipe his eyes with the back of his grimy hand. Another hour passed, filled with the ceaseless croaking. His nerves were stretched to the breaking point when Murdock passed again, a rifle in his hands and a glint of tears on his grizzled cheeks. A deafening explosion silenced the pitiful croaking. When Murdock returned once again, Philip heard a muffled sob. There was nothing he could do. The comforting would need to come from Sazie. He turned over in the new silence and fell asleep.

Luke rode hard, searching for water. Sometimes he was gone two or three days, taking only his bedroll and a meager supply of biscuits, jerky and water. More often than not he would ride back into camp dirty and exhausted, avoiding the hopeful eyes of those watching. Sometimes he brought game and small varmints, but as temperatures soared to over a hundred and ten, tongues became almost too swollen to swallow. The travelers ate because they knew it would be folly not to. Water was rationed one cup at a time; by the wagonmaster's decree, the extra water that some carried was put into a common barrel so that all could share.

This was the hardest requirement yet for Philip. He had sacrificed bringing other items to add extra water barrels. Now, folks who had not exercised the same caution were allowed to share his bounty and he had to stand aside and watch. Mary felt more accepting on this score. She watched mothers whose tears no longer fell for their children, endure misery like dumb oxen, plodding to the next stop with down-turned heads and dull eyes.

One scorching afternoon, Luke rode into camp in a tempestuous mood. Bill Weems growled, "Where's the water? Don't know why we bother to pay you if you can't do your job. We're thirsting to death here, man." For the space of a half-dozen heartbeats, Luke glared from the back of his mount. Without speaking, he leaped to the ground.

Weems waited, his knife glistening in the harsh sunlight as he crouched and began circling. He seemed to have forgotten his last lesson, but he seemed determined to have a piece of Luke.

Mary bit back her panic. "Lucas, he's sun-crazed. Fighting him isn't going to solve anything. He's only scared, and he has the right to be. Come over to the wagon. I've made some tea."

At the sound of Mary's voice, Luke straightened. "Put your knife away, Weems. I'll go out again after it cools down. There's one other spot I have to check." He left Weems sputtering and followed Mary to her wagon. "That fellow won't be satisfied until he has a piece of my hide on his wagon cover. It isn't going to happen if I can help it." He stole a glance at Mary and felt the tension of the past minutes ease. She seemed so thin and strained.

Sensing his eyes on her, Mary turned and smiled. "We haven't seen enough of you lately to know if the buzzards got you or if you're courting an Indian maiden."

He managed a wry smile. "I've been out early. Have to find water soon or it'll be too late for a lot of these animals. It's my job, like the man said, and I'm failing at it."

"No, Luke," Mary placed her hand on his arm. "You haven't failed. If there's water out there, you will find it. I know it, and so do the others." Her eyes shone soft and sincere. Suddenly, the sun did not seem so hot, nor the day quite so hopeless. He would ride back out again.

The tea she served went a long way to curbing the trail dust in his raw throat. He sipped while he studied her over the rim of his cup. She had brushed her hair back the way she had done at the waterhole. Hiding his smile, he feigned indifference, careful to watch her only when her head was turned.

When he could bear the deception no longer, he sat the cup down, thanked her and went off to give Leverenz his report.

Chapter Twenty

June 23, 1848. The toll this journey has taken on my fellow travelers is close to breaking my heart. We have been forced to harden ourselves and pass by scenes that would have earned our deepest sympathy back home.

CAMPFIRES DOTTED THE little valley where Leverenz's wagon train camped for a few days of rest. The sycamores and aspen provided shelter for the weary travelers, and lush grass for the cattle and mules. A sparkling underground river emerged from its journey, bringing snow-fed waters from some distant range that waited unseen in the western horizon. No longer chilled by the glaciers of the mountains, the waters flowed beneath the low-lying prairie floor into a natural sink.

Finding the valley had been a stroke of luck on Luke's part. He was out hunting when his stallion broke for the little glen. At first, he thought it was a mirage, just another disappointment in the harsh ground they traveled, but the smell of the trees was real and the taste of pure, sweet water made him toss his hat in jubilation.

The wagon train had to detour six miles from the track, but the mules and oxen smelled the change. They picked up their paces long before the glen came into sight. Within viewing distance the mules stampeded, leaving grown men to follow with tears streaming down their faces and shouts of "Hallelujah!" on their swollen tongues.

Men, women and children ran forward and threw themselves in face-first, as they pounded the running water with whoops of joy. Women packed their babies into the sink, giving the little ones a treat they so badly needed. In the previous fortnight's trek, the little ones had endured trials that had broken grown men.

Mary approached more slowly, turning in a wide arc to study the treeless hills and the sky. She sat on a fallen log and removed her worn boots and stockings, lifted her gritty, tattered skirts to her knees and paddled her pointed toes on the surface like a beaver tail on a pond. Almost reverently, she cupped her hands and let the water reach her lips and run down her arched neck, pooling in the recesses of her collarbone. She cupped more water and let it run in rivulets over her face, eyes, and cheeks. Finally, after satiating her other senses, she tasted the water. After drinking her fill, she leaned against a tree, closed her eyes and breathed the scent of water.

Luke stood beneath a scrub cottonwood and watched. The travelers had cursed and blamed him when water was scarce and he would be surprised if any of them came forward to thank him for finding this place. He held no bitterness. He understood the tension that drove them and was glad, for their sakes, that he had found it.

Across the way he spied Mary. Another time he would have gone to her like a bee to nectar, but today he was content to watch her. His eyes followed the drops where they ran down her neck and he could almost taste them as they fell. He had kept a wide berth of her by dint of pure will, but he had spent hours secretly watching her; taking the memories into his bed at night and onto his solitary rides. True to his resolve he had stopped waylaying her for a look, a touch or a word.

Mary noticed Luke in the shade of the tree and willed him to join her. She arched her back and paddled, trying to draw him nearer, but he remained where he was, leaning against the tree, smoking his cheroot and acting as though he had not seen her. She puzzled at his coolness. He had been a stranger since Philip's recovery. She could count dozens of times when he could have spent some time alone with her, but he had avoided her to spend his time with the men and sometimes even with the young women at the campfires. She had made excuses for his actions at the time, but now as she added them together, she could think of only one reason—he was avoiding her. She had spent hours wondering what she had done to discourage him and she always came back to the same conclusion; she must appear quite the hussy, being married to one man but willing to entertain the attentions of another. *How ironic that I play my role as wife so well that I have ruined my chance at happiness.*

Slowly gathering her shoes and stockings, she headed back to the wagon. The water had lost its attraction. There was no purpose in joining the group of laughing young women downstream who were enticing the young men with their antics. There was no arguing against it this time; Luke could have come to her and he had chosen not to. She walked slowly, not trying to hide her tears of shame. Never had she felt so lonely. That he considered her to be beneath his regard hurt to the core. There was nothing she could tell him that would change his mind.

The day had its compensations. Supper that night included fresh watercress and plenty of cool water: water for drinking and for brewing into coffee, and wet sand for scrubbing caked dirt off of the dishes. The water soothed tempers. Folks made up their differences, and after supper the fiddles rang once more.

Cattle nibbled and mooed in the meadow. Crickets and frogs sounded in the marsh grass as the moon rose over the knoll and cast its shadow on the meadow below. A pair of lovers stole off, unnoticed by all the other campers, save one. They headed toward the bushy creek to enjoy each other and the night. Each had waited long for this chance and caution held no place in their figuring as the rest of the camp danced and made merry without noticing that they were gone.

Luke was settling in for the night when an irate father burst into his camp shouting, "Sayer, my daughter's gone and so is that no-account Jim Tyler. He's been making sheep's eyes at her for weeks now and he's up to no good, I know. When I find him I'm going to give him a taste of this here birdshot."

"Now, Mr. O'Brian, I'm sure it's not as bad as all that. I'll go looking for them, but she's probably on her way to bed right now." Luke pulled on trousers and boots over his un-ion suit. "Keep calm and I'll do the looking. Folks are abed and could use the rest tonight." He knew where the errant couple was, and he knew what they were doing, but he wasn't about to add fuel to the already glowing coals of a father's wrath.

He headed straight to the grove of trees where a mound of flat rocks shone in the moonlight. Coughing loudly on his approach, he hoped to give them time to adjust themselves. "Miss Ida, your father's looking for you and he's hopping mad. Best you get on back, now."

She was flustered and embarrassed nearly to death he could tell. But if they had managed to find love out of all of this, then more power to them. Trying to spare them further shame, he said, "Jim, head on back for the camp. I'll make up a story about where Ida was and we'll come in soon. And Jim, if you've a love for this woman then face her father like a man and ask his permission for her hand. Do it the honorable way and you'll both be the better for it."

Jim Tyler blushed and stammered, "I aim to do that, sir. First thing tomorrow. And, thanks."

Luke nodded and started off for the other side of the camp with Ida alongside. She began shivering, probably as much from shame as cold, he figured. He put his arm around her in a gesture of support.

Mary stepped out of the circle of light to toss her wash water onto the grass. Hearing steps, she glanced up. "Oh, Lucas, you startled me." Looking closer, she noticed that he wore his underwear and had his arm around pretty Ida O'Brian, who looked as damp and washed clean as she had on the night he had taken her swimming. Apparently, he had found favor with another girl. No wonder he acted so aloof; he was trying to let her know his affections had changed. Stammering, she rushed an apology for disturbing them and turned back toward the wagon. Trying to restrain her tears, she halted when she heard Luke call her name, and without turning around, waited for him to speak.

"Mary, if anyone asks, Ida was with you and your husband this evening. I'd appreciate the favor."

"Philip's not back yet." She felt her face flame, but she forced herself to meet his gaze. Ida stared at the ground in shame, but Luke seemed almost oblivious. Wordlessly, she wiped her hands on the drying cloth and fled back inside her wagon. As she tied the canvas closure, she heard Luke lead the O'Brian girl into the darkness. Mary sought escape into her bedroll, where her tears fell in a silent flood.

Before sunrise the next morning, Luke appeared at her

wagon. He had chosen a time when Philip had gone to see to the oxen and the camp was busy with morning chores. Taking his hat between his fingers, he ran a hand through his still-damp hair, pressed his mustache over the corners of his mouth and cleared his throat while he waited for her to turn and acknowledge him.

She finished wiping the warm water from her face, her green eyes dark-lashed and dewy from her early morning swim. She had woken puffy-eyed, and sought a remedy for her tears in the chill of the river. Now she was glad that she had done so. She tried and failed to imagine a worse scene than having Luke standing before her, seeing the results of her caring. It would have been the final humiliation. Seconds passed while she straightened to her full height and tried to gain control of the fury growing inside her. She heard herself speaking as though the words came from a stranger. "Mr. Sayer, we have nothing to say to each other. You made yourself perfectly clear last night. Please get out of my camp."

The gravity in his expression held her captive. She tried to discern what he was thinking as he stood there, saying nothing, but with a disturbing hunger in his eyes. His lazy eye twitched and a hood fell over his face. Turning, he walked away.

The sun began its path across the scorched plains. Already the women were busy washing their clothes, beating them against rocks and washboards before hanging them on trees and bushes to dry. The children spent long hours in the water, trying to catch trout with their hands like the Indians, but without much luck. They rode slippery rocks over riffles, their giggles bringing gladness to the hearts of their watching mothers.

Men spread out to hunt ducks and other fowl that used this hidden glen to water. Deer trails led to the edge of the creek and rabbit burrows were thick in the hedges. Shots rang out frequently. Folks shared their bounty with neighbors they had been feuding with only days before.

True to his word, Jim Tyler approached Mr. O'Brian for permission to wed his daughter. The man exploded in fury, feeling his honor had been violated and wanting the boy to suffer for his rashness.

Mrs. O'Brian, normally a complacent woman who deferred to her husband's every wish, surprised him by speaking up in a voice that brooked no interference. "Semas," she told him in a soft voice, having pulled him to one side. "Wasn't no one in me family thought I should be marrying you, 'cause you had no prospects, me da said. And now look at you—in America and bound for a farm of our own, we are. And me da was wrong. Ida's been doin' the work of a grown woman for a year and more. You couldn't do nothing for her out in that god-forsaken prairie, 'twas her alone that got herself through. She can choose for herself what husband she'll be takin'—same as I did!" She stood with arms crossed, waiting his reaction. "I might not know what the next few months will bring, but I married for love, and so, by the saints, will me daughter."

Semas O'Brian gulped and gave young Tyler a handshake to seal the agreement.

The women planned the wedding for the next day to take advantage of the lovely glen that reminded them of Ireland. Mary made a pan of apple fritters, fried in hot lard and sweetened with honey from a wild hive that Luke found. She put in the last of her cinnamon because she recalled Luke saying it was his favorite. *I hope they're all gone before you get your chance. Then you can stand around and watch the others smack their lips. Will serve you right*! If Ida O'Brian and Luke had done something that compromised her reputation, it served him right that she'd spurned his advances for Jim Tyler. Tyler seemed the marrying kind, which was more than she could say for Lucas Sayer.

She shook the wrinkles out of the green dress Luke admired so much. Last time she had worn it he had been scarcely able to keep his eyes off the low-cut neckline. Along with the other girls, she washed her hair with water dipped from the stream, but while the others laughed and planned whom they would dance with, she listened to hear which of them made a claim for Luke Sayer. Surprisingly, no one had singled him out. *Maybe he holds himself aloof so he can spread himself around.*

She dried her hair and pinned it into place with her mother's tortoise combs and hairpins. Smiling into the tiny looking-glass, she ran her hand along her ribcage and noticed that she was as thin as the other girls. Her cheeks were naturally high-boned. Now, their prominence highlighted her emerald eyes, making her seem fragile and vulnerable. *Thank God for that horrible sunbonnet.* Still soft and creamy, her cheeks had just enough color from the open air to give her entire face a glow in the moonlight.

Philip came in to clean up and seconded her opinion. "Mary-girl, you've never looked better. All the men are going to be tripping over themselves to dance with you, and the ladies aren't going to talk to you for days. Too bad I'll be fiddling. Seems like I never get a chance to dance with you."

"Try tonight, Philip. It looks strange for us never to be dancing together. I would be content with your promise of a couple of dances."

"Maybe Luke Sayer will take a turn with you."

"I'd sooner touch a frog down at the river than to have his sweaty hands on me."

She missed Philip's smile as he backed away.

Ida's wedding was held in the late afternoon, after the crowd had rested and the sun began its descent over the little hillside to the west. Mary set her skillet on the table and looked over the collection of food. There were no other fried apple fritters.

She turned to greet Bethellen when she saw Luke sidle up to the makeshift table and pocket a fritter into his clean shirt. Winking at her, he made his way back toward his camp. "Lovely dress you're wearing, Mrs. Tate," he called to the woman at her side. "You look like a butterfly in spring."

He leaned against a tree at the edge of the gathering and took a bite of his stolen pie. Mary was watching him lick the crumbs when he glanced up. Making an "O" with his thumb and index finger, he signaled that it met his approval. "Swine," she muttered, and turned from his cocky grin. Working the crowd like an Irish politician, he chatted with the ladies, kissed the babies and accepted the compliments of the drovers on finding this spot. Several times she caught him watching her as he applied his charm.

The ceremony began, officiated by a Presbyterian minister traveling out to the territories to start an Indian mission—a poor choice for the Catholic priest the Irish bride would prefer, but they would remedy that when they found one. She watched the bride and groom and felt their happiness with such envy that she had to turn away. Even Ida's father was happy as he played the role of host. He seemed to have agreed to let bygones be bygones with his new son-in-law. Since Tyler was going to be in the family, O'Brian didn't want any breath of scandal attached to the young couple, so no hint of discord came from his lips.

Luke stood at the back of the crowd where he could watch Mary lean forward in rapt attention while the vows were spoken. She looked up, saw him and ducked her head. Fever surged through him at the thought of holding her in such a ceremony. He closed his eyes when the minister pronounced the couple husband and wife. When the new couple leaned toward each other for a first public kiss, he watched Mary's lips open in an involuntary response. By the time he returned his attention to the ceremony, people were surging toward the new couple, offering kisses to the bride and handshakes and enthusiastic back pounding for the new groom.

Mary held back as all the men gave Ida an enthusiastic hug. When it was Luke's turn, he spoke earnestly and quietly; to Mary it seemed a lover's farewell. As she watched, Luke pumped the groom's hand and moved on without a backward glance. She watched for some sign of regret on his part, but it seemed as though Luke had already forgotten about Ida. What sort of man was he? She made her way to the edge of the crowd, praying that the night would fly by. It was not possible for her to spend the evening alone in her wagon. Instead, she found a seat in the semi-darkness where she was able to shield her hurt from the people who might notice.

Philip and the others took up their banjos, fiddles and harmonicas. People made their way to the dance floor. Soon the area was filled with couples laughing, turning and promenading to the sounds of the music in the pale light of the setting sun. Mary danced with every young man who approached, tongue-tied and eager for the chance to squire her about the circle. She smiled and flirted, forgetting her woes while managing to keep one eye out for Luke. She wanted him to approach so she could snub him, but instead, he stood on the sidelines to himself. When he finally asked, it was for an impersonal Virginia Reel, where touching was at a minimum and the action was quick. They spoke only briefly while promenading down the center of the lined couples.

"Nice party, wouldn't you say?"

"Very nice," Mary said. "Ida looks happy. She made an excellent choice." Her feet felt wooden as she tried to follow his footsteps, but Luke didn't seem to notice. In fact, he treated her no differently than he did any of the married women.

Finally, the band took a break and supper was served. Skillets of new-caught trout were set alongside large wooden bowls of crisp greens, wild mushrooms and herbs found in crevices near the stream. There were pine nuts, roasted in the frying pans, dried apple compote, fried bread and venison haunch roasted to a turn. None of the cows were still giving milk, so there was no butter or cream, but the women managed to create magic with their limited means.

The children stared at the platters and bowls with wide eyes, excited by an abundance they hadn't enjoyed in weeks. Mary helped a young boy put a few items on his plate and he lisped through missing front teeth, "My Ma says my eyes is bigger'n my belly." She solemnly nodded, trying to hold back a smile while the child looked longingly at the empty skillets left after the men had eaten. When it came her turn, Mary helped herself to what was left, not surprised that the men had eaten most of the best as they did each night. The worst offenders were the hired hands, the single men with no regard for the children.

Philip escorted her over to a fallen log, stepping past children who sat on clumps of grass and tattered quilts. They sat across from a pretty girl and her brother who seemed to be enjoying the Indian sign language Luke was teaching them. The girl laughed and swished her curls in a coquettish way and he responded. It irked her to notice that, cleaned up and rested, he looked as handsome as she'd ever seen him. He said something and the girl put her hand over his and smiled. He glanced up and found Mary watching, and his eyes tarried a moment before he returned to his story. She managed a wan smile and returned her eyes to her plate. At that moment, Nellie and her young man sat down beside her and she turned her attention to what Nellie was saying, glad for the diversion.

Philip helped himself to a cup of coffee and Mary watched him swallow with his eyes closed. When he added a dram of his carefully hoarded whiskey and offered her a sip, she started to shake her head, but then thought, *why not?* The first sip slipped down her throat, numbing her. She took another sip, then another until Philip shook his head and returned his jug to safekeeping.

Mary was not used to spirits, and it was affecting her more than she realized. When the music resumed and new partners crowded around, she felt as light as thistledown. "This is nice," she giggled to a ham-fisted mountain boy in red suspenders who took her hand for a slow dance. A bout of dizziness assailed her and she clung to him more tightly than she realized. Giggling from a near miss with another couple, she tightened her hold on the eager young buck and was surprised when he mistook her intentions and moved his face a little closer to her own. She pushed back, putting her hand on his chest, and felt his heart pounding with excitement. "Oh, my," she babbled, "it seems to have gotten warmer, with the crowd so close."

When her partner grabbed her hand and eagerly guided her out of the circle into the dark, she opened her mouth in protest, but the pounding in her head confused her, and she figured they would stop at the edge of the clearing. Instead, they walked beyond the campfire, toward the creek with its benches of flat rocks nestled under low branches, but she was too dizzy to protest.

One man watched the mountain boy strong-arm Mary into the dark while she seemed not to care where she was heading. By the time they reached the rocks, Mary felt woozy and begged to sit. Adam Harsh, the young swain, found a flat rock near the river's edge and moved to sit beside her. He leered at her neck where her low-cut bodice left her exposed. With eyes closed, he moved into position for a kiss when he felt a firm hand on his shoulder. It yanked him backward and left him sprawled on the ground. "What in tarnation?" he sputtered.

"The lady's married. I suggest you get yourself back to the dance and find someone who isn't." Luke stood legs spread in a stance that brooked no argument. Apparently, Harsh wanted no fight with the strapping guide who had fought Indians in hand-to-hand combat. Muttering an oath, he decided to high-tail it back to camp to try another sip of moonshine his Pap had packed along for just such an occasion.

Mary made the mistake of giggling at the picture Luke made, standing like an angry mother with an errant child. This was the final indignity for Luke, who had spent the evening watching Mary flaunt her body and flirt with every man on the dance floor until his nerves were raw. He had been waiting for this very thing to happen, and now, when he had saved her from an unwanted groping, she laughed at him.

He stood fuming while she leaned back on both arms to steady herself. Her curls had loosened into a shining mass that looked as relaxed and tumbled in the moonlight as the rest of her. Her dress had suffered little from her exuberance; she reminded him of an Indian princess, sitting in haughty splendor. Frustration snapped the fragile string that held his reason in check and he reached for her. She came, leaning unsteadily against him, adjusting to this sudden change by putting both her hands on his chest in a steadying move he took for a caress. His grip expressed his weeks of frustration while his mouth moved on hers. His hands roved across her back, her sides, anywhere he could find to stem the feelings raging through him. It was impossible to get enough of the feeling.

He felt her soften under his grip and what began in anger shifted to wanting more. She leaned against him and he recalled that he sought to punish her—and himself. When she tried to return his caresses, he broke away. "Don't care who you're with, just as long as he's warm and willing, huh?" He clung to his anger to cover his reeling emotions and railed again. "It's all right for you to drink, just not with the half-breed, right? Best watch what you're doing, or you'll find yourself out here in the dark with the whole wagon train." He silenced her protests with a demanding kiss. While he could silence his words, he had no such luck with his body. Stopping was as abrupt as a plunge into an icy pool.

With shock pulsating through him, he grabbed her arm, half dragging her back to the dance, not even caring that her feet struggled to keep pace. Ignoring her sputtering protests, he deposited her outside the ray of lantern light and stalked off into the night to try to quell the frustration that rocked his entire body.

Mary stood for a moment, trying to gain her bearings on legs that threatened to collapse. Gathering her soft yellow skirts she fled to her wagon, climbed under the wagon and threw herself onto her bedroll where her memory of the evening returned in a flood of humiliation.

She was glad that the wagon train rode out the next morning and Luke was not among the point riders.

Chapter Twenty One

July 4, 1848. Celebration! Time to forget our woes and share a night of revelry among strangers. I shall look back on this night forever.

JULY FIRST SAW the wagon train coming off a torturous section of trail, fifty miles of uphill country that cut through steep ravines where the slopes had been treacherous and water was nowhere to be found. The guide books were filled with names of rock formations, some that they had passed and some that were coming up: Chimney Rock, Scott's Bluff and Eagle Rock in Nebraska Territory, Register Cliff, Independence Rock, and later, Devil's Gate in Wyoming Territory. These were tributes to the power of nature, but where nature bestowed beauty it also overpowered in a wild, magnificent and breathtaking way show that the emigrants had never before witnessed.

Water was not to be taken for granted. Piles of dead animals lie strewn around in places where the waterholes smelled like bad eggs. Luke found springs with coffee-colored water that smelled worse than anything Mary had ever known. "Alkaline," Leverenz warned. "It will sicken your horses quicker than eating poison. It *is* poison. You'll pay hell trying to keep them back once they catch the smell of water." Animals that bolted and drank died a lingering death. Many of the wagons had to be abandoned because their draft animals died at the springs.

"Look at those pitiful souls," Mary lamented as she struggled alongside Philip, using canes to beat the oxen from bolting to a bad spring. Throughout the wagon train came sounds of cursing and shouting from other drovers trying to keep their animals in line. She watched a trio struggling in the blazing heat with packs dwarfing their slumped shoulders. "They are down to the things they can carry on their backs, poor things."

Philip nodded. He, too, watched the little family stagger along. "They let their animals drink and now they're afoot. Some have made their wagons into carts. Others like them will have only what they can carry. It's going to be hard on them, now."

Mary's attention lingered on an exhausted mother and her three little children. There was no husband in sight. "Oh, Philip, can't we help them?" Tears blurred her vision as she watched the family struggling with their loads. "They aren't going to make it two more miles and we have plenty. Please?"

"Think hard now, Mary. There's hundreds stuck with bad luck on this trail. We can't help them all." He watched her warily. "You plan to toss out the farming implements and stack children in the wagon?"

"Maybe we could just give them a ride for a while, or pack their things so they could walk unencumbered," she suggested, her eyes back on the small group.

"Well, maybe until we get to the hill country, then it's going to be hard enough for the oxen to haul our own load. We've been lucky so far—but part of that luck is from caring for the animals." He motioned to the woman. "Ma'am, we'll be glad to give your children and your things a lift. You too, if you want, leastwise 'til we get to the Independence Rock."

"Oh, thank you, sir." The woman showed signs of tears. "My husband drowned right before our eyes back at the Bessemer Bend. I didn't have much experience with the mules and they bolted on me and drank from that poison spring afore I could get any help. Now we're down to what we can carry, and I don't know if we're even going to make it. Oh, how I wish we had stayed back in Missouri."

Mary looked closer. She had assumed the woman was in her late forties, but close up, she was scarcely thirty. The ages of her children seemed to bear that out. The woman looked worn and tired. She'd lost her sunbonnet and her lips were blistered and swollen. All of them suffered from sunburn.

"Climb aboard, ma'am," she offered quietly, hoping her offer would not reveal the terrible pity she felt. "We'll put your children in the back, and you can ride on the seat. It'll soon be suppertime. I have the remains of a buffalo stew." She gave the woman a hand up, noticing how little she weighed.

After settling the children, the woman slumped in exhaustion. Through closed eyes she murmured, "Missus, I don't know how we can thank you. It's not so much for myself, but to see my babies suffering like this…" Her voice trailed off. After a bit, she began again, "Enoch was a good man, but he had his ways. I wasn't wanting to come on this trip. It seemed like we had good and enough back home. All our folks within hailing distance. But one after another, our folks got the bug for free land in the Oregon Country. Enoch got to chomping at the bit to go, and finally I gave up and started packing. Now look at us—Enoch gone and not even the comfort of seeing him buried. My young'uns footsore and old before their time. All of us stuck out here on this prairie without so much as a mule to carry us. And for what? I ain't no farmer, and I don't expect we'll even make it that far. Maybe we'll be just more of those graves we been seeing along the track." She stared with unseeing eyes from the shock of the past days.

Mary put her arm around the thin woman. "Get some rest. We'll think about what we can do after we've eaten tonight." Reaching behind her, she handed the woman a crumpled scrap of cloth. "Here, this will do to shield your eyes. We'll rig something up for the children tonight. They're asleep."

"Bless you, Missus Rodgers. My name's Letha Clark." Tying the bonnet under her small chin, she leaned back and closed her eyes.

Mary turned to the woman, but she had already fallen asleep. She glanced back at the children, crowded on top of the crates and barrels, looking satisfied in their slumber.

"We still have to cross the mountains." Philip glanced off into the distance where Independence Rock slowly rose to resemble the back of a huge whale. "We'll be camping there tonight with a hundred or more wagons. Maybe we'll find someone to carry these folks. I don't intend to toss those implements out."

He glanced at the plow he had strapped onto the side of the wagon. During long evenings while other men rested and napped, he had jacked up his wagon and taken off the wooden wheels to swell them overnight. In the mornings, he replaced the rims. He'd worked hard so that he wouldn't experience the breakdowns that some of the others had—men who wedged a chunk of cottonwood into their loose rims rather than go to the extra work of doing it right. When the wagon hit a chuckhole, often the wedge would fly out and the rim would roll off.

Leverenz hadn't exaggerated back at the start when he

told them that harness and wheels would be plentiful. Some of the abandoned wagons had decent wheels and they passed harnesses lying in the sun—most still connected to the rotting corpses of animals covered with maggots.

Mary put her apron to her face to stem the stench. "Why don't people pull out of the road when they see their animals staggering? It's as if they want to get that last ten feet from the poor beasts and they don't care how many of us have to ride around them." She looked with disdain at the bloated, reeking mound of horseflesh that partially blocked the track.

"People are getting fractious. I've heard men who have traveled peacefully for a thousand miles quarreling over the right of the road. Just human nature, I guess."

"Why is that?" Mary asked, wondering why the women didn't argue as much as the men.

"Well, back on the prairie, we could travel twenty wagons abreast and no one had to eat someone else's dust. Now, we're forced to go single-file. There's more dust and not enough water to slake our thirsts. It's miserable going, and if a man thinks another traveler is adding to his misery he's pretty quick to let him know. You might not be able to strike out at the land, but you can strike out at the poor coot that's blocking your trail. Even the animals are surly." He pointed to a mule trying to jump its harness.

"It will be nice to travel alongside the river." Mary had heard rumors that the river was coming up again, and she hoped it was true. All day long they were plagued by flies that swarmed around their eyes. The sharp, stinging bites drew blood and nearly drove them mad—man and beast alike. The women pulled their bonnets forward to shield their eyes, but the men weren't so fortunate. Some cut slits in their kerchiefs and wore them like masks. A few did the same for their horses. Traveling alongside a river lessened the fly problem, but it increased the mosquitoes. Still, given a choice, she would take the mosquitoes. And traveling along the river would mean that Luke would be able to ride with the wagons again. She had not seen him in days; she had heard that he was off looking for buffalo.

Independence Day was exciting, with the magnificent Independence Rock looming in the distance like a beacon. Leverenz staggered the camps so that a short day's travel brought them through the last of the sage to the base of the rock. The children were wild with excitement when they heard there would be fireworks; young people hurried through chores so that they could mingle with new acquaintances from the other wagons.

The Rock was covered with travelers' names and dates scratched into the rock and then blackened with soot from the campfires—a record of passage. Each new arrival made a pilgrimage to the base of the rock, in order to carve their name and to search for names of family and friends who had passed earlier. It was encouraging to read names of the living for a change, and not the endless markers of the dead.

She and Philip had not found a solution for the Clarks. The children, especially, suffered from exposure. Mary's medicine basket contained menthol camphor for the chiggers that had bitten the children's legs until they were bloody from constant scratching. Their lips were blistered from the sun and their faces were peeling from sunburn. They walked barefoot over rocks and clumps of grass and their feet were bruised and pitiful. Mary spent the better of the evening doctoring as best she could, but even that wasn't enough. The children ate like they hadn't tasted food for several days, and even Philip had to look away when his pity threatened to humiliate the mother's pride.

As they cleaned up the remains of the supper, Mary remarked, "Letha, a few nights ago we parked alongside the train ahead of us. There was a Mr. Parkman, who has a new-born he's trying to care for, along with his team and the wagon. His wife died in childbirth and he buried her the previous day. One of the folks on our train was giving him goat's milk, and he was appreciative, but he seems in a sorrowful way. Maybe you could assist him with his baby."

"I couldn't travel with a single man. Ain't right."

"Even to save your children and his?"

"Ain't lookin' for a husband. Just buried mine." Letha stared off into the horizon as if she were seeing again the river swallow up her man while she screamed for help.

"Well, I'll introduce you after supper."

They made camp in the shadow of the rock, wagons crowded together in no semblance of order. In Independence, back at the start, everyone had spoken of spending the Fourth at the rock and, by the looks of it, most had managed. Firewood was non-existent, but the Sweetwater River ran nearby and that meant grass for the animals. Joining the women for a thorough soaking, she scrubbed herself and then her dresses—clothing that grew more threadbare with every laundering.

Remarking to no one in particular, she said, "There is not enough water on this earth for me. When I build my house, it will be on a river."

Virginie, scrubbing nearby, agreed. "That's why Pa says we're settling in the Willamette Valley. It's green and wet all year long, with more trees than a man has the need for. And fresh water for the asking."

The women cleaned themselves up while keeping watch for peepers. It was always hard, trying to find privacy with so many men around. Most of them would leave a wide berth when they heard the sounds of women at the river, but there were always those who would hide in the bushes for a peek. To Mary's mind, they were as welcome as rattlesnakes.

Darkness fell and the musicians began tuning guitars, banjos, fiddles, wash boards and a whole array of homemade instruments. Periodically, men fired off their pistols into the night, whooping and hollering with pure joy and the effects of whiskey. Even the women joined in, taking turns firing off their husband's guns. Someone packed gunpowder in the cracks of the big rock and touched it off, creating a sparkling burst of fire for the thrill-starved youngsters.

Whiskey flowed in good measure, ensuring that the celebration was noisy and rowdy. Many of the men had restocked when they passed Fort Laramie several days past. Judging from the availability of spirits on this night, they must have decided that one great celebration was worth the coming drought of the final leg of the journey. Some of the women complained that their provisions money had been spent on the devil's whiskey instead of flour.

Mary enjoyed the luxury of a few dances with Philip. With so many travelers camped at one spot, there were enough musicians that he could be spared, and she was grateful for the chance to quiet some of the wagging tongues. Unfortunately, her plan was ruined when they were interrupted by a tap on Philip's shoulder and she found herself facing a spruced-up Luke Sayer.

"Mind, Philip?

Philip stepped off with a nod of his head and Luke took his position. He kept his gaze fixed on Mary, but neither of them managed a conversation while she followed his lead in a wide swing and puzzled over his unfathomable mood. He took a risk out on the dance floor among strangers. Too many of the men took exception to having their wives and daughters touched by anyone other than a white man. In an inebriated stage they might take issue with what they saw as an insult to their women. She did her best to avoid any conflict. With a wide smile fixed on her face, she attempted to make anyone watching understand that she took no offense. But her tone didn't match her cheery façade.

"Why, Mr. Sayer, I wasn't sure you were still on the wagon train." In spite of her promise not to let him know how his aloofness hurt, she found herself saying what was forefront in her mind.

"Were you looking for me?" Luke studied her with a lazy smile and she felt herself heat from her neck to the top of her head. She met his eyes, meaning to break off with a coy laugh that revealed nothing of her feelings. Instead, she found herself lost in his gaze. She tried to resist, but in that single moment the truth dawned. She would go anywhere with this man—would trust him with her life. It was Lucas that she owed her loyalty to. It was him that she loved.

When the dance was over, Luke returned her to the ring of spectators and disappeared into the darkness. She spent the next hour pressed into endless dances while she watched for him. She wasn't surprised when he didn't return. Suddenly, she was weary of the noise, the press of bodies, and the turmoil inside her. She didn't want to dance, but she didn't want to return to her bed and wonder what might have happened if she had stayed. She headed to the outer ring to watch Letha Clark and her children stealing a bit of joy from the hard luck that plagued them.

When Mary rose the next morning, she went off to find the Parkman wagon. She found Bethellen trying to dress and feed the newborn while her own family's breakfast needed cooking. Mr. Parkman worked with an embarrassed frown as he fed hastily gathered twigs for a smoldering breakfast fire. His mules milled nearby, needing to be harnessed.

"Mr. Parkman, I'll be happy to spell Bethellen so she can attend to her own family.

"I hate to be a burden, but this here baby's all my Belva left me. She gave her all in the doing. I've wracked my brain to figure out how I'm going to be both mother and father on this trip. I thought I was hard-pressed before, but now, I've really got my problems."

Bethellen handed over the baby and a cup of goat's milk, and hurried back to her wagon. Mr. Parkman thanked her, laid the baby in a nest of blankets and set to sorting harness.

"You're welcome to come on over for breakfast. We have plenty. I'll take the baby over to our wagon and finish up the meal. You be sure to come, you hear?" He nodded, apparently grateful for a hot meal. Mary smiled at the surprise he would find there. Rested and bathed, Letha had cleaned up amazingly well; surely Mr. Parkman would be able to recognize a Godsend when he saw one.

Letha had a plentiful pan of fried cornmeal ready. The children were already eating when Philip and Mr. Parkman came walking in together. "Found another guest for the table. Says he's joining us today." Philip cocked an eyebrow at Mary. It was his concern about running out of food rather than lack of hospitality that made him nervous.

At the sound of men's voices Letha looked up, shy at the prospect of meeting more strangers. She was feeding the baby the last of its milk as she cooed to it in a practiced mother's way. Mr. Parkman stared, mesmerized.

Mary hid a smile. "Oh, my poor manners. Letha Clark, this is Mr. Parkman, whose baby you are holding. The poor man lost his wife in the birthing and is at loose ends."

The baby's father shook his head as if to clear himself of confusion. "Right nice of you, ma'am. I sure appreciate the extra hand."

Mary felt her plan quail in the face of Letha's nervous confusion—and his. Letha and the tall man fiddled with their buttons and tasks, unsure what needed to be said next. Clearly, they were not used to social situations. She stepped in. "Missus Clark lost her husband only a few days ago. Her mules ran off and drank the poison water, and now she and her little family are afoot."

Mr. Parkman gave closer inspection to the woman and to the children gathered about her skirts, playing with the baby's hands and feet. "Baby seems to take to you. If you'd not mind tending it today, ma'am, I'd trade supper tonight for you and your little ones."

Letha seemed to search for her answer in the surrounding air, a bright flush in her cheeks. "I'd be honored. She's a beautiful baby, and so contented. It might soothe her to hear a woman's voice."

Soon they were packed up and underway, with Letha perched firmly beside Philip on the wagon. She had confided to Mary that she didn't feel it was proper to be riding alongside an unmarried stranger, even if she was tending his child. The Clark children walked alongside with Mary, who spun a long, involved yarn, embellishing it with every twist she could think of in order to pass the time. Letha took care of the Parkman baby as tenderly as if it was her own; they seemed to share a bond of loss that both understood. Mary watched with amazement at how a little hope had restored Letha's will to live.

On the fourth day, Mary settled herself on the wagon seat and waited for Letha and the baby to join her when she heard voices from the edge of the camp. Mr. Parkman spoke in a low voice. "Would you be agreeable to riding in my wagon today? I could use the company."

Letha Clark answered something that apparently satisfied

the man because she climbed up into the wagon and they rode together for the rest of the day. In the evening, she insisted on cooking Mr. Parkman's meal. She was a light eater, and Mary smiled when she heard him admonish Letha. "You could use a little more fat on those bones." *So it's come to noticing what's on her bones already?* She was glad for the way things were turning out. They might find each other out of shared tragedy, but there was hopefulness in each of them that hadn't been there before. Life was short and unpredictable—they might all drown at the next crossing. Better to take some comfort from each other today.

No more was said about Letha riding in the Rodgers family's wagon.

Chapter Twenty Two

July 11, 1848. Mama, Papa, how I wish you were here. I long to share my happy news.

IN THE DAYS that followed, the dance with Luke replayed itself at odd moments: when she saw a lone rider galloping toward the wagons or when she heard a burst of man's laughter in the dark. An image haunted her, that of him standing aloof in the cluster of mixed-blood and Indian scouts at the edge of the circle. He had danced only once, with her, and some of the men had scowled at her choice of partners. She had accused him of being a womanizer, when the truth seemed to indicate that women shunned him.

During the day's trek she walked alone, hoping for sight of him while she chastised herself for having added to his poor opinion of women. She made sure that she was alone at night, easily available should he choose to approach. But he did not.

One afternoon she walked a distance from the train, alone with her thoughts. As the day's light waned, the train began to circle into camp position. From across the valley floor, a lone figure galloped toward them. It was Luke, his shoulder-length hair unfettered under a wide-brimmed black hat while the setting sun caught his high cheekbones and made his skin shine like warm honey. For long minutes, she watched him circling toward the wagonmaster until he altered his direction and headed toward her. The horse slid to a halt and Luke sat astride, his stirrups nearly touching Mary. She felt herself drawn into his brooding eyes, sensed the hunger behind his silence as if he were waiting for something to be said between them.

"I never meant…"

"I know."

"Lucas, we need to talk." Suddenly, nothing mattered but that they have some time alone.

He nodded. From nearby, a shout interrupted and he glanced at the approaching rider. "Tonight. At the river."

After the dinner dishes were finished, she waited at a stand of willows. Her entire life seemed to hedge on the next few minutes. Suddenly he was there, bending to miss a limb. His face nearly touched hers and she felt a shiver of anticipation, but he straightened, oblivious to his effect, and guided her downstream to a spot where they could be alone.

"This looks like paradise." She found herself cottonmouthed.

"It is." He stood beside her and searched the banks until he was satisfied that they were alone. Finally, he turned. "You all right with this?"

She spoke in a trembling voice. "Oh, Lucas! Better than *all right*. But it's time I told you about Philip and me." Slowly, she revealed the arrangement, her voice wavering while she struggled, not wanting to defend or soften her words with excuses. "So you see, Philip was not to blame for any of this. It was only in promising that I would tell no one, ever, that I convinced him to take me." Luke didn't seem shocked, so she plunged on; "There hasn't been a day I haven't longed to tell you the truth, but I couldn't do that without betraying Philip."

Luke's eyes narrowed. "Why tonight? Why at all?"

"You were so distant. As the days went by and you stayed away, I thought I had lost you." She made no effort to wipe the tears rolling down her cheeks. "I decided I would say nothing because I could not bear to have you without your complete faith in me."

Of all the things she might have expected, she found him smiling. "I could say the same. Happens I've known about your deception since that husband of yours took an arrow in the attack."

"You knew? How?"

"He told me."

"He wouldn't do that! He promised. Made *me* promise."

"Said he owed me that favor."

"All this time, you knew?" Mary's voice grew louder.

"Yes, ma'am."

"When you were flirting with those other girls, and ignoring me, and not coming by to see us—you knew?" Mary's words were punctuated by a series of jabs to his chest.

Flinching every time she chucked him with her balled-up fist, Luke tried to keep his voice low. "Wait just a minute. What'd I do wrong? I was just trying to protect your honor. Everyone seemed determined to keep me from the pretty little bride."

"Without telling me? It was so cruel—you could have told me and let me make my own choice. I was miserable." Even as she accused him, she began to understand his reasons. He could be saying the exact things to her. She studied her folded hands in silence. She was not sure where to look. She felt so young, so stupid and selfish.

"I wanted the same from you. I wanted you to trust me."

She whispered, "Lucas, I was so jealous."

"I claimed my woman the night I brought her back from the Ute village. And it was a good thing—because, as I recall, she wasn't exactly dressed for company."

"That's not true and you know it, Lucas Sayer. I was decent, and you better remember that when you tell the tale to our children."

"Are you asking me to marry you, Mary Rodgers?"

She stamped her feet and tried not to blush. "I thought you and Ida O'Brian were having a tryst out in the meadow. Then you asked me to fib to her pa!" Her eyes were black with the memory.

"Did you?" Luke's eyes held an inscrutable expression.

"Did I what?"

"Did you tell him she was with you?"

"Of course I did. He came high-tailing and I made up some cock-and-bull story about braiding her hair and having girl talk. Next thing I knew, she was being married off to some fellow I didn't even know she was interested in." Mary was not ready to forgive him on this score. "You were wearing your underwear and she was still wet, just like when you took me to the waterhole."

Luke chuckled. "Mary, her pa came into my camp after I was in bed—alone. He was going gunning for Tyler. I figured to head them back before he could find them. I sent Tyler back on the run and I came in a little later with Ida."

"But you were embracing her."

"Holding her up before she collapsed. She was trembling, scared out of her mind, and you were the only one I could trust."

"Then why didn't you come by later and explain?" Then

she remembered—he had tried. And she had run him off.

"And what about you, Mary Rodgers? Why didn't you explain that you weren't married? It nearly killed me every time I came calling, thinking that you and he were—"

"You weren't just doing your job?"

"You really need an answer?"

Mary had one last issue to settle. "Lucas, remember what you said about starting a stud farm when you got to Oregon?"

"Reckon."

"Your old stallion hasn't given my filly a minute's peace. And now he's managed to do his worst and she's going to have a foal. What have you got to say about that?" Her look of disgust didn't quite ring true.

Luke laughed. "Now, we're partners. You'll have to marry me."

"Oh, you bully! And what about all your warnings about women not getting…in a family way. You were so rude that I wanted to die."

"We can't have that." He pressed his mouth against hers. When he finally broke away, the sound of his winded breathing broke the silence. He faced the river in an effort to gain control of his thoughts and body; like a man thirsting, he'd gotten a drink of pure, sweet water, and he could easily drink himself to death.

"I have something keeps me awake at night, worrying." He held up his hand to silence her when she started to interrupt. "It isn't right, you sleeping next to Philip, even if you are related."

"People would think it odd if we didn't sleep close. We hang a blanket between us. I don't even see him."

"Can't you sleep in the wagon?"

"You know it's too full. Besides, what will the neighbors think?"

"They'll think you're sleeping there to avoid the snakes. If you want, I'll catch one and toss it near your bed. That'll give you reason enough. Or have Philip complain that you snore."

"Never! Who says I snore? Back home, a gentleman would never reveal such a thing about his girl."

"Are you my girl?" His eyes searched hers.

"Philip might have an objection." she feigned indifference while she casually brushed her skirts to eliminate any twigs or other signs of their dalliance.

A scowl replaced his hopefulness. "Philip change his mind about you keeping company with a 'breed'?" he growled.

"Lucas Sayer, stop it." Fury flashed from her eyes. "Don't you ever say that again. Ever."

A weight he had carried across a continent and halfway home again disappeared in the light of her anger. A slow, easy peace filled him as he led her back though the darkened meadow. She stumbled and his hold tightened. "I'm glad Philip is a peaceable man. Anybody else would take a shotgun to me, courting his wife. Think I could win against him?"

It took a second before she realized that he was joking. "Now, you stop it. You men are terrible. I have never heard so much bickering and quarreling as in the past month. You all argue about who will drive in front, whose ox kicked whose, whose drink first at the water hole, who gets the venison haunch and who gets the ribs. If there is anything to fight over, you men will find it."

"You're right about that, Mary. The tension is rising and

so are the accidents. We've had three deaths in as many days; losses that weigh on the mothers maybe more than the fathers."

"Mothers feel responsible for their children," Mary said. "I would be the same. But you haven't promised yet. Do you agree not to fight Philip over my honor?"

Luke nodded. "I like Philip. Fact is—I was coming to see him all those nights till I noticed you trying to get my attention."

"That's not true and you know it."

"Then prove it."

"Luke, we're too close for another kiss. Someone will see." She made the offer hesitantly. "If you want a lock of my hair, you can have one. Some of the other girls have given theirs to their fellows."

"Truly?"

For a grown man, he seemed shy about receiving a present. The joy in his eyes made her wish she had a real gift for him. "Go ahead. It's only hair. It'll grow back."

She waited while he pulled his skinning knife from its sheath and lobbed off a curl from the underside where it wouldn't show, and slowly replaced the knife. "I will add this to my medicine bag. It will be big medicine." A few minutes later, they arrived at a small herd of cattle browsing on the sage prairie. He released his hold and whispered, "Mary, I haven't the willpower left to say goodnight one more time. You walk in alone and I'll follow in a bit."

Luke returned to find Leverenz waiting beside the fire, a coffee cup in his hand and the remains of a whiskey bottle nearby. Luke glanced at his friend, surprised to see him drinking alone in the dark.

"John—thought you'd be at the celebration."

"Nah. Ran into the mail courier today on his way back east. Had a letter from Nancy in his pouch." He paused to take a sip from his mug.

"Anything wrong?" Luke added a drop of whiskey to his own coffee and settled onto the ground beside a wagon wheel.

"Depends on your viewpoint, I suppose. Nancy and the farm are fine. She had some local news might interest you."

Luke sipped and settled for what was coming. He didn't have to wait long.

"Nancy writes that Clara Halsey—that gal was smitten with you on the last train? Well, she's got herself a new baby. Her father has run her off. Seems the baby has some Indian blood in it. Clara's claiming it's yours."

"What the hell!" Luke jerked to his feet. "Where's that letter?" Leverenz obligingly unfolded it from its resting place in his breast pocket and waited while Luke searched through the lines, pausing only when he came to the part that concerned him. "She's named him Ramer."

"Your father's name. Course, she can't use your surname. Uses her maiden name for a bastard. Ramer Lucas Halsey. That's what she named it." In the silence, Leverenz took a long draw from his mug.

Luke stared from the letter to the fire while rage kindled inside him. "Son of a gun." He tried to recall what Clara Halsey looked like, and found the memory faint. He did remember telling her his father's name.

He recalled the sound of her father's anger when he found them together—not doing anything they shouldn't—making small talk while he rubbed down one of his mares. The rest came later, when Clara was seeking revenge for the tongue-lashing she had received from her father. Luke recalled the night she sought him out in the row of trees where he was enjoying a late night smoke. But it wasn't tobacco she'd had on her mind.

He had been surprised that she would want to see him again, after her father had dragged her home like a twelve-fingered shoplifter. "Your pa going to object?" he'd asked. He'd never been with a white woman that he hadn't paid for. This one was white, but he wasn't sure she was a woman yet until he watched her lift her skirts to reveal smooth, satiny legs from ankle to thigh. When she leaned toward him and began unfastening her bodice, button by agonizing button, any remaining doubt disappeared.

Later, when he lay next to her in the shadow of the river willows, he recalled her last words. "I'm never going back to my father. I'm going to dance in the moonlight without a stitch of anything on, and anyone who wants to watch me can, because I won't ever have my pa telling me what I can and can't do. I'm going to stay with you."

With her declaration, the scorch of the fire that Clara had built hit him with the force of a firestorm. "Clara, I've got a job to do and you're—" He tried to think of a way to explain that she was young, frivolous and the furthest thing from his future that he had ever envisioned. "You better get back to your father. I'll look you up in Oregon City when the trip's over."

"We'll be perfect together, Luke. Wait and see."

He'd seen clearly enough when he ran into her and a greenhorn farm boy lying in the grass a few days later. What disturbed him most was the look in her face—she was pretty pleased with herself that she'd been caught.

The words of the letter rang in his ears. Leverenz knew why he had done it; the answer was in his eyes. She was the first woman to come to him without the stain of his heritage lying between them like blood on a bridal sheet. The thing was too sweet to let go of. He'd known better, but just once in his life, he figured, he wanted to know how it could be between a man and a woman without having it be between a woman and an Indian. Now, he knew.

"Where'd she take the baby?"

"Nancy says she's working in a bordello in Oregon City."

Luke winced. "Hell." The fire crackled with the image of a baby lying in its mother's workroom. It didn't matter that a lot of babies grew up in the same place; Luke Sayer's would not. "Hell," he repeated.

Chapter Twenty Three

July 16, 1848. A most remarkable memory of this journey has been meeting the native women. It would seem that we share more in common than our differences.

AFTER THE CAMPOUT at Independence Rock, life on the trail took a subtle turn. Although the wagon train had agreed to keep together for mutual support, except for the one incidence with the renegades, there had been no further reason to fear the Indians. Indeed, the emigrants found the tribes to be unfailingly helpful and curious, as long as the animals were secured by an armed guard.

Each night, even before the travelers settled into camp and unhitched the animals, Indian women would appear seemingly out of thin air, carrying goods to barter. Some of the vegetables were familiar, some strange, but greatly appreciated by travelers trying to stretch their meager supplies as the journey neared its halfway point.

Some of the Indian traders brought plump pheasants and geese that hung limp in their brilliant plumage. Others brought squash, corn, salmon, ground acorns leached to remove the poison and bitterness, and leather goods and knives made from obsidian, with handles of stag antler, encased in buckskin sheathes. The natives seemed eager to trade for the red flannel shirts, tools, sugar or whatever met their fancy. Mary was grateful that Philip had brought extra shirts for trading, as the guidebooks had advised.

The Indian women admired the hair combs that Mary and the other women wore, even the bright pins that decorated their bodices. Often, however, the object that an Indian demanded was something the men didn't want to part with, so the bartering was spirited. The absence of a common language didn't seem to matter, but Luke intervened if things became a little testy. More than once he helped to avert a calamity, but overall, the Indians were friendly. The tribes seemed fascinated by the fair-skinned, blonde children. The Indian women, especially, liked to stroke the soft blonde curls, so different from their own. It became a common fear among the white women that their children might be stolen. Each evening, the harried mothers would press their children into the back of the wagons whenever the Indians appeared so that they had one less thing to worry about.

Mary spent an evening showing a few Indian women how to make bread with fine wheat flour from her supply. They were fascinated with the bread's taste and texture. While she mixed up a batch of biscuits, the women dipped into the bowl and licked their fingers, cooing and smacking their lips while she placed small, light balls into her Dutch oven. Squatting on their haunches, they indicated they were willing to stay for as long as it took to cook, and they did. She was surprised at how well they could communicate. They exclaimed over her white sugar, and tittered at her bloomers when she swatted at a spark that flew from the fire. She understood their guttural sounds and long faces when they showed scorn for a vile, obnoxious drover in the wagon train. Obviously they shared her opinion of his profanity.

When the dough was cooked, she removed the lid from

the circle of coals to a chorus of ooh's and ah's. The biscuits had risen to over twice their original size. To a people used to flat bread, this fluffy, leavened bread seemed a feat of magic. When they left that night with biscuits in their baskets, the women patted her on her hand, giving her as heartfelt a compliment as she had ever received.

Letha Clark found a stash of knitting yarn left behind by the late Mrs. Parkman and started to knit a hooded sweater for the baby. One of the Indian women watched, clearly intrigued by the speed at which the needles flew, and the pattern of the stitches. After several minutes, the woman broke out of her trance-like concentration. Rummaging among her things, she pulled out a beaded bag. Letha put down her handiwork to admire it. None of the emigrants had ever seen anything like it. A delicate buckskin with fringe at the bottom, it was encrusted with shell beading of a most intricate nature, spiraling around from a point in the center.

"Where do you suppose she got the shells?" Letha asked Mary.

"Maybe they traded with the coast Indians, or even the trappers. Lucas says there are old lakes nearby with fish bones marked in the stones." She answered the question, not sure she knew the answer. "I'll ask him when he comes back."

That night, Mary cooked a butternut squash in the coals, the steam bringing a tangy, buttery scent that made her mouth water. "I traded that extra wooden spoon for it, Philip. I'm glad I brought it along." She still had a sizable number of trading items and figured she got the best of the trades she made. They cut the squash in half and dug into the pulp like children in a watermelon patch. She kept an eye out for Luke so she could share her treasure, but he didn't appear.

Philip ate hurriedly, anxious to get back to his animals.

"Some of these folks were in such a gol-darn hurry to set off, they didn't attend to the little things such as shoeing their oxen. Now they're walking on bare pads. A heavy animal like that gets footsore. Some of the men are resorting to greasing buffalo hide onto the pads, anything to cushion the granite rock. Even the sandstone takes its toll. Some of the women are going to have to throw off more of their belongings as we start to climb."

"How can you tell?" Mary hadn't noticed the terrain rising, only the vastness of the Wyoming prairie.

"Down the road a spell we're coming to a turnoff. There's three ways to go. Those short on supplies will have to go on to Fort Bridger. Some, whose animals are in good shape and want to chance it, will take the road to the Sublette Cutoff. Others will follow the main trail, which is longer, but it follows a better water source."

"Which way will we go?" Mary was more concerned with which way Luke would travel. If they got separated now, their chances of meeting up again were slim. There were message trees and rocks where travelers left notes for each other, but she didn't want to rely on a scratched message.

"Haven't decided. I figure we'll see how the animals are holding up by then, and what the temperature is. The men will discuss the situation at the campfire tonight."

• ♥ •

The trail began a slow, winding ribbon toward the South Pass. Everyone over the age of ten walked because the animals needed all their strength to drag the load over the rocks and slopes. The wagons rolled slowly along the Sweetwater River with its plentiful supply of water, fish and fowl. Mary and Philip were amazed at Devil's Gate, where the Sweetwater had carved a narrow gorge through a ridge of solid granite, leaving a spectacular chasm. At the base, Leverenz halted the wagon train while everyone hiked to the top. The chasm was too narrow for the wagons to negotiate, so they had to detour by ridging a crest nearly a half-mile to the south.

Luke seemed preoccupied with his duties. One afternoon, he rode near and she thought she saw a look cross his face, as though he wasn't pleased when he recognized her wearing Bethellen's pokebonnet instead of her own. He glanced around and dismounted, as though checking his horse's hooves was the purpose of tarrying. She stood waiting, and when he stood, he seemed resigned to her company. Surely, she was wrong in her observation; the sun had made her overly sensitive.

"Isn't it strange, Lucas," Mary remarked while they walked side-by-side. "I know that these great big rocks are fixed in the ground and aren't going anywhere, but we've been living in these wagons so long that by now it's the only home I know. I watch the rocks and think they are rolling by—and my wagon is the one standing still."

"I know what you mean. I've seen these sights my whole life, but they never fail to stir me." Luke stood gazing across the land while he eased the stiffness in his shoulders. He didn't even glance at her. It was as if the only thing on his mind was appreciating the patches of buffalo grass, bright patches of yellow sage, rock outcroppings and the river below. "I started coming this way when I was a youngster with my father. This vastness is my people's blood."

"It's not natural for us farm people. Sometimes, I could choke on the loneliness out here. Sazie says she feels like a bug on a tabletop. Too exposed."

"The Eastern people will claim this land. There will be settlements all along the trail, with army outposts, trading posts and farms to support them. White men's towns will hold the folks who make a living off the emigrants."

"You really believe that?" Bethellen had approached and joined them.

He tipped his hat. "Afternoon, ma'am. The first time I rode across the big prairie with my father, there was no Oregon Country. Everything beyond the Missouri was Indian land. Now, people come from the East and they want to own this land. What will become of the native people who live there now? These are people of my people." They rode in silence, contemplating what civilization might mean. "There's talk in the East about running a telegraph line through, like the ones they're starting to put up in Boston and New York. If that happens, then Oregon will be just a tap away."

Mary thought about what Luke had said. His predictions seemed too grand, but the people traveling to Oregon were nothing if not determined. "How do you figure into this future?" she asked.

Lucas hesitated. "I'll do what I must. But how do you see you and Philip?"

She felt frivolous and free. "Oh, I'd take a simple mansion on the banks of the Willamette River, with a different colored mare to ride every day of the week. Perhaps an upstairs maid and someone to grow me peaches."

"Is that all? I suppose my wife will expect a teepee."

She hesitated. He was in a strange mood today. As if he were deliberately taunting her with his Indian heritage. She continued as though she hadn't heard him. "A sprung carriage so I'll never have to bump over a hard road. Oh, and a shade cover for the weather."

"If you were a proper squaw, you'd make yourself a travois."

"A dress for breakfast and another for supper, every day of the week." She was warming to the game.

"I'll hunt fat deer, and my wife will scrape their hides."

"And a featherbed to sleep in, and five children to climb into my bed every morning."

Luke watched her with hunger in his eyes. "An Indian does not fill his teepee with babies. One must be reared before the next is born."

Bethellen laughed, flustered. "Mr. Sayer, you are in a singular mood today. I don't often think of you as Indian. But it seems your thoughts linger in that direction. I would think you would make a fine husband and father."

Luke gave a hollow chuckle while he studied Mary with a strangeness that left her confused—and a little frightened. It seemed to her that he had been preoccupied since the night at Independence Rock. Maybe he had other things on his mind. Maybe she was oversensitive. His next words seemed to dispel her foreboding. "I have no thoughts but to get you all to Oregon. Most days, it's not water I seek, but the end of the trail."

Bethellen left them to attend to one of her sons. In the silence, Mary realized that this day would be a memory. She had too few stolen moments with him and she treasured every one. "Lucas, when the day arrives that we can speak freely, I hope to understand the Indian that rages inside you, like a restless cat. That will be my greatest wish." Her smile faded when Luke returned to his horse and sprang into his saddle.

He looked down at her with that strange, sad smile that he wore of late. "Be careful what you wish for. You could do better than me."

"Better, Lucas? I don't think the man exists that is better than you."

He sounded almost bitter. "Maybe you better take your time and look around. We have a few weeks left before we get to Oregon City."

His expression left Mary chilled. "I best get back to the wagon. It looks as though we are stopping for the noon meal and I haven't even gathered fire chips." Already tired drovers were dismounting and stretching their legs, eager for a hot meal.

"I may end up disappointing you, Mary."

Mary started in the direction of the wagons, calling over her shoulder, "It's not disappointment I'm feeling, Lucas. It's impatience!" She urged her horse into a quick trot.

Luke watched her ride off, a sense of foreboding in his gut.

• ♥ •

In the following days the emigrants saw Split Rock, a huge monument resembling Devil's Gate, but with the split up at the top where no water had ever run. The sensory-starved travelers, men and women alike, spent hours discussing the monument as they made their way slowly toward it. Natural phenomenon seemed bigger and more spectacular than back home.

One scorching afternoon, Luke rode into camp with a bundle under his arm. "Mary, have you any cold coffee you could spare? I'm mighty thirsty this afternoon, and it would sure hit the spot." He waited while she hopped from the wagon to do his bidding.

"You're in luck, Lucas. I do. It's warm, as usual, but there's nothing I can do about that. Tepid is the best I can offer." Holding a clean tin cup, she brought a covered coffee pot from its hook on the back of the wagon.

"Here, this might make it better." Luke nonchalantly pulled the cloth away to expose the surprise that he held. His hands were half-frozen and dripping with melt from a piece of ice the size of a ham.

Mary's hands flew to her mouth. "Oh, Lucas, where did you find it? You are a wonder. I can't believe it. Is there more?" Laughing and waving the ice for the others to see, she acted like a child at Christmas while he stood apace and savored the moment. "Ice in the middle of a high-plains desert? Luke, how did you manage?"

"There's a place we're coming up on, called Ice Slough. The ice is just under the water, free for the taking." While he explained, the children managed to reduce the ice block to a single dripping sliver in Mary's hand. "There's plenty for everyone up ahead. We'll camp there for tonight and let everyone cool off."

He carried his report to Leverenz, pleased for the excitement he had created, for the children, especially. They suffered enough.

That night the group made camp at the Slough. Leverenz explained that the ice was a remnant of the river that winter-froze in the peat moss along the Sweetwater River. It remained frozen through mid-August and early arrivals like his wagon train could have their fill until it was used up. The evening entertainment was dedicated to stomping among the peat moss with bare feet and a hammer, chipping off blocks of ice while others thought up ways to use it. Some, whose cows still gave milk, made ice pops while others packed it into wooden boxes. A few hardy souls leaped into the slurry, claiming that it cooled their blood. Others set wedges under their hats and let the melt-off run down their necks. Altogether the mood was one of intoxication, a Saturday night tippler without the whiskey—although there was some of that, too, served up in frosty coffee cups throughout the camp. Even Philip imbibed.

The next morning, the emigrants set out on a track that brought them to South Pass. Most had read about it in their guidebooks, but they didn't recognize it when they arrived, so gradual was the climb. It had been the goal of every traveler to reach this spot where the waters would eventually drain into the Atlantic Ocean from whence they had come. A hard day's walk across the pass brought them to the other side of the Continental Divide where the water drained off into the Pacific. The peaks were taller than anything they had ever seen, with grass of verdant green with freckles of wildflowers, even in July.

Despite the fuss made in the guidebooks Philip had brought, and the press clippings he had tucked in, the pass was nothing more than a thirty-mile wide plain that sloped ever so slightly to the east on one side and to the west on the other. In the morning, the emigrants had their celebratory cup of water on the east then pushed their wagons for twelve hours, stopping only after they rolled down the western slope to Pacific Springs. Nothing really changed in one day, but the travelers felt they were now in the West and that was a mighty happy thing to them all. The guidebooks showed that they were nine hundred and twenty-five miles from Independence. They were halfway home.

In the distance, Mary could see the snowy peaks of the Wind River Mountains standing sentry to the north. She spent long minutes gazing at the reminder of things to come. "Philip, does the air feel different to you?" She sniffed, thinking she could sense a change. Certainly the humidity was gone. She could stand the heat, but the combination of humidity and dust had given them no relief.

"There's more of a chill in the air, but I'd say it's the same air we breathed yesterday," he teased, setting his plate down and rising to stretch.

"I'll welcome the chill air. Even cold will be better than this infernal desert."

"Be careful what you wish for—we'll get our share of cold soon enough. You'll be wanting some of that desert heat in due time, I'll wager."

The last rays of the sun disappeared over the mountains and the night air turned brisk, but even as she wrapped herself in her shawl she was not convinced that she would miss the heat. Later, as she sat beside the crackling fire listening to the far-off howls of wolves or coyotes, her heart was glad for the feel of the West. They were on their way now and nothing would hold them back.

Luke was stymied by the openness of the plain that gave him no chance to even speak to Mary. He could do little more than glance across the darkness to watch her under the light of her campfire. It seemed that she never sat down; always cooking or doing something for the neighbors or their children, or mending or patching up someone who got themselves hurt. He tried to recall Clara's face, her laugh, her body—anything to diffuse the attraction Mary held—but nothing seemed to help.

The hour after supper was the hardest. Tonight, his wagon was positioned within sight of Mary and Philip's. Sitting at his camp, watching her, he forgot time and space in his musing until he felt the pain. "Ouch," he yelped. Pulling free from the coffee pot, he jumped back and caused the pot to spill at his feet.

"Woolgathering there, Sayer?" Leverenz followed the direction of his friend's gaze and thought the younger man deserved his burn. Frowning, he tapped his cold pipe against a rock and stalked off into the dark, looking for better company than a lovesick fool with a burned thumb.

The oldest of the Tate boys heard Luke's yelp and dropped the horseshoe he was playing with. "I'll quick fetch Missus Rodgers and her medicine box. I'll tell her you've been burned bad. Don't worry, sir, I'll do it."

Luke started to protest, but instead, he pulled a penny from his pocket and handed it to the boy. The boy stared hard at the shiny coin and took off as though his hero's life depended on him.

He heard the boy calling across the circle; "Hurry, Missus Rodgers. Luke's been hurt bad. Needs you."

"What is it? An arrow? Snakebite? Is it cholera?"

"He just needs you to hurry."

Mary grabbed her box of salves and wrappings and hurried around the outside of the wagon train. When she drew closer to his campsite she braced herself for whatever she would find, but she could see no cause for concern; but neither did she find a patient. She turned the corner and shooed Nathan Tate away while she searched again.

In the flickering of his fire, she saw a shadow and twirled to find Luke leaning against his cook wagon, calmly puffing on his cheroot and smiling like a brown leghorn cock that had swallowed a cricket.

"You scared me to death." Mary studied him for any sign of harm and found none. As the truth dawned, she dropped the medicine box on the wagon tailgate and planted angry fists on her hips while she hoped the devil would take him once and for all. "You better have a good explanation, Lucas Sayer!"

"Whoa, there, Mrs. Rodgers. I had nothing to do with this. The lad fetched you. But come to think of it, when I consider how you manage to hover over everyone but me, my thumb started throbbing from the injustice of it all. Since you're here, maybe you could tend it for me." He looked irresistible.

"You big prevaricator. You're no more injured than I am. Shame on you." She didn't care that her words came out the hiss of a cat. On the outside of the wagon they were well hidden in the darkness even though people were moving about inside the ring, intent on their own business.

"I'd heal faster with a kiss." The words came without bidding, but he wasn't sorry.

Mary lost her bid to keep a straight face. Her laughter was lost in the noisy confusion of the camp. It seemed that she laughed at his ridiculous ploy, her fright and the sheer deliciousness of being together until it was all she could do to keep her medicine box upright. Drying her eyes with a corner of her apron, she gasped. "Lucas Sayer, I ought to shoot you. Then you could have all the tending you wanted. This was a rotten trick."

His eyes were hungry as he lowered his voice to a whisper. "You'd be doing me a favor. I'll loan you my gun. But women don't have the gall to kill men outright. They have other ways."

She studied him, her laughter caught in her throat. "Lucas, what's wrong? Is it something I've done? Said? If so—"

He withdrew slightly and his voice turned serious. "It's neither. Just something that's wearing on me. Nothing to concern yourself about."

"Well, that's a relief. From the past few days, I thought maybe you had changed your mind about us."

He ran his thumb across the frayed, dusty lace on her cuff and she moved to cover his hand with her own. He allowed it to rest there for a moment while he promised himself that he would resist. "Maybe I have. Maybe I've been keeping company with Philip's little cousin as a favor to him."

She tried to hide her surprise. "In that case, I might just marry some scrubby-faced drover that brings to bed the smell of a skunk and spits tobacco juice from the side of his teeth. That'll show you."

"He'd have you smoking a pipe in no time. I always admired a woman who could handle a pipe. Suits your manner, now that I think of it." He offered her a draw of his cigar, "Care for a puff?" His voice barely audible, he stepped closer.

"Lucas Sayer, you wouldn't know a lady from a muleskinner, and that's a fact. I don't know what to do with you."

"I do." Frustration festered into anger. Looking around, Luke pulled her to him for a hungry kiss. If the Halsey girl was going to claim her due, he'd have this moment with Mary. He kissed her again, lighter this time, knowing they were pressing fate. When it seemed that luck wouldn't hold out forever, he broke off. "You better go." He folded her into his arms and brought his mouth down again.

A nearby footstep tore them apart. Swiftly, Mary grabbed her basket and turned toward the light. "Goodnight, Mr. Sayer. I hope that balm will help your injury." Her voice shook with unshed tears.

Luke's chuckle felt strained, but he wasn't sure who was listening. "Just what the doctor ordered. Yours is a healing touch, Missus Rodgers. Truly."

Mary fled toward the wagon.

Luke sucked in a lungful of air and expelled it in a rush. He turned away from the camp and strode out into the prairie, to wander among the sleeping livestock. He felt himself being swallowed by a fear that stalked him whenever he thought of his future. He'd rather face hostile tribes and snow packed mountains than a five foot tall girl named Clara with expectations for the future. In the darkness, his thumb throbbed.

Chapter Twenty Four

July 21, 1848. No matter how prepared we think ourselves for our next travail, we find ourselves taxed to the limits of our endurance. Today, it would seem a Divine mercy to join Mother and Lillian and be at peace.

SLEEP CAME EASIER some nights than others. Sometimes they camped on rocky ground. Other times, prairie storms brought wind so terrifying that it took the canvas wagon tops and blew them over acres. Rain fell in sheets that folded the earth into a sheet of blackness so suffocating that the babies' cries did not carry beyond their cribs. Some nights the thunder and lightning vibrated the earth so near that death seemed certain. On those nights, no one slept. Sometimes, the buffalo herds moved in such earth-shaking numbers that the ground rumbled and fires had to be stoked to show the outline of the wagon train against the darkness.

This night had been a long one for Mary. In the morning she rose, stiff and red-eyed from crying. She bent and touched her toes to ease her muscles. The camp was buzzing with early reports that Leverenz had called for a fifteen mile pace today because somewhere ahead was a brutal uphill climb that would slow their progress.

At breakfast, Philip remarked, "Was over to the Stoberson wagon last night. Seems they're down on supplies. Those boys eat everything in sight. They plan on joining the group looping south, later on today. They'll be restocking at Fort Bridger and maybe catch a glimpse of Big Jim Bridger himself, if the old trapper happens to be around. It'll be seven days out of their way. Most likely we won't see them until they reach Oregon City."

Mary's coffee cup dipped. "Oh, Philip, not the Stobersons. Can't we go with them?" Her tears fell inexplicably; fortunately, Philip assumed he knew the cause.

"They may be taking the Applegate Trail, but don't worry, you'll see them again. They wouldn't be taking the loop if they didn't have to. I'll wager prices'll be sky high down there, but they don't want to hit the mountains low on supplies. This will be their last chance." The bad news continued; "I was talking with Luke. The grass and game is giving out in places and the Indians hereabouts would rather fight than trade. Since we can't count on bartering, folks like the Stobersons have no choice but Ft. Bridger."

"What are we going to do?" Mary wouldn't complain. She had to trust Philip.

"Luke was telling us about the Sublette Cutoff. It's fifty miles across with no water to be had. Heat'll be fierce, once we're off this pass. We'll have to run dry for three days across the desert until we get to Bear River. We'll be traveling all night, resting in the heat of the day then starting out again in the evening, but it'll save us a whole week of travel. Think you're up to it?"

"Which way is Luke going?" Of course she would make it, but Buttercup was carrying a foal.

"Luke would follow you into a prairie fire. He was worried that I would go around to Fort Bridger and take you with me." Philip peered over the rim of his coffee cup while Mary lifted the lid on the Dutch oven. "If the situation were different he'd be over here courting you in front of the whole train. Don't let this situation cheat you any more than it must."

"He's acting like we're strangers," she admitted, meeting his gaze for the first time.

"He promised to stay away and he's kept his word. But it's a shame you can't get two minutes privacy. I know how I'd feel if it were Laurel."

Mary remembered Ida O'Brian and her young man, now happily married, sharing a wagon and awaiting the birth of their child. "Maybe when we get out of these flatlands we can find somewhere to talk."

"Be sure that's all you do, Mary. Those are deep feelings he has for you."

Humiliation flared in her voice. "Philip Rodgers, whatever you're suggesting, keep it to yourself. I don't need your advice." She took hold of the pot and started for the creek.

Midday saw the trail splitting in different directions; those who chose the shortcut went straight and the others forked south to Fort Bridger. "Bye girls, good luck," Mary called out a last time. Although she had said her farewells earlier in the day, she watched the Stobersons until they disappeared around a bend. "You keep safe. Hear me?" she whispered. Turning, she started walking behind Philip's wagon toward Big Sandy Creek.

That night she prepared for the tough days ahead with practical tasks to keep her mind occupied. She filled every barrel and crock. She helped Philip cut grass from the basin and lay it into the wagon so the oxen would have feed during the three-day travel across barren ground. One enterprising man packed grass into his boots and then filled them with water to keep his feet cool on the coming sand.

Philip spent the evening making sure that the two iron plates he had shod each oxen with were in good shape. He checked the six tiny nails and replaced those that showed signs of wear. Then he laid down near Mary to try to rest.

By midnight, they were on the trail again, hoping to make as much headway as possible while the oxen were fresh and watered. All night they traveled with only the moon to guide them. At five in the morning, when the sunrise peeked over the eastern horizon, they took a twenty-minute break for breakfast—coffee and dry bread with bacon—before they continued.

Leverenz had explained that their fastest travel would occur in the first day, but the oxen set a pace of only two miles an hour, a speed that frustrated Mary, especially when the mules outpaced them from the first hour. By mid-morning the heat was fierce. Leverenz called for the drovers to halt in irregular groups, using their wagons for shade while they waited for evening. The day was strangely quiet while people conserved their energy.

Mary endured the burning sand by putting extra leather in her boots, grateful that she still had a spare pair in her trunk. She walked with measured steps and tried to lend encouragement to the oxen. Philip walked alongside, flicking his cane. He had reminded her so many times that the team might halt in the middle of the trail. In this heat, stopping would mean certain death.

They drank sparingly, rationing cold coffee for themselves and saving the tepid barrels for the animals. By the second day, man and beast alike suffered with tongues swollen from dehydration. Buttercup staggered along without need of a lead rope. Out of consideration for the foal she carried, Philip didn't require the filly to help pull the wagon and Mary was grateful. She tried recalling the day at Ice Slough, but nothing helped quench her thirst. Reality was heat waves and burning sand.

She dozed fitfully during the mid-day stops and kept watch for Luke, but he didn't ride by to check on her. The oxen grew footsore. Back on the trail they had learned to lie down at each rest break, to rest their hooves and legs, but now the burning sand forced them to stand, night and day, and they suffered horribly for it. Despite the extra leather she had laid over the soles of her shoes, Mary hobbled along with bleeding blisters. Those who had failed to heed the advice of the guide books to bring three or four pairs of sturdy boots, or those who had already worn out their last pair, were reduced to walking barefoot with burlap or canvas tied about their feet like moccasins. She wondered about the man with the wet grass in his boots.

On the second and third days, they rolled past skeletons and broken wagons, signs that some weren't as lucky in their calculated risk.

On the third day, with temperatures soaring at one hundred and twenty, they caught sight of the Bear River. The rag-tag group staggered to the water and plunged in, grateful that Leverenz promised they would rest for two days to allow the animals time to recover.

Philip used the time to jack up the wagon and remove the wheels once more so that he could soak the parched wood in the river overnight. He had gained a reputation for being one of the more dependable members of the train and his gear was as much a point of pride as a physical necessity. Some of the more careless had already lost all their possessions. Gone were their stock, their tools and the seed they would need to start a new life—they would be lucky to hire out to one of the luckier families for room and board for the winter. Philip intended to be one of the fortunate ones

At Bear River, farmers among the group whooped and tossed their caps into the air when they bent down and scooped a handful of rich virgin soil dirt into their fingers and saw the promise that it offered. But no matter that the trees grew nearly to the sky, the free land they had been promised was still weeks off. Mary and Bethellen joined the other women in picking bright pink and periwinkle wild-flowers. Afterwards they sat down in the grass and watched the men free their animals and turn them loose to eat. It was a land of lushness and strangeness, and they watched idly, knowing the time would come when they could call a grassy patch like this "home."

It was much later, after a quenching swim, that Mary rose from resting to follow the call of a meadowlark squawking its familiar warning in the brush. From the sound, it was probably chasing a predator from its nest. Curious, she started along the bank, expecting to find the bird hiding in the grass, but the sound seemed to move further away. Just as she was ready to return to the safety of the train, something shook the bushes between her and the water. Whether white man or Indian, she couldn't tell. "Who are you? What do you want?"

She turned and started walking quickly back toward camp. A stick snapped behind her like the day at the North Platte. Panic drove her and she began running. She ran until she was out of air and fighting a stitch in her side when she heard the sound of moccasins pounding hard on the dirt behind her. Desperate, she darted under a tree limb and pulled it toward her. With the moccasins only steps behind, she released the limb and heard the sound of a branch slapping against skin, followed by a muffled oath. She hid behind a cluster of bushes and watched the dark form roll down the river bank and into the water A minute later, the man appeared, soaked to his knees, holding a dripping hat out in front of him like a muskrat. She remained motionless, but even though she made no sound or movement, she sensed that he realized she was hiding. Suddenly he was standing in front of her. She caught a glimpse of black hair and tanned skin.

"Lucas!"

His voice was angry. "How many times have I warned you about wandering away? The camps are easy pickings at night. Next time, it could be someone you don't want to meet in the dark."

"I was following a bird."

"Then where's your gun?"

"I wasn't going to eat it!"

"Mary, if you're not searching for food then you should be back in camp." The sternness left his voice. "I'm sorry. I know I scared you, but you need to remember the lessons that will save your life." Mary's knees were still shaking. He turned her around in the direction they had just come. "You need to go back. People will be looking for you."

His hands swept over her shoulders, leaving a trail of heat that he longed for his lips to follow; he breathed in her scent and tried to satisfy himself with just that. But the image of another girl brought a chill. It was so cursed hard. The last three days, over the Sublette Cutoff, he had forced himself to stay away. Philip saw to her needs, but he had watched every weary step she took, ready to pull her into the shade if she showed signs of flagging. He had no right to tell her any of this; tender promises would steal her strength on this last difficult part of the journey. Her anger was what would see her through to the end.

"Lucas? Where were you the last three days? I thought you would come by to see if we needed anything."

"Did you?"

"Well, no. But where were you?"

"I had others that needed help. That's what I'm being paid for." He closed his eyes against the image of the Halsey girl's baby.

When Mary returned to camp, Luke remained where he was, trying to capture her in the smoke of his cheroot. He closed his eyes and relived the stupidity of letting Clara Halsey undress for a half-breed who didn't have a clue about what he was buying. He thought about his actions with Mary tonight, recalled the lust he'd had for Clara, and felt the gall of his predicament. *I've got to leave Mary alone until I get this settled. There's no sense in leading her on.* Mary had the right to know what kind of man she'd set her cap for. If she decided he was a debaucher of innocent girls—his thoughts ended abruptly. Clara wasn't innocent by a long shot. But her—*their* baby was.

Chapter Twenty Five

August 2, 1848. We travel now along the Snake
River. The name is misleading, for it is straight
and deep and very fast running. At times we
travel the whole day, thirsting along with the animals. The river runs alongside, but more than a
hundred feet below, with no way to reach it.

MARY FINISHED HER journal entry while they traveled on
a section of the track where the dense rocks didn't stick up as
bad and cause the wagon to creak and torque over the mur-
derous trek. "Philip, the guidebook says we'll travel three
hundred miles on this road. Our animals will never make it."

"I'm more concerned about crossing this river and the Indians than I am about the road. Our wagon is stout, even if
the rims and frame have been used hard. We're nearly two-
thirds of the way there. Luke says we'll be climbing from
here on out and this last section will be the hardest on animals and equipment." He paused to wipe the sweat from his
brow and carefully replaced his hat. "You know what the
papers back in the States say about us?" He spoke half to
himself. "They say that, 'if hell were in the west, we would
cross heaven to get to it.' Lots of the Easterners think we are
mad. Maybe we are, at that." He finished slaking his thirst

with a drink from the barrel and returned to his team.

All they could do was press on, checking for stress cracks in the wagon, and tending to the hooves of the faithful beasts that were walking on worn shoes. He had already reshod his oxen with curved iron plates that reminded her of crumb catchers nailed to each side of the split hooves with small shoeing nails. Once in a while, one of them would throw a shoe, but more often they simply wore them out on the rocks.

"We're going to have to help others when they need it or we'll find ourselves too strung out along this stretch," Philip warned one day, when they passed the third wagon of their group stranded with a broken wheel.

"We haven't lost as many cattle to the Indians as some of the trains we've passed. Why worry now?"

"Not all the tribes think alike. Some, the Umatilla, Nez Perce, and the like, are happy to trade. For the present. But they're gotten used to the easy takings. Shoshone renegades have taken the fight one step further. They do it for revenge."

The train had taken a vote to stop over for two days at Fort Hall and by the time they pulled out, everyone had the latest news, brought by riders and freight haulers. The advice from all quarters was to press on hard and to expect an early snow. The Hudson's Bay trading post was no kind of fort, more a picket fence enclosure around a number of tents that had been built as a trading post for the fur trade. Philip had taken advantage of the blacksmith shop, with its crimps and forges, to have the oxen shod and the wagons repaired.

Mary bought some extra coffee, less than she had planned, because the prices were marked up six hundred per cent over Illinois. It was a sorrowful family who had to do major restocking, but when a wagon overturned and the flour barrels came apart in the dusty road, or the water from a river crossing soaked into the saleratus and flour, or the bacon was gone, folks still had to eat. Like Philip said, *an army marches on its belly*. A family could eat cornmeal so full of weevils that they plucked them out for fish bait. They could eat moldy bacon, but when it went rancid from the heat, it could cause intestinal problems that were not worth the risk—so it was with sad heart that some families tossed the last of their provisions onto the track for the coyotes. Mary had seen families eat weevil-infested flour until it petered out, or share their bacon with maggots, drink sulfur water, and even add grass to the stewpot to provide roughage for their diets. People did what they had to do to keep themselves alive.

A few days out of Fort Hall, Mary noticed a rider coming toward them, his horse kicking clouds of dust on the trail below. "I wonder what's his hurry?" She joined Bethellen and her baby while the rider whipped his horse toward them. "Maybe there's been an Indian attack up ahead."

"We'll know soon enough." Bethellen wrapped her baby tighter in its blanket, a protective gesture that showed her fear for her children. She didn't say much, but she probably was counting the days until her family was off the trail.

Soon, they could hear the rider sharing his news with the first wagons in the train before he rode on toward the others. "Gold, gold!" he shouted, sliding his horse to a stop. Travelers gathered around and the mere word seemed to breathe energy into the quarrelsome group. "They found gold at Sutter's Mill in California. Piles of it. They're picking it off the ground with their bare hands. Ain't nobody left in the towns to cook a meal or saddle a horse—they've all gone up to the mountains to fill their pockets with gold."

"Make us a map, fellow."

"We'll pay good money for directions, mister."

He ignored the interruptions and shouted to the crowd, "You folks will be wanting to take the cutoff down the road a spell, takes you to California—won't anybody be wanting to go on to Oregon now that they can make a fortune overnight. Those strike it rich, they can buy a farm anyplace they choose."

Questions went up. Each man shouted to be heard above the rest. The rider answered as best he could above the din.

"Where's this here Sutter's Creek?"

"What do you mean, 'picking it up'? Like buffalo chips off the ground?"

"How come you ain't back there if the pickings are so good?"

"Where's the turn-off? I'm going!"

By the time the man spurred his horse and it took off running in the direction of Fort Hall, the emigrants were already split in their opinions. Arguments mounted between partners, each owning a share of the wagon and grub, but each wanting to go a different way. Some husbands were determined to go on alone to California, with wives arguing that they weren't about to go on ahead to set up a household in Oregon. Some wives were adamant that they wouldn't be separated, and others laid down ultimatums. Arguments raged about how much money could be made, but nothing much was said about how they would survive if the rumor didn't prove to be true.

The debate raged into the night, with few facts to back anyone up. Like a fever, the desire to head off to California swept through the camp. Folks who had planned on being neighbors in the Willamette found themselves arguing about the wisdom of each other's decision. Voices were raised. Friendships crumbled while the camp chose sides in the great gold debate.

Mary watched and listened, afraid for them all. The change had been too sudden, based on too little information. A terrible thought occurred and she voiced it to Philip. "What if Laurel's family decided to head south? Seems as if Oregon would have gotten the news first. What if she's not there when you get to Oregon City?"

"She will be! By damn, she will be!" Philip stomped about the camp, spilling coffee in the process and Mary could tell he had been wondering the same thing. "Even if her pa goes down to search out gold, her ma and her will stay behind to wait for me. They'd know a goldfield would be no place for women. It'll be like an army encampment, coarse and primitive. They'll have the sense to wait."

Mary remembered something her mother had told her. "Philip, when a woman is ready to take a man to her heart forever, she leaves the counsel of her parents behind. Laurel has done that. I'm sure she regrets not fighting harder to marry you. She'll be waiting for you."

Philip raised his head from the cradle of his arms. "Mary-girl, I'd travel this road twice to find her."

Something in his tone reminded Mary of her father. Surprised, she glanced at her cousin and saw changes that the months on the road had wrought. The journey had tempered him, hardened the edges of his blue eyes. She recalled her mother's words from years past; "It's a wonder you two youngsters come from common stock. Your fathers are so alike, but you two cousins are like a hummingbird and an owl. One flits and the other sits and deliberates." Mary knew she was a hummingbird. But Philip was no longer a fence sitter.

They embraced each other while the world around them went crazy.

"You two seem to have come to an understanding." Luke had approached from the rear and stood smiling, but his eyes betrayed his uneasiness. "What's it to be, Oregon or California?"

"That depends on you," Mary answered firmly. "I will go where you go."

Luke's relief caught at her heart. "I was afraid you would be getting the fever, too. I've seen this happen before. People hear rumors that turn out to be false and they take shortcuts that lead to nowhere. Some of these folks will never be seen again."

"So you're not going to try your luck at the gold?" Philip's question indicated he thought Luke might have been tempted.

"What would an Indian need with gold? Besides, I've had more than my share of hard luck for one lifetime. I won't push for more." He avoided Mary's gaze. "I'm thinking this may be a Godsend for the folks who are going on to Oregon."

"Why is that?"

"Well, we need to hurry the pace, but so many folks are on the trail that we get bogged down at the bottlenecks. The more wagons that take the cutoff to California, the fewer will be traveling on to Oregon."

"You've got something there," Philip agreed. "Let's hope it works out that way and doesn't leave us with too few to stand against the Indians." When he got no response he glanced over and saw Luke's attention focused on Mary. He probably hadn't heard a word. Philip stood and gave an exaggerated yawn. "Guess I'll be turning in now. Could use the extra rest. Night, you two."

To anyone glancing over, it appeared the Rodgers were still at their fireside. "Um…this is so nice," Mary murmured, slipping her hand into Luke's. "Feels like we're a family and this is our camp and our wagon. I wish it was."

"We'll be to Oregon soon enough."

"Luke, it seems as though you dread getting there. Your voice changes every time you mention Oregon City. Why is that?"

He flinched under the weight of her questioning. Now would be the time to tell her, but once it was done, there'd be no going back. No one would fault her for thinking he was a womanizer; but on the other hand, no one would blame him for choosing Mary over a lifetime of hell. He had a world to lose and another to gain. He took a deep breath and his good intentions disappeared. "If the wagons get jumbled up—new folks join us and the old ones leave for California—we could get married right here on the trail. I'm getting tired of sneaking around."

"It's true. This lie gets heavier every day." She gave a rueful laugh. "The idea sounded so simple back home, but living it is another matter. I hate lies."

Luke ignored the twist that was forming in his gut. "Wonder what your folks would have thought of all of this? You haven't talked much about them. What was your father like?" He broke off, watching her reaction while he pretended to study the fire.

Mary smiled. "You resemble him in a lot of ways. That's what I first noticed. Well, except for that stinky cigar you always had in your mouth."

"So your pa didn't know the value of a sweet cigar. What

a pity or he would've been even more like me," Luke smiled. "How was he like me?"

"He had your humor…your sense of honor."

"Honor?"

"Yes. He knew which way truth lay and he never wavered. You're like that and I'm glad. Philip, too. He would be relieved to ride into Oregon a free man."

Mary watched Luke's eyes draw distant. He seemed to turn into his Indian mother's son in front of her eyes.

"A free man. Is that where a man goes to be free? Oregon City?"

Luke's scornful laugh turned the night chilly for Mary. She couldn't talk about weddings to this man; he was a stranger tonight. What had he said about trust? "Maybe I better say good night. It's getting late and people are setting off to bed."

"Yeah. Maybe." He studied the dying embers. "Maybe I'll go find myself a free man."

A shiver went down Mary's spine. She waited for Luke's kiss, but he was brooding and didn't notice. "We're the last ones awake. We'll be paying for it come morning," she murmured, confused because he seemed glad for the dismissal.

He started off toward his wagon, lost in thought. Seconds later he stumbled over someone's doubletree in the dark. Stifling a curse, he grabbed for something to right himself and his foot struck a three-legged tripod. A coffeepot tumbled into the dying embers of someone's campfire.

"Who's there?" a sleepy voice demanded. "Is that a bear?"

"Go back to sleep!" Luke snarled and limped off to bed.

Chapter Twenty Six

> August 23, 1848. It is beyond comprehension to lose our friends to water when we nearly perished from a dearth of it. Is there no moderation to this vast wilderness?

BY TEN THE next morning, men's wagons were jostling for a better position and men were yelling as they approached a pitiful excuse of a waterway the map named the Raft River. It was really only a creek, barely wide enough to float a raft on, hence the name. It was not the water, but its significance that had the men so excited, for the river represented the last turnoff to California. Those turning south onto the Raft went off to the goldfields. Those who crossed it continued on to Oregon.

Mary watched the wagon train divide—two wagons to California, one to Oregon, three to California, two to Oregon, three, none, two, one. It seemed as though half the world was turning away from the dream that had sustained them for so many miles. For the women, it was another in a long line of sorrowful good-byes. Mary hugged friends who cried their disappointment into her shoulders. She watched them take the turnoff with a pain in her heart.

Bethellen and her husband struggled with the decision. At first, it seemed that they would leave, but at the last minute, they voted to continue on to Oregon. She felt limp with relief when Bethellen announced their decision. They had one last hope; farther down, the trail would divide again. Maybe some would reconsider and continue on to Oregon on the newly laid Applegate Trail. If so, maybe she would see them again.

A new wagon train formed from the small group that remained. From the original fifty-six wagons, the number dropped to only twenty-three. They had been lucky so far; many of the horses and cattle had survived, and they added more from the trail-worn cattle and horses abandoned by the gold-seekers who were in too much of a hurry to be bothered anymore. The young men unencumbered by wife or family couldn't get to the gold fields fast enough. They took off on fast horses and left their staples and tents with the wagons, figuring to purchase what they needed with the workings of their claims.

"They're all fools," Luke muttered. "What do they think they'll be eating up in those mountains? Can't eat gold."

With a heavy heart, Mary helped Philip start the footsore oxen onward through another stretch of the volcanic rock that stretched as far as they could see. For two hundred miles they had followed the Snake River, but its twists and turns were now in canyons far below, inaccessible to the thirsty travelers. The landscape around them was something she could imagine finding in hell, if it came to that; jagged, rocky walls of lava, devoid of plant life, fed by a battering torrent of a river that would claim every single soul in their wagon train if given a chance.

The rocky trail across lava rocks wrought havoc on the wagon wheels and endangered the oxen with each step they took. She took care, because a twisted ankle would be dire at this stage, but it seemed as though some days they fought mile by stubborn mile, sometimes, foot by foot.

"I wish we could have traveled this part first and then en-joyed the flatlands and the spring wild flowers after we tuckered out," Mary commented.

"I heard someone describe this place as 'Hell with the fires put out'," Philip responded from where he was guiding the oxen through a particularly bad part of the trail.

The roar of a waterfall caught their attention and gave Mary something to think about besides her misery. Luke rode up as she stood appreciating its stark beauty. "What is it? Does it have a name?" She stared at the awesome specta-cle that nature had set in the middle of hell. A rock tower split in two, where the Snake River poured over the lip with a crashing roar that she could hear from a mile away. "I've never seen anything so magnificent."

"Twin Falls. Lives up to its name, wouldn't you say?" Luke smiled as though he had provided it especially for her enjoyment.

Later in the day they came to other falls, but none held the enjoyment of this moment shared with Luke. Several days later, she heard a roar and wondered at first if the buffalo were returning to shake the dry earth. The tempo and rhythm continued and she recognized the sound as a gift of the river. For three miles, the oxen plowed slowly ahead un-til she could barely stand the suspense. Suddenly, there, ahead, was the granddaddy of all waterfalls; a plunging stream that fell two hundred feet straight to a canyon that had been carved by eons of constant wear on the rocks be-low.

"Look, Mary," Philip called out. "We're witnessing new sights at every turn." In silence, they watched the hypnotic pull of water pouring over the canyon wall.

Mary knew what he was trying to say—the same idea

tugged deep inside her, an appreciation for the life she was experiencing in this new and astounding way. "We will have this memory inside us forever, won't we, Philip?"

Standing on the breezy bluff, Philip could only agree. "This has been the journey of a lifetime. I doubt I'll be back this way."

Straight across the river, they could see a waterfall flowing, not over the cliff, but from a point high on the rock face. Fed by an underground river, it poured out a spigot from the side of the mountain, collecting in the river below. Some previous traveler had named it the Thousand Springs and the name had stuck.

Too soon, the wagonmaster gave the signal to continue. Leverenz had warned them that they were going to have to cross the Snake River, and dread filled Mary's steps when the trail dropped to a ford where wagon tracks showed it was possible to cross. The guide book called it Three Islands Crossing, but it looked more like giant stepping stones across the deep, swift river. They arrived at the spot in the afternoon and the waning sun lent urgency to the event. Leverenz had warned them that if they made their river crossings late in the day when their animals were tired and used to the day's commands, they were less likely to balk at the cold water. Their crossings so far had proven him right.

"Listen up, men," Luke shouted against the river's backdrop, "bunch up as tight as we dare. The hostiles are watching from those bluffs. If night catches us strung out on both sides of the river, we can't defend ourselves. No matter what happens, keep going. If your team balks, pull aside. Those that want to can share teams and double or triple team. It's safer that way, but it will take longer." He paused, watching the drover's faces, closed, stoic and determined. Each had probably witnessed wagons swept away in rivers less dangerous than the one they faced today. "If someone gets washed downstream, swallow hard and come on ahead. Worst thing you can do is hesitate. This river's swift and deep—the animals need your confidence. So does the man who's following you." He looked around and wondered what the next three hours would bring.

Luke led the train toward the channel, taking the shortest line to the first island. Plunging into the frigid water he steadied his oxen with his voice while they rolled their eyes in terror. On the seat, his hired drover shouted and flicked his whip.

Mary waited on the bank, utterly powerless to do anything but watch the wagon pitch and roll with the current. As soon as Luke gained the first island, Leverenz signaled another team into the water before the driver had time to think. Having seen the waterfalls behind them, no one wanted to speculate on what might lay beyond the next bend should their team fail in midstream.

Finally, it was Philip's turn. Luke had already swum his oxen back across. He yoked them to Philip's then climbed aboard to handle the whip. Mary clutched the wagon seat and turned to check Buttercup who was tied to the end of the wagon with a rawhide lead. The wagon hit a dip at the edge of the bank and began its slow decline.

"Hold on, Mary! Say a word to your Maker, then sit back and enjoy the ride," Luke said.

She felt the rush of the current at the same moment the first set of oxen lost contact with the bank and lurched into the depths. The flow pulled them several feet downstream before the second team of oxen got its footing and the wagon corrected itself. In what was probably a minute—but seemed like twenty—the oxen traversed the channel and hauled the wagon onto the first small island. Without pausing, Philip urged the team across to the other side and back into the river.

Behind her, wagons were backed up on the trail like a serpent, each waiting its turn while above, in the bluffs, hostile Indians doubtlessly watched. She clutched the wagon as they forded to the next island. The third and final island was smaller, and before she realized it, they were back into the channel. When they reached the other side, Luke leaped to the ground while Philip kept the team moving forward.

"Go on ahead and find a camp—no use clogging the trail here. We're in Paiute country now, not as much to worry about. The rest of the train will come in behind you."

Philip nodded. For once, the oxen were eager to put the sound of the river behind them. Luke had been right in his estimation. It seemed as though there were always teams that crossed water better than others. By sending the most confident teams across first, the other animals followed.

Mary looked back to watch Letha Clark, sitting beside her new husband, Mr. Parkman. Mary saw her tie the children to boxes inside the wagon, as safe a place as anyone had managed to find for their little ones. Their mismatched set of cows and mules entered the river in a jangle of thrashing horns and flailing hooves. From the moment they felt the water, the lead mules began to fight each other for control. Instead of working as a team, they seemed determined to return to the bank while the set of half-wild steers behind them plunged ahead. Mary jumped to her feet and screamed, "Letha, be careful!"

From the shore, Luke threw a lariat into the air that sailed over the tops of the cows and caught one of its horns before the thrashing animal thrust it off into the water. Luke pulled it back, hand over hand in a desperate effort to throw it again, but by then, the wagon had drifted out of reach.

She could hear Mr. Parkman shouting to his leaders, urging them forward while the wagon began to list to the left. He leaped from the wagon and grabbed the mule's harness. A thrashing hoof caught him in the midsection and he hollered in pain before slowly disappearing into the churning foam. She heard Letha scream, saw the terrified whites of the cows' eyes as they slowly disappeared, dragged under by the weight of the wagon behind and the mules in front. Mary heard their panicked bawls as the wagon listed and began to topple. She watched Letha grip the side of the wagon cover and climb inside, intending to untie her bound children, but she lost her seating and slid into the water. She managed to grab hold of a wheel and cling desperately to it as she tried to climb back inside. In a hopelessly lonely motion, the wagon capsized and began drifting downstream, accompanied by the screams of Letha and the children.

Mary couldn't force herself to look away. She began praying as the wagon slowly broke apart. In the seconds that followed, the river seemed to go silent. She heard no roar of the falls, no braying of animals, only the sound of her heart beating before she felt the rush of darkness. When she came to, another wagon had descended into the water and was crossing to the first island.

Philip turned the oxen away from the water and began walking. "We've learned a lot in the last few months," he said. "But our skill was hard won."

"We just lost a family." When she closed her eyes she saw the Parkman wagon capsizing all over again. *Hard won* didn't begin to describe the experience. Those who had lost their lives at the Snake didn't need recounting; their names would be seared in the memory of every emigrant who made the crossing that day. Later that night, when a baby in a nearby wagon cried, she crumpled onto the crosstree and sobbed until she was numb.

After supper, Luke walked from wagon to wagon greeting the new families and asking where they were from. The variety was surprising; a wealthy family from Georgia, a New York mercantile man, a Missourian hoping to farm, a burned-out family with little more than the clothes on their back, from New Orleans.

• ♥ •

The Snake River Valley gave way to the lush Boise Valley with its dense virgin forests where friendly tribes were willing to trade salmon for whatever belongings the emigrants could spare. Mary loved the rich, oily flavor of salmon steak broiled over coals, unlike anything she had ever tasted.

She had days where she could walk alone and think about the losses she'd endured in the past months. Her mother's death, her father's, Toby's, Lillian Stoberson's, Letha Clark's; their images ran together in her head like a patchwork memory quilt. She felt that she carried a piece of each of them on her heart into this vast land. Some days she could feel them walking alongside her.

One day, she discarded her worn-out shoes and donned her last good pair. Silly as it might seem to anyone watching, she wept as she tossed the scraps of worn leather into the fire.

She and Bethellen agreed; the women fared better now that they were off the odious lava rock, although they could hardly appreciate their good fortune for worrying about the ominous Blue Mountains that lay ahead. Their wagon train had yet to undergo the test of mountain hauling; the ranges they had crossed so far had been little more than hills. From the looks of the road ahead, it wouldn't be long now.

"I dread the coming mountains," Bethellen confessed one morning while she nursed her baby, wrapped in a shawl as they walked side by side. "I'm always wondering which of these perils will claim us. I fear them all."

"Do you think we're been spared so much only to die in the days ahead?" Mary reached to feather the soft blonde hair of the baby girl they had named after Lillian.

"It seems so. The road will claim its toll."

Mary walked in silence until her friend's words seemed like an omen of things to come. She thought of Luke and the chances he took every day. He was now walking beside his own oxen, after their cook deserted in the middle of the night for California.

"Didn't even think to take his last month's pay," Leverenz grumbled when he turned out one morning to find the coffeepot still hanging on the wagon and the fire pit cold.

The Parkman drowning had changed something in Luke's resolve. He sat one night watching the camp settle in and recalled the stillness of the Blue Mountains in the first hours after a snowfall. The wilderness sang in his bones, penetrating the stench of civilization that assailed his nostrils: campfire smoke, animal excrement, burned beans, even leftover coffee. He was tired of talking, tired of meeting strangers. His mother's people were within a week's ride, and he fought the urge to mount his stallion and ride toward the mountains. He longed to spend the winter among his mother's people, watching the earth slumber in its winter blanket. But he knew that he would spend his days wandering the camp, restless, dissatisfied and with a need to return. The journey would bring him no peace. He would watch the maidens' dark eyes and imagine taking one to wife, but none of them would satisfy his longing.

His vision quest had not included eagles or wolves; he had seen the white camps. The knowledge had brought suffering to his grandfather and to himself. Now, listening to an emigrant woman chastising her child in an exhausted harangue, he wasn't so sure. The dichotomy of his dreams mocked him. He wasn't white, but he wasn't Umatilla anymore; his father had seen to that. When he dreamed, he saw his stepmother standing beside his birth mother and they were each smiling at him, but in his heart, he no longer smiled back.

He untied the medicine bag that his mother had given him when he was a boy, and removed the datura seeds that he had collected in the full moon a few weeks earlier, when the thunderclouds were forming and lightning flashed in the Wyoming desert. That night, the white flowers of the jimson weed had shone in the golden August moon like a ghost dancer and he picked the seeds, intending to visit the ways of his mother. Tonight the seeds burned on his palm. He lifted them to his lips and tried to swallow, but his mouth tasted of cotton, like it had on that day when he had taken them the first time, a boy on his vision quest, with the help of a shaman who had guided him through. He was told that he lay in the sun for a day until the old man dragged him into a cave and kept him from wandering off the cliff because he believed he could fly.

For three days, he lay sightless and helpless while his head throbbed with nightmarish images of demons. He remembered screaming when insects and serpents entered his ears and crawled through his brain, eating, purifying, dissecting him until he knew that the demons controlled the earth and nothing in his life was what he had thought it was.

Tonight, sitting on the ground where the Snake River had devoured Letha Clark and her family, he felt the white serpent slithering across his chest like the day of his vision. He was a man now, but life was a still a thin thread.

He saw the skies light up, and for a moment he was afraid

that the heavens would flash with vivid reds, blues and yellows like those in the datura moon. But tonight, it was only lightning. He felt himself flowing like the Snake River, pulsing and surging through the crevices, then widening and slowing. He felt himself relaxing and his body warming until he wanted to run and plunge into the river to cool off. Instead, he reached for the medicine bag and returned the seeds. He would need his wits about him if they were to find their way through this valley of hostiles. Too many had lost their lives; he would not be the cause for more.

His legs felt weak and his mouth parched by the time he found the coffee pot that Leverenz had left hanging with the leftovers cooling in the night air. He drained the pot before he crawled into his bedroll.

In the morning, he hired a young man of color to handle the team for meals and cash. The Negro had begun the journey as a slave to a Southern businessman, John Grant. When Grant and his family drowned in a river crossing, he had fared as best he could, feeding his belly with grass and whatever he could scrounge from abandoned wagons. With no one to claim ownership of him, his first act of freedom had been to change his name from Buck Grant to one of his own choosing, William Livingston, and to hire on with Luke. His hopes were to hire out, save enough money to buy his own mules and wagon, and start a freight company. The land bill circulating through Congress didn't include free government land for Negroes, but already some were having success as free men and women of trade, as seamstresses, haulers, and liverymen. Some had made their names as mountain men, scouts, and soldiers.

"No matter," Livingston told Luke, "ain't no man's law going to fret me, now I got myself this far. I figure I got as much chance as the next man."

The slave hunter had not returned. Now that they had crossed the Snake, no slaver in his right mind would risk the perils of a crossing for a crippled Negro boy. The boy emerged from the wagon and began hobbling around camp on a crutch that Luke whittled from the crotch of a cottonwood limb. His name was Lazrus, he told Mary when she asked, like the man that Jesus had raised from the dead. She taught him to spell it the way it appeared in her Bible, but he dropped the middle syllable the way his mother had spoken it.

"If we want to take the Barlow Road, we're going to have to make up lost time. Otherwise, it's the Columbia River for us," Leverenz announced one evening. It was fortunate that no snow had fallen at this point, for it would be nearly impossible to traverse the mountains in such conditions.

Mary pitied the poor travelers who were coming behind them, late from previous mishaps and having to face the daunting sight of a snow-covered Blue Range. At least they were in Oregon Country. The knowledge lifted their spirits in a way that nothing else could. *Oregon.* Even the wind seemed to whisper the name, blowing off ridges filled with the most majestic trees that she had ever seen. The farmers were doubly excited about the trees. To them, the sheer size of the forests meant soil of inestimable quality. Any soil that could grow a tree that tall, they reasoned, could do a fine job of nurturing corn, wheat and sorghum.

That opinion was seconded when they climbed a ridge that overlooked the Grande Ronde, a mountain-encircled valley where only the want of seed seemed to keep it from reaping a bounty in the virgin soil. Many of the emigrants came from cotton and tobacco-worn lands that now produced little, and the farmers were looking to this new soil to begin anew.

As they inched their way over the mountains and into the valley, Mary had the feeling she was home. One evening, she stood absorbing the smells and the feel of the land when Luke came strolling into camp with a man for her to meet.

"Mary, this is Reverend Henry Mossler. He's a minister, convicted to his calling. He's willing to marry us. I think it's time."

Mary turned with surprise. What was Lucas's hurry? They had scarcely talked during the past week, and certainly not about marriage.

"It is extremely good to see such devoted and hardworking young people in pursuit of a spiritual life together," Reverend Mossler began. He peeled his tiny gold spectacles from his ears and proceeded to wipe them with the corner of his waist coat. "How long have you known each other?"

"Nearly five months."

"Five months and more."

"Well, exactly how did you come to meet each other?" he asked. Mary could see that he was used to performing weddings under such hurried circumstances.

"We met on the train," Luke began. "She's what I want for a wife. Let's do this."

Mary heard the edge in his voice. When Reverend Mossler glanced up sharply at Luke, she added quickly, "Lucas is a good and generous man. He will be a loving husband."

The Reverend appraised her over his wire-rim spectacles. "Are you certain you aren't making a hasty decision? He is…of a different culture. You seem to be a gently reared woman of Christian virtue. Do you have family to help you in this matter?"

Mary heard her voice go hard-edged. "My family is deceased."

"Is there anyone who might object to this union? Have

you a guardian?"

She tried not to let her fear show in her voice. "I have only my cousin. I suppose you could consider him my guardian."

At that moment, Philip came walking back into camp, fresh from a swim, clad only in his dampened trousers.

Mary felt her heart drop. "Reverend Mossler, meet my cousin, Philip Rodgers."

The minister studied him, his little eyes blinking rapidly. "You're the *guardian*? Somehow I expected a much older man. Whatever induced her parents to name you as her guardian? Unless, of course there is a Mrs. Rodgers around?" He peered about in a vain attempt to locate a possible wife for Philip. Finding none, he rephrased the question. "Are you a single man, Mr. Rodgers?"

Philip accessed the situation: Luke stood with his arms folded across his chest, defiance in every muscle. Mary was toying with her bonnet string, creasing it with her teeth as she watched him in trepidation. The reverend was assessing him with suspicion. He hastily donned his wet shirt and tried to decide what he had ventured into. He met Luke's defiant gaze and realized why the minister was standing in their camp.

"Uh, yes I am. I don't guess Mary's folks figured on dying so soon. Besides, she's a biddable young lady. I haven't had one problem with her since we left Independence. She's meek and mild and truly a help about the camp. Never gives her opinions on issues that don't concern her, and she makes a delicious apple pie."

"Well, this is highly irregular. You paint a different picture than does Mr. Sayer. It would appear that your relationship with her is based on more appropriate attributes for a young lady than the coarser things Mister Sayer apparently finds appealing. You share a similar cultural background.

Perhaps, in naming you guardian, it was her parents wish that the two of you be wed."

Luke leapt forward with an angry growl. "Reverend, I'm not looking for your opinion. Just your assistance."

"Tut, tut, Mr. Sayer...I fear you're an impulsive man of dubious Christian merit." He scrutinized Luke with a frown. "You are apparently of mixed blood. I presume you are a Christian?"

Luke started. "I'm no heathen, if that's what you're worried about. I was baptized." His stepmother had insisted. It had been one more confusion for a nine-year-old boy with the old ways still ringing in his ears. His idea of Jesus had blurred with drum songs and the scent of burning feathers and sage. Unfortunately, his glare had an unintended effect.

With finality born of conviction, the minister adjusted his spectacles. "I must think a bit before I can, in good conscience, inflict a lifetime of your influence on Mary's gentle ways. I shall sleep on the matter." Gathering his notebook and pen, he strolled from the camp.

Mary recovered first. "Lucas, what were you thinking of?"

"I'm tired of waiting. Have you changed your mind?"

"That's not fair. You know I haven't.

Philip glanced at the strangers at the next wagon. "Maybe we better keep it down. But you can't marry her out here. What got in to you?" He glanced from Luke to Mary and back again. "Why didn't anyone let me in on this plan? It's true, some of the people we know are gone, but I'm not taking any chances. You took a lame-brained chance just now. You must be desperate."

Luke paced the ground between them, agitation raising his voice. "Maybe I am. If Mary doesn't want to marry me out here, I've got a mind to head for the back country. Find me a wife among the tribes." He stalked from the wagon, frustration trailing his words. A few minutes later, he galloped past the wagon, bareback, clad only in his buckskin trousers and moccasins, his hair loose around his shoulders and his medicine bag bouncing around his neck. Mary watched with a feeling of foreboding.

She picked her way across a rocky field to the water's edge where she could sit and try to solve the conflict that raged in her. She had felt Luke's desperation.

In another man, she might have thought it was fear, but that didn't seem possible. She thought of other marriages that had been performed on the journey by Protestant missionaries on their way to convert the Indians. Ida O'Brian, Irish to the core, had accepted a minister's blessing rather than none at all. She hadn't been the first bride to find herself in a practical dilemma. She'd heard of couples who lived for years until a proper wedding could be managed. Luke seemed eager to make himself a married man. Maybe she would have to accept marriage in whatever form it was offered.

When Luke returned, after dark, he found her still sitting at the river. He approached with obvious hesitation, but not before he caught the sheen of tears. "Mary, I've got something to tell you."

Her fears were captured in his tone. "What is it?"

Luke crouched on his heels and toyed with his hat. "I have a child. A baby boy. He has my name. Mine and my father's."

Mary felt a dull roar fill her ears. "What are you saying? When? Where?"

"It's a long story. I just found out. There's a girl involved."

"Obviously." Her scorn made the word sound mean,

hard-edged, the way she felt.

"I met her on the last train west." He gave a wry smile. "Guess you were right about me. Maybe I am a womanizer." Mary stared while a contradiction formed inside her brain. She said nothing. "It's not exactly how it sounds. But John Leverenz tells me it's true, so I have to believe him."

"Where is she?" Mary felt the underlining being ripped from the fabric of her future. She could almost hear the rending as it tore.

"She's…her father threw her out when she had an Indian baby. She's living up-top of a saloon in Oregon City."

"A brothel."

"If you want to call it that."

Mary's scorn spilled out as she tried to think of what she knew of such places. "Does it really matter what you call it?" Another thought occurred. "Don't those girls…entertain several men in a night? How would you know it's yours?"

Luke winced as he hesitated. "Because I was her first."

Mary's anger merged with more fear than she had ever known. Her question was scarcely a whisper. "Oh, Lucas…how could you?"

He touched the brim of his hat and wished he had an answer that would satisfy her. Maybe there wasn't one. "I don't know."

Mary waited for more. When it didn't come, she whispered, "What are you going to do?"

"I'm going to see my son. Clara can go to hammer for all I care. She was bound there long before I met her. I just scratched her itch on the first try."

Mary shifted on the hard ground and focused on the single word she'd just heard. "Is that her name—Clara?"

"Name's not important."

"It is to me. I want to know." She could imagine running

into her on the street one day, or worse yet, wondering if every young mother she met was *the one.*

"Clara Halsey. She rode with us last year. It wasn't what you think. I didn't have any feelings for her."

If he thought to relieve her, he was wrong. That was even worse. "Lucas—no feelings? Then, how could you—"

His guilt flared into anger at the accusation in her voice. "I don't know. Maybe it's just my nature. I'm half Indian. I probably can't handle liquor very well, either. Hell, I probably couldn't handle *you* for that matter." He rose to his feet and found his hat. "Anyway, there's a lot of men looking for wives. You shouldn't have much trouble finding a decent one."

Mary allowed her anger full rein. "Don't worry on my account." She tried to swallow the lump in her throat, determined not to give him the satisfaction of seeing her cry. "You better get back to the camp. You'll probably want to get an early start for Oregon City, to see your—your family!" Watching him stalk to his horse gave her no satisfaction, nor the sound of pounding hooves as he rode away.

Chapter Twenty Seven

August 28, 1848. The trail is crowded with a strange assembly of travelers. Some have become our dearest friends while others try us sorely. Privacy is afforded only to the gravely ill.

MARY SAT HUDDLED in the wagon, too weary to walk. Fragments of conversation interrupted her melancholy mood and she tried to catch the snatches coming from fifty feet downwind.

"Hold up there, man...what you doing in Thurley Hartzell's wagon? He ain't been seen today, and you look a mite quiet, sneaking out of camp like a snake 'neath a bush. Whereabouts you bound, and where be the owner of this here rig?" The speaker was Bill Weems. He seemed sure enough about the ownership of the wagon to call the stranger out, right in the middle of the track. She'd seen him argue with nearly every man on the train, but apparently he had made one friend. To hear him talk, the missing man was a fellow Kentuckian, probably a rough-mannered man like himself who had shared the miles and all its tragedies. They had made a pact and he was sticking to his part of the deal.

The stranger seemed intent on getting out of camp. He didn't stop to answer but kept heading east, back in the direction they had just come.

278 ♦ ANNE SCHROEDER

"What's going on?" Philip straightened and wiped the hoof pick he was using on Rankle's hoof. From his point of view, the whole thing looked a little strange.

Apparently, Bill Weems agreed. "Hold up there, stranger, I'm talking to you." As the man shifted on the wagon seat he found himself facing Weem's Colt revolver. Yielding to common sense, he pulled the team to a halt and set waiting for Weems to catch up. "I asked you where Thurley Hartzell be. We ain't seen him since yesterday, and now you all come sashaying down the trail with his rig, looking like you might be heading on back to the trail that sets off for California. That's fine by me, 'cept the owner of this here wagon should be sitting right 'long side of you, else I'm liable to smell a skunk. Talk up there, stranger."

Philip followed Mary toward the edge of the gathering crowd.

"Don't know nothing 'bout no Thurley whoever," the man grumbled, looking down at his unlaced boots as he twisted the reins in his gnarled fingers. "Found this outfit down the road a piece with the man all played out what drove it."

"He didn't have no sickness. Was healthy as a horse yes-terday—what have ya done with him?"

"Ain't done nothing. He's dead, I tell you. Maybe of the cholera, for all I know. Fact, that's probably what it was. I'll be lucky not to get it myself. Shouldn't be using his gear 'cept I figure to be dead myself, one way or the other if I don't get myself some grub and a ride. Saw this one. Didn't figure no one was needing it now so I helped myself."

"Well, now, that might sound fine and dandy to another fellow, but I knowed old Thurley, and I says he ain't dead of his own accord. I reckon we all just mosey on down the road and find out where you left him. I'd lay odds you didn't even sod him under afore you made off with his gear. Man like you ain't a man, he's a critter."

By now, a crowd had gathered; angry voices rose until the scene had the markings of a mob. The stranger was set on a spare horse with his hands bound to prevent his escape while the crowd discussed what they should do.

He sat there, a hawk-eyed skeleton of a man in a flannel shirt that had probably fit him once, but now hung about his frame in folds that billowed in the evening breeze. A mustache drooped at the corners of his mouth. Needing a trimming, it formed a mournful expression on his haggard face. His hair lay ragged and untrimmed in its shaggy black thickness, about the only thing on the man that wasn't gaunt and spare. His eyes, almost steel color, watched the crowd, seeking a friendly face who might plead his case. He caught Mary's eye and she saw his despair. He had the look of a man who would never do the pleading himself.

Weems led the group down the road, holding the horse's reins while the others followed. Mary had made Bill Weem's acquaintance, but neither she nor Philip knew Thurley Hartzell. It didn't matter. She tried to choke back a feeling of foreboding as they traveled west, scanning the sides of the road for signs of the fallen man. "Philip, maybe we should go get Mr. Leverenz." She didn't consider asking Luke for help. She hadn't spoken to him since that night; tried to ignore the fact that he prowled the outskirts of camp looking wounded in the moonlight shadows. She'd convinced herself that she didn't care.

"Nah. He's not back yet. Those fellows will take care of it themselves. Let's stay out of it."

Too many wagons had passed to be able to detect where Thurley might have pulled off, whether sick and weak or the victim of a desperate man. The stranger had the look of someone who hadn't eaten in a while and didn't know where his next meal was coming from. Just possibly, he'd seen Thurley as his meal ticket to California. He didn't speak unless forced to answer a question, and even then, his answers were more grunts.

Philip and Mary followed the crowd that accompanied the man down the road. With the setting sun in their faces, they forced their way past wagons, the drovers shouting at them to clear the trail. Finally at a bushy pass where a rocky overhang forced the road into a narrow opening, someone spotted a naked foot sticking from an overgrown bush at the side of the road.

"Hold up!" the tracker shouted, dismounting. "Could be someone sleeping in the shade, but unlikely."

Shouts of "It's him! It's Thurley!" rang out from the men who helped part the bushes and roll the body over. They recognized their friend in the swollen, blackened-faced man who lay stiff and wide-eyed, his expression frozen in a look of astonishment. Flies buzzed about. It didn't take much convincing for the men to leave the corpse and back off a pace.

"Stay back. He may have the fever."

"Nah, I don't think that's what done him in," Bill Weems countered, having seen Thurley up close and personal. "It might be, cause I ain't no doctor, but I think this here knife slit across his throat did more harm than the fever. Quicker, too. Gentlemen, this here bushwacker's a murderer!"

Cries of "String him up!" came from every man in the group.

"Wait a minute," Philip interrupted. "There's no cause for haste. This man's entitled to a trial."

"Hell, he's getting one," someone said with a laugh.

"Shut up, you meddler," another added.

"Mary, go get Luke."

"What can he do?" Her scorn caused Philip to scowl in surprise. "Anyway, I haven't seen him around."

Weems's voice broke in. "Stranger, you are going to die. Mind telling us why you done this foul deed? Thurley lost his wife and young'uns on this trip, and he ain't never done nothing to no one. You killed him for the wagon he was driving. At least say something for yourself before you swing."

Mary watched as the stranger looked around at the angry faces. Faces that looked well-fed and cared for—probably by someone back at the camp tending supper right now. The stranger hesitated when he saw her, the only woman in the group, and she read his story in his eyes. He had been born poor, had eaten dirt and grass to keep himself alive long enough to get to Oregon Country. Probably wasn't anyone in the whole world who cared if he lived or died, and when he saw his chance to get to California disappearing the night his partner took off in the dark of night with everything they owned, he did the only thing he could. He had spotted a lone wagon that was traveling back a pace, lagging behind the rest of the folks and decided that it was a sign. Made his way to the top of the rock, drew his knife and slit the drover's throat before anyone was the wiser. It was an easy matter to push the drover off into the bushes, and easier still to sit atop the sturdy wagon, packed with staples and bedrolls to ease his way to the gold country. He had only to catch up with a group of strangers and tag along, and no one would be the wiser.

Only the bad luck of running into the drover's friend now stood between him and freedom. He should have known it would go this way—it had been so for all of his life. Now, he would swing for fifteen minutes of hope. Well, let them hang him, his expression challenged. He would die, but he would never tell them how low and driven he had become. He would take his secrets to his death.

His words were directed at Mary. "Weren't no one cared about me when I was alive," he growled and spat a brown wad of saliva to the side. "Ain't none of you going to start now." Shaking his head at the man who had asked for a confession, he sat facing front with stony, resolute blankness and the dead steel of his eyes.

"Weems—you better wait for Leverenz."

"No need. He ain't the law around here. We know what needs doing. And we'll do it."

"You won't be any better than this fellow...just a murderer."

"Stay or go, Rodgers. It's your choice. But we're doing what we have to. Stranger, you best give us your name. We won't even have a name to mark you with." Bill Weems glanced belligerently at Philip.

"Ain't no one going to be searching out my grave," the stranger muttered. "No one a'tall."

"Suit yourself." A rope was slung over the stout branch of a cottonwood. Mary heard herself pleading for them to halt as the stranger's horse was led beneath the rope. In the space of seven minutes his body had ceased its struggle, and hung swaying from the utility rope that one of the wives used to hang her laundry on wash day.

The group stood silent. Each stared mutely at the body, not regretting their action, only the deed that made it necessary. "Thurley Hartzell was a good ole boy," Bill Weems stated softly, an epitaph for a fallen friend as his murderer swung to and fro in the roadway. "I reckon he would have been real proud of us finding his killer so quick. We done good, boys."

Leaving the stranger in his noose, the crowd started back

to the wagons. Time enough for supper before they set to the grisly business of burying the two. Besides, they didn't have the tools for the job. The pick and shovel were still on Thurley's wagon.

Mary felt the sting of bile in her throat. She followed Philip back toward their wagon, unsure if they could have made a difference. Maybe if Luke had been around. But maybe not. She thought about turning for one last look and decided against it.

She was starting supper when she heard Leverenz bellowing from down the row of wagons. "Weems, you scarlet-arsed rodent. I want you out of this wagon train tonight. I'm filing charges at the next outpost. That was the meanest trick I ever saw done. Damn weasel. Now get your gear packed up and get out of my sight."

He and Luke strode from Weems's camp toward the lynch tree. With sharp, angry stabs they dug two graves in silence. When the holes were deep enough they placed the bodies inside and shoveled the dirt back.

After supper, Mary walked to the graves to see what Luke had carved on the two boards he ripped from Thurley's wagon. On one, he had carved Hartzell's name and the date of his death. On the other he scratched the words *Stranger. He had a hard crossing*. Thurley Hartzell and his murder would lay side-by-side in the untamed land.

Chapter Twenty Eight

September 2, 1848. Determination is our daily companion. It will be good to reach our destiny. We are exhausted in mind and body, and we find no solace in anything but to struggle onward.

THEY HAD MADE it across the Cascades; the wagons rolled across flat, gentle lands that once again made for easy travel. Luke stood gazing out at the miles of grassland. "This will be a land of wheat and barley someday," he told Leverenz. "Sheep will graze the stubble after harvest. Whoever sees his way to plow and plant this land will provide bread for the whole territory. Soon enough, the people from the East will build towns and farms. The buffalo and the people who depend on it for their lives will be forced to go south. Time will tell if there is enough space in the west for everyone. But there sure as hell isn't enough room for me."

"Something brooding you lately, Sayer?"

"Nothing I didn't expect would happen when I read your letter."

"Not the end of the world." Leverenz's words hit a hollow chord. Luke could see Mary over in the camp preparing supper for Philip as though nothing was amiss in her world. She had apparently not confided his sins to Philip. Luke thanked her for that.

He returned to his camp and ate his supper in silence while Leverenz made a valiant effort to leave him in peace.

The campfire talk that night was filled with debate about which way they should proceed when the trail branched up ahead. Those who had money and wanted to chance it could travel the Columbia River, floating their belongings and ferrying the cattle and oxen. At The Dalles, unneeded oxen could be traded to the Indians as boat fare for the two-day trip and wagon beds would be smeared with tar to waterproof them—sometimes buffalo grease, ox tallow, or anything else penniless travelers could get their hands on. For those who still had money, white trappers or Indians could be hired to help ferry the cargo for a stiff share of the emigrant's start-up money.

The guidebooks warned about the Columbia River waterfalls and in one place, a narrow canyon that would require travelers to unload their canoes, boats and wagons. The wheels would need to be reattached and the animals harnessed to portage the load around the obstacle. After they reached a solid bank again, the wheels could be taken off, the goods reloaded and—a day or three later—they could resume their journey.

There were other drawbacks. As with nearly every choice on the journey, decisions came with consequences. In the case of the river, the water ran swift. For travelers who had witnessed wagons being swept away and people drowning at other crossings, the wide, unpredictable river caused much anxiety. There was also the cost. Freighters and ferrymen extracted a heavy toll. Even those with means were hard-pressed to part with their coin, but those whose cash had been depleted at the forts and the trading posts had no choice but to take another route.

Some people simply preferred to take their chances on an

overland route, trusting what they knew. Philip and Luke were among this group. They decided, after hearing the arguments, to strike out directly for Oregon City by way of the Barlow Road. Not really a road, but a trail that Samuel K. Barlow had chopped, blasted and burned through the Cascades and over the shoulder of Mt. Hood, practically into the lap of Oregon City.

Luke was guarded in his enthusiasm. He'd made the trip before and it was rough going. On paper it looked shorter, more direct, and the route had plenty of huckleberries, blackberries and nuts to sustain the travelers and to provide food for the animals, but he warned Philip, "It will be the hardest part of the trip."

Philip listened in disbelief. They had endured some backbreaking situations so far. They had dug out wagons that were stuck to their axles in sand, had climbed mountain passes where they had to hitch eleven yoke of oxen to a single wagon and drag it over an incline. They had forded rivers where the wagon in front of them was swept away and sank from sight. They had waited out one-hundred-ten-degree heat in the questionable shade of a wagon until the sun set and they could continue. They had pried boulders out of the path, cut trees and strained to pull wagons stuck in muddy bogs. Now Luke was telling them that the worst was yet to come.

"How bad can a toll road be?" Mary directed her question to Philip. "Seems the man should provide some convenience for our money; otherwise we could just take another route and bypass his rutty road."

"At least we won't have to fell trees or blast rocks every step of the way," Luke said without looking at her.

Even though she ignored him, his words got her to thinking. They might get through on the Barlow Road, but at what cost? Most of the youngest and strongest men were gone to California. In their place were older and weaker men, and strangers who might turn out to be just fine, but traversing the mountains was not the best way to test their mettle. Both Luke and Philip had suffered the loss of some of their animals. One of Luke's horses had become so footsore on the high desert he'd been forced to destroy it.

Fortunately, they had other meat that day and didn't have to eat it, although there were others who did. Meat was important—meat and water, and they were constantly on the search for both. There were days when they suffered an oversupply of fresh cow, mule and horse meat and they traded some of the excess to the Indians. Other days, the excess rotted in the sun if there was no one to claim it, but that was rare these days.

Many of the more impoverished travelers existed almost entirely on carcasses of deceased horse or cow. She saw women and children and wondered how they survived. Some of the wagons were now pulled by a comical mix of animals: an ox, the family cow, two horses and the remaining mule tied to harness. Philip was lucky to have his oxen team still intact. She popped out of her reverie and heard him talking.

"My beasts can make the rest of the trip. They're thin, but no more so than the others." He watched over his team like a prideful mother.

"We have the rest of the day to graze them. The grasses here are some of the best I've seen." Luke acted like she wasn't even standing there. But she had to admit; he had the instincts of a rancher. He looked first to maintaining his herd and then, if there was time, to his own needs. "So it's set— the Barlow Road for us."

"That's good to hear."

Although Luke directed his words to Philip, it was to Mary that his gaze flicked. They hadn't spoken since the night they'd met with the minister. The next day, Reverend Mossler's wagon had been seen traveling west with another group.

"Mary…"

Mary turned to meet his gaze and the sight of him made her heart leap as it did every time she came across him un-expectedly. His words, spoken low and personal, caused something good and warm inside her, but she folded her arms in a protective stance and tried to mask her conflict.

"Mary," he continued, "we're still weeks out. You take care of yourself. "

"I'm so weary." She felt tears clotting in her eyes. Seeing him here alone was almost more than she could bear. She studied him surreptitiously and wondered if she looked broken.

"Why aren't you riding anymore?"

She raised her hands to her gaunt cheekbones and was surprised at how thin she had become. "Buttercup is too far along with her foal."

"Ride one of my horses until we hit the high country. You look like you're ready to drop."

Mary tried to summon the strength to object, but she was too weary. She remembered a scene she had seen a few days earlier; a wagon burning unattended. The woman, middle-aged, with no children in sight, had ignited it in despair or madness. She knelt in the middle of the trail staring straight ahead, heedless of her husband's admonitions while a half-dozen wagons pulled around her. He shouted and implored her to get into their remaining wagon. From wherever her mind had gone, she sat unspeaking while drovers and teams backed up behind them, impatient to clear the trail. The husband regarded his burning wagon and his distraught wife while teamsters shouted oaths for her to clear the road. Slowly, out of anger and despair, he turned his remaining wagon west and continued on alone.

"What will happen to her?" she had asked, craning back at the disappearing trail.

"Isn't likely we'll ever see her again," Philip had answered quietly.

The next morning they began the cutoff to the Barlow Road. At the tollgate, a ragtag group mingled, waiting for someone to pay their toll or for the tollmaster to take pity on them. Philip pretended not to notice the eager eyes and expectant expressions that reminded him of vagabonds seeking a lift to town.

"Leave them be," he warned Mary. "We'd spend more time getting these people out of the mountains than we'll spend on our own teams. I wish we could strike out alone and spare ourselves the trouble." He turned to gaze at the snowy peaks in the distance.

Luke rode up and heard this last. "Snow comes early this year. Have to get over the passes soon."

Philip cast a sideways glance at Luke. "Things all right with you and Mary?"

Luke kept his attention on the oxen. "Right enough. I suppose. She has some sorting out to do."

"Don't let her shut you out, Luke. She'll be a fool if she does."

At the John Day River crossing, emigrants bound for the Columbia Gorge set off in a trail of dust, accompanied by many hearty farewells. Mary watched with envy. It would have been heaven to lay back and float the last few hundred miles into Oregon City.

Philip laughed. "If it were as pleasant as all that, there

wouldn't be a land trail. Everyone would be lined up, waiting to take the Columbia."

Mary was not in the mood for humor. "Don't be such a
sour sport. It's no sin to dream."

The tollmaster extracted a fee for each wagon, horse, oxen,
cow, mule, sheep and person using the road. Some of the emigrants argued about the steep fares, but they had little
choice. Mary saw one woman tearfully part with her butter
mold, a cherished memento to have made it this far. While
her husband scrounged for his remaining cash and came up
short, the woman slowly relinquished her mold and turned
away.

Philip reminded Mary, "She just might come across it
again, some day. The shops in Oregon City will be filled with
the like."

He and Luke paid quietly. As soon as they could escape,
they started toward the waiting mountains.

Mary took a deep breath and steeled herself for what was
to come. "At least," she said aloud in Luke's hearing, "This
will mark the end."

Her words brought a shadow over his features. Two
weeks of caution, weighing every move with Mary had given
him cause to hope. Now, she seemed to be saying that nothing had changed.

Chapter Twenty Nine

September 10, 1848. We have gained the Barlow
Road. The trees are majestic. Tall as a cathedral
and the trunks bigger than four men forming
hands. We are hard pressed to see the sun. An
ominous feeling has descended upon us.

ON THEIR FIRST day into the Cascades, some of the women
were outspoken in their dismay. "It beats the prairie, I suppose. Out there I felt as exposed as a bug on a table, what
with the horizon stretching clean out of sight," Sazie Murdock muttered as she lifted her muddy shirts to ford a rivu-
let.

Water flowed everywhere. Huge ferns grew in the shad-
owy canopy, in fissures and washes left by the violent rush
of melting snow. Trees diffused the light, shutting out the
heat that might have evaporated some of the dampness. Waterfalls and crossings left the trail muddied and prone to ero-
sion. The trail was merely two tracks ground deep into the
soil where wagons rolled, sunk to axles and oxen bogged to
their knees. It was hard work, getting the oxen to haul the
loads up the continual climb. Tempers frayed when oxen
balked. Wagons got stuck, holding up the entire column.
Mud slid across the road, causing washouts, and wagons
overturned on steep passes. A child became separated from

his mother and somehow got caught under the wheels of the following wagon. The little boy had a leg broken and several ribs cracked from the weight of the wheel passing over him. The fact that he had fallen into one of the deep ruts saved him from certain death. What a tale he would have to tell his children, Mary thought. She saw men killed and animals drop dead from exhaustion; all day long the sound of whips punctuated the animals' movement up the mountain.

The snows held off, but the nights got colder and the winds never ceased. In the distance, Mt. Hood stood like a sentry, both beckoning and threatening. Leverenz told them they had to pass within the shadow of the mountain, but they would do so on its terms. He directed them to meadows where the grass grew lush and water ran in clear streams.

One area, which the emigrants called the "Big Deadening" was formed in a basin of pine and fir trees, burned off by Indians in a contest with the forest for food and grass. Periodic burning opened the sunlight and let the blackberries and grasses flourish so that the deer returned, bringing larger game to the meadows and waterways. The area of the "Big Deadening" covered over fifty acres, the fires that cleared it, probably extinguished by the rains. Wildflowers of every hue bloomed in the peaceful meadow, and the air smelled of jam.

Mary trudged into the clearing and soon the smoke from her campfire blended with the lowing of cattle and oxen grazing alongside the wagons. Here and there a bell tinkled from a milk cow.

What a relief to be free of the woods for even a night. No matter how majestic the forests, they extracted a toll and she was tired of paying it. Only today, a wagon had toppled from the ridge, crushing the driver and killing the mules in a tangle of blood and spilled goods. Fortunately, the woman and her children had been walking at the time, but everything they owned lay scattered about the broken body of her husband. The women collected what they could while the men dug a grave for the body. At least the widow had one consolation, Mary decided, watching the man being lowered into his resting place; she could be glad she wasn't forced to abandon her husband to the wolves and dust of the prairie. *Strange how little death upsets us now.* Even the widow and her children struggled on in a numb sort of peace, as though nature had taken its course and there was nothing to be done for it. Maybe their tears would fall when they had time and energy, but for now, survival was a full-time job and no one spared the energy for grief.

Luke passed by the wagon without seeming to notice her. He was limping as he led his horse to the camp he shared with Leverenz, exhaustion in every muscle. She had watched him rescue a handful of emigrant wagons earlier in the day when the wagon slid off the trail and overturned. She wanted to call to him, but he was gone before she worked up her nerve.

• ♥ •

"Mary, help me with these fellows." Luke was sweating and straining as he tried to coax two worn-out steers into the extra effort of pulling a wagon over an incline. They had but two weeks before the snows came—if they didn't come early—and each man, woman, and child knew the cost of being caught in the mountains. Snow would turn the slippery road into an impassable track where ropes would have to be tied to every tree and the wagons inched up the hill, step by step. Mary was glad they had resisted the urge to stay awhile in the lush Kansas wildflowers or the streams and rivers that had been won by hard struggle. It had been difficult at the time to pack up and leave, but now the group reaped the benefit of the grueling pace Leverenz had set.

When it seemed that they would perish in a muddy sump within hailing distance of their goal, they reached the final mountain. From camp, Mary could see only downward slopes. She closed her eyes and tried to smell the ocean.

In a half-hearted attempt to celebrate, she tried to cook a special meal, amid relentless winds that blew the ashes from her cooking fire. She had found a patch of blackberries earlier in the day and traded some of her bounty for a scant cup of milk to ladle over biscuits and fresh berries. The smoothness trickled down her throat in a burst of sweetness, all the more precious for months of craving it. She thought of the times that Luke had shared their meals, but she was too peeved with him to suggest it. He and Philip could polish off a gallon pot of berries. Instead, she saved aside a helping for a widow whose husband had perished that day.

The tone of the camp was silent, filled with concern for the coming dawn. Even the animals sensed the danger and went about their business, cropping grass with subdued watchfulness. As soon as the camp chores were complete, everyone settled in for the night. No fiddle played, no deck of cards appeared before the flickering campfires; the atmosphere was that of a wake. They had conquered the mountain but they weren't down it yet, and before the next day's sunset, there might be more funerals. The unspoken question was, *whose*?

Luke spent a quiet hour at the campfire with Philip, while Mary silently oiled her boots nearby. Luke must have told Philip about their estrangement because he showed little curiosity about the situation. The scene seemed almost too comfortable for coincidence. A thought nagged at her: if Philip knew and didn't consider Luke's transgression an impediment to their happiness, maybe she was making more of it than need be. Luke included her in his conversation. Abandoning her indifference, she responded. She'd missed their talks.

"Mary, when this is done we will have made a part of history. Your journal will be read by your children and theirs. Lives will be changed because of what we did out here. A new country will be formed. Have you thought about that?"

"Often. Sometimes it's the only reason I can find for the misery we've been through. I wonder how many women back home are planning for an easy trip as I did?"

"There's no turning folks back, Mary, even if they knew the truth. The human spirit has to expand. We're lucky to live in times that permit it. Someday, the land will be settled and there will be nowhere for people to go. Kind of sad, really."

She understood. For Luke, every white man who arrived was a kind of death for his people. "The guidebooks either give glowing reports or they paint a picture of gloom every mile of the way. The truth is somewhere in the middle," she said.

Philip held up a dog-eared copy of his *Prairie Traveler*. "Many of them were written by men who never set foot into Oregon Country, just sat in some fancy eastern mansion and wrote to make money. Look at the book that claims a fellow can hunt all his food along the trail. Right now there's enough game for us and the Indians, but next year—well, you saw the way those fellows rushed off to the gold field. When news reaches the East, it'll be a stampede. Poor fools will likely starve."

"I'm glad we left when we did," Mary said.

"Only because you won't get trampled by gold hunters?" Luke asked.

Mary tossed her head. "Think of all the handsome men on

the trail next year. More to choose from."

"Maybe you should."

Mary glanced up at the irony in Luke's voice. Philip removed his boots and disappeared into the darkness in preparation for bed. The moon crested and moved overhead; somewhere, an owl hooted its wake-up call. The grasses rustled with the sounds of the night critters looking for their supper. Everywhere was the promise of life and industry. Below the moon, two people sat in the fire's glow, each with their own private thoughts. When the silence grew burdensome, Luke rose and excused himself.

Daylight dawned cold, the sun's rays blocked by the mountains, Women were forced to break camp by the light of their fires, with whatever oil remained for their lamps. The men gave the animals time to crop. In their hunger the cattle and mules had become uncaring about what they ate. Several of the horses had fallen victim to poisonous weeds, ignoring the instincts of their breeding in a frantic effort to fill their bellies. Today, the herdsmen had an easy job.

Luke yoked his oxen early and motioned to Philip to do the same, intending to be in the lead so the slower wagons would not bog them down.

At the first downhill he rode his brake hard, pulling back on the lever as the wagon made a slow descent. "Take care the weight of the wagon doesn't catch the animals. Whole team will go down. I've seen it happen before. Not a pretty sight—between the broken legs and the mangled horns."

Sometimes the steep road gave way to a bit of flatland, a respite for man and beast alike. At such places they took their rest, unyoking the oxen to forage among the trees. There was no fear the animals would wander; they were numb to anything but forward movement, rest, and finding food. Water was so plentiful that they used some of the water barrels to fuel the fire at night.

Mary walked now, slipping and sliding down the muddy track, but preferring it to the danger of riding the wagon. From behind, she could hear drovers cursing and shouting, trying to burn off their own tension as much as to berate the animals. It was nerve-wracking work, this creeping down the mountainside. Time and again, she wondered how Mr. Barlow had the gall to call it a road—let along charge folks for the use of it. But it wasn't really his fault. He could hardly flatten the mountain. Until something better came along, this was the best trail to Oregon City.

Each step contained plenty for the men to fuss about. With oxen buried in ruts up to their bellies, the men worried that they would break a leg in a false step. Wheels broke under the weight, brakes failed, and neighbor struck out against neighbor in the process. The women mostly bore the strain in stony silence.

The routine took on a weary horror. Nothing helped to break the exhaustion—not food, not rest. Luke watched Mary from a distance, but he offered little encouragement except to fuel the fire of anger that kept her moving. *Surely there is an end to this trail,* Mary thought, as each turn of the bend brought a repeat of the last.

On the last morning, they arrived at the final hill before the trail opened onto Oregon City. At the precipice, Mary halted and stared at the decline. Surely, there was some mistake. They had heard about this last hurtle, *Little Laurel Hill,* a gently named killer that led down the forbidding slope of Mt. Hood. A trail so steep that even the oxen backed away in panic as their eyes rolled in crazed fear and they refused to go forward.

Men trembled at the magnitude of the task before them. Women cried out that the trail was not possible and they would have to go all the way around to the Columbia, after all. The grade of the mountain had been surveyed at thirty-eight degrees. Off to the side of the trail, splintered wagons rested beside belongings crushed in previous attempts to gain the base. The stench of rotting animals lay alongside, still harnessed in blood-soaked leather straps.

Luke chose to be first down the mountain. Taking his axe, he selected a tree with a trunk about as thick as his torso. Cutting it to a length where two men could roll it in place, he and Philip tied it with ropes to slow its descent. Taking another, smaller tree—called a brake tree—he instructed a volunteer to push it though, and in front of the wheels, and used it as a drag to keep the wheels from turning if the wagon descended too fast. He sought out another man, Philas Murray, a skillful teamster, and asked him to handle the brake tree.

Philip insisted on the most dangerous job of all, riding the wagon down the hill and manning the hand brake. Luke would have done that himself, but his place was at the head of his team, encouraging them. "When I get you off this mountain, boys, I'm going to retire you to a life of clover and grain—at least when you're not pulling a plow. But your hard work will be done...you hear me, boys?" Stroking their necks and speaking softly, he finally overcame their resistance and they started down the mountain, one tentative step at a time. His last thought was for the girl watching with arms wrapped around her midsection in an effort to contain her trepidation. "Wish us luck, Mary."

Mary nodded, her eyes wide with fear. A bolt of realization nearly brought her to her knees; she faced the possibility of losing the two men she loved. The thought made her disagreement with Luke seem petty and unworthy. She tried to control her trembling as she watched her future inching away. Her words conveyed more than a warning; they conveyed a promise. "Luke…be careful." She saw the comprehension dawn in his face and his answering smile was magnificent. "I love you, Lucas…be safe." When she mouthed the words he nodded and reluctantly broke his gaze.

The oxen slid to the side, correcting before the wagon could jackknife. Luke talked them down, slipping and sliding, straining with every fiber of muscle until sweat dripped from both he and his animals. Halfway down, the brake began to smoke and the oxen began to get restless from the strain.

"We're in trouble!" Philip called from the wagon seat. "I can't hold the wagon back."

"How's the log doing?"

Philas Murray's voice showed his tension. "Not good. This is a long mountain. I'm giving it everything I've got."

"You men at the top—bring ropes. Now."

A half-dozen men tied ropes to sturdy hooks on the wagon box and wrapped the other ends around trees on either side of the trail. They fed the ropes out to full length, easing the wagon another thirty feet before they had to disconnect and slide to another tree to reposition the rope. With agonizing patience they made it down the mountain. On the next wagon, they unhitched all but one set of oxen and harnessed the rest behind, figuring the weight would hold it back. Using the ropes again, they got the wagon down without mishap.

Then, it was Philip's turn. Again they repeated their labors, with fresh men to replace those that collapsed in the grass.

As the fourth team started down, the mules began rearing. "Hold them back…get them down!" someone yelled, while many hands dragged them back to the flat. Luke headed back up the hill. "Here, move aside. The rest of the teams are spooked and they can smell the fear. If we don't do something quick, we'll be in trouble. Get the next wagon down and let the animals see that it can be done."

He made the trip two more times before Leverenz called him aside and said, "Sayer, you've done more than your share. That's enough for one day. Let the men take responsibility for their own." He turned to the others who were waiting to have their wagons brought down. "You folks are going to have to get your own animals calmed down or wait until tomorrow morning. It takes eight men to get one wagon down the mountain. That means every one of you has to help seven others besides your own. If you have two wagons, double the number. But we won't do it for you. Now, get the next wagon ready."

Luke looked over the cluster of waiting men. Some of the older or more timid ones were not suited for the frontier. It always seemed to fall to someone else to fix their wagons when they broke, dig them out when they got stuck, or like today, bring their wagons down off the mountain. He only hoped that when he had need of an apothecary or a merchant, these gentlemen would remember it was he and Philip and their kind who had brought them through.

Mary led Buttercup down, slipping and sliding in the wheel tracks. When she tried to hurry, her feet slid out from under her. By the time she reached the base of the mountain she was trembling with the strain. She saw Luke lying in the shade of a pine tree and led her horse toward him, unmindful of who might be watching.

When he could speak, Luke's words were muffled. "Ah Mary, I've missed you." She could say nothing for the clot of tears. "We'll talk tonight…after supper."

She nodded.

Another wagon train had arrived at the top of the mountain. Luke saw Leverenz turn his back on the newcomers and pick up a brake tree to help the last of his train just as the sun was setting. Too tired to speak, Luke struggled to his feet to watch the last wagon descend. He was walking up to congratulate Leverenz and the drover when he heard a commotion. Up on the mountain, men were cursing. Frightened, desperate screams of mules followed the thunderous sounds of crashing wood, blended with women's cries, then silence.

He raced toward the sound and saw Leverenz running beside him. At the bottom of the hill, one of the new arrivals had attempted a descent, taking with it the lives of eight mules that had no say in the matter. With disgust clenching his gut, Luke pulled out his sidearm and unloaded a shot into the head of each pain-crazed animal. The reports filled him with anger at the waste of such loyal beasts. He found the driver crushed by the wagon box. It was Bill Weems. He was already dead.

From the top of the hill, a man shouted, "He was in a fearful hurry to get to his holdings. Said his team was faithful critters and they could hold the wagon back."

Another of the group added, "Wagon run smack into the back of the mules. Serves him right. He was fixing to catch up with you and save himself the effort of helping the rest of us down." The price of Weems's greed was borne by the survivors; they would have to clean up the wreck before they could start their own descent. "Wish we were in you folks' shoes," one of them shouted.

"Could be worse. You could be in that poor fellow's! Good luck, and we'll see you in Oregon City tomorrow," Leverenz called. Turning toward their wagons, he and Luke held their thoughts to themselves.

• ♥ •

The little group of one hundred and fifteen people summoned energy for a celebration that night. "End of the trail," one of the women said. They pooled the last of the whiskey, the fiddles, and what little they had left to eat, sharing with each other in a spirit of thanksgiving. Later, Luke and Mary walked out into the forest. By the time they returned, a look of peace had replaced Luke's haggardness. Philip looked up from his fiddle and frowned, but no one else noticed. Luke escorted Mary to the line of women and disappeared into the darkness. She looked calmer than Philip had seen her in weeks. With renewed energy he began another verse of *Durang's Hornpipe*.

By three o'clock the next afternoon, smoke could be seen from Oregon City. In the distance, the roar of the Willamette Falls could be heard ahead. The emigrants celebrated their last few miles with as much diversity as they had the journey. Some men fired off their guns and rode pell-mell into the town. Others continued almost sedately, holding their excitement until they actually set foot on the Abernathy Green.

Philip could scarcely bridle his impatience, but his oxen plodded with mind-taxing indifference while all around, faster horses and mules raced to finish the journey. Mary felt her legs protesting the last miles, but she hurried to keep up while Luke stalked beside her with feather-light steps, his moccasins making scarcely a sound in the brittle grass. He was lost in private thought, but his scowl was that of a worried man. She was sure that Clara Halsey figured into his mood. She studied his face and his features seemed all the more precious for their trail dust; he seemed in every line of his face to belong to her. Their marriage commitment had been made a thousand miles back; if it was meant to be, the coming hours would have the answers. As though Luke read her mind, he looked over and smiled.

Philip scowled, darkly. "Whoa there, man. Dashed if I'll watch the two of you celebrating until I can see my Laurel again."

"You're right, my friend. After all, think of all those nights we got to spoon under the stars—" Luke grouched.

Philip ignored this last comment. Somewhere in the town, a girl waited. He was tempted to let his oxen forage on their own at the edge of town while he went in search, but Luke reminded him, "Make a proper finish to your journey. This girl will find you."

They arrived at the Green to find a frenzy of celebration. People lined the roads watching the new arrivals for kinsmen and friends they had separated from on the trail. Some of the emigrants got down on their knees and kissed the soil, tears streaming down their faces. One lady fainted. Another went into labor when her water broke. The ladies of the Emigrant Society produced a midwife, a real bed and a stack of fresh towels. "I'll be calling it 'Abernathy' if it's a boy," the woman laughingly promised.

Townsfolk served up a hot meal that brought tears of joy to even the toughest men. Children ate watermelon and spat the seeds into the Green that, by next summer, would mark the spot of their rebirth. Young children who had shown signs of exhaustion earlier in the day ran around in circles while their mothers and fathers sank to their knees, too overcome to walk another step. Merchants passed out handbills advertising their shops, where the newcomers could restock at their convenience.

304 ◆ ANNE SCHROEDER

Chapter Thirty

October 4, 1848. Today, for the first time I wept.
Tears I would not allow myself to shed in pity, I
do now in relief. Relief and pride for a job well
done. I will celebrate my nineteenth birthday in
Oregon.

LUKE HAD SCARCELY brought his team to a halt when he
turned to Mary. "We've made it." He took her in his arms for
a first public embrace, little caring who watched.

Clearly, Mary relished her feeling of homecoming. She
had crossed a continent to be here, and found herself in the
bargain. She had earned the right to her happiness and she
was going to find it in full measure. Luke released her and
looked around, scanning the crowd. He tried to hide his concern from Mary, but the look in her face reminded him that
their arrival was bittersweet for her, as well. She didn't need
to ask who he was searching for. His dark mood said it for
him. Fortunately, Philip came walking up.

The town was crowded with noisy people camped near
the river under the protection of their wagons, restless to
move on. Some of the recent arrivals had already set up
shops. Some had taken jobs as craftsmen, working for black-
smiths, leatherworkers, wagonwrights to replace the young
men who had left their employers for the goldfields. Some of

the new arrivals had money left; the sound of bartering added to the cacophony of sounds.

Mary stood taking in the neatly built houses and hastily thrown-together shacks next to tents and wagon camps perched on the hillsides and crowded onto the flatland. Sounds of the town competed with the roar of the river falls at its back door. The town was a verdant array of grass and trees. Brightly dressed women and their husbands bustled about with energy and industry.

Dusty, worn-out families moved through the streets past people offering squash and potatoes for sale. Fresh baked bread and fresh apple pies sent their aromas into the air, here and there mixed with the smells of roasting meat. Mixed among the smells of comfort food and safe arrival, the offal of human and animal wastes fouled the air and gave the town the air of an army camp just settling in for a siege.

Hollow-eyed children and gaunt horses stood watching, unsure of what to do with themselves with no trail to walk. At the edge of town, pens held animals for sale or trade, with other pens crowded with the remnants of small herds that would head out to new land holdings in the Willamette Valley once the spring rains ceased.

Luke walked alongside Mary and Philip, dodging the horse manure and taking in the stench of campfire smoke. The place reeked of white man's civilization. Every fiber in him longed for solitude, but he had a score that needed settling. He was lost in his own thoughts while Philip and Mary searched for Laurel in the crowd. He heard bits of conversation:

"Do you think she is here on the Commons?"

"I pray so, cousin. I plan to put up a message at the public houses and reading boards," Philip answered, trying to sound casual.

Apparently, they heard a voice they recognized shouting over the din, because Philip turned toward the sound, his head going back like a buck sniffing the wind. From out of the crowd a pretty girl ran toward them in a clean white shirtwaist. They met in an open area, the girl flying into Philip's outstretched arms with wonder-filled eyes and an embrace that said everything about their loneliness and longing.

Luke felt like an intruder as he stood off to the side, not sure if he should go or stay.

"Laurel, let me look at you." Philip held the girl with an iron grip on her narrow shoulders. He tilted her back to get a closer look and his expression clearly said that she'd turned into a woman in the year's time they had been apart. "My Lord, Sweetheart, I should've run my team across the country and not even stopped for supper." He brought her close again as if he couldn't get enough of the sight, the smell, the touch of her.

"Meaning you tarried because you forgot about me?" she teased.

"Never." He spoke with quiet intensity, no longer teasing. Mary broke the spell with an awkward cough and he gave his cousin a quick glance. "Sorry. I forget the world when I'm looking at her." He turned back to his fiancée. "Mary's here. And Luke Sayer..." he hesitated and caught Mary's curt shake, "our friend. Luke, my friend, meet Laurel Marie Chapman."

Luke smiled at the pretty girl, taking in her blonde hair and blue eyes, so like Philip in looks, and apparently in her depth of feelings as well. "Miss, I'm pleased to make your acquaintance."

"Likewise, Mr. Sayer." She wasted the briefest glance on him before her attention reverted to Philip.

Mary bided her time and now pressed forward. "Hello,

Laurel."

"Why, Mary, what a surprise. Philip didn't write to say you were coming. Who did you travel with?"

Mary and Philip exchanged looks. "The story will be long in the telling. Maybe we should save it for later."

Laurel linked arms with the cousins. "We've taken lodgings at the outskirts of town. You must bring the wagons around back. There isn't room enough in the house for all of us, but there's grass nearby. And supper as soon as Mother knows you're here."

"How did you guess we'd arrive today?" Philip pressed her hand into the crook of his arm.

"I didn't."

"You're here all day long? Alone?"

"I volunteered for the welcoming committee until you came. That's how I saw you, over by that table," she explained. "The rules are different here in Oregon. We're stronger on sensibility and a lot less set on useless convention." She walked between them pointing out sights that Luke had seen many times. "We found a house. Mother and Father have started a small tack and feed store and he spends most of his time over there. Mother, too, for there is little enough else to do here."

Supper that night was fresh vegetables and juicy salmon. Dessert was tiny raspberries and cream over a thin slice of poundcake, and coffee brewed in sweet water. Afterward, everyone made plans for a wedding.

"Father Laroquette will be here on Wednesday. He's already expecting to marry Philip and me," Laurel told them. "I've seen the way the two of you look at each other. Maybe he will have to perform two marriages."

In the uncomfortable silence, Mrs. Chapman turned to Mary. "So the two of you met on the wagon train. How wonderful. A real trail romance. Your mother and father would be so pleased, don't you think so, Philip?" Mrs. Chapman's questions were light and teasing, but her maternal concern was hard to ignore.

Philip disengaged himself from Laurel's eyes. "Luke is the one man in the world that Uncle Henry would have approved of. Aunt Ruthie, too. Have no fear about that."

Luke ducked his head and sipped his coffee to settle his nerves.

The men slept under their wagons while Mary shared a mattress and a thistledown coverlet with Laurel. Freshly scrubbed and wearing one of Laurel's old nightgowns, she felt like a stranger in her own skin.

"Mary, how did you meet Luke?" Laurel was too excited to sleep.

"Why? Don't you like him?"

"Of course I do, silly. He'd be perfect for you. You've always been so high-spirited. I despaired of you ever finding a proper husband." She squeezed Mary's hand. "It's just that he's so—well, I don't know. So aloof. Not the type to settle down."

"That may be true. He has some decisions to make, that's for sure."

"Mary?"

"Hum?"

"Maybe you'll marry him and we'll have babies the same age."

"That would be nice." Mary drifted off to sleep with the image of another baby sleeping in the same town.

Mary spent the next day trying to boil the trail grit out of her clothing. The men had gone downtown to arrange for the sale of their extra oxen and to see what the shops offered in the way of supplies. Luke came back with a haircut, a shave and a bath, and the sight of him did things to her insides. When the meal was over, he wasted no time in idle conversation. "Let's take a walk, Mary." He picked up his hat and held the door for her.

"So you're already feeling the pinch of civilization?" she teased.

"Don't tease, Mary. There's something yet to be settled between us."

She chose her words with care. "You need to be settling your business. One way or another, you find her and finish this thing. I won't have it hanging over us. Even if she's the one you choose, you settle it tomorrow."

"I already have." They stopped in the moonlight to watch the river explode over the waterfall.

She found herself dreading what he was going to say. Instead, she began babbling about the first thing that came to mind. "It's different, watching a river you don't have to fear—"

"Mary—I've had word about Clara and the baby."

Mary felt her heart drop.

"She's gone. Took the baby and ran off to California with a mulatto fellow she met here in Oregon City. They're bound for the goldfields. The madam claims she stole some stuff from the—from the place she worked."

"Why didn't she wait for you?"

"I told you, she's bound for adventure. She probably doesn't want a husband. She wants to see the world. Leverenz said she was using me to get away from her father. If that was the case, it worked."

Mary saw the pain mirrored in the blackness of his pupils. They had come so far; the next part of his journey was up to him. "Lucas. I'm no Clara Halsey."

"I know you aren't. You're so fine that I haven't the right

to ask what I want to ask of you. It's been worrying me for weeks. I feel like I've ruined your chance at happiness."

She allowed him to lead her to a spot beneath a cottonwood tree where someone had placed a rough bench. The waterfall of the Willamette River roared in the background, but that was not the sound that she heard.

"Will you marry me, Mary? Take me as I am, and make something finer of me? I promise that I am not—"

She placed her hand over his lips. "Shhh, no more. What is in the past is forgiven. We will have only tomorrows, agreed?"

Relief shone in his eyes before he took her in his arms and brought his lips to hers. Later, he vowed that he'd find a way to make it all up to her. "I intend to find my son one of these days."

• ♥ •

Mary took a small pair of scissors and plucked the stitches from her ragged camisole that contained the proceeds from the sale of her father's farm, along with the savings her father had put aside for a rainy day. The pile of gold poured out onto Laurel's mattress with a resounding *thunk*. The subject of her worth had never come up. She hadn't mentioned it to anyone, but she couldn't continue to wear her wealth in her underwear forever.

Wednesday dawned bright, with a crispness that spoke of fall. The apples were ripe and there was a smoky tang to the air when Mary prepared to leave the house. Laurel had already stepped out into the dawn. Philip caught her padding to the outhouse in her wrapper. Mary ducked back inside to give them some privacy, but the walls were thin and she couldn't help but hear what he was saying.

"Whoa, there, little filly, whereabouts you going this fine morning?" Tweaking a pretend mustache in a bad version of a stage villain, he teased, "How about a little nibble for a hungry man?" He brought her into his embrace and chased the cold from her cheeks.

"Philip, you are a terrible actor. For one thing you have your lines mixed up from 'Little Orphan Nettie.' And you aren't a very good actor."

"But my leetle peegeon, I am very good at this, no?" His kiss was intended to demonstrate his true talent.

"Yes, you are very good at *that*. Probably the best," Laurel giggled, nuzzling up. "Definitely the best."

"That's better. A man does not like to be laughed at on his wedding day. It undermines his confidence."

"You have enough confidence for two men," she whispered.

"Well, you shall find out tonight, my love. You have driven me to distraction with your ploys. Tonight, you will be mine, and I will have you like the fearsome beast I am." Taking her into his arms, he proceeded to show her just what she had to fear.

Laughing at his antics, Laurel finally broke away. "Philip, I came out here for a reason and you better let me go."

"Later, my dear. Much later…and you will be mine." Tweaking his imaginary mustache again, he rounded the corner toward the house.

Mary ducked back behind the door before Philip entered.

The wedding was planned for two o'clock on Saturday. By eight in the morning, wooden slats were laid out in the front yard for the reception. Mary had run into George, Bethellen, and the children the previous day. Baby Lillian looked pink and happy in her tiny shawl of knitted worsted. She objected, but Bethellen insisted on bringing a dish for the potluck supper.

On her way back to the house, Mary took a stroll along

the river to escape the press of bodies in the house. She thought about the people who would not be there—the Parkman-Clark family, Lillian, her mother, her father, and Toby. She imagined dancing with Toby. Her father would have walked her down the aisle. She was happy that Mr. Chapman had offered to escort his "two girls," but his generosity didn't eliminate her sense of loss; he had squeezed her hand and with a wink of his eye, had let her know that he understood he was a poor substitute for her father.

She went to the Abernathy Green, even though she knew the Stobersons could not possibly make up the extra miles in so short a time. When they were not among the new arrivals, she strolled back through town while her eyes blurred with unshed tears. At a plain little dressmaker's shop, she stopped to look at a dress displayed in the window. It was made of the thinnest lawn, rose colored, overlaid with thin strips of lace. The sleeves were full at the top, tapering to a fitted wrist with layers of cream colored ribbons at the tight bodice. Fortunately, it had no train and had been cut slightly shorter than the Eastern fashions to accommodate the mud and lack of improvements in the frontier town.

She stared at the dress, knowing that she had to inquire. It might be too rich for her blood. It might be the wrong size, it might be sold, but she would never know if she didn't open the door and ask. With fingers crossed, she entered and rang the bell. A beautiful, petite woman with a handsome coil of ebony hair pulled aside the drape from the back room and entered smiling. She removed several straight pins from her teeth and called out a greeting. Mary gawked at her cotton batiste shirtwaist that she wore tucked into a black satin skirt with the tiny waist she had ever seen. The woman appeared to be French, and when she opened her mouth to speak, her accent removed all doubt. "*Bon jour, Madame.* Good Day."

Mary hesitated. "Ma'am, about the dress in your window—"

"Oh, yes. Made precisely for someone of your coloring. It would be perfect."

"How much?"

"Let us see if it fits, first. Then, we shall talk of cost." The dressmaker went over and deftly removed the pins that held it fast. Taking the dress down, she led Mary into the tiny dressing alcove where she helped unhook her worn dress. "I am Marietta Stewart, the proprietress. You have just arrived, no?" She must have recognized the frayed look of the dress with its faded colors and the ingrained dust that would remain with the garment until it was relegated to the ragbag.

"Yes. I'm getting married today."

"Oh, what a happy day. This will be just the thing. Already I know it will fit you like a princess." Fastening the tiny buttons, she led Mary to the looking glass. "You see? Made with you in mind."

Mary faced herself in the shiny mirror and couldn't check the flow of tears that ran with a will of their own. "I'm so— so sorry. I must…seem impossible. But I'm so weary. And I want…my mother and nothing—"

"My dear, I understand. Truly. Have a good cry. And then we will see you reborn and everything will be all right. Yes?"

"How…how much?" Mary asked the question again, afraid of the answer.

When pressed, Marietta named a price. Mary looked again at the dress and weighed the consequences of buying it against the disappointment of not.

Marietta watched Mary contemplate the purchase. "I tell you what. You buy this for your wedding and I will sell you the green linsey-woolsey I have just finished for less than I would usually ask. That way, you will have two new dresses."

Mary looked at the serviceable green dress that would set off her eyes and hair to perfection. More importantly, the darker color would travel in Luke's open wagon in the rain, and that would have to be considered.

"And," the woman continued, "I will give you a good price on a fine linen nightgown. If you are fortunate, your groom will prefer you in your natural state, but you will need something to tantalize him, no?" She smiled knowingly. "You have something in mind already?"

Mary blushed to her roots at the woman's frank manner, but the proprietress acted as though this were an everyday occurrence. Mary murmured, "I wanted to bring nice things, but there was no room in the wagon."

The woman nodded. "It is the same with every woman. What is to be done?" She went to the trunk where her white nightgowns were stacked and selected one with a yoke buttoned with tiny pearl buttons. "This one. It's heavy and will be good for the winter. Not too expensive, but plenty fancy to make you feel the seductress when the lamp is low, no?" I sell them for a widowed woman and it would be a kindness to her if you would buy one so that she might feed her four small children." Marietta laid the gown against Mary so she could see for herself the effect.

The onslaught was too much for a girl who had been tumbled by prairie winds and sunburned to a crisp for the past six months. Marietta smiled encouragingly and Mary purchased the entire lot. She had the money and, after all, it was her wedding day. When asked about stockings and shoes, she held a firm line. She had brought her mother's wedding shoes and they would suit until she could find a plain bootmaker.

When she returned home with her packages, Mrs. Chapman met her at the door with a look of dismay. "Mary, we've been so worried. Your bath is ready and you have yet to dress. Thank goodness you washed your hair yesterday, or it would never dry in time. Laurel is all ready. You best hurry now."

Mary undressed and lowered herself into the hipbath with a sigh of appreciation for the feel of warm water over her skin. She felt her parched skin absorbing the soothing water on her arms and legs. Mrs. Chapman had offered a vial of scented bathing oil and she watched the oil merge with the water—it was wonderful. On the day of her arrival she had attended to the serious business of scrubbing the trail grime from her skin. Rubbing hard with the washrag, she had moaned, "It's no use. I will never be clean again." Nevertheless, she felt renewed when she stepped from the tub and dried herself in a scrap of real cotton toweling. Today her skin felt soft and delicate, like a bride's should.

Donning the dress, she found a bottle of scent on Laurel's shelf and applied it to her throat and behind her ears. *I look so thin.* She had walked nearly twenty-five hundred miles and she was afraid that she looked like it. But she was fortunate to be alive.

She allowed Mrs. Chapman to do up her buttons, tie the ribbons and arrange her hair in tight coils. She glanced at herself in a small hand mirror and realized that Luke would prefer it unfettered and full, but this was her wedding day and she would look proper for her mother's memory. Drawing a deep breath, she gave herself a last look and turned to the door.

Mr. Chapman was waiting in the parlor. "My stars, I'll be the envy of every man around, squiring the two prettiest ladies in town."

"Father," Laurel protested. Mary heard herself laughing.

Everything was perfect. Everything would be perfect, even if it rained. The low-sprung buggy he had borrowed was waiting outside.

They pulled up to the tiny mission where the priest held services on alternate weeks. There were only two priests in Oregon. This one ministered to Christians of every denomination as the need arose, to the Indians—and on muleback, to the rest of the far-scattered townships that were beginning to spring up.

Mr. Chapman started into the chapel with a girl on either arm. Mary watched the way Luke's mouth dropped at the sight of her. She had no way of knowing that her eyes glowed with the light of a thousand candles, but she saw Luke's approval and love, and she felt her mother's presence. She was not alone on this day.

While Father Laroquette prayed over them, Luke's gaze never faltered, nor hers on him. In a dream, she felt him slip her mother's ring onto her finger and heard the priest pronounce them man and wife. When he turned to seal their troth with a kiss, Luke whispered, "I'll cherish you until the sun no longer rises."

She was nearly as happy for Philip when she heard him repeating the words that she had just uttered to Luke. Finally, the ceremony was over and the two couples passed through the group of well-wishers.

Mary turned to kiss Philip through a haze of tears. "Thank you for bringing me—for everything."

Philip's own happiness was apparent as he pulled her close. "You were right about us never getting separated, Mary-girl."

At the reception, they greeted old friends and made new—and shared the bounty of a table that reminded her of Ida O'Brian's wedding. She smiled at Luke's surprise when he saw the plate of apple fritters that she and Mrs. Chapman had made in the early morning.

Philip made a long-winded explanation of how he happened to leave Ohio with one wife and arrive to another. Their friends seemed to take it as a good joke on their parts, now that the trip was over and the deed done. Of all the guests, John Leverenz seemed the happiest. After all his hours of fretting, seeing Luke and Mary wed seemed a miracle. He even delayed a day before setting off for his farm—and his Nancy—so he could dance at the celebration.

Mary had steeled herself against the absence of her parents and Toby with the hope that the Stobersons would show up in time. When they did not, she tried to blink away tears that threatened to ruin her day. Across the room, Mrs. Chapman was explaining that the Stobersons would need another week of travel. There was no point in wishing for something that could not be.

Mary turned to accept Luke's request for a first dance. The fiddles and banjos sang while Luke twirled her and she circled, her head tipped back while she laughed and fought the dizziness that made her legs weak. On their last turn, she caught a glimpse of a man standing across the crowd and she blinked, afraid she imagined it. Slowing, she looked again and saw that it was no illusion. It was Orv Stoberson and Virginie and Nellie and the boys and their new wives—all come to wish her well.

"How did you know to come? How did you get here so fast?" She laughed and cried by turns, caught up in a whirlwind of hugs and kisses. The older boys were not shy in their affections. They had traveled alongside Mary for months and with the perfect excuse they didn't waste their opportunity for a kiss.

"Sit and eat. And tell me about yourselves," she implored

them, taking Luke's hand and bidding him to join her.

"Tell you about *us*? Why, we left you with one husband and now he's dancing with another bride at your wedding. You better start by telling us about yourself!" They had heard about the wedding from a mutual friend who read the notice on the common post, but they seemed a little confused about just what they were here to celebrate.

Luke and Mary filled them in on the facts, leaving nothing out while their friends laughed and gaped in turns.

"You should've confided in us. We wouldn't have told a soul. Surely, you know that." Virginie sounded hurt that Mary, of all people, hadn't chosen to confide in her.

"It wasn't that I didn't trust you. I gave Philip my solemn word. It was not mine to tell. Had it been, you would have been the first to know. After Lucas, that is."

"Well, we're awfully glad things worked out. Ma used to comment on the sparks you and Luke set off each other, and she thought it was sure a pity you two weren't hitched."

"I thought so, too," Luke admitted. When the laughter subsided, he asked, "How'd you get here so soon? We left you slanting off to Ft. Bridger. Did you grow wings?"

"We backtracked down the trail a spell, took the Columbia route and paid some Indians to raft us here. We're flat-busted and looking at a hard winter, but we figured we'd had enough, what with Lill's passing, and all. We just wanted it over."

They danced into the night, drinking distilled spirits and letting loose from the tight discipline they had been forced to maintain. Finally, the weary newlyweds took their leave. Thanking the Chapmans, Luke took Mary's arm and pointed her in a direction that was neither toward the wagon nor the house. "Where are we going?" she asked, not really caring.

"I thought you might like the chance to clear your head

before we turn in." Wondering at his strange reluctance for bed after all his teasing, Mary fell in alongside him.

"Mary, honey, you could have knocked me over today. I never saw anything so pretty in my whole life. I can't even remember, was someone else in that church with us?" He took her arm, feeling the delicate fabric with his thumb. "Where did you get this?"

"I bought it. You didn't think I was going to come to you like some pitiful little ragamuffin, did you? You didn't bring me a doeskin so I had to make do."

He laughed. "You'll get your hide. Then, you'll have to learn to tan it. A good Indian wife keeps her husband in clean buckskin shirts."

"Oh, you clean up well enough. For a trapper, you spruce up pretty nice. I wasn't sure I had the right man there in the church."

"Well, you already married the other groom and I was the only one left, so I was a pretty sure bet," he teased. They stopped and Luke opened a door for her.

"Where are we going?" Mary asked again, sure now this was no evening stroll. They were standing on the main street where the lamps of a dozen establishments merged with the tinkle of piano keys.

"This is the Oregon City Hotel. I thought you might enjoy a little privacy. It was filled up, but I paid a gent to vacate for the night and he's sleeping under our wagon. Said it was the least he could do. I even invited him to the wedding. Did you see the little man in the green bowler who was dancing with the heavy-set woman in the feathery hat?"

"Why, Luke, what a fine gift." Her voice stilled at the bottom of the stairs and she craned to see into the restaurant just off the stairwell.

"We—uh....can eat there tomorrow if you want." Luke

had to clear his throat as they climbed the stairs. He led her down a short hallway until they came to the last room. Taking a key from his pocket, he unlocked the door with trembling hands. They entered the small room and he lit the lamp, turning it so that it cast a soft light on the bed.

In a single motion he locked the door, tossed the key on the vanity and turned to remove the pins so that he could splay her hair loose. "I love your hair like this."

Mary felt her words catch in her throat. "I know."

Moving his hands to cup her face, he murmured, "It feels good, seeing you so pretty and fine after the hell you went through." He kissed her softly. "You look fine, Mary," he added as he lifted her hair with his fingers.

"I'm too thin."

"You're beautiful."

With the rush of long waiting they came together in a kiss that, for once, brooked no stopping. Taking their time through the process of tight buttons and laces, they found themselves breathless, and Luke incredulous at the piles of clothing they left on the hotel floor. Until he pulled her onto the bed and they found the true end of their journey.

The next morning the two sleepy occupants eyed the sun as it peaked through a crack in the window blind. Mary cast a lazy glance at her stockings, half hidden under his trousers. "Is this the way you intend to spoil me? The sun's nearly straight up. I could get used to this."

He coiled a stray curl around his finger. "Not unless you want breakfast. But that would suit me just fine."

On their way out of the dining room, Luke nodded at a gentleman in a green bowler who was having his breakfast at a table near the door. Their tousled hair and soft, sleepy eyes brought a satisfied smile to the small man who had spent the night under the wagon tossing on unfamiliar ground. He left the breakfast room a satisfied man.

• ♥ •

"To think that I once thought you were shy!" Luke complained one night, pleading his need of rest in their wagon at the rear of the Chapman house.

"Well, if it's a calm, domesticated wife you want, then I will try to comply." Mary buttoned her nightgown to its topmost, affected spectacles on her nose and said, "Really, Herbert, I see no further need for this dissipation. If you do not desist, then I shall have a lock affixed to the door."

Laughing, Luke turned her toward him and lavished a kiss on her prudishly covered throat. "Oh, Mary. I can't even remember life without you."

Chapter Thirty One

October 9, 1848. I feel such a bond with my
mother, as if she is here to share my joy. In preparing me to be a good wife, she gave me the finest gift of all.

"WAKE UP, SLEEPYHEAD! Philip and I are bound for the
Willamette. Good land with room for expansion. We'll be
back in a week's time."

Mary stretched a slow, reluctant arch, sorry that she had
been awakened from the dream of her old home and the river that wound through the meadows. "Where will you be
looking?" she asked.

"Someplace where the grass is plentiful, the trees are tall,
and the river is clear. Where we can raise forage and have
babies and grow a garden. I'll know it when I see it." He was
in an expansive mood as he moved about the wagon, gathering his gear. "If we're lucky, we can start building before the
rains set in."

"Philip's going with you?"

"He's going to winter here in town to help his father-in-
law expand the feed store. But my mares need a home, and
your filly's going to be a mother any day now. She needs a
warm shed." He pulled a gold coin from his pouch. "While
I'm gone, you may need to buy some things."

The days passed slowly while she and Laurel waited for the men to return. They spent the time cutting new shirts; Mary managed to stitch one up while Mother Chapman made aprons for each of them. Mary put up jars of gooseberry and blackberry preserves from the late-blooming berries on the bushes out back. She dried apples and tried in every way to build up her store of food against the uncertain winter. She took bread starter from Mother Chapman, made vinegar, and dug potatoes from the garden to be used for sets when spring allowed for planting. Mother insisted that she dig plenty, claiming she had planted extra for Philip's arrival. Mary didn't remind her that no one had expected her; it obviously pleased Mother to share her larder with a new bride.

At supper time on the eighth day, the men rode into the yard. Luke led Mary to a secluded spot under the trees while Philip ladled warm water into the basin and soaped himself up to his elbows. As he took a chair, he leaned over and gave Laurel another kiss.

"Luke and I agree. We've never seen anything like it. Virgin trees of every kind, bigger around than five men outstretched. Topsoil so deep the thistles grow over a man's head. The water is clear and runs deep all year long." Luke followed Mary back inside and took a place at the table.

Philip paused to fill his mouth with savory, molasses-flavored beans before he continued. "The game's thick around there, and the snow doesn't fall more than a foot or so every year. We talked to several others who settled there last year. They looked far and wide before they chose the land. Say they'd welcome neighbors."

Luke addressed his words to Mary. "It suits our needs." He paused for a gulp of coffee before continuing, "We'll be leaving in two days. Can you be ready? We're claiming a full six hundred and forty acres as soon as Congress gives us permission. It may not happen for a year or so, but we'll be in good shape when it does. Enough for the horses and a few crops. Later on, we can add to that if we come up with the money."

Mary sat, stunned at how fast her life was changing. Nodding to her husband, she folded her hands in her lap to contain her excitement.

Talk went on until late that night, and by bedtime even Philip had convinced Laurel that, come spring, this was the land for them.

Luke waited until he entered the wagon to share his plans with Mary. She listened for a few minutes and then covered his mouth with her hand. "Lucas dear, you aren't a landowner yet, but you *are* a husband." He stopped in midsentence, realized the direction of her words, and lowered himself into their bedroll.

The next morning, Luke pulled her out of the wagon before she was finished coiling her hair. "Mary, we're burning daylight. I've got the oxen yoked and ready. We'll purchase what provisions we can afford, but it will be a hard winter for us."

He waited to hand her up onto the seat, the act of gallantry causing her to smile when she recalled the hundreds of times she'd jumped down unaided. She breathed in the sweet smell of pine and the misty morning fog while she waited for him to join her. Then she reached into the deep pocket of her skirt and brought out a fist-sized sack of paper money and gold coins.

"What's this?" Luke stared. "Good Lord, Mary, where did you get those? Have you been carrying these since you left Illinois?"

"Where else would I have come across them?"

He hefted the gold and glanced around to see who might be watching. "Let's get inside." He pulled her under the rainfly and sat her on an empty flour barrel. "Mary," he repeated, "Where did you get this?"

"From the sale of the farm. From Father's savings account, from the sale of the animals. From Mama's inheritance. I don't know. It's what I had left after paying Philip for my share of the provisions."

He gave her a funny look and continued counting. "I thought you had to sell the farm to pay taxes."

"Well, we were frugal. I had some left over."

Another thought occurred. "Why didn't you say something back on the trail? You wouldn't have had to take the Barlow Road. You could have floated down the river."

"Luke Sayer, don't you blame that on me. You and Philip were determined to test your mettle against that mountain." At least he had the grace to blush. But she'd had her fill of sitting on flour barrels; she gathered her skirts in her hands and stood up. "Now, let's go buy what we need. You can decide later whether I'm to be forgiven."

Luke held his hands up between them like he was warding off evil. "Good news. Word from the States is that Congress is working on a plan they're calling the Donation Land Grant. It may take a year or so, but it will give us rights to six hundred and forty acres if we live on it for four years."

"Then I intend to spend my money on a wood stove."

The first stop was the mercantile where they loaded up Mary's purchases, adding scrap iron, a hammer, shot and a new two-man saw. Luke added six glass panes to be set into the cabin he planned to build. "No sense in having the prettiest view in the valley if we can't admire it," he explained.

The store was filled with people looking longingly at goods they probably couldn't afford. Most of the things that

caught their attention were basics that they were going to
need. Some of the women looked haggard and hopeless as
they slapped the hands of their children for wanting to touch
things that they might never be able to afford. Mary took a
handful of gold coins and dropped it into the hand of one
such mother. The woman started to protest, but Mary moved
out of hearing.

The sun was nearly overhead by the time they were ready
to say their good-byes. She managed to get Nellie and Virginie aside and gave them each a gold coin to set aside for
their own weddings. "You need something of your own,
your mother would agree."

Laurel's mother was waiting with a pot of fresh baked
beans and cornbread. In the misty rain, the sight of her ma-
tronly profile brought a pang of longing. "Mother Chapman,
I'm so tired of farewells. It seems like I've had to leave behind everyone I love." Mary pressed her cheek to her friend
and vowed they would return often to visit.

"Mary, think of this as a beginning. One of these days the
roads will be better and you'll be able to drive a proper buggy. There will soon be a stage connecting the valleys. And
we'll keep in touch by letter, I promise. Who knows, with
both you young couples living down there, Father might be
persuaded to take his business down the Willamette."

As they rolled away, Mary turned back to wave. Mother
Chapman was right; Philip and Laurel would be coming in
the spring. Even the Stobersons were heading down that way
and had agreed to stop by and see for themselves the land
that Philip had raved about. They had agreed to help raise
Luke's cabin and fences in return for his help a few weeks
later.

Behind them, the town disappeared in the trees; and with
it all the noise and confusion. Mary tried to remember, had

she ever been this carefree? Thinking back to the Ohio farm, and the Kansas prairie with its wildflowers, she remembered a day when she thought she had been. But little did she know. *Maybe the trail is like life itself. If you knew what was in store up ahead, you might not even have the nerve to start, but having no choice, you do your best; and in the end, you triumph through your own grit.*

A few days later, they lumbered into the central part of the great Willamette Valley and the oxen made their final stop. Later, as Mary lay under her mother's wedding quilt with her husband, she made her final journal entry. When she finished, she closed the cover and placed it inside her wooden hope chest beside the oval photograph of her parents. Turning to Luke, she drew herself against him and felt her body absorbing his warmth. A wolf howled somewhere in the distance. She closed her eyes and drifted off to sleep in the quiet of her new surroundings.

> October 23, 1848. We are home. The trip that started exactly six months ago is done. I have traded my old life for a new one, and have gained the better bargain. We have brought everything we need to make a success, now the rest is up to us.

About the Author

A fifth-generation Californian, Anne Schroeder's love of the West was fueled by stories of bandits and hangings; of her great-grandfather and his neighbors working together to blast the Norwegian Grade in Southern California out of solid rock; of Indian caves, and of women who made their own way. She worked her way through Cal Poly University with a variety of odd-jobs that included waitressing at a truck-stop café in Cholame, near the spot where James Dean died. Anne recently served as President of Women Writing the West. Her short stories and essays have appeared in print and online magazines. She lives in Southern Oregon with her husband, dogs, and several free-range chickens.

http://anneschroederauthor.com
www.facebook.com/anneschroederauthor

Other books by Anne Schroeder: Maria Inés, Cholama Moon, Gifts of Red Pottery, Ordinary Aphrodite

Made in the USA
Monee, IL
13 August 2021